ALL RHODES LEAD·HERE

MARIANA ZAPATA

I don't know how I could have gotten through this last year without you.
Eva, thank you for everything.
Especially your friendship.

CHAPTER 1

*M*y eyes burned. Then again, they hadn't *stopped* stinging since it had gotten dark a couple of hours ago, but I squinted anyway. Coming up ahead, on the very, *very* edge of my car's headlights, there was a sign.

I took a deep, deep breath in and let it right back out.

WELCOME TO
PAGOSA SPRINGS
World's Deepest Hot Springs

Then I read it again just to make sure I hadn't imagined it.

I was *here*. Finally.

It had only taken an eternity.

Okay, an eternity that fit into a two-month period. Eightish weeks of me driving slowly, stopping at just about every tourist attraction and two-star hotel or vacation rental along the way from Florida through Alabama, Mississippi, and Louisiana. Spending time in Texas and then skipping to Arizona, exploring towns and cities I hadn't had time to check out in the past when I'd come through. Even visiting an old friend and his family too. I went to Vegas while I was at it because it was somewhere else I had been to at least ten times but had never truly gotten to see. I spent almost three weeks in Utah. Last but not least, I took a week to check out New Mexico before circling back up toward the mountains. To Colorado. My final destination—I hoped.

And now I'd made it.

Or just about made it.

Letting my shoulders sink down, I pushed them back against the seat and relaxed a little. According to the navigation app, I still had another thirty minutes left to get to the place I was renting on the other side of town in the southwest part of the state most people had never heard of.

Home for the next month, or maybe longer if everything worked out the way I wanted it to. I had to settle somewhere after all.

The pictures online of the rental I'd booked were just what I'd been looking for. Nothing big. Not in town. Mostly though, I'd fallen for it because the rental reminded me of the last house Mom and I had lived in.

And considering how last minute I had reserved it, right smack at the start of summer and tourist season, there hadn't been a whole lot left to choose from—as in, there had been next to nothing. I'd come up with the idea of going back to Pagosa Springs two weeks ago in the middle of the night while the weight of every choice I'd made in the last fourteen years rested on my soul—not for the first time either, more like the thousandth—and I'd fought not to cry. The tears weren't because I'd been in a room in Moab all by myself with no person who gave a shit about me within a thousand miles. They had sprouted because I'd thought about my mom and how the last time I'd been in the area had been with her.

And maybe just a little because I had no clue what the hell

to do with my life anymore and that scared the hell out of me.

Yet that was when the idea had struck.

Go back to Pagosa.

Because why not?

I'd been doing a lot of thinking about what I wanted, what I needed. It wasn't like I'd had anything else to do being by myself nearly nonstop for two months. I'd thought about making a list, but I was done with lists and schedules; I'd spent the last decade listening to other people tell me what I could and couldn't do. I was over plans. Done with a whole lot of things and people, honestly.

And just as soon as I had thought of the place that had been home once, I knew that was what I wanted to do. The idea just felt *right*. I'd gotten tired of driving around, looking for something to set my life back into some semblance of order.

I'd figure it out, I had decided.

New year, new Aurora.

So what if it was June? Who said your new year had to start on January 1st, am I right? Mine had officially started with a lot of tears on a Wednesday afternoon about a year ago. And it was time for a newer version of the person I'd been back then.

That's why I was here.

Back in the town I'd grown up in, twenty years later.

Thousands of miles away from Cape Coral and everyone and everything in Nashville.

Free to do whatever I wanted to do for the first time in a long, long time.

I could be whoever I wanted to be. Better late than never, right?

I blew out a breath and shook my shoulders to wake myself up a little more, wincing at the ache that had taken them over, back when I'd gotten the rug pulled out from under me, and never left. Maybe I had no *real* idea of what I was going to do long term, but I was going to figure it out. I couldn't find it in me to regret my decision to drive here.

There were plenty of things in my life I regretted, but I wouldn't let this choice be one of them. Even if I didn't end up staying in the area long term, the month I had reserved in Pagosa Springs was going to be nothing in the grand scheme of life. It was going to be a stepping stool for the future. Maybe a Band-Aid for the past. A boost to the present.

It's never too late to find a new road, as my friend Yuki sang. I had driven all this way to Colorado for a reason, and nothing was going to be in vain—not my butt cheeks hurting, my shoulders aching, my sciatic nerve acting up, or even how much my eyes needed a light bulb and a nap.

And if I could feel the start of a headache right above my eyebrows, then that was just part of the journey, a building block for the fucking future. No pain, no gain.

And if I didn't get into my car again for another month, that would be great too. The idea of being behind the wheel for another minute made me want to puke. Maybe I'd buy another car while I was at it now that I thought about it. I had the blood money for it. Might as well use it for something I would actually need and use since my existing one didn't have four-wheel drive.

Now. New. Present.

The past was staying where it was, because as much as I would've liked to light it on fire and watch it burn, that couldn't happen.

Mostly because I'd go to jail for double homicide, and that kind of thing was frowned upon.

Instead, I was moving on without a criminal record, and this was the next step. Bye, Nashville and everything there. See you later, Florida, too. Hello, Colorado and mountains and a peaceful, hopefully happy future. I was going to will that shit into existence. Like Yuki would also sing, *if you put things out into the universe, hopefully someone will listen.*

The hard part was over. This was my future. Another step in the next thirty-three years of my life.

I should thank the Joneses for it, really. Maybe not for taking advantage of me, but at least I knew now what I'd been in—who I'd been surrounded by. At least I had gotten out.

I was free.

Free to go back to where I'd spent the first part of my life, to see the place where I'd last seen my mom. The same place she had loved so much and that held so many good memories, as well as the worst.

I was going to do what I had to do to keep going with my life.

And the first step was to make a left down a dirt road that was technically called a county road.

Gripping the steering wheel as hard as I could as my tires drove over one pothole after another, I pictured the last blurry memory I had of my mom, the image of her greenish-brown eyes—the same ones I saw in the mirror. Her very medium brown hair, not dark but not light, was another thing we shared—at least until I'd started coloring my hair, but I'd stopped that. I'd only started coloring it because of Mrs. Jones. But mostly, I remembered how tightly my mom had hugged me before she had given me permission to go to my friend's house the next day instead of going with her on the hike she had planned for both of us. How she had kissed me when she'd dropped me off and said, *"See you tomorrow, Aurora-baby!"*

Guilt, bitter and sharp, as fine and deadly as a dagger made out of an icicle, jabbed me in the stomach for just about the millionth time. And I wondered, like I always did when that familiar sensation came over me, *What if? What if I'd gone with her?* Like every other time I wondered, I told myself it didn't matter because I would never know.

Then I squinted hard into the distance again as I drove over a bigger pothole, cursing the fact that none of these roads had streetlights.

In hindsight, I should have stretched this last part of the drive over another day so that I wouldn't end up wandering through the mountains in the dark.

Because it wasn't just the ups and the downs of elevation that came at you. There had been deer, chipmunks, rabbits, and squirrels. I'd seen an armadillo and a skunk. All of them decided at the last minute to run across the road and scare the living shit out of me so bad I slammed on my brakes and thanked God it wasn't winter and there weren't many cars out on the road. All I'd wanted to do was arrive to my temporary home.

To find a person named Tobias Rhodes who was renting out his garage apartment at a very reasonable rate. I'd be the first guest. The apartment didn't have any reviews, but it fit every other thing I wanted from a rental, so I was willing to go for it.

Plus, it wasn't like there had been anything else to choose from other than renting a room in someone's house or staying in a hotel.

"Your destination is approaching on the left," the navigation app spoke up.

I squeezed the steering wheel and squinted some more, just barely catching sight of the start of a driveway. If there were more houses around, I couldn't tell in the darkness. This really was in the middle of nowhere.

Which was just what I wanted: peace and privacy.

Turning down the supposed driveway that was only

marked by a reflective stake, I told myself that everything was going to be okay.

I would find a job... doing something... and I'd go through my mom's journal and attempt to do some of the hikes that she'd written about. At least her favorites. It was one of the biggest reasons why coming here had seemed like such a good idea.

People cried over endings, but sometimes you had to cry over new beginnings. I wouldn't forget what I'd left. But I was going to be excited—at least as much as I could be—about this start and however it would end.

One day at a time, right?

A house loomed up ahead. From the number of windows and lights on, it seemed smallish, but it wasn't like that mattered. Off to the side, maybe twenty, maybe fifty feet away—this night driving bullshit was crap on my astigmatism—was another structure that looked an awful lot like a separate garage. There was a single car parked in front of the main house, an old Bronco I recognized because my cousin had spent years rebuilding one just like it.

I turned the car toward the smaller and less lit-up building, spotting the big garage door. Gravel crunched under my tires, rocks pinging and hitting the undercarriage, and I reminded myself again of why I was here and that everything would be okay. Then I parked around the side. I blinked and rubbed at my eyes, then finally pulled out my phone to reread the check-in instructions I had taken a screenshot of. Maybe tomorrow I'd go and introduce myself to the homeowner. Or maybe I'd just leave them alone if they left me alone.

I got out then.

This was the rest of my life.

And I was going to try my best, just like my mom had raised me to do, like she would have expected from me.

It only took about a minute with my camera's flashlight to find the door—I'd parked right beside it—and the lockbox hanging from the knob. The code the owner sent me worked on the first try, and one single key sat inside the tiny box. It fit and the door squeaked open into a staircase on the left with another door perpendicular to it. I flipped on a light switch and opened the door directly in front of the one I'd just come through, expecting it to be the entrance into the garage and not being disappointed.

But what did surprise me was that there wasn't a car inside.

There were various forms of padding along the walls, some of it the kind of foam I'd seen in every recording studio I'd ever been in, and other parts of it, blue floor mats that had been nailed in. There were even a couple of old mattresses pressed against the walls. In the center, there was a big, black, four-by-four speaker with a banged-up old amp, two stools, and a stand with three guitars on it. There was also a keyboard and a basic, starter drum set.

I swallowed.

Then I noticed two posters taped to the mats and released my breath slowly. One was for a young folk singer, and the other was for a big tour of two rock bands. Not country. Not pop.

And most importantly, no need to overthink it. I backed out the way I'd come in and shrugged off the practice space, closing the door behind me.

The stairs turned once, and I made it up, flipping on more lights and sighing with relief. It was just like the pictures had advertised: a studio apartment. There was a full-sized bed tucked against the wall on the right, a heater made to resemble a wood-burning stove in the corner, a small table with two chairs, a fridge that looked to be from the 90s but who cared, a stove that also had to be from the same decade, a kitchen sink, a set of doors that looked like they might be a closet, and a closed one that I hoped was the bathroom that had been in the listing. There was no washer or dryer, and I hadn't bothered asking. There was a laundromat in town; I'd looked it up. I'd make it work.

Scarred wood floors covered the layout, and I smiled at the small mason jar sitting on the table with wildflowers in it.

The Joneses would have cried that this wasn't the Ritz, but it was perfect. It had everything I needed, and it reminded me of the house I'd lived in with Mom with wood-paneled walls and just the... warmth of it.

It really was perfect.

For the first time, I let myself feel genuine excitement over my decision. And now that I did, it felt *good.* Hope sprang up inside of me like a Roman candle. It only took three trips to carry my bags, box, and cooler up.

You would figure that packing up your life would take days, even weeks. If you had a lot of belongings, it might even take months.

But I didn't have a lot of stuff. I'd left Kaden just about everything when his lawyer—a man I'd sent Christmas cards to for a *decade*—had sent me a thirty-day notice to move out of the house we'd shared, the day after he'd ended things. Instead, I'd left hours later. All I'd taken with me were two suitcases and four boxes worth of belongings.

Good. It was good it had happened, and I knew it. It had hurt then, hurt like a son of a bitch, and afterward. It didn't anymore though.

But... I still sometimes wished I'd sent those traitors a pie made of shit just like in *The Help.* I wasn't that good of a person.

I had just opened up the fridge so I could put the sandwich meat, cheese, mayo, three cans of strawberry soda, and single beer inside when I heard a creak from downstairs.

The door. It was the door.

I froze.

Then I grabbed my pepper spray from my purse and hesitated—because the owner wouldn't just walk in, would they? I mean, it was their property, but I was renting it from them. I'd signed an agreement and sent a copy of my license over, hoping they wouldn't do a search of my name, but oh well if they did. At a few of the rentals I'd stayed at, the owners had come over to see if I needed anything, but they hadn't just strolled in. Only one of them had done a search and asked a lot of uncomfortable questions.

"Hello?" I called out, finger on the pepper spray trigger.

The only response I got was the sound of feet on the stairs, these loud clunks that sounded heavy.

"Hello?" I called out a little louder that time, straining to hear the steps continuing up the stairs and making me clench the pepper spray in my hand just a little tighter.

In the time it took me to hold my breath—because *that* was going to help me hear better—I caught sight of hair and then a face a split second before the person must have taken the last two or three steps in a leap because they were *there*.

Not a *they*. A *he*. A man.

The owner?

God, I hoped so.

He had on a khaki-colored, button-down shirt tucked into dark pants that could have been blue, black, or something else, but I couldn't tell because of the lighting.

I squinted and laced my hands behind my back to hide the pepper spray just in case.

There was a gun at his hip!

I threw my hands up and squealed, "Holy shit, take whatever you want, just don't hurt me!"

The stranger's head jerked before a raspy-rough voice spit out, *"What?"*

I held them up even higher, shoulders around my ears, and gestured to my purse on the table with my chin. "My purse is right there. Take it. The keys are in there." I had insurance. I had copies of my ID on my phone, which was in my back pocket. I could order another debit card, report my credit card as stolen. I couldn't care less about the cash in there. None of it was worth my life. None. Of. It.

The man's head jerked again though. "What in the hell are you talking about? I'm not trying to rob you. *What are you doing in my house?"* The man shot out each word like they were missiles.

Hold on a second.

I blinked and still kept my hands where they were. What was going on? "Are you Tobias Rhodes?" I knew for a fact that was the name of the person I'd made my reservation with. There had been a picture, but I hadn't bothered zooming in on it.

"Why?" the stranger asked.

"Uh, because I rented this garage apartment? My check-in was today."

"Check-in?" the man repeated, his voice low. I was pretty positive he was scowling, but he was under a gap in lighting and shadows covered his features. "Does this look like a hotel to you?"

Ooh, attitude.

Just as I opened my mouth to tell him that, no, this didn't look like a hotel but I'd still made a legal reservation and paid upfront for the stay, a loud creak came from downstairs a split second before another voice, a lighter, younger one, shouted, "Dad! Wait!"

I focused on the man as he turned his attention down the

stairs, his upper body seeming to expand in a protective—or maybe defensive—gesture.

Taking advantage of his change in focus, I realized he was a big man. Tall and broad. And there were patches on his shirt. *Law enforcement patches?*

My heart started beating loud in my ears as my gaze focused back on the gun holstered at his hip, and my voice sounded oddly loud as I stuttered, "I... I can show you my booking confirmation...."

What was going on? Had I gotten scammed?

My words had his attention swinging back toward me right at the same moment that another figure appeared with a wild jump to the landing. This one was a lot shorter and thinner, but that was about all I could tell. The man's son? Daughter?

The big man didn't even glance at the new arrival as he said, anger definitely seeping from his pronunciation, from his entire body language really, "Breaking and entering is a felony."

"Breaking and entering?" I croaked, confused, my poor heart still beating wildly. What was going on? *What the fuck was happening?* "I used the key someone gave me a code to get." How did he not know this? Who was this? *Had I really gotten scammed?*

Out of the corner of my eye, because I was so focused on the bigger man, the smaller figure I'd barely paid attention to muttered something under their breath before basically hissing, "Dad," again quietly.

And *that* had the man turning his head down toward the figure that was his son or daughter. "Amos," the man grumbled in what sounded an awful lot like a warning. Fury there, active and waiting.

I had a terrible feeling.

"I gotta talk to you," the figure said in almost a whisper-hiss before turning to me. The smaller person froze for a second and then blinked before seeming to snap out of it and saying in a voice that was so quiet I had to strain to hear it, "Hi, Ms. De La Torre, umm, sorry about the mix-up. One sec, uh, please."

Who the hell was this now?

How did they know my name? And this was a mix-up?

That was good... wasn't it?

My optimism only lasted about a second, because in the dim lights of the studio apartment, the man started to shake his head slowly. Then his words made my stomach drop even further as he muttered, sounding deadly, "I swear, Amos, this better not be what I think it is."

That didn't sound promising.

"Did you post the apartment for rent after I literally told you not to the fifty times you brought it up?" the man asked in this crazy still voice that hadn't gone up at all in volume, but it didn't matter because somehow it sounded even worse than if he had yelled. Even I wanted to flinch, and he wasn't even talking to me.

What the hell did he just say though?

"Dad." The younger person moved under the ceiling fan, light striking him, confirming he was a boy—a teenage boy somewhere more than likely between twelve and sixteen based on the sound of his voice. Unlike the broad man who was apparently his father, his face was lean and angular, and long, thin arms were hidden mostly by a T-shirt two sizes too big.

I got a bad, *bad* feeling.

The reminder that there hadn't been anywhere else to stay within two hundred miles popped up front and center in my brain.

I didn't want to stay in a hotel. I was over those for the rest of my life. The idea of staying in one made me feel sick.

And renting a room *in* someone's house was a hard no after that last time.

"I paid already. The payment went through," I pretty much shouted, panicking suddenly. This was where I wanted to be. I was *here* and tired of driving, and suddenly the urge to settle down somewhere filled just about every cell in my body insistently.

I wanted to start over. I wanted to build something new. And I wanted to do it here in Pagosa.

The man looked at me. I was pretty sure his head reared back as well before he focused again on the teenage boy, hand flying through the air once more. This sense of anger exploded across the room like a grenade.

Apparently, I was invisible and my payment meant nothing.

"Is this a joke, Am? *I told you no.* Not once or twice but every time you brought it up," the man spat, straight-up furious. "We're not going to have some stranger living in our house. Are you shitting me, man?" He was still talking in that inside-voice way, but every word seemed like a quiet bark somehow, tough and serious.

"It's not technically the house," the kid, Amos, whispered before glancing at me over his shoulder. He waved, his hand shaking as he did.

At me.

I didn't know what to do, so I waved back. Confused, so confused, and worried now.

That didn't help the pissed-off man. Like at all. "The garage is still part of the house! Don't play that technicality game with me," he growled, making a dismissive gesture with his hand.

That was a big arm attached to that hand now that I got a look at it. I was pretty sure I'd seen some veins popping along his forearm. What did those patches say though? I tried to squint.

"No means *no*," the stranger went on when the boy opened his mouth to argue with him. "I can't believe you did this. How could you go behind my back? You posted it *online?*" He was shaking his head like he really was stunned. "Were you planning on letting some creeps stay here while I was gone?"

Creeps?

Me?

Realistically, I knew that this was none of my business.

But.

I still couldn't keep my mouth shut as I tossed in, "Umm, for the record, I'm not a creep. And I can show you my reservation. I paid for the whole month up front—"

Shit.

The boy winced, and *that* had the man taking a step forward under better lighting, giving me my first real good look at his face. At the whole of him.

And what a face it was.

Even when I'd been with Kaden, I would have done a double take at the man under the lights. What? I wasn't dead. And he had that kind of face. I'd seen a lot of them, I would know.

I couldn't think of a single makeup artist that wouldn't call his features chiseled, not pretty by any means but masculine, sharp, highlighted by his mouth forming a tight scowl and his thick eyebrows flat across his remarkable, heavy brow bones. And there was that impressive, strong jaw. I was pretty sure he had a little cleft in his chin too. He had to be in his early forties.

"Rough handsome" would be the best way to describe him. Maybe even "ridiculously handsome" if he didn't look about ready to kill someone like he did right then.

Nothing at all like my ex's million-dollar, boy-next-door looks that had made thousands of women swoon.

And ruined our relationship.

Maybe I *would* send that shit pie eventually. I'd think about it some more.

Basically, this man arguing with a tween or teenage boy, with a gun on his belt and wearing what looked to me to be some kind of law-enforcement-type uniform, was unbelievably handsome.

And… he was a silver fox, I confirmed when the light hit his hair just perfectly to show off what could have been brown or black mixed in with the much lighter, striking color.

And he didn't give a single *shit* about what I was saying as he snapped words out in the most level, talking-voice volume I'd ever heard. I might have been impressed if I wasn't so worried I was about to get screwed.

"Dad…," the boy started again. The kid had dark hair and a smooth, almost baby face, his skin a very light brown. His limbs were long under a black band T-shirt as he slid into place between his dad and me like a buffer.

"A whole month?"

Yeah, he'd heard that part.

The kid didn't even flinch as he replied, very quietly, "You won't let me get a job. How else am I supposed to make money?"

That vein on the man's face popped again, color rose up along his cheekbones and ears. "I know what you want the money for, Am, but *you know what I said too*. Your mom, Billy, and I all agreed. You don't need a three-thousand-dollar guitar when yours works just fine."

"I know it *works* fine, but I still want—"

"But you don't *need* it. It isn't going to—"

"Dad, please," the Amos kid pleaded. Then he gestured at me with a thumb over his shoulder. "Look at her. She's not a creep. Her name's Aurora. De La Torre. I looked her up on Picturegram. She only posts pictures of food and animals." The teenager glanced at me over his shoulder, blinking once before shaking himself out of it, his expression turning almost frantic, like he too knew this conversation wasn't going well. "Everybody knows sociopaths don't like animals, you said, remember? *And look at her.*" His head tilted to the side.

I shrugged off his last comment and focused on the important part of what he'd mentioned. Someone had done his research... but what else did he know?

But he wasn't wrong. Other than those and some selfies or shots with friends—and people I used to think were my friends but weren't—I really did only post pictures of food and animals I met. That reality, and the bags and boxes sitting on the ground close by, were just another reminder that I wanted to be *here*, that I had things I needed to do in this area.

And that this kid either knew too much or really had fallen for the façade that I'd presented to the world. For all the lies and smoke and mirrors I'd had to employ to be around someone I'd loved. A reminder that I hadn't deleted pictures off my Picturegram of a life I used to have. I had been careful on my account to never take any romantic-looking pictures—or fear the wrath of Mrs. Jones.

Maybe I should make my page private, now that I thought about it, so that the Antichrist didn't snoop. I had only posted a handful of times over the last year and hadn't tagged any place I'd been. Old habits died hard.

The man's eyes flicked to me for maybe all of a second before they went back to the boy, and he said, "Does it look like I care? She could be Mother Teresa, and I still wouldn't want anybody here. It isn't safe to have some stranger hanging around our house."

Technically, I wouldn't be "hanging around." I'd stay *here* in this garage apartment and never bother anybody.

Seeing my opportunity disappearing with every word that came out of the man's mouth, I knew I had to act fast. Luckily for me, I liked fixing things and was good at it. "I cross my heart I'm not a psycho. I've only gotten one ticket in my whole life, and it was for going ten over, but in my defense, I had to pee really bad. You can call my aunt and uncle if you want a character reference, and they'll tell you I'm a pretty good person. You can text my nephews if you want, because they won't answer even if you blow up their phones."

The boy looked over his shoulder again, eyes wide and still frantic, but the man... well, he wasn't smiling at all. What he was doing was glaring at me over his son's shoulder. Again. In fact, his expression went flat, but before he could say a word, the kid jumped on my train of defense.

His voice was still low but impassioned. He must really want that three-thousand-dollar guitar. "I know what I did was shady, but you were gonna be gone a whole month, *and she's a girl—*" There were female serial killers out there, but now didn't seem like the right time to bring that up. "—so I figured you wouldn't, like, have to worry. I bought an alarm system I was gonna install on the windows anyway, and nobody was gonna get through the deadbolts on the door."

The man shook his head, and I was pretty sure his eyes were wider than they normally would have been. "No, Amos. *No.* Your sneaky shit is not winning me over. If anything, it's just pissing me off even more that you'd lie to me. *What the hell were you thinking?* What were you going to tell your uncle Johnny when he came over to check on you while I was gone? Huh? I can't believe you'd go behind my back after I told you no so many times. I'm trying to protect you, man. What's wrong with that?"

Then that intense face focused down as he shook his head, shoulders dropping so low I felt so obtrusive for witnessing it, for being here to notice the sheer disappointment that was so apparent on every line of this father's body as he stood there, processing this act of betrayal. He seemed to exhale before glancing back up, zeroing in on me that time, and said, gruffly, and I was pretty sure genuinely hurt by the actions of the teenager, "He'll get you a refund the second we get back in the house, but you aren't staying. You shouldn't have been able to 'make a reservation' in the first place."

I choked. At least inside I did. Because *no*.

No.

I hadn't even realized when I'd dropped my hands from the position they'd been, still in the air, but they were down and my palms were flat on my stomach, the pepper spray in my fingers, the rest of my body consumed by a mixture of worry, panic, and disappointment at the same time.

I was thirty-three years old, and like a tree, I'd lost all of my leaves, so much of what had made me *me*; but just like a tree, my branches and my roots were still there. And I was being reborn with a whole new set of leaves, bright and green and full of life. So I had to try. I had to. There weren't any other rentals like this.

"Please," I said, not even wincing at just how croaked that one single word sounded out of my mouth. It was now or never. "I understand why you're upset, and you have every right to be. I don't blame you for wanting to take care of your son and not risk his safety but...."

My voice cracked, and I hated it, but I knew I had to keep going because I had a feeling I was only going to get one shot at this before he kicked me out. "Just... *please*. I promise I won't make a peep or bother anyone. I took an edible once when I was twenty and got so high I had a panic attack and almost had to call an ambulance. I took Vicodin once after my wisdom teeth got removed, and it made me throw up so I didn't take more. The only alcohol I like is really sweet Moscato and a beer every once in a while. I won't even look at your son if you don't want me to, but *please*, please let me stay. I'll double the rate the listing was set for. I'll send it over right now if you want." I took a breath and gave the man what I hoped was the most pleading face ever. "Pretty please."

The man's facial expression was hard and stayed that way, that square jaw locked tight even at this distance. I didn't have a good feeling. I didn't have a good feeling at all.

His next words made my stomach drop. He was staring straight at me, those thick eyebrows flat on his absurdly handsome face. He had the bone structure you could only find on old Greek statues, I thought. Regal and defined, there was nothing weak about any part of his features. His mouth —his full lips the kind of inspiration women went to expensive doctors to try and replicate—became a flat line. "I'm sorry if you got your hopes up, but it's not happening." Those hard eyes moved toward the maybe-teenager as he growled in a voice so low I almost couldn't hear it—but I had great ears and he didn't know that—"It's not about the money."

Panic rose up inside of my chest, steadily, and I could see this opportunity disappearing before my eyes. "Please," I repeated myself. "You won't know I'm here. I'm quiet. I won't have any visitors." I hesitated. "I'll triple the rate."

The stranger didn't even hesitate. "No."

"Dad," the boy cut in before the older man shook his head.

"You have no say in this. You aren't going to have a say in anything any time soon, are we clear?"

The kid gasped, and my heart started beating faster.

"You went behind my *back*, Amos. If they hadn't found

another warden last minute, I would've been in Denver right now without a fucking clue you did this!" the man explained in that murderous, not loud or quiet voice, and honestly... I couldn't blame him.

I had no kids—I'd wanted them, but Kaden had kept putting it off—but I could only imagine how I'd feel if my child went behind my back... even if I understood his reasons. He wanted an expensive guitar, and I guessed he was too young to work or his parents wouldn't let him.

The kid made a weak, disgruntled noise of frustration, and I knew my time was just about to run out.

Rubbing my fingers together because they suddenly felt clammy, I tried to clamp down on my panic because it was more powerful than my strength. "I'm sorry about all of this. I'm sorry this wasn't done with your blessing. If some stranger moved into... well, I don't have a garage apartment, but if I did, I wouldn't be a fan of it. I value my privacy a lot. But I don't have anywhere else to go. There's no other house for short-term rental nearby. That's not your problem, I get it. But please, let me stay." I sucked in a breath and met his eyes; I couldn't tell what color they were from this distance. "I'm not a drug addict. I don't have a drinking problem or any weird fetishes. I promise. I had the same job for ten years; I was an assistant. I got... divorced, and I'm starting over."

Resentment, bitter and twisted, rose up over the back of my neck and shoulders like it had daily since things had fallen apart. And like every other time, I didn't brush it off. I tucked it into my body, real close to my chest, and babied it. I didn't want to forget it. I wanted to learn from it and keep the lesson for myself, even if it was uncomfortable.

Because you had to remember the shitty parts of life to appreciate the good.

"Please, Mr. Rhodes, if that's what your name is," I said in the calmest voice I was capable of. "You can make a copy of my ID, even though I already sent one. I can get you character references. I don't even kill spiders. I would protect your son if he needed it. I have teenage nephews who love me. They'll tell you I'm not a creep too." I took a step forward and then another, keeping our gazes together. "I was going to see if I could rent this out for longer, but I'll move on after a month if you could find it in your heart to give me a chance for now. Maybe another place will open up. I'd rent a place in town, but there isn't anything short-term, and I'm not ready to sign something for long." I could buy something, but he didn't need to know that; it just created too many questions. "I'll pay you three times the daily rate and won't bother you at all. I'll give you a five-star review too."

Maybe I shouldn't have added that part. It wasn't like he'd wanted this place up for rent in the first place.

The man's gaze narrowed just a little I was pretty sure because his eyebrows didn't move much, but I thought I noticed a difference. A notch appeared between his thick, dark eyebrows, and that terrible feeling intensified.

He was going to say no. I knew it. I was going to be fucked and living out of a hotel. Again.

But the boy joined in and said, talking just a little louder, genuinely sounding excited by the prospect, "Three times the price! Do you know how much money that would be?"

The man, maybe Tobias Rhodes, maybe not, glared at his son as he stood there, tense and still pissed. He really was furious.

And I braced myself for the worst. For the *no.* It wouldn't be the end of the world, but… it would still suck. A lot.

Instead though, the next words out of his mouth were aimed at the teenager. "I can't believe you'd lie to me."

The boy's entire body seemed to soften and fall, and his voice turned smaller than ever. "I'm sorry. I know it's a lot of money." He paused and managed to say even more quietly, "I'm sorry."

The man ran a hand through his hair and seemed to deflate too. "I said no. I told you we'd figure it out."

The kid didn't say anything but nodded after a second, looking like he felt about an inch tall.

"And this isn't over. We'll talk about it later." I didn't miss the boy's wince, but I was too busy watching the man turn to me and stare. He lifted a hand and scratched at the top of his head with long, blunt fingers. The man I was pretty sure might be a game warden at this point based on the patches I'd zeroed in on when they had hit the light perfectly, watched me.

I thought about waving but didn't. Instead, I just said, "Pretty please can I stay for triple the rate?"

I'd be lying if I said that I didn't purposely make sure to turn both my arms out so he could see that there weren't track marks on them. I didn't want him to think I was hiding anything. Well, the only thing I was hiding were details, but they really weren't any of his business or anyone else's. They wouldn't hurt him, his son, or anyone else other than me. So I tipped my chin up and didn't try to hide my desperation. It was the only thing possibly working in my favor.

I wasn't too proud for that.

"You're here on vacation?" the man asked slowly, still basically growling but testing the weight of every word out of his mouth as it came out.

"Not really. I'm thinking about living here permanently. I just want to make sure, but there are other things I want to do while I'm here." A lot of them but one day at a time.

"What?"

I shrugged and told him the truth. "Hikes."

A thick eyebrow went up, but his pissed-off face went

nowhere. I was on thin ice. "Hikes?" he asked like I'd said orgies.

"Yes. I can give you a list of the ones I want to do." I'd memorized the names of the trails based off my mom's journal, but I could write out the names of them if he wanted. "I don't have a job yet, but I'm going to get one, and I have money. It was my... divorce settlement." I might as well give him details so he didn't have to ask or think I was lying about being able to pay.

The man just kept looking at me coolly. The fingers of his free hand flexed open and closed. Even the nostrils of his strong nose flared. He didn't say anything for so long that even his son glanced at me over his shoulder again, eyes wide.

The boy just wanted my money, and that was fine. I actually thought it was pretty funny and smart of him. I remembered what it was like to be a kid without a job and want things.

Finally, the man tipped his chin up a little higher, and his nostrils flared again. "You'll pay triple?" he asked in a voice that told me he still wasn't totally convinced about this.

"Check, card, PayPal, or money transfer right now." I swallowed and, before I could stop myself, added with a smile I'd used plenty of times to try and diffuse difficult situations, "Do you offer cash discounts, because I can get you cash if that's the case." I stopped right before I winked, only just barely stopping myself. This man was probably married after all, and he was still pissed. Rightfully so to be fair.

"A money transfer is faster," the teenage boy volunteered in his quiet, whispering voice.

I couldn't hold back; I snorted and slapped my hand over my mouth when I snorted again.

The man glanced at his son with an expression on his face confirming he was still upset with him and didn't think his suggestion was funny, but to give him credit, he focused back on me and might have even rolled his eyes like he couldn't believe what he was about to say. "Cash. Tomorrow or you're out."

Was he...?

"I don't want to see you. I don't want to remember you're here unless it's seeing your car," he stated, still sounding and looking pissed but...

But agreeing! He was agreeing! Maybe!

"You got the month, but you're out after that," he stated, holding my gaze the entire time, trying to get his point across that there wasn't going to be any talking him into staying longer, that I should be grateful he'd agreed to this much.

I nodded. I would take a month if that's all I had and not cry or pout about it. If it came down to it, it would give me more time to figure out living arrangements. More permanent ones depending on how things went.

I wasn't getting any younger, and sometimes you just had to choose a path in life and go with it. That was what I wanted. To go and go.

So... I could start worrying about that tomorrow.

I nodded, and then I waited to see if he said something else, but all he did was turn toward the teenager and point him at the stairs. They started to head down in silence, leaving me in the studio apartment.

And maybe I shouldn't bring more attention to myself, but I couldn't help it. Just as the only thing visible about the man was the silvery back of his head, I called out, "Thank you! You won't know I'm here!"

Andddd he stopped walking.

I knew because I could still see just the top part of his head. He didn't turn around, but he was there, and I almost expected him not to say a word before he exhaled loudly—

maybe it was a grunt actually—seemed to shake his head, then called out in what I knew was an annoyed voice because that was something my sort of mother-in-law had mastered, "I better not."

Rude. But at least he didn't change his mind! That got tense there for a second.

Finally letting myself exhale, parts of my body I hadn't known were tensed, relaxed.

I had a month. Maybe I would end up staying longer and maybe I wouldn't. But I was going to make the fucking best out of it.

Mom, I'm back.

CHAPTER 2

J checked my phone for about the twentieth time the next day and did what I'd done the other nineteen times after I'd done the same thing.

I set it back down.

There was nothing new—not that I got a whole lot of texts or emails in the first place anymore, but regardless…. There was nothing to check in the first place.

As I'd learned last night, the only place I got cell phone reception was standing right by the window beside the table and chairs. I'd figured that out when I'd wandered away and lost the call I'd been in the middle of. It was an adjustment, but no big deal. A few of the smaller towns I'd stayed in had been the same way. My phone picked up *one* router, with two little bars, but it was password protected. I'd bet it was the family's home one and figured there was zero chance in hell of me getting that password. But it was all right. Part of me I guess had hoped that it had been a fluke and maybe a cell tower had been down, but that didn't seem to be the case.

There was nothing I really *needed* to check. I wanted to

look at my phone less anyway. Live my life instead of watching other people live theirs online.

The only message that had come through this morning had been from my aunt. We'd talked for an hour last night. Her text had made me grin.

Aunt Carolina: Go buy bear spray this morning PLEASE

Just in case I'd forgotten the five other times she'd insisted on the same thing during our phone call. She'd gone on and on about bears for at least ten minutes, apparently assuming that they randomly killed people just because. But I tried to take it as she was scared for me and had been nonstop for the last year. She had seen me when I'd moved back in with them, brokenhearted and feeling so lost that no compass in the world could redirect me.

That seemed to be the story of my life: going to my aunt and uncle's when my world fell apart. But as disastrous as splitting up with someone that I'd thought I'd be with for the rest of my life was, I'd known with my entire heart that nothing held a candle to losing my mom. That helped me keep things in perspective and reminded me of what was important.

I was so lucky to have my aunt and uncle. They had taken me in and treated me like I was theirs. Better, honestly. They had protected me and loved me.

And as if she had read my mind while we'd talked, she had griped, "Leo"—one of my cousins—"came over yesterday and helped me give that thief a one-star review for his new album. We set up your uncle an account and did the same. There were a lot of them too. Heh, heh."

I loved them both so much.

"I talked to Yuki a week ago, and she said it deserved for someone to give it a big shit emoji instead of any stars," I had told her.

In the background, my uncle, who wasn't a big talker but was a big listener, called out, "I bet he and his momma are freaking out now that their golden goose is gone."

I'd smirked.

Because I might know everything that happened had been for the best, but it didn't mean I was a good person who wanted the best for her ex.

He was going to pay for what he and his mom had done. Eventually. I knew it. He knew it. It was just a matter of time before everyone else did. Kaden could find someone else to write his music for him… but he was going to spend an arm and a leg when, before, I'd done it out of love. For free.

Well, not really, but it could have been.

But whoever helped him wouldn't let him take all the credit for their hard work. Not like I had.

My aunt had sighed and seemed to hesitate before saying, "Ora, I heard through Betty—do you remember Betty? The lady that does my hair?—Well, she said she saw a picture of him with that Tammy Lynn at an event recently."

Something had ticked at the back of my throat at the mental image of the man I'd been in a relationship with for nearly half my life with someone else.

Now he could have pictures of himself taken with someone. Huh. That was convenient.

It wasn't jealousy I felt. But… it was something.

The faint taste of bitterness had stayed with me during the rest of our conversation while my aunt had circled back around to talking about bear spray and blizzards and having to revert to cannibalism because people weren't prepared in the mountains for a snowstorm.

I figured I could explain to her later just how "mild" of a winter Pagosa Springs got versus most other places, so she wouldn't worry so much.

In the meantime, I had spent the morning deciding what I

needed to do and in what order everything would be the most efficient. I needed to get cash for the rental, and even though I was financially fine for now with my blood money, it wasn't like I had anything else to do. I also had a friend to visit.

Besides that, I needed more groceries because I'd eaten my last slices of turkey breast and cheese for breakfast and had nothing to eat for lunch or dinner. And since I was going to be here for a while and needed to make this place home, I might as well start chipping away at things that needed to be done ASAP.

Might as well get to it now.

Down the stairs and outside, I had to stop beside my car door. I'd driven in so late, I had missed the view of the surroundings, so I wasn't ready for the landscape ahead of me. The pictures of the garage apartment had focused mainly on the inside; there had only been one of the building.

Back when we'd lived here, we had been closer into town, in the midst of the huge pine trees that made up so much of the national forest in and around the town. But I could remember that on the outskirts, it had been more desert-like. And that was the exact kind of scenery here. The bright greens and dense forests were predominant here in Pagosa, but the craggy beauty that came with being so close to New Mexico and the desert-like area was an exception. Scattered cedar trees and brush filled the hills around the house.

It was incredible in its own way.

I stood there for a long time, then finally looked around. The SUV was still parked there. That was it though, vehicle-wise.

But just as quickly as I glanced in that direction, I looked away. The last thing I needed was to risk the maybe Mr. Rhodes seeing me looking at his house, period, and think I was doing something he didn't like. I didn't need to get kicked out. I'd walk to my car with my eyes closed for the next month if I had to.

I was here for a reason, and I didn't have time to waste since I wasn't sure how long I'd really be staying.

I wouldn't be staying if I didn't give myself a reason to.

And that's what got me sliding into my car and heading out, not totally sure I knew what I was doing but knowing I had to do something.

I waited until I got to way down the county road before looking up directions for the bank. I knew there was a branch in town; I'd checked to be on the safe side before coming. Five hours from Denver and four from Albuquerque, it was basically in the middle of nowhere, surrounded by small towns that even fewer people had ever heard of. There were two grocery stores, a few local banks and one major one, a tiny movie theater, and a pretty good amount of restaurants and breweries for the town's size.

Considering how booked the rentals were, I should have expected how busy town would be. It wasn't like I didn't know that Pagosa Springs relied heavily on tourism. As a kid, my mom used to complain about all the tourist traffic at the height of summer, getting frustrated at the grocery store when we'd have to park at the back of the lot.

But the rest of my memories of Pagosa were cloudy. So much of it looked different; there were a ton more buildings than I remembered, but there was something about it that was still... familiar. The new Walmart was the exception.

Everything changed over time, after all.

Hope again flared in my chest as I navigated my way down the highway. Maybe it didn't look totally like what I remembered, but there was enough there that felt... right. Or maybe I was just imagining it.

More than anything, this place was a fresh start. That was what I wanted. Sure, one of my worst memories had taken place here, but the rest of them—the best of them—overrode that.

Life in Pagosa had begun, and time was ticking.

The bank. Groceries. Maybe I could walk around and check out a few shops, see if anywhere was hiring or find a paper to look for ads there. I hadn't had a normal job in over a decade, and it wasn't like I had references I was willing to give anymore. Maybe I could stop by and see if Clara was working.

And if I had time, I could log on and give Kaden a one-star review too.

∼

THE SMALL WHITE sign in front of the shop said "HIRING" in bright orange letters.

Tilting my head back, I read the name of the business. THE OUTDOOR EXPERIENCE. Peeking through the window, there were a ton of people inside. There were racks of clothes, and a long counter formed an L-shape across two of the opposite walls. Inside, there was a woman zipping around from side to side behind the counter, looking exasperated as she helped as many people as she could who were all pointing at signs mounted to the walls. The most I could read was something about rentals.

I hadn't really had any expectations of what kind of job I could get, but after spending the last two hours ducking into one shop after another to explore, I was glad I didn't have my heart set on anything. The only places with signs had been a fly fishing store—I hadn't been fishing in years, so I didn't even bother asking—a music store that had been playing a song I knew too well and I'd turned around and walked back out instantly, and a shoe store. Both employees that had been working at the time had been in the back arguing so loud I heard every word, and I hadn't bothered asking for an application there either.

And now, on the opposite end of town from where I was going to be staying, I'd ended up here.

From memory, I knew The Outdoor Experience was an "outdoor outfitter"—aka store—that sold and rented everything you might need for outdoor activities—fishing, camping, archery, and more. It depended on the season.

I didn't know anything about... any of those things. Not anymore. I knew there were different types of fishing, fly-fishing, bottom fishing... other kinds... of fishing, but that was it. I knew about bows and... crossbows. I knew what a tent was, and many, many years ago, I'd been a pro at setting one up. But that was the extent of my knowledge of the outdoors. I'd lived in a city with people who weren't outdoorsy for too long, apparently.

But none of that mattered because I was here for another reason. Not for a job or to buy anything. And honestly, I was just a little nervous.

I hadn't reached out to Clara in almost a year, not since everything had gone to shit, and even then I had only messaged her to tell her happy birthday. She didn't know I'd split up with Kaden.

Well, she probably knew now since apparently he was dating someone else and taking pictures with them.

Yeah, he was getting that shit pie eventually.

Deciding I'd thought enough about him for the week, I shoved Kaden out of my head and went in.

I'd looked up pictures of the store when I'd still been in Utah and had been bored one night. Back when I'd been younger and would go home with Clara after school, sometimes her dad would bring us back to work with him and we'd play in the store if there weren't customers or would hide in the back and do homework. From the looks of it though, the store had gotten renovated sometime recently. The flooring was tile, and on top of that, now everything was new and modern. It looked great.

And very, very busy right then.

Moseying through the store, I zeroed in on the woman behind the counter. The same one I'd spotted through the window. She was helping another family out. Beside her, a teenage girl was helping a couple. I had no clue who she was, but the woman, I did recognize. We hadn't seen each other in person in twenty years, but we'd kept up enough over time that we were friends on Facebook and I recognized her.

I smiled and figured I might as well wait. There was no rush getting back to the garage apartment. Sidestepping through racks of clothes, I wandered toward the back of the store where a big FISHING sign hung... and where there were a lot fewer people.

Tiny, clear bags with all kinds of feathers and beads hung from waist-height rows of hooks. Huh. I picked up one bag with what looked like some kind of fur in it.

That's when I heard, "Can I help you with something?"

I didn't recognize Clara's voice, but I'd creeped through the windows enough to know the person speaking was either her or the teenage girl. And the person talking wasn't a teenager.

So I was smiling already as I turned around and came face-to-face with a person I recognized from the Facebook and Picturegram posts she'd made over the years.

But I knew she didn't recognize me when her mouth formed a pleasant, helpful smile of a person who owned a business. Clara had grown a few inches, and her curvy figure had hit voluptuous territory. She had inherited her Ute father's rich brown skin and high cheekbones, and I could already tell she was as cute and sweet as she used to be.

"Clara," I said, grinning so wide my cheeks hurt.

Her eyebrows went up just a little, and her voice was steady, "Hi. Do you...?" Her eyelids came down quickly, and I was pretty sure her head bobbed a little before her dark brown eyes moved over my face and slowly she said, "Do I know you?"

"You used to. We were best friends in elementary school and middle school."

My old friend's eyebrows knit together for a moment, these thin, dark arches, before suddenly her face fell, her mouth hung open, and she gasped, "Oh! You stopped dyeing your hair!"

A small reminder of the life I'd left behind. One where Mrs. Jones talked me into coloring it blonde "because you look so good that way." But I let it go in one ear and out the other as I nodded. "It's back to my natural color." I'd hacked off the blonde that hadn't finished growing out a couple months ago; it was why my hair was shorter than it had been in forever.

"I haven't heard from you in a year, you jerk!" she hissed, poking me in the shoulder. "Aurora!"

And in the next blink of an eye, her arms were around me and my arms were around her and we were hugging.

"What happened? What are you doing here?" she gasped, pulling back after a moment. We were about the same height, and I caught a little glimpse of the small gap between her two front teeth. "I tried texting you a few months ago, but the message bounced back!"

Another reminder. But it was fine. "It's kind of a long story, but I'm here. Visiting. Maybe staying."

Her dark eyes moved over my shoulder, and she seemed to be thinking about what I hadn't said. Only because she'd looked behind me for the person who should have been here with me... if he wasn't an asshole. "Are you by yourself?" she asked.

And by that, she meant, *Is Kaden with you?* She was one of the few people who knew about him. "No, we're not together anymore." I smiled, thinking about that shit pie for a second.

Clara blinked, and it took her a second to nod, but she did, her own smile taking over her face. "Well, I hope you'll tell me the long story eventually. What are you doing here?"

"I was in town; I just got here last night. I was walking around looking for a job, and I figured I might as well drop by and see you." While we hadn't been active-active in each other's lives for a long time, we had managed to keep in touch. We'd texted each other Happy Thanksgiving and Merry Christmas and Happy Birthday for two decades.

And since I'd split up with Kaden... I'd kind of fallen off the face of the planet. I hadn't felt like talking about anything more than I already had.

"You're really planning on staying?"

"Yeah. That's my plan at least."

Clara looked pretty damn surprised.

I knew how it seemed. No wonder she looked surprised.

But I'd have to explain that I hadn't really had a choice, even if I saw that it had been the best thing that could have happened.

She blinked again and then smiled a little more brightly before gesturing toward the counter where the younger girl was, looking at us with a curious expression on her face. Her ponytail was lopsided, and she seemed just as tired as Clara. I knew she didn't have kids, so maybe she was just an employee. They might have been going full speed all day. Based on the time, I'd bet all those rentals would be coming back pretty soon too. "Step into my office," Clara suggested. "Let's have a chat. I need to keep an eye out in case anyone else has any questions, and I want to hear about *stuff.*"

I cracked a smile at her office and nodded, going to stand across from where the teenager was leaning and watched as

Clara went around the counter to face the store. "Aurora, this is my niece, Jackie. Jackie, this is Aurora. We were best friends a long time ago."

The teenage girl's eyes went a little wide, and I wondered why, but she waved.

"Hi." I waved back.

"Where are you staying? You said you got here last night?" Clara asked.

"I'm staying closer to Chimney Rock." That was a national monument on the opposite end of town. "And, yeah, I drove in last night. I came into town to buy groceries and check out some of the shops. I figured I might as well come say hi while I was at it."

All I knew about Clara was that about a year ago her dad had gotten really ill, and she'd moved back to Pagosa from... Arizona? She had been married, and about eight years ago, her husband had died tragically in a drunk driving accident. I'd sent her flowers for the funeral when she'd posted about it.

"I'm glad you did," she said, still smiling wide. "I still can't believe you're here. Or that you're even prettier in person than in your pictures. I'd kind of hoped it was an app with a really great filter, but it's not." Clara shook her head.

"I didn't do anything to deserve it. Anyway, how are you? How's your dad?"

It was only because I'd gotten so in tune with people's suffering that I caught a hint of her wince. "I'm good. Really busy here. And Dad is... Dad's doing okay. I've taken over running this place full-time." Her face was tight. "He doesn't come in here that much anymore. But I'd bet he'd love to see you if you're planning on staying a while."

"I am, and I'd love to see him too."

Clara's gaze strayed to her niece before returning to me,

eyes narrowed. She looked at me a little too closely. "What kind of job are you looking for?"

"What kind of job are you hiring for?" I asked her, joking. What the hell did I know about outdoor activities? Nothing. Not anymore. Just walking through the fishing section had been eye-opening.

Mom would be so disappointed with me. She used to take me fishing all the time. Sometimes it had been the two of us, and sometimes her friends came too from what I remembered.

Yet that was all a blank wall for me now.

I wasn't exaggerating. I didn't recognize half of the stuff inside the store. More than that probably.

The last twenty years without my mom had turned me into a city girl. I hadn't been camping once since leaving here. I'd gone fishing a handful of times with my uncle on his boat, but that had easily been fifteen years ago since the last trip. I wasn't even sure I could name ten different kinds of fish if I had to.

The surprising part was, Clara looked... well, she looked surprisingly interested. "Don't mess with me right now, Aurora... or do you go by Ora now?"

"Either one." I blinked. "And I was kind of joking. I don't know anything about any of this." I gestured behind me. "If I did though, sign me up."

Her gaze hadn't stopped being narrowed since I'd joked around. If anything, her chin had tipped up a bit. "You don't know anything?"

"It took me a second to remember the flies and fishing lures back there weren't called 'fishing thingies.'" I grinned. "That's bad."

"My last guy that quit on me used to tell people they could catch salmon in the San Juan," she said drily.

"You... can't?"

Clara smiled, her little gap flashing at me, and I had to grin back at her. "No, you can't. But he also showed up late every day he came in... and never actually called in when he wasn't planning on keeping his shift..." She shook her head. "I'm sorry. I'm jumping all over you. I've just been looking for help, and I feel like I've hired everyone looking for a job in town."

Oh.

Well.

I closed my mouth and processed what she was saying. What this could mean. Working for someone who I had a relationship with. We all knew how that had gone last time.

Great until it hadn't, but that was life.

I was sure I could find something elsewhere, but I was also pretty sure Clara and I could get along. I'd followed her enough over the years to see her happy, upbeat posts online, which could have been a ruse and part of her highlight reel, but I doubted it. Even when her husband had passed away, she had been gracious in her grief. And we'd always joked around just fine online.

What did I have to lose? Other than making an idiot out of myself since I didn't know anything?

"No, don't apologize," I told her pretty cautiously. "I just... I don't know anything about camping or fishing, but... if you're willing... I can try. I'm a fast learner, and I know how to ask questions," I threw out, watching her facial features go from open to straight-up calculating. "I'm punctual. I work hard, and I almost never get sick. It takes a lot for me to be in a bad mood."

She lifted a hand and tapped her index finger against her chin, her pleasant face thoughtful, but it was her slightly widened eyes that gave away her continued interest.

But I still wanted her to understand the extent of what

she'd be dealing with by hiring me so that there weren't any surprises or anyone ended up disappointed.

"I haven't worked retail in a really long time, but I did used to have to deal with people a lot at my, uh"—I did quotations with my fingers—"last job."

Her mouth puckered, eyes sliding toward the teenage girl —Jackie—before flicking back to me and ending up with a tight nod.

She wasn't going to bring up Kaden in front of her, I guess, and honestly, that was totally fine with me. The fewer people that knew, the better. The Joneses had bet on me keeping my word about not talking about our relationship, and they'd been right.

But I only didn't want to talk about him because I didn't want to be Kaden Jones's ex-girlfriend for the rest of my life, especially not if I didn't have to. Damn, I hoped his mom got hot flashes tonight.

"I just want you to be aware of my absolute lack of knowledge."

Clara's mouth twitched. "The second to last employee I hired lasted two days. My last one was here for a week before she ghosted me. The last ten before that were the same story. I have two part-timers that are friends with my dad who show up once or twice a month." Clara's chin went high, and I swear she winced. "If you can show up when you're sched-uled and do *something*, I'll teach you as much as you're willing to learn."

Yeah, that was hope blooming in my chest. Working with an old friend? Doing something that my mom would have killed at? Maybe this wouldn't be such a bad thing. "I love learning," I told her honestly.

I'd spent so much of my life seeing hopeful, cautiously optimistic faces, that I recognized her expression for what it was: that.

She must really be desperate if she was willing to hire me, old friendship or not.

"So…" Her hands wrapped around the counter. "Do you want to work here then? Doing odds and ends?"

"As long you don't think it will be awkward." I paused and tried to smile at her brightly. "I'm a good listener; I know business is business. But if you get tired of me, will you tell me? If I'm not doing a good job? And real talk, I have a room booked for a month, and if things are going okay, I'll stay for longer, but I don't know yet for sure."

Clara glanced at the teenage girl who was too busy staring at me intently before nodding. "I'll take it as long as you show up and, if you don't feel like coming in, you'll at least give me notice?"

"I promise."

"I have to warn you though, I can't pay you much hourly." She gave me an amount that wasn't much over minimum wage, but it was something.

And with someone I liked and had known me before, it was fucking fate slapping me in the face.

And when fate pushed things into your life, you should listen. I had my ears ready. My future wide open. I had no clue what I wanted to do anymore, but this was something. This was a step. And the only way you could move was by taking that first step, and sometimes it didn't matter which direction you took it as long as you did.

"I can teach you how to use the register, and we can figure out what other things you can do. Rentals. I don't know. But it isn't going to be a whole lot of money; I want you to know that. You sure that's okay?"

"I've never wanted to be a millionaire," I told her carefully, feeling something that felt an awful lot like relief crawl over my skin.

"Want to start tomorrow?"

Some more of that blooming hope flowered in my chest. "Tomorrow works for me." I had exactly nothing going on.

I held my hand out between us. She slipped hers forward too, and we shook on it, roughly.

Then slowly, we both smiled and she dipped her chin down and asked, with her mouth twitching again, her dark eyes bright, "Now that that's over, tell me everything. What have you been doing?" Her face fell, and I knew what had come into her mind again—the same thing that loomed over just about every relationship I had with people who were aware of what had happened—my mom.

I didn't feel like talking about my mom or Kaden, so I changed the subject. "What have *you* been doing?"

Luckily, she took the bait and told me all about what she'd been up to.

∼

I WAS FEELING PRETTY DAMN good as I drove back to the garage apartment that evening. I'd spent two hours hanging out with Clara and Jackie. The fifteen-year-old had been quiet but extremely watchful, soaking up everything Clara shared about her life with these wide eyes that made me like her already.

Those hours together were the highlight of the last two months of my life—probably even longer than that. It was nice to be around someone who *knew me.* To have a conversation in person with someone who wasn't a total stranger. I'd been to so many cool national parks, major tourist destinations, and so many other places that I'd only seen in magazines and in travel blogs, that I couldn't regret how I'd spent my time before getting to Pagosa. It had been what I'd needed, and I was fully aware my free time had been a luxury.

Even if it was a blessing that had come with what had felt like such a huge price tag.

Fourteen years wasted for two months of doing whatever I wanted to do. And still more than enough money in my bank account that I wouldn't have to work for... a while. But I knew that time was over.

There was no point in waiting to settle in to get my life back on track.

But getting to catch up with my old friend gave me hope that maybe... there was something for me here. Or at least that if I gave it some time, I could make there be something here for me. There were bones, and that was more than I could say for just about every other place in the United States that wasn't Cape Coral or Nashville.

Why not here? Ran through my head all over again.

If my mom had been able to live here with no family and a few friends, why couldn't I?

I pulled my car into the driveway like my navigation instructed and spotted two vehicles in front of the house. The Bronco and a truck that said "Parks and Wildlife" on the sides. Lights blazed through the big windows of the main house, and I wondered what the father and son were doing.

Then I wondered if there was a girlfriend, wife, or mom in there with them too. There might be a sister. Or even more siblings. Maybe not though, because if he had thought about trying to pull off renting out the garage apartment, it would've been a lot harder with a sibling who could rat him out.

I would know. My cousins used to pay me not to tell my aunt and uncle about things that would get them in trouble. Who the hell knew though?

I could snoop and perv from a distance. I was a sucker for a gorgeous face—usually dog faces or baby animals but human ones too from time to time. It wouldn't be a hardship to check out my landlord.

Parking my car alongside the garage apartment, I picked up the envelope with cash that I'd gotten from the bank and got out. Not wanting to get caught by the hot dad who didn't want to know I existed, I pretty much ran to the front door, knocked on it, then stuffed it halfway under the mat before I got caught.

I collected the bags of groceries I'd bought after leaving Clara and Jackie, grabbed the right key, and hustled for the door.

What had been supposed to be a quick trip to the grocery store ended up taking almost an hour since I had no idea where anything was, but I managed to get more sandwich supplies, cereal, fruit, almond milk, and things to make a few quick dinners. Over the last decade, I'd mastered about a dozen versions of quick, easy dinners I could make with a single small pot—most of the time I would rather eat my own food than what I could have gotten through catering. Those recipes had come in handy over the last two months when I'd gotten fed up with eating out.

Closing the door with my hip, I glanced toward the house and spotted a familiarish face through a window.

A young face.

I paused for a second then waved.

The boy, Amos, lifted a hand shyly. I wondered if he was grounded for the rest of his life. Poor kid.

Back upstairs, in my temporary home, I put my groceries up and made a meal, basically inhaling it. After that, I pulled my mom's journal out from my backpack, setting the leather-bound book beside a spiral one I'd bought the day after I'd decided to head to Pagosa. Then I found the page I already had memorized but felt like seeing.

I'd driven by the house we'd lived in after the grocery

store, and it had left me with something that felt an awful lot like indigestion in the center of my chest. It wasn't indigestion though. I'd gotten so familiar with the sensation that I knew exactly what it was. I just missed her extra today.

I was lucky because I remembered a lot about her. I'd been thirteen when she'd gone missing, but there were a few things I could recall a lot more clearly than others. Time had softened so many details and watered other memories down, but one of the brightest memories of her had been her absolute love of the outdoors. She would've killed it working at The Outdoor Experience, and now that I thought about it... well, I guess it was the most perfect job I could have gotten. I was already planning on doing her hikes.

Maybe I didn't know anything about fishing, camping, or archery, but I'd used to do some of that stuff with her, and I was pretty sure if I'd hated it, I wouldn't have forgotten. That was something to consider.

Another thing I remembered as well was how much she had loved to catalog things she did. That included keeping track of what had been her favorite hobby in the world: hiking. She used to say it was the best therapy she'd ever found—not that I'd understood what that meant until I'd gotten a lot older.

The problem was, she hadn't written things down in order of easiest to hardest. She'd done random ones, and over the last two weeks, I had already done the grunt work of finding the ratings for their difficulties and figuring out how long each trail was.

Because I wasn't used to the altitude, and I didn't know yet how long I was going to actually be here, I had to start with the easiest and shortest and work my way up from there. I knew exactly what hike I would do first. Clara and I hadn't talked about long-term scheduling, but I'd eyed the shop's hours on the way out and saw it was closed on

Mondays. I figured that for sure would be my day off, obviously. Now I'd just have to see what other day I could get too. If she wanted me to only work part-time, that was good. We'd... see. And that was perfect.

My plan was to start jumping rope tomorrow to give my lungs some exercise in preparation. I'd been walking and jogging almost every day lately, when I wasn't driving somewhere new, but I didn't want to give myself altitude sickness my first week here—at least that's what all the travel forums I'd read had warned against. There really wasn't anywhere to walk around here though, other than driving into town to a trail or settling for the side of the road, which didn't exactly sound safe.

Either way, I set the two notebooks in front of me and reread my mom's entry. The one I was looking for was toward the middle. Mom only did entries for new hikes, but continued doing her favorites over and over again. She had started this particular journal after I'd been born. There were older journals she'd done before me, but all those had been extreme hikes and ones in other places she'd lived before having me.

AUGUST 19
PIEDRA FALLS
PAGOSA SPRINGS, CO
EASY, 15 MINUTES ONE WAY, CLEAR TRAIL
COME BACK IN THE FALL TO GET IN THE RIVER!
WOULD DO IT AGAIN

There was a heart drawn next to it.

Then I read it once more even though I'd already read the entry at least fifty times and had it memorized.

There was a photograph of Mom and me doing this hike when I'd been around six years old in one of the photo albums I'd been able to keep. It was an easy, short hike, only about a quarter of a mile in, so I figured it would be a good starting point. Tomorrow I'd talk to Clara about days off to be on the safe side and plan to work around them... if she didn't fire me an hour in because I had no clue what the hell I was doing.

I dragged my finger along the outside of the journal; I didn't do it over the words anymore because I was worried about smudging them or ruining them, and I wanted her notebook around as long as possible. Her handwriting was small and not all that neat, but it felt a lot like her. The book was precious and had been one of the few things that had never left my side.

After a little while, I closed it then got up to shower. Tomorrow I should take my tablet into town and go somewhere with Wi-Fi to download some movies or shows onto it. Maybe Clara had Wi-Fi at the shop. Stopping at the only other window in the house that I hadn't opened as soon as I got into the almost too-warm apartment—I'd forgotten most places around here didn't have air conditioning—I paused and glanced at the main house again.

It was even more illuminated than it'd been when I'd arrived. Light pierced through every huge window along the front and side. This time though, the Parks and Wildlife truck was gone.

For the second time, I wondered what my landlord's significant other looked like.

Hmm.

I mean, I was already right here, where there was service. Plus, it wasn't like I had anything else to do. I grabbed my phone and went back to the window.

I typed "TOBIAS RHODES" into the Facebook search box.

There were only a few Tobias Rhodes, and none of them were based in Colorado. There was one with a picture that looked a little old—and by old I meant maybe ten years or so from how blurry it was, like an old cell phone picture—of a little boy with a dog beside him. It said he lived in Jacksonville, Florida.

I wasn't sure why I clicked on, it but I did. Someone named Billy Warner had posted on his page a year ago with a link to some article about a new world record fish that had been caught, and after that was a post with an updated profile picture of an even younger little boy and the dog. There were two comments, so I clicked on them.

The first one was from the same Billy Warner, and it said: **Am got my looks**

The second comment was a reply, and it was from Tobias Rhodes: **You wish**

Am? As in... Amos? The boy? His skin tone was about right.

I went back to the posts and scrolled down. There were barely any. Three actually.

There was an even older profile picture of just the dog, this big white one. And that had been from two years before that.

The other post was from the same Billy person with another fishing link, and that one had comments too.

Being as careful as possible, because I was going to die if I accidentally liked an old post—I would literally have to delete my account and legally change my name—I clicked on the comments. There were six.

The first one was from someone named Johnny Green, it read: **When we going fishing?**

Tobias Rhodes responded with: **Whenever you want to come visit.**

Billy Warner replied with: **Johnny Green, Rhodes is single again. Let's go.**

Johnny Green: **You broke up with Angie? Hell yeah, let's do it**

Tobias Rhodes: **Invite Am too.**

Billy Warner: **I'll bring him.**

Who Angie was, I had no idea. Chances were, it was an ex-girlfriend or maybe even a current girlfriend? Maybe they had gotten back together? Maybe it was Amos's mom?

Who Billy or Johnny were, I had no idea either.

There was no other information on his page though, and I didn't trust myself to snoop through other profiles without getting caught.

Hmm.

I exited out of the window before I accidentally clicked on anything.

I'd just have to snoop through Picturegram and see what I could find. That was a good plan. Worst case, maybe I could invest in some binoculars to snoop on the outside.

Deciding that was a good idea, I went to take a shower.

I had a busy day tomorrow.

I had a life to start building.

CHAPTER 3

a gallon of water even though it was less than a one-mile hike? Check.

Brand-new hiking boots I had only tried breaking in walking around the apartment that were more than likely going to give me blisters? Check.

Two granola bars even though I'd just eaten breakfast? Check.

Two days later, I was ready to go. It was my first day off since Clara had hired me, and I was going to try and knock out the short hike to the waterfalls. I'd been guzzling down so much water in an effort to avoid getting altitude sickness that I'd woken up three times last night to pee. I didn't have time to get hangover-like symptoms.

Plus I was hoping that the hike would get my mind off how useless I was at the shop.

Just thinking about the shop got me to stop with the Spice Girls lyrics I'd been singing under my breath.

My first and only day had gone just as bad as I'd worried it would, as I'd warned Clara it could. The shame of staring blankly at one customer after another when they asked questions hurt me. Literally hurt me. I wasn't used to feeling incompetent, to having to ask one question after another because I literally had no clue what in the world the customers were referring to or asking for.

Beads? Leaded weights? Recommendations? Just thinking about how bad yesterday had gone made me cringe.

What I needed to do was figure out a solution, especially if I was planning on sticking around for much longer. A couple times—mostly when customers were extra kind when I didn't know things, especially when they were almost condescending telling me *not to worry my pretty head* because *that* got under my skin like nothing else could—I thought about quitting, letting Clara find someone who knew more about anything in the store than I did, but then all I had to do was look at the dark circles under her eyes, and I knew I wouldn't. She needed help. And even if all I did was ring people up and save her two minutes, it was something.

I think.

I had to suck it up and learn faster. Somehow. I'd worry about it later. Stressing over screwing up had robbed me of enough sleep last night.

Down the stairs and out the door, I stopped to lock it and headed around to get to my car, but I caught something moving out of the corner of my eye by the main house.

It was Amos.

I lifted a hand as he sat on one of the deck chairs, a game console clutched in his hand. "Hi."

He stopped, like I'd surprised him, and lifted a hand up too. His "Hi" wasn't exactly enthusiastic, but it wasn't mean either. I was pretty positive he was just shy.

And I wasn't supposed to be talking to him. Invisible. I was supposed to be invisible.

"See you later!" I called out before ducking into my car and reversing.

At least his dad hadn't caught me.

~

ALMOST FIVE HOURS LATER, I was pulling back up to the garage apartment and giving myself the middle finger.

"Fucking idiot," I told myself for at least the tenth time as I parked my car and tried to ignore the tightness in my shoulders.

I was going to be hurting soon. Very, very soon. And it was all my fault.

I'd taken for granted the fact that I was tanner now than I'd been in years. Mostly from all the outside time I'd spent in Utah and Arizona. What I hadn't done was take into consideration the change in altitude. How much more intense the UV rays were here.

Because over the course of the short hike to the falls and back, I'd gotten roasted despite having a base coat. My shoulders were hot and stung like a son of a bitch. All because my dumb ass had forgotten to put sunblock on and I'd spent too much time sitting on a rock, talking to an older couple who hadn't been feeling so well.

On the bright side, the drive toward the falls was the prettiest thing I'd ever seen, and I'd had to pull over a bunch of times just to take in the wilderness without pissing off the cars behind me. I had also taken advantage of the stops to pee while I was at it.

It was magical. Spectacular. The landscape was straight out of a movie. *How had I forgotten that?* I had a couple of blurry memories of going there with Mom before, nothing real concrete but just enough.

But none of that compared to the simple feeling and power of the falls. It wasn't extraordinarily tall, but it dropped so much water, it was pretty amazing to witness. It left me in awe, really. Only Mother Nature could make you feel so small. The trail and falls were pretty packed, and I'd taken pictures for a family and two couples. I'd even sent my uncle some pictures when I'd gotten into cell service reception. He'd texted me back a couple of thumbs-up, and my aunt had called and asked me if I was crazy for crossing the river over a big log that had been draped across it.

"Owwie, oww, oww," I hissed to myself as I got out of the car and went around the other side. I grabbed my little backpack and gallon of water and shut it with my hip, feeling the heat on my skin some more and groaning.

Like an idiot, I instantly forgot and slipped the strap of my backpack over my shoulder and just as quickly, slid that son of a bitch back off with a cry that made me sound like I was getting murdered.

"Are you okay?" a voice that sounded only *slightly* familiar called out.

I turned around to find Amos sitting in a different chair than the one I'd last seen him in on the deck, holding his game console in one hand and squinting hard while his other one hovered just above his eyes to block out the sun so he could get a good look at my lobster reenactment.

"Hi. I'm all right, just gave myself a second-degree sunburn I think. No big deal," I joked, groaning when my shoulder gave another throb of pain from contact with the strap.

I almost didn't hear him say, "We got aloe vera," quietly.

I just about dropped my bag.

"You can get some if you want."

He didn't have to tell me twice. Setting my bag down on the ground after grabbing my Swiss Army knife, I walked toward the house. Up the stairs, I headed over to where he was. In a ratty T-shirt and even rattier sweatpants with a couple holes in them, he gestured to the side, and I could see a medium-sized aloe vera plant in a plain orange pot next to a cactus and something that had once been alive but hadn't been in a while.

"Thank you for offering," I told him as I kneeled beside the pot and picked out a nice, thick leaf. I glanced at him and caught him watching me. He looked away. "Did you get in trouble over the garage apartment?" I asked.

There was a pause, then, "Yeah," he replied hesitantly, still quietly.

"Big trouble?"

Another pause before, "I got grounded." One more beat of silence then, "You went hiking?"

I glanced up at him and smiled. "I did. I went to Piedra Falls. I got roasted." The whole thing had felt a whole lot farther than a half mile. I'd started bitching about five minutes in, at how thirsty I was and how much I regretted refilling an old bottle I'd found on the floor of my car so that I wouldn't have to carry the entire gallon. I'd had a harder time breathing than I would have expected, but it was practice. So I wasn't going to beat myself up too much about how much I'd been panting and sweating while going through a canopy of trees lining the trail.

But I decided I was going to have to start doing some other kind of harder cardio because, holy shit, I'd die doing one of the ten-mile trips I wanted to take—if I stayed and could.

After the shit show that yesterday had been at work, I wasn't totally sure if things were going to work out... but I still hoped they did.

No one *really* missed me in Florida. They loved me, but they had gotten used to me living away for so long that I knew it had to be weird that I'd come back. My aunt and uncle had gotten used to living home alone, even though they'd accepted me with open arms and nurtured me back to a healed heart. Or at least a mostly healed one. My cousins all had their own lives too.

And my friends cared about me, but they had three thousand things going on as well.

"How'd you get burned?" he asked after another moment of silence.

"There was a couple there who had gotten lightheaded right at the base, and I hung out with them until they felt good enough to hike back to their car," I explained.

The boy didn't say anything, but I could see his fingertips tapping along the border of his Nintendo as I finished cutting through the leaf. "Sorry." He was focused on his console. "About Dad getting pissed. I should've told him, but I know he would've said no."

"It's okay." I mean, it wasn't, but his dad already bitched him out, I was sure. Something *could* have happened to him if he'd rented the place out to the wrong person. But you know, I wasn't his mom, and his sneakiness got me this place I liked, so I'd be a hypocrite to give him a hard time. "Did you get grounded for a long time?"

His "yeah" was so disappointed, I felt bad.

"I'm sorry."

"He deposited the money into my savings account." One slim finger picked at a hole in his sweatpants. "Can't use it anytime soon though."

I winced. "Hopefully your parents will change their mind."

He made a face aimed at his console that told me he wasn't holding his breath.

Poor guy. "I don't want to upset your dad any more; I'll let you get back to your game. Thank you for letting me get some aloe. Yell if you need something. I have the windows open."

He glanced at me then and nodded, watching me head

back down the deck and across the gravel toward the garage apartment.

I thought about Kaden and his new girlfriend for a split second.

Then I shrugged that loser off.

I had better things to think about. Starting with this sunburn and ending with just about anything else.

A WEEK WENT by in the blink of an eye.

I worked—crashed and burned half the time was more like it—and slowly started to get to know Clara again. Her niece, Jackie, came in and helped a few days a week;, she was nice but she kind of just stuck to herself and listened to Clara and me when we had time between customers, and I worried she didn't like me even though I'd brought her a Frappuccino and tried to share my snacks with her. I didn't *think* she was shy from the way she spoke to customers, but I was still working on her.

Clara, though, was a good boss and worked harder than most people, and as much as I knew I was terrible at my job, I kept trying because she needed the help. No one new had come in to apply for a job while I was there either, so I was well aware that didn't help.

I started jumping rope a little longer every day.

When I was "home" and wasn't in the middle of reading or watching something I'd downloaded onto my tablet, I spied on my neighbors. Sometimes Amos caught me and waved, but most of the time, I got away with it. I hoped.

What I'd learned was that his dad, who I'd confirmed *was* Mr. Rhodes because I'd used binoculars and read the name embroidered on his uniform shirt, was gone all the time. Literally. His car was missing by the time I left, and he usually wasn't back until seven most days. The teenager, Amos, didn't leave the house ever—I only saw him on the deck—and I guessed that was because he'd been grounded.

And in the little over a week that I'd been at the garage apartment, not once had I seen any other car show up.

It really was just Mr. Rhodes and his son, I was pretty sure. The time I'd read the older man's name, I might have also peeked at his hand to see there wasn't a wedding ring there.

Speaking of Amos, I was considering him my second friend in town even though we only waved at each other and he'd said about ten words to me since the day he'd saved me from my sunburn with his offer. Even though I talked a lot at work, asking a lot of questions to try and figure out what customers wanted because I didn't get half the shit that came out of their mouths—why some people chose to use water purifying tablets instead of buying a bottle with a built-in filter was still beyond me—I hadn't really made friends yet.

I was a little lonely. All the customers I'd dealt with had been too nice to give me a hard time for not being able to answer their questions, but I dreaded the day I pissed off the wrong person and smiling at them and trying to make a joke wouldn't work like it usually did to get me out of trouble.

No one ever told you how hard it was to make friends as an adult. But it was hard. Real hard.

I was working on it. Quality over quantity.

Nori, Yuki's sister and my friend too, texted. Yuki called. My cousins reached out and asked when I was coming back. (Never.)

Things were… coming along.

I had hope.

And I was in the middle of getting dressed, making a mental plan to go to the grocery store this evening, when my phone pinged with an incoming email. I stopped to take a peek at the screen.

The email was from a K.D. Jones.

I shook my head and bit the inside of my cheek.

There was no subject. I shouldn't waste my time, but... I was weak. I clicked on the message and prepared myself.

It was short and simple though.

Roro,

I know you're mad but call me back.

-K

Kaden knew I was mad?

Me? Mad?

Hahahahahahahaha

I would set his Rolls-Royce on fire if I had the chance and sleep just fine.

And I was thinking of a dozen other things I could do to him without feeling guilty as I got into my car a few minutes later and tried to turn it on.

There was no click. Not a slight turn. Nothing.

It was karma. It was karma, and I knew it, for thinking ugly things. At least that's what Yuki would say... if it was anyone other than Kaden I was wishing shitty things upon.

Squeezing my eyes closed, I wrapped my fingers around the wheel and tried to shake it with a "Oh, fuck youuuuuu." Then I tried to shake it again. "Fuck!"

I was so busy yelling at the steering wheel that I barely heard the knock on my window.

Mr. Rhodes stood there, eyebrows slightly up.

Yeah, he'd heard me. He'd heard it all. At least I'd had the windows up. I hadn't been paying attention and didn't notice he was still home.

Peeling my fingers off the stranglehold they had on the steering wheel, I swallowed my frustration and opened the door slowly, giving him time to back up. He took a single big step, giving me a view of a red cooler in one hand and a travel coffee mug in the other. He was even better looking up close and personal in daylight, I realized.

I'd thought his jaw and brow bones had been a masterpiece when I'd creeped on him before, but now, just feet away, they still were, but the gentle cleft in his chin got added to the list.

I'd bet if he was in a game warden calendar, it would sell out every year.

"…didn't work?" he asked.

I blinked and tried to figure out what he was talking about since I'd zoned out. I had no idea. "What?" I asked, trying to focus.

"Telling your car to fuck itself didn't make it turn on?" he asked in that same level, hard voice from a week ago, both of his thick eyebrows still up.

Was he… joking? I blinked. "No, she doesn't like being bullied," I told him, deadpan.

One eyebrow went up a little higher.

I smiled.

He didn't smile, but he did take a step back. "Pop the hood," Mr. Rhodes said, flicking his fingers toward himself. "I don't have all day."

Oh. I reached inside and opened it as he set his cooler down and his coffee, or whatever was in there, on top of it. He went straight for ducking under the hood as I circled around to stand beside him.

Like I knew what I was looking at.

"How old's your battery?" he asked as he tinkered with something and pulled it out. It was a dipstick. For the oil. There was some on it. I was pretty good at getting it changed on time. I figured it couldn't be that.

"Um, I don't know? Four years?" It might be more like five; it was the original. The Joneses had given me so much crap for not trading my car in every year like they did. Fortunately for me though, Mrs. Jones hadn't wanted me driving around a car under their last name in case I was pulled over, so I'd bought it on my own. It was and had always been all mine.

He nodded, attention focused on my engine, then took another step back. "Your terminals are corroded and need a clean. I'll give you a jump and see if that'll get you going until you get it fixed."

Corroded? I leaned in, coming in to step beside him, just inches away, and peeked inside. "Is it that white stuff?"

There was a pause and then, "Yes."

I peeked at him. He had a really nice voice... when he wasn't snapping out words like a whip.

Up this close... I guess he had to be six-three. Six-four. Maybe a little taller.

Why was this guy not married? Where was Amos's mom? Why was I so nosey?

"Okay, I'll get it cleaned," I said brightly, focusing before he got irritated with me for checking him out. I could just do it from upstairs tomorrow.

Mr. Rhodes didn't say another word before he headed toward his truck. In no time at all, he pulled it up alongside my car and then farted around in the back cab before coming back with jumper cables. I stood there and watched as he hooked them up to my battery and then opened his own hood and did the same.

If I was expecting him to stand there and talk to me, I would've been disappointed. Mr. Rhodes went and sat in his truck... but I was pretty sure he was looking at me through the windshield.

I smiled.

He either pretended not to see me or decided just not to smile back.

I stood there, looking at my car's engine like I recognized some of it when I damn well did not. After a minute, I leaned in and snapped a picture of the cables hooked up to my battery, just in case I ever had to do it. I should get an emergency kit while I was at it. I still needed to get bear spray.

What could only have been a couple minutes later, he hung his head out of the window. "Try her now."

I nodded and dodged inside, making a quick plead for her to not do this shit to me, and turned the key.

She squealed to life, and I fist pumped the air.

Mr. Rhodes slid out of his truck and quickly undid the cables from our batteries, going back around his truck in the time it took me to close my hood, and depositing his cables somewhere in his back seat. I reached up to try and close his hood but couldn't reach. He slid me a side look as he lifted a hand and slammed it shut.

I grinned up at him. His khaki-colored work shirt hugged the broad line of his shoulders and tapered into the grayish-blue pants it was tucked into. That hair of his was something else too, that silver with the brown…. He really was way too attractive. "Thank you so much."

He grunted. Then he crouched down, making me freeze because his face went right by my shoulder and side, but popped back up with his cooler and coffee mug. He was out of there, back around his truck, and then jumping in. He hesitated.

Mr. Rhodes nodded at me and then reversed so fast I was impressed.

He'd helped.

And hadn't kicked me out even if he'd looked like he would rather be just about anywhere else.

Something was something.

And I had to get to work.

CHAPTER 4

*T*he next three days of my life went by in the blink of an eye.

All right, a blink if you had pink eye.

I woke up, and each of the days, I tried to jump rope, had to stop every ten seconds then start again as I accepted I was nowhere near the top tier of physical conditioning above sea level. Then I had breakfast, showered, and went to work.

Work was... parts of it were good. The parts where I got to talk to Clara and catch up with her were my favorite. Rekindling a friendship with her was like breathing. It was effortless. She was just as funny and warm as I had hoped.

We didn't get to talk much. By the time I arrived every morning, she was hectic in trying to have everything organized before opening. I helped her as much as I could, and we squeezed in questions as she made explanations about stocking and what the store carried, which was everything imaginable and everything unimaginable.

Had I gotten my boobs done? No, they were the same C-cup I'd had since they'd stopped growing at fifteen, held up by what was basically a Wonderbra.

Did I bleach my teeth? No, I used straws all the time and brushed my teeth three times a day.

Had I ever gotten Botox done because she was thinking about it but wasn't sure? No, but I knew a lot of people who had and wasn't sure I would do it. I also told her she didn't need it.

I would have asked her things too, but she'd squeezed in so many details that first day I'd walked in, that there weren't too many other things I felt comfortable asking about so soon.

In the years since we'd last seen each other, she had gone to college in northern Colorado for nursing, moved to Arizona with her boyfriend, gotten married, and then he'd passed away too soon afterward. Since then, she'd moved back to help take care of her ill dad and run the family business, and—this was where she'd been vague and I'd bet it was because her niece had been there—shortly after that, Jackie had moved in. Her older brother got a job as a long-distance truck driver and needed somewhere safe and constant for her to stay.

Having worked for people that I cared about and loved before, I already understood how to listen and follow instructions without letting them get to me or affect my pride. But Clara was great. Literally great.

We'd made plans to hang out away from work sometime soon, but she had to get someone to stay with her dad because he couldn't be left alone for long periods, and the nurses and aides who usually stayed with him during the day were already working too many hours with her being at the shop literally all the time since she didn't have reliable help.

I remembered her dad and wanted to see him; she said that he would love to see me too. She'd told him all about how I was back, and that just made me want to help her that much more, even if I was pretty sure I was only one step above her previous shitty employees. My only saving grace was literally that, even though I was useless and constantly having to ask her questions eighty times a day, the customers were all sweet and patient. One or two were a little too friendly, but I was good—and unfortunately used to—ignoring certain comments.

When Clara wasn't running around the shop talking to customers, we talked about the store. When she asked about my life, I told her bits and pieces, tiny fragments that didn't exactly piece together properly and left plot holes the size of Alaska, but luckily the store was busy and she got distracted constantly. She hadn't grilled me yet on what happened with Kaden, but I had a feeling that she had an idea since I was avoiding the topic.

That part of my new start in Pagosa was great. The Clara part of it. The hope I felt in my heart. The possibility of new connections.

But actually working at the store....

I'd come into my new job being realistic. I had no idea what the hell I was doing working at an outdoor outfitter. For the first ten years after I'd moved away from Colorado, the closest I got to doing outdoor activities were the times I'd gotten on my uncle's boat. Over the last ten, I'd gone to a beach a few times, but we'd stayed at upscale resorts that served pretty and ridiculously expensive drinks.

My mom would have disowned me, now that I thought about it.

I had never felt more like an imposter than I did working at the shop though.

Today, someone had asked me about a wade trip, and I'd literally stared at them blankly for so long, trying to figure out what they were asking about, that they had told me not to worry about it.

Fishing. They'd been talking about a fishing trip, Clara had explained to me with a pat on the back.

An hour later, someone asked for recommendations on tent hammocks. *There were different kinds of tent hammocks?*

I'd had to run to ask Clara to help them even though she was busy with another customer.

What kind of fish are there around here? Little ones? I had no idea.

Which hikes could a sixty-five-year-old woman handle? Short ones maybe?

Was it too late in the season to go rafting? How should I know?

I had never felt so useless and dumb in my life. It was so bad that Clara had finally told me to work the register and run to the back if Jackie—a fifteen-year-old who was clearly more capable than me at everything—asked me to get anything from the storeroom.

And that was what I was doing, standing at the register, ready to check someone—anyone—out as Jackie handled some fishing rod rentals and Clara helped a family with some camping gear purchases—I'd been eavesdropping a ton and considering bringing a notebook with me to work to take notes I could go over at home—when my phone buzzed in my pocket. I took it out.

The notification wasn't for a phone call or a text but for an email.

Then my hackles rose.

Because it wasn't just some spam email or a newsletter from a company.

The name of the sender was K.D. Jones.

The man who had called me his wife in private and around loved ones.

The man who had promised to *really marry me one day* when his career was *just right and a relationship wouldn't hurt* his *wittle fanbase*. "*You understand, don't you, beautiful?*" he'd reasoned time after time.

That fucker.

Delete it, some part of my brain instantly said. *Delete it and pretend you didn't see it. Nothing he says is anything you want to hear.*

Which was true.

His last email was an example.

There was literally nothing I needed to hear from him. Nothing that would benefit me. Nothing I wanted other than to possibly hear him admit that he had gotten to where he was, at least in part, thanks to me. But honestly, I would have gotten a hell of a lot more satisfaction hearing those words from his mom's mouth than his.

Everything that needed to be said between us had been laid out almost a year ago.

I hadn't heard from him until recently.

Fourteen years and he'd dropped me cold turkey from one day to the next.

But the nosey motherfucker that lived in my body said, *Read it or you're going to wonder what he wanted.* Maybe someone had cast a curse on his dick that made him impotent and he wanted to see if it had been me so I could remove it. (I wouldn't.)

Then the smug inner voice inside of me that had reveled in how poorly his last two albums had been reviewed, reared her pleased face up and said, *Yeah, you know what he really wants.* I knew damn well what the most important thing in his life was. The voice in my head had a point. I *did* know. I'd been imagining this happening, even while we'd still been together, when he had first started to pull away. When I was pretty sure his mom had decided to start phasing me out slowly.

They had no idea what they'd done, what they'd almost completely taken from me, even though I didn't feel any grief over it.

Delete it.

Or... read it first and then delete it?

Maybe get mad if he was being an asshole? If that was the case, it wouldn't be unexpected and it would only be a reminder that I was better off now than I had been. I was a winner anyway, right?

I was here. I was without people who hadn't contributed to my happiness in too long. I had my entire future ahead of me, ready and waiting for me to take it.

There were a lot of things I wanted and nothing stopping me from them but patience and time.

But...

Before I could talk myself out of it, I clicked on the message and braced myself, pissing myself off so that whatever he said couldn't make me angrier.

But there were only a few words in the email.

Roro,

Call me.

And for one microsecond, I thought about replying to him. Telling him no. But...

No.

Because the best way to get under his skin would be to just not reply.

Kaden *hated* being ignored. More than likely because his mom had spoiled him every day of his life and gave him just about everything he ever asked for, and everything he didn't. He'd gotten too used to being the center of attention. The pretty boy everyone fawned over and fell over to please.

So instead of deleting the email, knowing I wouldn't be tempted to reply to him, I left the message where it was because Aunt Carolina would ask to see it. Yuki would too so she could cackle. Nori would tell me to keep it so one day when I was feeling down, I could look at it and chuckle to myself at how the mighty had fallen. I set my phone back into my pocket.

Yeah, he wasn't asking for me to call because he couldn't find his social security card or had a hex on his dick, and I knew it.

I smiled to myself.

"What's that smile for?" Clara whispered as she came around the counter where the register was.

The family she'd been helping waved as they went by. "We're going to think about it, thank you!" one of the two moms said before leading her loved ones out.

Clara told them to call if they had any more questions, waiting until they were out before turning to me.

I couldn't help but smile again and shrug. "Kaden just emailed me. He asked me to call him." I had thought this situation over in my head a few times since we'd reconnected, and I'd decided that sticking to the truth was the only way to go.

She knew about our relationship because I'd told her about him before he'd gotten famous, back when I'd been able to post pictures of us online, before his mom had come up with the idea of painting him as an eternal bachelor. Before they had asked me, so sweetly, so kindly, to please remove all the pictures I had up of us together.

Clara had noticed.

She'd contacted me and asked if we'd broken up, and I'd told her the truth. Not saying what the "plan" was but just that we were still together and things were fine. But that was all she'd known.

And I knew I had to explain it all to her, if I was planning on staying here.

Lies had fragile, little legs. I wanted a foundation.

Clara raised an eyebrow as she leaned a hip against the counter, stretching her dark green, collared shirt with the name of the business above her breast. She'd brought me one of her old ones and promised to order new ones. "Are you going to?"

I shook my head. "No, because I know it will bother him. And there's nothing he would need to tell me anyway."

Clara scrunched up her nose, and I could see the questions in her eyes, but there were too many customers still around. "Did he try calling you?"

"He can't because"—this was all part of Things She Could Know—"his mom disconnected my line the day after he said things weren't working anymore." Didn't even give me a warning or anything. I had been packing up to leave when it had happened. "He doesn't have my new number."

She winced.

"My family and friends would never give it to him either; they all hate him." Nori had said she knew someone who knew someone who could make me a voodoo doll. I hadn't taken her up on it, but I'd thought about it.

Clara's expression was still troubled, but she nodded seriously, flicking her gaze around the building quickly, like a good business owner. "Good for you. What a jerk—his mom, I mean. Him too. Especially after how long you were together. What was it? Ten years?"

True. Too true. "Fourteen."

Clara grimaced just as the door opened and an older couple came in. "Hold on. Let me go help them. I'll be back."

I nodded, and I was lingering over my hope that his mom was sweating his career when I happened to glance up to find Jackie staring at me strangely.

Very, very strangely.

But just as soon as we made eye contact, she smiled a little too brightly and looked away.

Huh.

~

I spent the car ride back to my garage apartment thinking more about everything that had gone wrong in my relationship.

Like I hadn't already done that enough and sworn not to do it again after almost every time. But some part of me couldn't move on from it. Maybe because I'd willingly been so blind, and it bothered some subconscious part of myself.

It wasn't like there hadn't been signs leading up to his declaration that *things weren't working anymore*. The highlight of that final conversation had been when he'd looked at me seriously and said, *"You deserve better, Roro. I'm just holding you back from what you really need."*

He'd been fucking right that I deserved better. I had just been in some serious denial back then, asking him to stay, to not give up on fourteen years. Telling him I loved him so much. *"Don't do this,"* I'd pleaded in a way that would have horrified my mom.

Yet he had.

With time and distance, I now knew exactly what I'd dodged in the long run. I just hoped my ultra-independent mom would forgive me for having stooped so low to keep someone around who obviously didn't want to be there. But love could make people do some crazy stuff, apparently. And now I had to live the rest of my life with that shame.

Anyway, done *again* thinking about it, I followed my navigation carefully back to the garage apartment because I still didn't have every turn memorized and the driveway to the house wasn't exactly well marked. A couple nights ago, I'd tried to drive back without it and had gone about a quarter of a mile farther than necessary and had to pull into someone's driveway to turn around. After that final turn off the dirt road, the crunch of gravel under my tires sang me a song I was slowly becoming familiar with. For one brief moment, it felt like a word started to take shape on my tongue, but the sensation disappeared almost instantly. It was fine.

I frowned as the main house came up through the windshield.

Because sitting on the steps was the Amos kid.

Which wouldn't have been a big deal—it was a nice day out, especially now that the sun wasn't directly overhead baking everything under its rays—but he was hunched over, arms crossed over his stomach, and it didn't take a mind reader to know that there was something wrong with him. I'd seen him yesterday on the deck again, playing video games.

I watched him as I parked my car off to the side of the garage apartment, tucked in as close as I could get it to the building so that his dad wouldn't be inconvenienced.

I got out, nabbing my purse and thinking about how the man, Mr. Rhodes, didn't want to be reminded that I was staying here....

But when I got to the other side, the boy had his forehead pressed to his knees, curled into a physical ball about as much as someone who wasn't a contortionist could be.

Was he okay?

I should leave him alone.

I really should. I'd been lucky not to have gotten busted the day he'd shared aloe vera with me or the other times we'd waved at each other. Leaving them alone was the one thing his dad had asked of me, and the last thing I wanted to do was get kicked out ahead of time and—

The kid made a sound that sounded like pure distress.

Shit.

I took two steps away from the door, two steps closer to the main house, and called out, hesitating and ready to hide around the back of the building if the game warden truck started coming down the driveway. "Hi. You okay?"

Nothing was exactly the response I got.

He didn't look up or move.

I took another two steps and tried again. "Amos?"

"Fine," the kid choked out, so raggedly I barely understood him. It sounded like there were tears in his voice. Oh no.

I sidled a little closer. "Usually when someone asks me if I'm okay and I say I'm fine, I'm not fine at all," I said, hoping he understood I didn't want to be annoying, but... well... he was curled up in a ball and didn't sound right.

Been there, done that, but hopefully for very different reasons.

He didn't move. I wasn't even positive he was breathing.

"You're kind of scaring me," I told him honestly, watching him as fear rose inside of me.

He *was* breathing. Too loudly, I realized when I took another two steps closer.

He grunted, long and low, and it took him over a minute to finally reply in a voice I still barely understood. "I'm good. Waiting for my dad."

My uncle had said he was "good" when he'd had kidney stones and had tears streaming down his face while he sat on his recliner, ignoring our pleas to go to the doctor.

My cousin had once said he was "good" when he'd jumped out a moving truck—don't ask—and had whatever bone consisted of his shin sticking out of his leg as he bawled in pain.

What I should do was mind my own business, turn around, and go inside the garage apartment. I knew that. This stay here was already on a rocky road, even if Mr. Rhodes had been decent and helped me with my dead battery—I still hadn't gotten the corrosion off, now that I remembered. I needed to do it on my next day off.

Unfortunately, I had never in my life been able to ignore someone in need. Someone in pain. Mostly because I'd had people who hadn't ignored me when I'd felt those ways.

Instead of following my gut, I took yet another two steps to the teenager who had gone behind his dad's back and given me the opportunity to stay here in the first place. It'd been a crazy, sneaky thing to do… but I admired him for it, especially if he'd done it to buy a guitar. "Did you eat something bad?"

I was pretty sure he tried to shrug, but he tensed up so violently and grunted so loudly, I wasn't positive.

"Do you want me to get you something?" I asked, eyeing him closely, alarm still bubbling inside of me at the noises he was making. He had another big, black T-shirt on, dark jeans, and worn, white Vans. None of that was alarming though. Just the shade of his skin was.

"Took Pepto," he gasped before I swear on my life he whimpered and clutched his stomach closer.

Oh, fuck it. I cut the distance and stopped right in front of him. I'd had the stomach flu more than a few times in my life, and that shit was something, but this… this didn't seem right. He was scaring me now. "Did you vomit?"

I barely heard his "no." I didn't believe him.

"Did you have diarrhea?"

His head jerked, but he didn't say anything.

"Everybody gets diarrhea."

Okay, what stranger—especially a teenage boy—wanted to talk about diarrhea with someone they had literally met less than a month ago?

Maybe just me.

"You know, I got food poisoning from a sandwich I bought at a gas station in Utah a month ago, and I had to spend an extra night in Moab because I couldn't stop using the bathroom. I swear I lost ten pounds that night alone—"

The kid made a choking sound that I couldn't tell whether it was a laugh or a groan of pain, but he sounded a little quieter as he muttered, "I don't." He made the savage, painful sound again.

Apprehension gripped the back of my neck as the kid hunched over even more a moment before he started panting through his mouth.

All right.

I crouched down in front of him. "Where does it hurt?"

He gestured toward his stomach somehow... with his chin?

"Have you farted?"

That choking sound rattled from his throat again.

"Does it hurt on the left, right, or the middle?"

His words were gritted. "Kinda right."

I pulled out my phone and cursed at the fact that I only got one bar of cell phone service in this spot. Not enough to use the internet but hopefully enough for a call. There was Wi-Fi, but... I wasn't going to ask what the password was when he could barely speak.

I hit the contact for Yuki, thinking she was the only person I knew who constantly had her phone on her, and fortunately she answered on the second ring.

"Ora-Ora-Bo-Bora! What are you doing? I was just thinking about you," one of my very best friends answered, sounding pretty damn chipper. But of course she should. Her album had hit the number one spot three weeks ago and was still hanging in there strong.

"Yuki," I said, "I need your help. What side is your appendix on?"

She must have heard the distress in my voice because the humor disappeared from hers. "Let me find out. Hold on."

She whispered something to what had to be her manager or assistant before putting the phone back to her face after a few moments and saying, "It says mid-abdomen, right lower abdomen, why? Are you okay? *DO YOU HAVE APPENDICI-TIS?*" she started to shout.

"Fuck," I muttered to myself.

"ORA, ARE YOU OKAY?"

"I'm fine, but my neighbor is sweating big-time and looks like he's going to puke, and he's clutching his stomach." I paused. "He doesn't have diarrhea."

The boy made another choking sound I wasn't totally sure was appendix-related and more than likely just me talking about diarrhea again. I had enough nephews to know that as savage as they could be, they got shy about bodily functions sometimes. And the way he'd been talking to his dad a couple weeks ago, how he'd talked to me too, I had a feeling that maybe he was just shy in general.

"Oh thank God. I thought it was you." She whistled in relief. "Take him to the emergency room if he looks that bad. Is he bloated?"

I pulled the phone away from my face just a little. "Do you feel bloated?"

Amos nodded before he let out another whimper and pressed his face closer to his knees.

Of course this would happen to me. I was going to get kicked out for talking to this kid, and I wouldn't even be able to regret it.

"Yes. Say, Yuki, let me call you back. Thank you!"

"Call me back. Miss you. Good luck. Bye!" she said, hanging up immediately.

Slipping my phone back into my pocket with one hand, my free one went to the boy's knee and I gave it a single pat. "Look, I don't know for sure, but it sounds like it might be your appendix. I don't know though, but honestly, you don't look well, and I think you're in too much pain for it to be, I don't know, something else." Diarrhea. But I think he was fed up with me saying the d-word in front of him.

I was fairly positive he tried to nod, but he groaned in this way that had my armpits starting to sweat.

"Is your dad on his way?"

"He's not answering." He let out another grunt. "He's at Lake Navajo today."

I knew the lake wasn't far from Pagosa, but service was sketchy all over Colorado, I was starting to learn. Is that why he thought his dad was on his way? "Okay. Is there someone else we can call? Your mom? Another parent? Family member? A neighbor? The ambulance?"

"My uncle—*Oh fuck.*" He let out a cry that somehow went straight into my heart and brain.

I couldn't hesitate anymore. This wasn't good. My gut said so. The only thing I knew about appendix issues was that, if one ruptured, it could be deadly. Maybe it was nothing. Maybe it was something. But I wasn't willing to screw around with his well-being.

Especially not when his dad wasn't answering and couldn't make an executive decision.

I stood up and then bent back over to slide my arm under his shoulder blades. "Okay, okay. I'm taking you to the hospital. You're scaring me big-time. We can't risk waiting around."

"I don't need to—*oh fuck.*"

"I'd rather take you and there's nothing wrong than having your appendix rupture, okay?" I would rather his dad kick me out for communicating with him than this kid die or something else terrible.

Oh my God. *He could die.*

Okay. Time to go.

"Do you have a wallet? ID? An insurance card?"

"I'm okay. It'll pa—*fuck! Holy fuck*," he groaned long and deep, the length of his body tensing with a cry that took another bite out of me.

"I know. You're fine, but come on anyway, okay? I don't want your dad to see me trying to put you in my car while you fight me and think I'm trying to kidnap you. He's not answering, so we can't ask him what to do. I can try and call your uncle on the way, is that okay? You said something about calling your uncle, right?" I asked, tapping his shoulder. "You can't die on me, Amos. I swear I won't be able to live with myself if you do. You're too young. You have too much left to live for. I'm not as young as you, but I've still got at least another forty years left in me. Please don't let your dad kill me either."

He tipped his head and looked at me with big, panicked eyes. "*I'm going to die?*" he whimpered.

"I don't know! I don't want you to! Let's go to the hospital and make sure you don't, okay?" I suggested, knowing I sounded hysterical and was probably scaring the shit out of him, but he was scaring the shit out of me, and I wasn't as much of an adult as my birth certificate said I should be.

He didn't move for so long I thought for sure he was going to keep arguing and I was going to have to call 911, but in the span of a couple of breaths I sucked in through my nose, he must have come to a decision because he slowly tried to climb to his feet.

Thank God, thank God, thank God.

There were tearstains down his cheeks.

He moaned.

He groaned.

Grunted.

And I knew I saw a couple fresh tears stream down his sweaty face. He had the beginnings of his father's sharp features, but leaner, younger, without the rugged maturity.

One day he would though. *He couldn't fucking have his appendix rupture on me. No way.*

The teenager leaned against me big-time, whimpering but trying his damnedest not to.

The fifty feet to my car felt like ten miles, and I regretted not driving over. But I got him into the passenger seat and leaned over to strap his seat belt on. Then I ran around the back and got behind the wheel, turning it on and then pausing.

"Amos, can I borrow your phone? Can I try to call your dad again for you? Or your uncle? Or your mom? Anybody? Somebody?"

He pretty much threw his phone at me.

Okay.

Then he muttered a few numbers I figured were his lock code.

He leaned against the window, his face this pale bronze that bordered on a shade of green, and he looked about ready to projectile vomit.

Fuck.

Blasting the air conditioning, I grabbed an old grocery bag from under my seat and set it on his leg. "In case you want to throw up, but don't sweat it if you don't make it. I was thinking about trading this in anyway."

He said nothing, but one more tear made its way down his cheek, and suddenly, I wanted to cry too.

But I didn't have time for that shit.

Unlocking his phone, I went straight to his recent contacts. Sure enough, his last call had been to his dad about ten minutes ago. There was still barely just enough cell service for a call, and I tried again. It rang and rang. This was my luck.

I glanced at the boy as a standard "The caller you are

trying to reach is currently unavailable" recording popped up, and I waited for the beep.

I could do this. It wasn't like I had another choice. "Hi, Mr. Rhodes, this is Aurora. Ora, whatever. I'm taking Amos to the hospital. I don't know which one. Is there more than one in Pagosa? I think he might have appendicitis. I found him outside with a lot of stomach pain. I'll call you when I know where I'm taking him. I have his phone. Okay, bye."

Well, that lack of information might come back and kick me in the ass, but I didn't want to waste time on the phone explaining. There was a hospital I needed to find and get to. Stat.

I backed up, made it to the road where I'd learned I got some cell reception, opened my navigation app, found the nearest medical facility—there was an emergency room and one hospital—and set it to navigate. Then with my other hand, I grabbed Amos's phone again, cast one more glance at the poor kid who was opening and closing his fist, his body faintly trembling with what I could only assume was pain, and asked, "What's your uncle's name?"

He didn't look at me. "Johnny."

I winced and turned the knob for the air conditioner as cold as it could get when I spotted a bead of sweat at his temple. It wasn't hot; he was just feeling that bad. Shit.

Then I pressed down on the gas pedal. As fast as I could, I drove.

I wanted to ask him if maybe he felt any better, but he wouldn't even lift his head, instead just resting it against the window as he took turns groaning and grunting and moaning.

"I'm going as fast as I can," I promised as we wound down the hill to the highway. Luckily, the house was on the side of town closest to the hospital and not clear on the other end.

One of his fingers lifted in acknowledgment. Maybe.

At the stop sign, I scrolled through his contacts and found one for an Uncle Johnny. I hit dial and put it on speaker-phone, holding it in my left hand as I turned right.

The "Am, my guy" came clear through the phone.

"Hi, is this Johnny?" I replied.

There was a long pause and then a "Uh, yeah. Who's this?"

I didn't exactly sound like a teenage girl, I got it. "Hi, this is Aurora. I'm, uh, Amos's and Mr. Rhodes's neighbor."

Silence.

"Amos seems really sick, and his dad isn't answering, and I'm taking him to the hospital—"

"*What?*"

"His stomach hurts, and I think it might be his appendix, but I don't know his birthday or if he has insurance—"

The man on the other end cursed. "Okay, *okay.* I'll meet you at the hospital. I'm not too far, but I'll be there as soon as I can get there."

"Okay, okay, thanks," I replied.

He hung up.

I eyed Amos again as he let out a long, low moan, and I cursed and drove even faster. What should I do? What could I do? Get his mind off the pain? I had to try. Every noise out of his mouth was getting harder and harder to bear.

"Amos, what kind of guitar are you wanting to buy?" I asked because it was the first thing that came to mind, hoping a distraction would help.

"What?" he whimpered.

I repeated my question.

"An electric guitar," he grunted in a voice I could barely hear.

If this were any other situation, I might have rolled my eyes and sighed. An electric guitar. It wouldn't be the first time someone assumed I knew nothing about music or instruments. But it was still a bummer. "But what kind?

Fanned fret? Headless? Fanned fret and headless? Double-necked?"

If he was surprised I was asking him about something as inconsequential as a guitar when he was trying not to throw up from pain, he didn't show it, but he did answer with a tight, "A... a headless."

Okay, good. I could work with this. I pressed down on the gas a little more and kept on hauling ass. "How many strings?"

It didn't take him as long to answer as it had a moment ago. "Six."

"Do you know what kind of top you want?" I asked, knowing I might be irritating him by forcing him to talk but hopefully distracting him enough with the questions so that he'd think about something else. And because I didn't want him to think I had no idea what I was referring to, I went more specific. "Spalted maple? Quilted maple?"

"Quilted!" he gasped violently, forcing his hand into a fist and banging it against his knee.

"Quilted is real nice," I agreed, gritting my teeth and sending a silent prayer up that he was okay. My God. Five more minutes. We had five more minutes, maybe four if I could get around some of the slow drivers in front of us. "What about your fingerboard?" I threw out.

"I don't know," he basically cried.

I couldn't cry too. I couldn't cry too. I always cried when other people cried; it was a curse. "Birdseye maple might look nice with quilted maple," I threw out in basically a shout like if I was loud enough to overpower his tears, they wouldn't come out. "I'm sorry I'm yelling, but you're scaring me. I promise I'm driving as fast as possible. If you don't cry anymore, I know someone who knows someone, and maybe I can get you a discount on your guitar, okay? But please stop crying."

This weak cough came out of his throat... that sounded a hell of a lot like a laugh. A butchered, pained one but a laugh.

A peek at him as I turned right showed there were still tearstains on his cheeks but maybe....

I took another right and pulled into the lot for the hospital, steering us toward the emergency room entrance, saying, "We're almost there. We're almost there. You're going to be okay. You can have my appendix. It's a good one, I think."

He didn't say he wanted it, but I was pretty sure he tried to give me a thumbs-up as I parked in front of the glass doors and helped Amos out of my car, one arm around his back, taking his weight into me. The poor kid felt like melting Jell-O. His knees were buckled and everything, and it seemed to take everything in him to put one foot in front of the other.

I had never been to an emergency room before, and I guess I had expected someone to come rushing out with a gurney and everything, at least a wheelchair, but the woman behind the counter didn't even raise an eyebrow at us.

Amos hobbled into a chair, groaning.

I had barely started telling the woman behind the desk what was going on when a presence came up to my side. I met dark brown eyes set into a dark face. It wasn't familiar whatsoever. "You're Aurora?" the stranger asked. It was another man.

And my God, this guy was handsome too. His skin was an incredible shade of milky brown, cheekbones high and round, his short hair a deep black. This had to be Amos's uncle.

I nodded at him, tearing my gaze away from the whole of him to just focus on his eyes. "Yes, Johnny?"

"Yeah," he agreed before turning toward the woman and sliding his phone across. "I'm Amos's uncle. I have his insurance information. I have a power of attorney to make medical decisions until his dad can make it," he rattled off quickly.

I took a step to the side and watched him answer more of the woman's questions then fill something out on a tablet. I learned as I stood there that Amos's name was Amos Warner-Rhodes. He was fifteen, and his emergency contact was his father even though, for some reason, his uncle had a medical power of attorney. I backed up right after that information dump and headed over to sit beside Amos, who was back in the same position I had found him: groaning and sweating, pale and terrible.

I wanted to pat his back but kept my hands to myself.

"Hey, your uncle is here. They should be coming to get you in a second," I told him quietly.

His "okay" sounded like it came from some deep, dark place.

"Do you want your phone back?"

He tipped his head farther toward his knees and groaned.

It was right then that someone in scrubs came out with a wheelchair. I was still holding Amos's phone when they wheeled him out of the waiting area, his uncle following after him.

Should I... leave?

It might be hours until they knew for sure what was wrong, but... I'd brought him here. I wanted to make sure he was fine; otherwise, I'd stay up all night worrying. I remembered to move my car before it got towed, then sat down to wait.

An hour passed with no sight of Amos's uncle or his dad. When I went to ask the employee at the front desk if I could have an update, she narrowed her eyes and asked if I was family, and I had to back away feeling like a stalker. But I could wait. I would.

I had just come out of the bathroom nearly two hours

after getting to the ER and was heading to my seat when the doors leading outside opened and a big mass of a man came storming in.

The second thing I noticed was the uniform he had on, which seemed poured over a whole lot of impressive muscles and bones. His belt was tight around his waist. Someone deserved a catcall.

What it was about a man in uniform, I had no idea, but I was pretty sure my mouth watered there for a second.

Mr. Rhodes's shoulders seemed broader, his arms beefier under the bright white hospital lights than they had under the warm yellow of the garage apartment. His scowl made him look even more ferocious. He really was a big, old hunk of a man. My God.

I swallowed.

And that was enough to have his gaze flick toward me. Recognition crossed his features. "Hi, Mr. Rhodes," I stated as those legs that were just as long as I remembered started moving.

"Where is he?" the man I'd spoken to twice demanded, sounding just as pleasant as he had before. And by pleasant, I meant not pleasant at all. But this time, his son was in the hospital, so I couldn't blame him.

"He's in the back," I told him instantly, letting his tone and words slide down my back. "His uncle is here, Johnny? He's in the back with him—"

One big, booted foot brought him closer to me. His thick, dark eyebrows knit together, faint lines crossing his broad forehead. The brackets along his mouth were deep with a scowl that might have burned the hair off my eyebrows if I wasn't so used to my uncle making faces every time someone aggravated him. "What did you do?" he demanded in that bossy, level voice.

Excuse me? "What did I do? I drove him here like I said in my voice mail...."

Another big, booted foot stepped forward. Jesus, he really was tall. I was five-six, and he towered over me. "I specifically told you not to talk to my son, didn't I?"

Was he kidding me? "Are you joking?" He had to be.

That handsome face dipped closer, his scowl plain mean. "I gave you *two* rules—"

It was my turn to raise my eyebrows at him, indignation flaring up in my chest. Even my heart started beating faster at what he was trying to imply.

Okay, I didn't know what he was trying to imply, but he was giving me shit for driving his kid to the hospital? *Really?* And had he tried to make it seem like I'd done something to make his kid end up here?

"Hey!" an unfamiliar voice called out.

We both turned to where it was coming from, and it was the Johnny man standing by the elevator bank, one hand on the top of his head.

"Why the hell aren't you answering the phone? They think he has appendicitis but are waiting for the scan results to come back," he explained quickly. "They're treating his pain. Come on."

Tobias Rhodes didn't even look at me again before he quickly walked toward Johnny. Amos's uncle, though, nodded at me once before leading the other man toward the elevators. They were talking quietly.

Rude.

But I guess that sort of counted as an update?

CHAPTER 5

*M*aybe it made me a creeper, but I pretty much sat by the window as much as I possibly could over the next two days. Mostly because the shop was closed on Monday. Clara had to go do inventory, and her face had turned red when she'd explained she couldn't pay me to help her. It had only made me want to help her more, but I understood she wouldn't be fine with it even if I offered to do it for free, so I'd kept the offer to myself. For now at least.

I'd been distracted anyway, worried about Amos and whether he was all right or not. Sure, I didn't know him, but I still felt responsible. He'd been curled up on the porch, waiting for someone to get him and….

It had reminded me of me when my mom hadn't picked me up from Clara's house that terrible day. How I had called home over and over again when she hadn't shown up at the time we'd agreed on. How I'd sat on Clara's parents' porch while I'd waited for her to arrive with some excuse about an emergency she'd had. Mom hadn't always been punctual, but eventually she had always gotten there.

One little tear had popped up into my eye at the memory of the days after she'd disappeared.

But just like every other time, I wiped it away and kept going.

My original plan for the day had been to go on a practice hike I'd seen online closer to Bayfield, the next nearest town, but the urge to make sure Amos was all right had seemed more important. Even Yuki had texted asking for an update. I didn't have one other than what I'd overheard the day at the hospital, and that was what I'd shared.

I also had his phone, which had vibrated on and off until the power had eventually gone dead earlier.

I'd almost given up hope of him coming home while I was reading a book I'd picked up at the grocery store, when the sound of tires on gravel came in through the open window. I got up and spotted a Parks and Wildlife pickup truck followed by a hatchback.

A familiar figure jumped out of the truck, and out of the car, another long, male figure came out. They both rounded the other side of the car and, after a moment, helped a much smaller person out. They sandwiched him between them as they disappeared into the house, and I was pretty sure I heard them bickering as they did.

It was Amos.

Relief tickled me right in the chest.

I wanted to go ask him in person if he was fine, but... I was going to wait.

Well, unless Mr. Rhodes came over and kicked me out. At least I hadn't totally unpacked my things yet. Just a few days ago, I'd gone to the laundromat and refilled my suitcase with clean clothes.

At the main house, every light inside seemed to get flipped on.

For about the tenth time, I wondered about a mom or

wife figure. No one had come by the house. I'd had the windows open and hadn't slept all that great; I would've heard someone on the driveway. Amos hadn't asked me to call his mom either yesterday.

But hadn't his dad mentioned something about her the first day?

Either way, Amos was lucky to have a dad and an uncle that would rush to the hospital to be with him; I hoped he knew that. Maybe his dad was strict... and maybe not the friendliest person on the planet, but he loved him. Loved him enough to blame me for some dumb shit. To genuinely worry about his safety.

I sniffled, feeling a little heartsick suddenly, and picked up my phone. It rang once before there was an answer.

"Ora! Any news?"

There was a reason why I loved Yuki—and her sister—as much as I did. They were good people with enormous hearts. I knew how busy she constantly was, and it didn't stop her from always being a call or a text away.

"He just got back home. His uncle and his dad helped him in, but he was walking on his own."

"Oh, good." She made a sound before saying, "You said it was your neighbor, didn't you?"

I snorted, the loneliness already ebbing away with just the sound of her voice. "Yes. The son of the guy renting me his garage apartment."

"Ohhhh. My assistant ordered a crystal for him. I'm sending it to the PO box address you texted me the other day. Tell him to put it on his left side. I hope he gets better."

See? The best heart.

"So, how are you doing? Are you settling in? How's Colorado?"

"I'm okay. I'm settling in. It's really nice out here. It feels good."

There was definitely hope in her voice as she asked, "You're happy then?"

Yuki, like my aunt and uncle, had seen me at my worst. I'd stayed with her for a month immediately after I was *told* my relationship was over. Partly because she lived down the street, but mostly because she really was one of my best friends. She'd been going through her own breakup at the time, and that month I'd stayed turned out to be one of the most productive periods of my life. And hers.

We'd written a whole album together in that time... in between listening to Alanis, Gloria, and Kelly so loud I was pretty sure we'd both lost some hearing.

But it had been worth it, obviously.

"Yeah. I got a job with a friend I used to have when I lived here."

"Doing what?"

"Working at an outdoor outfitter."

There was a pause on her end. "What's that?"

"They sell camping and fishing equipment. Stuff like that."

There was another pause, and then she asked slowly, "Um, Ora, no offense but—"

I groaned. "I already know what you're going to say."

Her crystal clear laugh reminded me a lot of her singing voice. It was beautiful. "What are you doing working there? What do you know about any of that? How long have I known you? Twelve years? The most outdoorsy thing you've ever done was... was hanging out in tents at festivals."

I laughed, but really, I cringed because she had a point. "Shut up. Who was going to go camping with me? Kaden? Could you imagine his mom? *You?*" I cracked up, and she started laughing hard too, imagining it.

Mrs. Jones, his mom, was notoriously high-strung as hell, which was funny because I'd seen the house he had grown up in. His dad had been a plumber with three kids and a stay-at-home wife. They had more money than I'd had when Mom had been around, but they had never been rolling in it. But over the last ten years, since his career had taken off, she had turned into a snooty monster that scoffed over hamburgers unless they were made of wagyu or Kobe beef.

"Good point," Yuki agreed after she'd stopped laughing.

"But seriously, I don't know anything about anything in there. I've never felt so stupid in my life, Yu. Customers ask me so many questions, and I just look at them like they're talking ancient Greek. It's the worst."

She went "aww" but still laughed.

"But my friend needed the help, and it's not like I can give references to get a better job." And it wasn't like I even knew what I wanted to do in the first place. This was just... something. Until I decided. A step.

That got her to stop laughing. "Use me. I'll tell them you've worked for me and about how you're the best employee I've ever had. And actually, it wouldn't be a lie. You have worked for me, *and* you've been my MVP. I did pay you. I'm going to keep paying you."

Her record label had insisted on giving me credit for my work so that I wouldn't sue them in the future. They were going to be wiring me money every quarter. *If they don't pay you, they just make more money, Ora. Take it.* And she had a point. Better me than the record label.

Honestly, I hadn't thought about doing that once: asking her to lie for me. But now that she mentioned it... it wouldn't be a terrible idea to have that on my resume once I found something else to do that I wasn't awful at.

But even thinking about leaving Clara made me feel terrible. She really was overwhelmed, and I wasn't sure who would help her once Jackie went back to school. I needed to get better and learn more before the teenager did leave. But this was all just in case. In the future. I wasn't planning on leaving anytime soon.

"Are you sure?" I asked her.

She sighed dramatically. "You need a spiritual cleansing, teddy bear. I think Kaden might have rubbed his dumb off on you."

I snickered. "You're dumb."

She laughed.

"If it comes to it, I'll take you up on it. I hadn't even thought about it."

"Right. Because of the dumb. I'll send you some sage."

I cracked up and heard her sigh.

"I miss you, Ora. When are we going to see each other again? I wish you'd move back and live with me. You know, *mi casa es tu casa.*"

"Whenever we meet up somewhere or you come here. I miss you too. And your sister."

"Ugh. Nori. She needs some sage too now that I'm thinking about it."

I snorted. "I think she needs it more than I do. Speaking of people who need cleansings, guess who emailed me?"

She literally choked. Like there was anybody else. "The Antichrist's spawn?"

The fact she called Mrs. Jones the Antichrist too never got old. "Yup. He asked me to call him. Twice."

"Mm-hmm. Probably because his album flopped and everyone is talking about how bad it is."

I smiled.

She hummed thoughtfully for a moment. "You're better off without him, you remember that, right?"

"I know." Because I did know. If I had stayed with him... we never would have gotten married, even if he'd been in his late forties. We never would have had kids. I would have been in the shadows the rest of my life. I would never have been a real priority to someone that I had supported with every inch of my soul.

I could never forget that. I wouldn't. I was so much better off without him.

We talked for a few more minutes, and I was just wrapping up the phone call when I heard a car door slamming shut outside the window and peered out.

The restored Bronco was leaving; I had only seen it gone twice in the time I'd been here. The other car was still there though, the hatchback that had to belong to Amos's uncle, Johnny. I couldn't see into the driver's seat, but I had a feeling it was Mr. Rhodes leaving. *Tobias.* Not that I'd call him that out loud. He didn't want me to call him anything from the way he'd acted two days ago.

But there was nothing wrong with making sure the boy was doing okay, was there?

With both his cell phone and mine in my pockets, I carried the single can of chicken noodle soup I'd been carrying around for weeks down the stairs and crossed the gravel leading toward the main house, eyeing the entry to the property to make sure the SUV didn't suddenly turn back. I wasn't even embarrassed by how fast I hustled up to the deck and knocked on the door, twice, hopeful.

I heard a "One sec!" from inside, and maybe three later, the door opened and the man I'd met at the hospital was standing there with a slight smile on his face that grew wider after a moment. "Hi," the good-looking man said. He wasn't as tall as Mr. Rhodes.... Was he a Mr. Rhodes too? He didn't look at all like him, not even a little bit. Their features and colorings were totally different. So were their builds. If anything, Amos looked like a blended-up version of both of them.

Maybe he was related to his mom?

"Hi," I told him, suddenly feeling shy. "We met at the

emergency room, remember? Is Amos okay?" I held up my offering a little. "It isn't homemade, but I brought him a can of soup."

"Want to ask him yourself?" He smiled so wide, I couldn't help but give him one right back.

Yeah, he and Mr. Rhodes were definitely not related.

I wondered *again* if I'd find out what the situation with Amos's mom was like. Maybe she was in the military, deployed. Or maybe they were divorced and lived far away? Hadn't Mr. Rhodes said another man's name when he'd brought up the boy's mom? I had so many questions and way too much time to think about business that wasn't mine.

"Can I?" I asked, hesitating, knowing I should damn well just go back to the garage apartment before I got in trouble. It wasn't like Amos's dad had been all that happy to see me yesterday.

Or the last time we'd seen each other.

Much less the first time.

Or never. He was never happy to see me.

Johnny stepped back with a nod. His eyes seemed to scan the area behind me, and a crease formed between his eyebrows like he was confused. But whatever he was thinking over must have not been that important because he seemed to shrug it off before gesturing me forward. "Come in. He's in his room."

"Thanks." I smiled and followed after him once he closed the door.

The house was the epitome of rustic and cute. Light-colored floors led the path through the foyer, past a cracked door that a quick glance in told me was a half bath, and straight ahead, a cathedral ceiling opened over an area that consisted of a living room and a kitchen on the right. In the living area was a single gray love seat and two scarred leather recliners. A wood-burning stove was set up in the corner.

There was a milk crate working as a side table with a lamp on it. The kitchen was small with green-tiled counters and cupboards the same shade as the log cabin walls with black appliances. There was a plastic coffee container next to a coffee maker, an old jar with sugar, and more things around the counters.

The place was really, really clean and organized. Or maybe every man I'd ever known and lived with was just messy, because for two males living here, it was pretty spectacular. It suddenly made me feel like a slob for having clothes scattered all over the garage apartment, hanging off doors and chairs.

It was cozy and homey and nice.

I really liked it.

I guess in a way it reminded me of people and things that had brought me comfort. And love. Because the two were basically the same, or at least they should be.

"Aurora, right?" the Johnny guy asked, making me look over at him.

"Yeah," I confirmed. "Ora if you want."

He flashed me a white smile that was... it was something. "Thanks for calling about Am," he said as he pointed through the living area and toward another short hall. There were three doors. Through one, I could hear a washing machine going. On the other side was another cracked doorway that was too dark.

"Thank you for letting me in. I was worried about him. I waited around at the hospital as long as I could, but I didn't see you or Mr. Rhodes again after you went down there to get him, and I went home." I'd been there until nine.

We stopped outside another cracked door. "He's awake. I was just in here."

Johnny knocked, and a raspy "What?" came through the door.

I tried not to snort at the warm greeting as his uncle rolled his eyes and pushed the door open.

I peeked my head inside and found Amos on the bed in boxers and a deep green T-shirt that said "Ghost Orchid" on the front of it. He glanced up from the game console he was holding in his hands and yelped before throwing his hands over his crotch, his face going red.

"Nobody cares what you got under there but you, Am." Johnny chuckled even as he picked up a pillow I hadn't seen on the floor and tossed it. The kid dropped it over his lap, eyes wide.

I smiled at him. "I really don't care, but I can cover my eyes if it'll make you feel better." I took a single step inside and didn't move closer. "I just wanted to check on you. You okay?"

The boy lowered his game console to rest it on top of the pillow, his features still showed his surprise as he muttered in that quiet, shy voice I figured was just part of him, "Yeah."

"Was it your appendix?"

"Yeah." His gaze moved to his uncle before returning to me.

"I'm sorry. I'd hoped it was just really bad gas after all."

He made a face, but he muttered, "I had it removed yesterday."

"Yesterday?" I turned to look at the uncle who was still standing there, and he tipped his head to the side, like it didn't make sense to him either that he was free.

"And they let you out already? Is that safe?"

The kid shrugged.

"Huh. I'd be wrapped up in a blanket, crying if I'd just had surgery and was out."

His mouth went a little flat. He really was an adorable kid. I'd bet he was going to be a real good-looking man someday.

Well, with a dad that looked the way his did, of course he would.

"Well, I brought you some chicken noodle soup. I figure your uncle or your dad can warm it up for you. Unless you're vegan. If you're vegetarian or vegan, I'll bring you something else."

"I'm not," he pretty much whispered, moving his attention over my shoulder briefly.

"Oh, good. I've got your phone too, by the way. It's dead now." I took a step and set it on the dresser next to me, right beside a mound of loose guitar picks and a few packs of strings. "Well, if you need anything, you know where I am. Just yell really loud. I'll be home the rest of the day, and tomorrow I'm gone from nine to six." He was still looking at me with these big, round eyes. "I'll let you rest. Hope you feel better!"

His "bye" was muttered, but hey, it was better than nothing. According to one of my cousins, one of his sons had gone through a one-month long phase of not answering with anything more than grunts and nods, so I figured this was normal.

Figuring my job was done, I took a step back and almost ran into Johnny.

He smiled down at me when I glanced up and gestured toward the hall. Johnny followed, so close to my elbow, it kept brushing his upper body. "You said you were a neighbor?" he asked suddenly.

"Something like that," I told him. "I'm staying in the garage apartment."

The way he asked "What?" made me peek at him.

He looked confused as hell, that notch back between his eyebrows. "It's a long story that Amos can probably explain better."

"He won't. He says about ten words a day if we're lucky."

Fair enough. I laughed. "To make a long story short, he put it up for rent behind his dad's back, and I reserved it. Mr. Rhodes found out and wasn't happy, but he still let me stay when I offered to pay extra." That was a lot quicker than I expected. "I'll be here about another two weeks."

"What?"

I nodded then grimaced. "He really wasn't very happy. Now he's not going to be happy I came over probably, but I was worried about Amos."

"I was wondering about the car out there." His laugh came out of nowhere and caught me off guard. "I'm sure he wasn't happy. At all."

"He was really, really mad, but I get it," I confirmed. "I don't want to piss him off anymore, but tell Mr. Rhodes that I was eight feet away from his son and you were around the whole time. Please."

Johnny opened the front door with a smile. "Eight feet away and you brought him soup and his phone. No problem."

I walked through, and he moved to stand in the doorway.

It had gotten a lot darker in the ten minutes I'd been inside, and I pulled my flashlight out of my pocket. God forbid I trip on a rock, break my leg, no one hears me screaming, and I get eaten by meat-eating bears and birds take my eyeballs. That was literally a scenario that my aunt had imagined and texted me about days ago.

"You're from Florida?" he asked just as I flipped it on and aimed the beam toward the driveway. It was faint. I should look into getting one with more lumens.

"Kind of. I used to live here, but I moved away a long time ago." I hopped down the steps and waved at him. "Thank you for letting me see him. Nice to see you again."

He was leaning against the doorway. "Thank you for taking him."

"No problem." I waved again and got a short one in return.

I didn't want to say I ran to the garage apartment, but I definitely walked fast.

And just as I shoved the flashlight under my armpit to aim it at the doorknob, I heard the crunch of tires on gravel and panicked. *Where was the key?* As long as I didn't see Mr. Rhodes, he couldn't tell me to beat it, right? Shoving my hand into my pocket, I tried to find it but couldn't. Damn it! Back pocket! Back pocket!

The headlights caught me just as my fingertips touched the cool key.

And I dropped it.

"You okay?" I heard Johnny holler.

He was watching. Probably laughing as I panicked. Did he know what I was doing?

"I'm fine! Just dropped the key!" I yelled back, sounding rabid and panicky *because I was* as I patted around the ground.

The headlights weren't moving anymore, I realized just as I found the damn key again.

I heard a door open and slam closed just as I pushed it into the lock.

"Hey," a gruff voice called out.

Play it cool. Everything was fine. He owed me, didn't he? I'd saved his son. Kind of. "Hi," I called back, resigned. *Busted.*

The lights caught a silhouette as my landlord slash neighbor crossed in front of his Bronco. "Aurora, right?" the man asked. Tobias. Mr. Rhodes.

I totally turned around, flipping off my flashlight when it hit him in the chest. He had a T-shirt on. His headlights lit him up from the back, but I didn't have that good of a view of his face.

Was he mad? Was he going to kick me out?

"That's me." I held back a gulp. "Can I help you with something?"

"Thank you for what you did" was his reply, catching me off guard.

Oh. "It was no problem," I told the shadowed part of his front. He'd stopped just a few feet away, arms crossing over his chest, I was pretty sure.

He didn't *sound* mad. That was a good thing. Then again, he had no idea I'd just left his house.

He took another step forward, but I still couldn't see him that well, just the overall shape of his frame, so wide at the top and narrow at the hips. Did he go to a gym? There was one in town. He had to. Nobody looked like that naturally.

The man's deep sigh had me trying to peer at his face.

"Look...." He seemed to struggle for his words, his tone just as stern as the first time I'd heard it. "I owe you. Am told me what happened." His exhale was loud but steady. "I can't thank you enough," he rumbled in his hard voice.

"You're welcome." The less I said, the better.

Another exhale. "I owe you. Big-time."

"You don't owe me anything."

Another sigh, then, "I do."

"No, I promise you don't," I threw back. "Please, really, you don't owe me anything. I'm just glad I could help and that he's fine."

He didn't say anything for so long I partially expected him not to, but what he did do was take another step forward and then another until he stood closer, arms loose at his sides, so near I could get another good look at that incredible face. The hard, sharply defined bones of his features were tight. He was in jeans, and his T-shirt had a fish on it.

He was definitely mid to late thirties. *Maybe* early forties.

An excellent mid-thirties to maybe early forties. I bet he'd

99

just gone gray young. It happened. There was a singer I'd known who had gone totally silver by twenty-seven.

And his age was none of my business.

There were other things I needed to worry about, and I might as well get them over with. He was going to find out anyway, and if he felt like he owed me, maybe he'd forgive me and not kick me out. I could only hope. "I went over to your house real quick, and Johnny let me in. I just wanted to check on your son. I stood at the doorway and was only there for ten minutes, if that. Johnny was there the whole time. Please don't get mad."

Again, he didn't respond fast enough to make me feel better. He just... looked at me. I couldn't see the color of his eyes, but I could see the whites at the edges.

That's what my honesty got me, I guess, and I squirmed.

"I'm not mad," my landlord said slowly before exhaling once more. His grumbling voice was still hard, but something about his features seemed to soften a microscopic amount. "I owe you. I appreciate what you did. I don't know how I'll pay you back, but I'll figure it out somehow."

He took another deep breath, and I braced.

"I'm... sorry for how I handled you being here."

He was apologizing. To me. Sound the alarms.

"It's fine," I told him. "If I think of something I need, I'll tell you." Then it was my turn to hesitate. "If you two need anything too, let me know." I'd be there until I... until I wasn't. Then I remembered. "Can I ask one question though? You know, just so I know. How many people live in the house with you?"

I could tell he was watching me carefully before he answered. "It's only Amos and me."

Exactly what I'd thought.

"Okay." At least he wasn't kicking me out. Since he wasn't, I was going to take advantage of it.

I extended my hand toward him, and a big, cool one slipped into mine, giving it a solid, slow shake.

I smiled at him. He didn't smile back, but that was all right.

Before he could change his mind and kick me out, I backed up. "Goodnight," I called out and slipped inside the garage apartment, flipping on the lights and the lock before running up the steps.

Through the window, I watched Mr. Rhodes pull his Bronco up into his usual spot in front of the house. He opened the passenger door and pulled out two white bags with the name of one of the two fast food places in town stamped on them. Then I kept on watching as he went inside.

Well, I was still here.

And hopefully would be for another two weeks.

Or at least as long as possible.

CHAPTER 6

"*B*less your heart, honey, you don't need to apologize," the older man said with a smile so filled with sugar I was going to get a cavity.

His friend, bless *his* heart, winked. "How could we ever get mad at such a sweet face, right, Doug?"

My whole body went rigid at their kind words. Words spoken by two very nice customers that I'd been trying to help but couldn't. I'd known from the moment they had walked up to the counter holding two fishing rods that they were going to ask me something I wouldn't be able to answer, so I'd been prepared.

Hell, the first thing out of my mouth had been, "Let me get someone who can help you with any questions you might have on those rods."

I had tried, and I knew I had tried to avoid having to stand there like a dummy. I'd memorized most of the prices for the models we carried. I even had a couple of the brands we carried burned into my brain, but that was absolutely it. What the differences between them were, much less why they should get a longer rod versus a shorter one, or even what kind of fishing—or angling as some customers had called it—they were used for, I had *no* clue.

So when the man who had to be in his early fifties ignored my words and went ahead and asked, "What's the difference between these? Why is this one twice the price?" I'd been pretty resigned.

If we'd been less busy, I could have yelled for Clara across the room. But she was behind the rental counter, talking to a small family about something. Jackie was in the back taking her break, and the only part-time employee I'd met—for the first time that morning—had hung around for about two hours before waving and saying he'd be back.

Clara and I had looked at each other from across the room, and I'd suddenly understood, even more so than before, how much of a pickle she was in with employees.

For the record, he hadn't come back.

The two men though kept on ignoring me trying to pawn them off on Clara.

I was glad and relieved that they weren't being mean or impatient, but I couldn't help but have my feelings be hurt anyway. I *knew* that I had gotten myself out of more pickles than I could ever count because some people found me attractive and I was pretty friendly by nature. Despite getting pulled over at least ten times, I had never gotten a ticket, even though some of my friends claimed I drove like a maniac. I just didn't like to waste time. What was wrong with that? My cousins had teased me nonstop for the way people treated me for something I'd had nothing to do with.

But at the same time, my genetics were kind of a curse. Some men tended to be misogynistic. Sometimes I got treated like I was an airhead. And a lot of times, I got more attention than I wanted, especially when it was the uncomfortable kind.

I listened and I tried my best at just about everything, and

I had a good heart—as long as you hadn't wronged me. And all those things were a lot more important to me than what was on the outside.

I didn't want to get babied. It made me uncomfortable.

And it took me a moment to collect myself enough to give the well-intentioned men a sweet smile. "Let me get my boss to help you. I'm new, and I haven't gotten familiar with everything yet."

The one with more gray hair than the other glanced at my boobs so quickly I was pretty sure he thought he was so slick I hadn't noticed. "Don't you worry, beautiful."

I wanted to sigh, but I just smiled all over again.

And that's when the door opened and the last figure I would have expected to come in, did.

Well, not the *last*, but one of them.

It was the uniform on that long, strong body that caught my eye first.

He was already looking at me. And if he was surprised, I wouldn't have been able to tell because of the sunglasses he had on. Well, that and the fact that the customers decided to keep talking.

"What's a pretty thing like you doing working here instead of a clothing store? Or maybe a jewelry store? I'd bet you'd sell everything in one those."

Pretty much any other job but this one was what they were hinting at.

I was trying my best. I really was. But it had only been a couple weeks.

I slid my gaze back to the less gray-haired man. "I'm not really that fashionable, and I don't wear much jewelry."

Out of the corner of my eye, Mr. Rhodes wandered farther into the store, but I could tell he was still looking at me.

"One of my friends is a lawyer in town; he might be

looking to hire a new secretary if I put in a good word for you," the one with the most amount of gray hair said.

Did he insinuate he'd hint at his friend to fire his current employee to hire me?

I shook my head and tried to give him another smile. "That's all right, I like it here." When I wasn't screwing up. And when people weren't petting me on the head like it was okay for me to not know things.

Fortunately, they settled on a rod on their own, and I rang him up and did my best to ignore the way they both kept staring at my face and boobs. When he took the receipt and rod out of my hands, I gave them both a smile and only let myself sigh once they were out of there.

But just as soon as the door closed, the reminder that if I was planning on staying—and yeah, I didn't *love* every part of the job, but one more glance at how tired Clara was told me I wouldn't be leaving any time soon—I needed to get my shit together. For her. I needed to learn so I could answer questions on my own and not feel like crap about being so useless.

That was when I looked around the store and spotted the man by the fishing accessories.

It hit me.

Who would know more about outdoor things than a game warden?

No one.

Okay, maybe someone, but I only knew very limited someones here, and it wasn't like I could ask Clara to sit me down and teach me anything. We barely had enough time to talk at the store, and she was always busy afterward. We'd made plans twice to go out for dinner, and she'd bailed both times because something had come up with her dad.

And sure, Mr. Rhodes didn't exactly seem to have a whole

lot of extra time on his hands either, considering I only saw his truck at home after seven most nights but...

I *had* saved Amos's life, hadn't I?

And he had said he owed me, even though I didn't plan on ever taking him up on the offer, right?

The more I thought about it, the more I settled into the idea of asking him for help. What would he say? That he had better things to do? Or he'd remind me that I didn't even have two more weeks left at his place?

Which reminded me that I needed to decide if I was staying so I could find another rental.

Or not.

I rang out a couple more customers as I thought about it, and by the time he strolled up after saying something to Clara and saying something to Jackie that I couldn't hear— how he knew them, I wasn't sure, but I wanted to find out— he slowly walked up to the counter and set down two spools of line. I should really figure out what the point of one being thicker than the other was.

"Hi, Mr. Rhodes," I greeted him with a smile.

He'd taken his sunglasses off and slid them through one of the gaps between the buttons of his work shirt. His gray eyes were steady on me as he said in that same uninterested, stern tone from before, "Hi."

I took the first package of fishing line and scanned it. "How is your day going?"

"Fine."

I scanned the next package and figured I might as well go in for the kill since no one was around. "You remember that time you said you owed me?" A day ago.

He didn't say anything, and I peeked up at him.

Since his eyebrows couldn't talk, they formed a shape that told me exactly how distrustful he was feeling right then.

"You do, okay. Well," and I lowered my voice, "I was going to ask if I could redeem that favor."

Those gray eyes stayed narrowed.

This was going well.

I glanced around to make sure no one was listening and quickly said, "When you aren't busy... could you teach me about all this stuff? Even if it's just a little bit?"

That got him to blink in what I was pretty sure was surprise. And to give him credit, he too lowered his voice as he asked slowly and possibly in confusion, "What stuff?"

I tipped my head to the side. "All this stuff in here. Fishing, camping, you know, general knowledge I might need to work here so I have an idea of what I'm doing."

There was another blink.

I might as well go for it. "Only when you aren't super busy. Please. If you can, but if you can't, that's okay." I'd just cry myself to sleep at night. No biggie.

Worst case, I could hit up the library on my days off. Hang out in the grocery store parking lot and google information. I could make it work. I would, regardless.

Dark, thick, black eyelashes dipped over his nice eyes, and his voice came out low and even. "You're serious?" He thought I was shitting him.

"Dead."

His head turned to the side, giving me a good view of his short but really pretty eyelashes. "You want me to teach you to fish?" he asked like he couldn't believe it, like I'd asked him to... I don't know, show me his wiener.

"You don't have to teach me *to* fish, but I wouldn't be opposed to it. I haven't been in forever. But more about everything else. Like, what is the point of these two different kinds of line? What are all the lures good for? Or are they called flies? Do you really need those gadgets to start a fire?" I knew I was whispering as I said, "I have so many random questions, and not having internet makes it hard to look things up. Your total is $40.69, by the way."

My landlord blinked for about the hundredth time at that point, and I was pretty sure he was either confused or stunned as he pulled his wallet out and slipped his card through the reader, his gaze staying on me for the majority of the time in that long, watchful way that was completely different from the way the older men had been eyeballing me earlier. Not sexually or with interest, but more like I was a raccoon and he wasn't sure if I had rabies or not.

In a weird way, I preferred it by a lot.

I smiled. "It's okay if not," I told him, handing over a small paper bag with his purchases inside.

The tall man took it from me and let his eyes wander to a spot to my left. His Adam's apple bobbed; then he took a step back and sighed. "Fine. Tonight, 7:30. I've got thirty minutes and not one longer."

What!

"You're my hero," I whispered.

He looked at me, then blinked.

"I'll be there, thank you," I told him.

He grunted, and before I could thank him again, he was out of there so fast I had no chance to check out his butt in those work pants of his.

Either way, I couldn't help but be relieved.

That had gone better than I'd expected.

I WAS STILL in shock over my tutoring lesson when the alarm on my phone went off at 7:25 p.m.

I'd set it so that I'd have more than enough time to finish whatever I was doing—that was putting together a puzzle I'd bought at the dollar store—and walk next door.

Was it dumb that I was nervous? Maybe. I didn't want to say or do anything to get me kicked out ahead of time.

But I hated screwing up.

And I hated being in a position where I was unprepared.

Most of all, I didn't like to feel dumb. Yet that was exactly how I'd felt way too many times while working at the shop. I was fully aware there was nothing wrong with me not *knowing* things—because I was sure I knew a hell of a lot more about a lot of things than other people did. I'd like to see most people work in a music store. Personally, I'd kill it. I'd spent the last decade of my life around musicians. The amount of random knowledge I'd picked up over the years, surprised me. I could keep time and decently play three instruments.

Yet none of that benefitted me at all anymore. I hadn't even felt the urge to write since that month with Yuki. My words had dried up; I was pretty sure. That part of my life was done now. It wasn't like I knew what I wanted to do with the rest of my life anyway. No pressure, right?

So in the meantime, I might as well help my old friend.

If I was going to do that, I wanted to do it well. My mom hadn't half-assed things, and I had never been the kind of person to do that either. She would have told me to study, to not give up.

And that's what led me down the stairs and across the gravel driveway, holding a container of blueberry muffins I'd bought from the grocery store after work and the notebook I used to take notes for the hikes I was planning on doing. I thought about the box full of notebooks that I hadn't opened in a year, then shook the thought away.

I eyed Mr. Rhodes's truck as I walked past it and knew I was going to the right person.

I hoped.

I knocked and took a step back. About three seconds

later, a shadow of a figure appeared down the hall before lights were flipped on, and I took in the size of the body. It definitely wasn't Amos.

That thought alone made me smile just as he opened the door, didn't say a word, and gestured me in with a tip of his head.

"Hi, Mr. Rhodes," I said as I crossed the doorway and beamed up at him.

"You're on time," he noted, like that surprised him, as he closed the door behind us. I waited for him to walk ahead so he could tell me where to sit. Or stand.

Maybe I should have just googled all this. Or gone to the library. But I wasn't a resident yet, so more than likely I wouldn't be able to get a library card.

"I was worried if I was a minute late, you wouldn't open the door," I told him honestly.

He slid me a long look with that stony, hard face as he went around and headed down the hallway. I was pretty sure he even went "hm" like he wasn't disagreeing. Rude.

I eyed the house again as we moved, and it was just as clean as last time. There wasn't a single coffee cup or glass of water lying around. Not even a dirty sock or napkin either.

I should probably clean the apartment before he had an excuse to come over and saw the war-zone reenactment that was going on across the driveway.

Mr. Rhodes ended up leading us toward the table in the kitchen that was so scarred, I knew from enough Home Remodel Network that it needed to get sanded and a layer or two of stain. Don't ask me how it would be done, but I knew it needed it. But what caught me off guard was the way he walked around the back of it and pulled a chair out before taking the one next to it.

I plopped down on it and realized this was the steadiest chair I'd ever sat in. I peeked down at the legs and tried to wiggle; it didn't move. I knocked on a leg. It didn't sound hollow.

When I sat back up, I found Mr. Rhodes watching me once again. His raccoon face was back. I bet he was wondering what I was doing with his furniture.

"This is nice," I told him. "Did you make it?"

That snapped him out of it. "No." He scooted the chair closer, set two big hands with long, tapered fingers and short, trimmed nails on top of the table, and leveled me with a heavy, no-nonsense gaze. "You've got twenty-nine minutes. Ask your questions." His eyebrows went up about a millimeter. "You said you have a million. We might get through ten or fifteen."

Shit. I should've bought a recorder. I pushed my chair in closer. "I don't really have a million. Maybe just about two hundred." I smiled and, like I expected, didn't get one in return. Worked for me. "Do you know a lot about fishing?"

"Enough."

Just enough that friends and family posted about fishing stuff on his Facebook page. *Okay.* "What kind of fish can you catch around here?"

"Depends on the river and the lake."

I didn't mean to say, "Oh shit," but I did. *It depends?*

His eyebrows went flat. "Do you know what you're doing?"

"Nope, that's why I'm here. Any information is better than no information." I smoothed my hand across the blank page. I tried to give him my most charming smile. "So, uh, what kinds can you get in the rivers and lakes around here?" Time to try again.

It didn't work. Mr. Rhodes sigh then told me he was wondering what the hell *he'd* gotten himself into. "We had a dry winter and water levels are very low, which makes fishing conditions not that ideal already. That and the tourists have probably fished out most of the rivers. Some of the lakes are stocked, so that's most people's best bets—"

"Which lakes?" I asked him, sucking up his information.

He rattled off the names of a handful of lakes and reservoirs in the area. "What are they stocked with?"

"Large-mouth bass, trout. You can find perch...." Mr. Rhodes named a few other different kinds of fish I'd never heard of, and I asked him how to spell them. He did, leaning back against the chair and crossing his arms over his chest, the raccoon-watching face back on his features.

I smiled, feeling a little too pleased with myself for making him wary, even though I didn't want him to think I was some weirdo creeper. But the truth was, it was good when people didn't know what to expect from you. They can't creep up behind you if they don't know what way you're going to look.

I asked him if there was still good bass fishing and got a lengthy answer that was way more complicated than I'd anticipated. His eyeballs were lasers aimed on my face the entire time. His shade of gray was pretty incredible. The color looked almost lavender sometimes.

"How much are licenses and how can people buy them?" I asked.

I ignored the way his eyes widened like this was common sense. "Online, and it depends on if they're out of state or residents." He then told me the prices of the licenses... and how much the fines were if someone was caught without one.

"Do you bust a lot of people for not having licenses?"

"Do you really want to waste this time asking me about work?" he asked slowly and seriously.

It was my turn to blink. *Rude.* What was that? Three for four times now? "Yeah, otherwise I wouldn't have asked," I muttered. I really did have better things to ask but fucking attitude. Jeez.

One of those dark eyebrows rose, and he kept his response simple. "Yes" was his informative answer.

Well, this was going well. Mr. Friendly and all that.

Too bad for him I was friendly enough for both of us.

"What are the different kinds of line you use for fishing?"

He instantly shook his head. "That's too hard to explain without showing you."

My shoulders dropped, but I nodded. "Which of those lakes would you still recommend?"

"Depends," he started as I jotted down all the information I could handle. He was in the middle of telling me what places he didn't recommend when we heard, "Hey, Dad—oh."

I glanced over my shoulder at the same time Mr. Rhodes looked in the same direction to find Amos standing halfway into the living area, holding a bag of chips in one hand.

"Hi," I greeted the kid.

His face turned red, but he still managed to say, "Hi." His hand slid out of the bag and hung at his side. "Uh, I didn't know anyone was here."

"Your dad is helping me with some fishing questions," I tried to explain. "For work."

The boy wandered closer, rolling the top of the bag up to close it. He looked really good. He seemed to be walking just fine, and his color was back to normal.

"How's your missing appendix?"

"Fine." He came to stand beside us, eyes going straight for the notebook I'd been in the middle of writing in.

I angled it toward him so he could see what I'd written. "I meant to tell you that you could play... music... in the garage any time you want. It won't bother me at all," I said.

The teenager's gaze flicked toward the man sitting there.

"I'm grounded," the teenager admitted. "Dad said I can start going into the garage again soon if it's okay with you."

"It's totally okay." I smiled. "I brought some muffins if you want one." I gestured to the container in the center of the table.

"You got five minutes left," Mr. Rhodes interjected suddenly.

Shit. He was right. "Well... just finish telling me what you don't recommend then."

He did.

And I wrote down just about everything he said. Only when he'd stopped talking did I set my pen down, close my notebook, and smile at both of them. "Well, thank you for helping me. I really appreciate it." I pushed back from the chair and stood up.

Both of them just kept on watching me silently. Like father, like son, I guess. Except Mr. Rhodes didn't seem shy— just grumpy or guarded, I couldn't tell yet—and Amos did.

"Bye, Amos. Hope you keep feeling better," I said as I backed away from the table. "Thank you again, Mr. Rhodes."

The stern man undid his arms, and I was pretty positive he sighed again before muttering, sounding so reluctant his next words surprised the shit out of me. "Tomorrow, same time. Thirty minutes."

What!

"You'll answer more questions?"

He dipped his chin, but his mouth was pressed down on the sides in a way that said he was already second-guessing himself.

I backed up some more, ready to run before he changed his mind. "You're the best, thank you! I don't want to wear out my welcome but thank you, thank you! Have a good night! Bye!" I shouted before basically running toward the door and closing it behind me.

Well, I wasn't going to be any kind of expert at anything any time soon, but I was learning.

I should call my uncle and dazzle him with everything I'd learned. Hopefully tomorrow someone would come in and ask something about fishing so I could answer them correctly. How great would that be?

CHAPTER 7

It was during one of our rare slow moments at the store the next day that Clara finally saddled up next to me and said, "So...."

I tipped my chin up at her. "So?"

"How do you like Pagosa so far?" was what she decided to ask.

"It's good," I answered, carefully.

"You gotten around? Seen some of the sights again?"

"I've driven around a little."

"You been to Mesa Verde?"

"Not since that field trip half a century ago."

She rattled off the names of a couple more tourist activities that we had pamphlets for in the corner of the shop. "Been to the casino?"

"Not yet."

She frowned and leaned a hip against the counter. "What have you been up to on your days off then?"

"Not going anywhere fun, apparently. I've done a little hiking"—not enough—"but that's about it."

Her face went a little pale at my mention of the h-word,

116

and I knew her mind had gone to the same place mine had. My mom. Once we'd reconnected online, we had never actually brought up... what happened. It was the elephant in the room in most conversations that could be turned around and tied into her disappearance. It always had been. When I'd lived with my aunt and uncle, they had purposely avoided any movie or show about missing persons. When that movie about the man who had gotten his arm stuck had come out, they had changed the channel so fast, it had taken me a couple days to figure out what they'd been doing.

I appreciated it, of course. Especially for probably the first decade afterward. And every time I'd had a bad day in the time after that.

But I didn't want the people I cared for having to walk on eggshells because of me. I was doing better dealing with it all, for the most part. I could talk about it without the world falling out beneath my feet at least. My therapist had helped me get there.

But she seemed to realize she'd reacted because her expression lasted about a second before she said, "I'm not much of a hiker or a camper anymore, but Jackie is when she's in the mood. You need to get out while the weather is good and see some things."

"I just started hiking again, and I haven't gone camping in twenty years."

Her expression changed once more, and I knew she was thinking about my mom again, but just as quickly, she recovered. "We should do something. What are you doing on Monday? I haven't been to Ouray in a while."

Ouray, Ouray, Ouray... It was a town not too far, I was pretty sure. "Nothing," I admitted.

"It's a date then. As long as I don't have to cancel on you. Want me to pick you up or meet here?"

"Meet here?" I couldn't see Mr. Rhodes being happy with

me having her come over to his property, and I wasn't willing to piss him off, even if I wasn't going to be around too much longer.

She opened her mouth to tell me something before she leaned forward and whistled.

I turned around to see through the big windows I'd peeked through weeks ago, too.

"You see that?" she asked as she made her way around the counter and headed toward the front.

I followed her. There was a truck out there, a truck that looked awfully familiar... And beside it was a man on a cell phone, and there was another man standing beside him in the same uniform.

Clara whistled at my side again. "I've always been a sucker for a man in uniform. Did you know my husband was a police officer?"

Sometimes... sometimes I forgot I wasn't the only person to have lost someone they really loved. "No, I didn't know that," I said.

A wistful expression came over her face, and it made my heart hurt only imagining what she could be thinking of. Hoping it wasn't the what-ifs. The alternate realities. Those were the worst.

"Police officers are cute, but I've always had a thing for firefighters," I told her after a second.

Her mouth formed a little smile. "With their little pants and hats?"

I looked at her. "I like their suspenders. I'd give them a snap or two."

Her laugh made me smile, but only for a second because the man on the other side of the glass had turned, and I finally got my confirmation that Mr. Rhodes's butt was fantastic in his work pants. "Did you meet him the other day when he was here?" Clara asked.

"Which one?" I knew exactly who she was referring to even as I eyeballed the other man in the same kind of uniform. He was about the same height as my landlord but leaner. I couldn't see his face though. I could see his butt though, and it was a good one.

"One on the right. Rhodes. He comes in sometimes. He was just here yesterday. He used to date my cousin a million years ago. His son is best friends with Jackie."

No shit? I wanted to tell her the truth, but she kept on talking.

"Dad said he moved back here when he retired from the Navy to be closer to his son and—oh, he's about to get into his truck. Let's move before he sees us and things get awkward."

He had been in the Navy? Well, that was another piece of the puzzle. Not that it mattered.

And actually, the way he talked now made total sense. That bossy voice. I could totally picture him bossing people around and giving them the stare down he'd given me. No wonder he was so good at it.

"He's my landlord," I told her as we moved away from the window before getting caught spying.

Her head whipped around so fast, I was surprised she didn't end up with whiplash. "*He is?*"

"Yeah."

"That's the garage apartment you're renting?"

"Uh-huh."

"*He* let you rent it?"

"You're not the first person to ask me that that way. But no, it was more like Amos did behind his back. Why?"

"It's okay. He's a good dad. He's… quiet and private is all." Her eyes widened. "This suddenly makes so much sense. That's why Amos got grounded."

So she'd heard from Jackie. Was that why she had been

giving me funny looks when she thought I wasn't looking? "Yup."

It wasn't until we made it back around the counter that she asked really quietly, "Have you seen him without a shirt on?"

I grinned. "Not yet."

Her smile in return was pretty damn sly. "Take a picture if you do."

~

I WAS EARLY AGAIN that night. Two minutes ahead of schedule and holding a plate with a few Chips Ahoy cookies I was going to try and pass off as homemade unless one of them asked. It was the thought that counted, right?

My notebook was tucked under one arm, the beautifully wrapped crystal that Yuki had sent Amos was under my other arm, and I had a pen shoved into the back pocket of my jeans alongside my cell and key. I'd written out a bunch of questions while I'd eaten dinner and marked them in order of what I should ask, depending on how much information we could get through.

Hopefully a lot.

I'd only gotten one chance that day to use my newfound knowledge, and I'd been so damn proud. It had helped curb the edge for every other time I had to go bother Clara or pass a customer off on her. She was a fountain of information, and I admired her so, so much for it. Sure, she'd grown up in this business and lived in the area way longer, but it didn't make it any less impressive. She had moved away; anyone else would have forgotten most of what they knew.

In my dreams, Mr. Rhodes would do me another solid and invite me over tomorrow too, but I wasn't holding my breath. I thought about the way Mr. Rhodes had looked in his uniform earlier when he'd been across the street.

It sure wouldn't be a hardship.

Was he divorced? Did he date a lot? I didn't think he had a girlfriend since no one ever came over other than the Johnny/uncle figure, but you never knew. From everything I'd gathered about him, he was really overprotective of his half-grown son. Maybe he had a girlfriend but never brought her over.

That'd be a bummer.

Not that it should matter.

I really did need to start getting around to possibly dating. I wasn't getting any younger, and I missed having someone to talk to in person. Someone who was... mine.

Being single was cool and all, but I missed companionship.

And sex.

Not for the first time, I wished I had an easier time with one-night stands or friends with benefits.

For one brief second, my heart longed for the easiness and effortlessness that had been such a staple in my relationship with Kaden. We'd been together so long and knew everything about each other, I had never thought for a second that I'd ever have to find someone else to become my new best friend. Someone else to get to know me and love me.

And I missed that a lot.

But we weren't together anymore, and we were never going to get back together.

I missed having *someone* in my life, but I didn't miss him.

Sometimes, maybe even more often than just *sometimes*, you were better off alone.

Sometimes you had to learn to be your own best friend. To put yourself first.

One tiny tear pooled up in my eye at yet another reminder that I was starting over again—at the magnitude of what lay in front of me—when the door swung open. I hadn't even realized the hallway light hadn't gotten turned on. Mr. Rhodes was right there, one hand gripping the door, his frame filling the rest of the doorway. His gaze landed on my face and he scowled, lines etching their way across his broad forehead.

I left the tear where it was and forced a smile onto my face. "Hello, Mr. Rhodes."

"You're on time again," he stated before taking a step back.

I guess he was letting me in. "I didn't want to get in trouble with the principal," I told him with a side look, joking.

Nothing about his expression changed.

I didn't let him get me down as he closed the door and then headed down the hallway toward the living area, aiming straight for the table again. I set the plate down in the middle, Amos's gift next to it, and watched as he pulled out the same chair I'd sat in the night before, then taking out the same one he'd been in and settling into it.

Maybe he wasn't Mr. Warm and Fuzzy, but he had some manners.

I beamed at him as I took the seat and plopped the notebook down before pulling my green pen out. "Thank you for letting me come over again."

"I owe you, don't I?" he asked, eyeing the round object wrapped in white tissue paper critically.

Could I tell him what it was? Sure. Was I going to? Not unless he asked.

"That's what you keep saying, and I sure could use your help, so I'm going to take advantage of it." I winked at him before I could stop myself, and fortunately he didn't frown. Instead, he just pretended I hadn't.

Smoothing out the page I'd left off on with my notes the day before, I scooted my chair in a little closer. "I have a million other questions."

"You've got twenty-nine minutes."

"Thank you for keeping track," I joked, not letting him get me down.

He just kept right on looking at me with those purplish-gray eyes as he crossed his arms over his chest.

He really did have some impressive biceps and forearms. When the hell did he work out?

I stopped thinking about his arms. "Okay, so… camping. Do you know what the hell a tent hammock is?"

Mr. Rhodes didn't even blink. "A tent hammock?"

I nodded.

"Yes, I know what a tent hammock is." He might as well have called me Captain Obvious from his tone of voice.

I eyed the cookies for a second and snatched one up. "How do you use one? What kind of trees do you hook them up to? Are they practical?" I paused. "Do you camp?"

He didn't answer my question about whether he camped or not, but he did listen to my other questions. "You put the hammock between two sturdy trees," he offered. "Personally, I don't think they're practical. There's a lot of wildlife around here. Last thing you want is waking up to a bear sniffing around your site because most people don't know how to properly put their food away, and even with a good mummy bag"—what was a mummy bag?—"the rest of you is going to be too cold most of the year. There's only about two good months here you could pull one off. Depends on where you're going camping too. I've been up at 14,000 feet in June before with layers on early in the morning."

"In June?" I gasped.

That chin with its cute cleft dipped.

"Where?"

"Some of the peaks. Some passes."

I was going to need to ask for specifics. Maybe later once I was walking out. "So hammock tents are no good?"

"Seem like a waste of money to me. I'd say get a tent instead and a good pad. But if someone's got the money to throw away, go for it. Like I said, bears are curious. They'll run, but after you, each scare the hell out of each other."

I really needed to get some bear spray. And never let my aunt find out about curious bears. She had started sending me texts about mountain lions now.

"What kind of bears are there?"

"Black bears, but they aren't always that color. There's a lot with brown and cinnamon fur around here."

I swallowed. "Grizzlies?"

He blinked, and I think I might have seen part of his mouth quiver a little. "Not since the 70s."

I didn't mean to, but I whistled in relief, then laughed. "So tent hammocks are stupid unless you really want to use them and have the money to spend and are willing to put your life at risk. Got it." I scribbled down part of it, even though I doubted I'd forget. "So tents...."

He sighed.

"Okay, we don't have to talk about tents if you don't want to. Where do you recommend going camping? If you wanted to see animals?"

Mr. Rhodes ran a hand through his short, salt and brown pepper hair once before crossing his arms over his wide chest again, bringing to attention the way his pecs were squeezed together on his lean chest.

How old *was* he?

"This is southwest Colorado. You can go camping in your backyard and see a fox."

"But other than a backyard, where? Within an hour from here?"

His hand slid to his cheek, and he rubbed the short bristles there. I bet he had to shave twice a day—not that it was any of my business to wonder.

Mr. Rhodes went into a description of several marked trails close to water sources. He stopped to think a couple times, and a little notch formed between his eyebrows as he did. He was handsome.

And he was my landlord. A grumpy—or distrustful—one at that, who didn't want me hanging around and was only being nice because I'd taken his son to the hospital. Well, there were worse ways to get to know people.

He suddenly said a name that made my hand pause over the paper.

"It's not well-marked, and it's difficult, but if someone has experience, they can do it."

A knot formed in my throat, and I had to glance down at my notebook as discomfort lanced me straight through my chest. A beautiful, perfect arrow with a jagged arrowhead.

"Need me to spell it out for you?" he asked when I hadn't responded to him.

I pressed my lips together and shook my head before glancing up, focusing on his chin instead of his eyes. "No, I know how to spell it." But I still didn't write down the name. Instead, I asked, "And all the rest of these are close to water you said?" That was exactly what he'd said, but it was the first thing I thought of to change the subject.

He didn't want to hear about how well I knew that hike.

"Yes," he confirmed, stretching the word out in a weird way.

I kept my attention down. "Do you and Amos go camping a lot?" I asked.

"No," he answered, his attention a little too focused, that crease still there. "Amos isn't into the outdoors."

"Some people aren't," I said, even though it was a little funny that he lived in one of the most beautiful places on Earth and didn't care for it. "So—"

"Why are you here?"

I froze, surprised he was curious. I wanted to glance at my watch—I really did have a lot of things I wanted to know —but if he was asking… well, I'd answer. "I used to live here as a kid, but I had to move away a long time ago. I… got a divorce and didn't really have anywhere else to go, so I decided to come back." I smiled at him and shrugged like everything that had happened was no big deal, when they had been the two biggest events of my life. They'd been the dynamite that restructured my entire existence.

"Denver is more most people's style."

"Most people, sure, but I don't want to live in a city. My life was really hectic for a long time, and I like the slower pace. I forgot how much I love the outdoors. The clean air. My mom used to love it here. When I think about home, it's here, even twenty years later," I told him honestly before plopping the rest of the cookie in my mouth and chewing it quickly. When I was done, I kept going. "I don't know if I will end up staying forever, but I'd like to try. If it doesn't work out, then it doesn't work out. I just want to try my best in the meantime." Which reminded me again that I needed to look for some other place to stay. I hadn't had any luck searching so far, and part of me hoped someone would cancel their reservation at the last minute.

For a long time, I'd thought I was pretty damn lucky. My mom used to say all the time how lucky she was, for every-thing. Every occasion. Even when things went wrong.

She saw the best in everything. A flat tire? *Maybe we would have gotten into an accident if we hadn't stopped.* Someone stole her wallet? They needed the money more, and at least she had a job and could make more! The highs with her had always been so high. Now, more often than not—and especially when I felt down—I felt more like I was cursed. Or maybe my mom had taken all my luck with her.

Mr. Rhodes stayed leaned back in his chair, lines back across his forehead, watching me. Still not in that way I mostly ignored from other people, but with that raccoon did-I-have-rabies-or-not face.

"Are you from here?" I asked, even though Clara had told me earlier.

All he said was "yes," and I knew that was all I was going to get. Well, that wasn't going to tell me how old he was. Oh well. Maybe I could ask her in some subtle, sneaky way.

"Back to camping then... do any of these places have fishing?"

～

"TIME IS UP," he said at eight o'clock on the dot, focusing on the top of his right hand, which was resting on the table.

How the hell had he known what time it was? I'd been watching him; he hadn't looked at the heavy watch on his left wrist or at his phone. I didn't even know where his phone was. It wasn't on the table like mine.

I smiled as I closed up my notebook and clipped my pen to the front cover. I picked up another cookie and bit off half. "Thank you so much for the help," I said as I pushed the chair back.

He grunted, still not sounding like it was what he would have picked to do today. But he had.

"Hi, Aurora," another voice spoke up suddenly.

Glancing over my shoulder, I noticed Amos making his way into the kitchen, a vase full of flowers in his hands, his big T-shirt covering everything until halfway down the baggy basketball shorts he had on. "Hey. How are you?"

"Fine." He came to a stop beside the chair his dad was in. I didn't miss the quick glance he shot the man before focusing back on me. "How are you?" he asked slowly, like he felt awkward.

It just made me like him more. I grinned. "Fine. Your dad was just helping me again." I eyed the mixed bouquet of pink and purple flowers. "Those are pretty."

Amos held them out. "They're for you. From my mom and dad. Thank you for taking me to the hospital."

"Oh." I took the vase and was surprised at how heavy it was. "Thank you so much. They're beautiful. You didn't have to do that, Mr. Rhodes."

I didn't see Mr. Rhodes's face or Amos's because I was too busy looking at the arrangement, but it was the teenage boy who said, "No, my other dad."

"Ohhh." I glanced up at him. Where were they? I wondered. His mom and other dad? "Tell them I said thank you. I love them. And they're very welcome for taking you. I'd say any time, but I hope not."

Neither one of them said anything.

But I remembered what Clara had told me earlier as I set the vase down on my thighs and peered at the teenager. "I got something for you too, actually." I picked up the crystal from the table and held it out to him. "You might have been too out of it to remember, but I called my friend before we went to the hospital, and anyway, she sent this. She said it promotes healing and to put it on your left. She hopes you feel better."

His eyebrows rose steadily with each word out of my mouth, but he ended it with a nod, not unwrapping it or anything. I figured he'd do it in the privacy of his room, I guess. "Hey, did you know I work with Jackie?" I asked him.

Amos nodded, still holding his gift and testing the weight.

"I didn't know that you knew each other. Clara said you're best friends." I paused.

"Yeah," he answered in that quiet voice of his before slipping the gift into his pocket. "We play together. Music."

"Really?" I asked. She hadn't said a word about music, but then again, we only talked about work when we chatted. Twice we'd talked about movies, but that was the extent of our relationship. She just always seemed really hesitant around me, and I hadn't figured out why.

"She plays guitar too," he added, almost shyly.

"I had no idea."

"We play in the garage when I'm not in trouble." He shot his dad a pointed look that the older man didn't see, and I had to force myself to keep a straight face so he wouldn't catch on either.

"He plays the blues," Mr. Rhodes threw in. "But he doesn't like to play in front of other people."

"Dad," the kid scoffed, his cheeks going straight to red.

I tried to give him an encouraging smile. "It's hard to play in front of other people, thinking of how they're judging you. But the best thing to do is not care what they think or if you mess up. Everybody messes up. Every time. No one is ever flawless, and most people are tone deaf and can't hear a flat note if you poked them with it."

The kid shrugged, obviously still embarrassed his dad had ratted him out, but I thought it was cute.

Mr. Rhodes wouldn't have said anything if it didn't please him to a point.

"Exactly, Am. Who gives a shit what other people think?" Mr. Rhodes egged him on, surprising me again.

"You're always correcting me every time you come hear us," he muttered, face still flamed.

I bit back a smile. "I know a lot of musicians, and honestly, most of them—not all of them—but most of them like it when people are honest and correct them. They'd rather know they're doing something wrong, so that they can make a correction and not keep making the same mistake over and over again. That's how everyone gets better, but I know it sucks. That's why I'm here bothering your dad. Because I'm tired of being wrong at work."

Amos didn't make eye contact, but he did shrug.

I caught Mr. Rhodes's gaze and lifted my eyebrows as I smiled at him. His stoic expression didn't change at all, but I was pretty sure his eyes widened just a little, tiny bit.

Amos, either not wanting to be the center of conversation anymore or in a talkative mood, placed his hand on the back of his dad's chair and ran his fingernails along the top of it, focused on that as he asked, "Are you... doing another hike?"

"I think I'm going to do this river trail next."

The boy's gaze flicked up. "Where at?"

"The Piedra River." It was arguably the most popular one in the area. I tapped the tips of my fingers against the vase. "I'll get out of your hair. Thank you again for tonight, Mr. Rhodes. Keep feeling better, Amos. Have a good night." I gave them one more wave and headed out, neither one of them following to lock up behind me.

It was only eight, and I wasn't really tired yet, but I took a shower, flipped off the lights, and climbed into bed with a drink, thinking about the damn trail Mr. Rhodes brought up earlier.

The one my mom disappeared on.

The one that killed her.

At least we were pretty sure that was where she had gone. One of the witnesses that the police were able to find had claimed that they'd passed her on the trail when they'd been heading out and she'd been going up. They had said that she'd looked fine, that she'd smiled and asked how they were doing.

They were the last people to ever see her.

This tiny, bitter ache stretched across my heart, and I had to release a deep, deep breath.

She hadn't left me, I reminded myself for about the millionth time over the last twenty years. I had never cared what anyone had tried to say or hint at. She hadn't left me on purpose.

After a moment, I pulled up my tablet and started a movie I'd downloaded the day before, and I watched it distractedly, snuggling under the single sheet I slept under. At some point, I must have fallen asleep because the next thing I knew, I woke up with the tablet on my chest and with this intense urge to pee.

Usually, I tried to stop drinking fluids a couple hours before bed so that I wouldn't have to wake up; I had this fear of peeing myself even though that hadn't happened in like thirty years. But I'd sucked down a strawberry soda while I'd watched my movie.

Now, waking up in the pitch-black studio apartment, I groaned at the pressure on my bladder and rolled up to sitting.

It took me a second to reach around and find my phone plugged in under my pillow. I yawned as I took it off and tapped at the screen as I stood up, turning on the flashlight feature to get into the bathroom. I stumbled in on another yawn, not turning on the light so that I wouldn't wake myself up, and used it, peeing what felt like a gallon out, then washing my hands.

I was yawning all the way back, blinking at the faint light of the microwave's clock and adjusting to the moonlight that came in through the windows that were constantly cracked.

And that was when I felt the whoosh over my head.

I yawned again, confused, and lifted my hand, trying to cast the beam of light from my phone upward.

Out of the corner of my eye, something flew.

I *ducked.*

The flying thing did a turn in flight *and came right fucking at me.*

I screamed as I threw myself to the ground and, swear to God on my life, felt it go inches above my head.

Right beside the bed, I yanked on the thin blanket I kept by my feet because it was too warm to cover myself completely with it and covered my head as I blinked up and tried to look for what I was pretty sure was a bat because a fucking bird couldn't be that fast.

Could it? Could one have snuck in while I'd opened and closed the door? Wouldn't I have noticed? There was a screen on the window, so it couldn't have gotten in through there.

I crawled toward the wall where the light switch was on my hands and knees. "What the hell?" I liked to think I said but was pretty sure I shrieked as I lifted my hand just enough to feel the switch and flip it, the overhead lights illuminating the living room.

Confirming my worst nightmare.

Yeah, it was a fucking *bat* swooping.

"What the fuck!" I pressed my back even more against the wall.

What kind of bullshit was this?

Had I been sleeping in this damn room with it *every night?* Had he been landing on my face? Pooping on me? What did bat poop even look like? I'd seen some dark shapes on the floor, but I'd assumed they were mud off my shoes.

The bat dropped in height as it flew... and it came right toward me again, or at least it looked like it did.

Later on, I'd be disappointed in myself, but then again it was a goddamn bat, and I screamed.

And after that, I'd be even more disappointed in myself for the fact I crawled down the stairs on my hands and knees, but I did it. Only after grabbing my keys and shoving them into my shirt. Fuck this!

And in a way that pretty much summed up my life, I opened the door outside and ran out in my socks, tank top, and underwear—totally and completely unprepared—and saw another bat fly right in front of my face, aiming back up toward the endless, dark sky... where it belonged.

I still ducked anyway.

I might have screamed again, and I was pretty sure I yelled, "Fuck off!" but I wasn't positive.

What I was positive of was yelping my way over the gravel, holding my cell phone in one hand as a flashlight, clutching the blanket over my head but under my chin, and pretty much diving into my car the second I was close enough.

I was sweating, big-time. The shower I'd taken had gone to fucking hell. But what else was I supposed to do? Not sweat? There was a goddamn bat in the garage apartment!

It took way too long for me to stop panting, and I had to wipe my armpits with the corner of the blanket after locking the doors.

I needed some water.

More than that, I had to do something. I had more than a week left here. It wasn't like the bat was going to open the door and let itself out.

Shit, shit, *shit.*

It was either do something or do nothing... and for now, the only thing I was going to do was sleep in my car because there was no way in hell I was going back in there. Not for water. Not for a bed. I'd pee in an old water bottle if I had to. Bats were nocturnal, weren't they? God, I needed internet.

I shivered and tucked the blanket under my chin tighter.

Had Mom and I ever had bats at our house? Did she take care of them on her own? I wondered.

What in the hell had I gotten myself into?

CHAPTER 8

That next morning, I rolled up to the store and found Clara standing beside her car—a new Ford Explorer—and talking to a man a lot taller than her while Jackie stood off to the other side, messing with her phone.

It took me a moment to realize why his light brown skin and build seemed kind of familiar.

It was Johnny. Amos's uncle.

Pulling in to park on the other side, I finally spotted the Subaru parked behind the store. I grabbed my purse from the passenger seat before getting out.

"...it's fine. Just bring me the money tomorrow," Clara said in that soft, steady voice of hers.

"Can't tell you how much I appreciate it, Clara," Amos's uncle replied. I could see he was smiling at her, this sweet, easy one.

Jackie glanced over her shoulder and smiled tightly. "Hi, Ora."

She was one of the only people to call me that here. Even Clara only called me Aurora. Probably because it was my aunt and uncle who had started calling me Ora.

"Hi," I greeted her. "Are you coming with us?"

She blinked, and her smile dropped just a tiny bit. "Is that okay?"

I smiled extra wide, hating that for some reason she'd think I wouldn't want her around, especially since things were fine between us but just a little awkward for whatever reason, and nodded. "Yeah, it is."

Her smile back was timid but brighter.

Johnny happened to glance over then and made eye contact with me.

"Aurora," Clara called out over her shoulder. "This is Johnny, Amos's uncle."

I couldn't help it, I said, "We met at the hospital." I forgot I hadn't told her about all... that.

I walked around the Explorer and came to a stop beside Clara who smiled at me.

"Nice to see you again, Aurora," the man drawled.

"Nice to see you too."

I wished I put more makeup on now. I hadn't gotten around to it because I'd been so tired thanks to the chaos last night, I hadn't exactly gotten a good night's sleep. And it wasn't like Clara—or Jackie—cared if I had bags under my eyes.

"Did Rhodes give you a hard time the other night?"

I grinned and shook my head. He had to be referring to the night I'd snuck over to see Amos. "No. He said thank you. I figured that was pretty good."

The way he tilted his head said he thought so too. "Have fun on your trip. Clara said you're going to Ouray; it's nice up there. See you around?"

"Sure," I agreed, figuring I'd probably see him around the store since I wouldn't be at the apartment too much longer.

Clara gave him a quick hug, Jackie and I waved, and then

we were loading into her Explorer and Johnny was getting back into his car.

Her little sigh had me leaning between the two front seats —Jackie was in the front passenger—and peering at her.

Was that a dreamy look on her face or what? I glanced at Jackie to find her smirking. I wasn't imagining it.

Clara looked at us and instantly frowned. "Yes?"

Neither one of us said anything, and she sighed again and turned on the car.

"He's a sweetheart, okay?" She started to reverse. "And he's cute."

I leaned back into the seat and put the seat belt on. "He is cute."

"He just split up with his girlfriend about a month ago...." She trailed off.

"Aunt Clara's been wanting to get in his pants," Jackie said out of nowhere.

"Jackie!"

I laughed.

"He is cute," she confirmed, not exactly sounding happy about it though. "But I'm not saying I want to marry the guy or... or... get in his pants. I don't even want to date him. I'm not ready yet to be with anyone else, but I can still look."

Something in my chest churned at her own step she was admitting to. We were all trying to take small steps in our lives, trying to get somewhere.

I guess the good thing was, there might be a finish line with a specific time we needed to get there but none of us knew what it was.

Clara kept talking. "And, Jackie, quit telling people about Johnny."

The teenager blew a raspberry. "*You* said sex wasn't a big deal."

"It isn't for a lot of people, but only when you're ready.

Some people believe that it's a transfer of energy, and you don't want to pick up on anyone's bad energy. *And* I told you you can have sex with whoever you want once you're eighteen."

"You're so weird."

"Why am I weird?"

"Because you're supposed to tell me that I should wait until I get married!" Jackie argued back.

"You don't have to love every man you're with. Right, Ora?" Clara said with a peek over her shoulder.

I *had* loved every guy I'd ever been with. All whopping three of them. Two had been puppy love, but the last one... well, it had been real. Until it got burned alive and to a crisp. But that wasn't the point Clara was trying to make. "Exactly. No one ever tells a guy to wait for someone special. My uncle used to just beg my guy cousins to wear a condom. A skinny sixteen-year-old with bad acne isn't going to be a prince charming. At least just wait until you make sure the guy isn't a total immature douchebag."

"Uh-huh. And boyfriends just bring problems," Clara kept going, gesturing to me for my own input.

Considering none of my past relationships had worked out... she wasn't wrong. "I haven't had that many boyfriends, but yeah, they're a pain in the ass."

Jackie's turned around in her seat to peek at me. "You haven't had a lot of boyfriends?"

I shook my head.

"You look like you'd have a lot."

Clara tried to cover her snort at the same time I burst out laughing. "Thank you?"

She blanched. "Not like that! Because you like.... You're so pretty! You look like a princess! That was, like, the second thing Amos ever told me, and he never says stuff like that."

Amos thought I was pretty? What a sweet kid.

"I was with my ex for a really long time. And my other two boyfriends were in high school." One of them, I had kind of kept in touch with. He messaged me on Facebook every birthday and Christmas, and I did the same. He was still single and apparently some kind of workaholic engineer. The last I'd heard from the other one, the one between the guy I'd lost my virginity to and Kaden, was that he was married with four kids; at least that's what I'd seen the last time I'd stalked him online out of boredom. "You're so pretty too, Jackie, and you're really smart. That's a lot more important and useful than looks are."

Suddenly, I missed Yuki and Nori. We used to take turns pumping each other up when we were having bad days. When Yuki had broken up with her boyfriend about a month before Kaden had kicked me to the curb, we had sat around her living room—while he'd been on tour—and yelled at her. *You're beautiful! You treat people with respect! You haggled with your label for more money! You sold one hundred million records because YOU worked hard! You've got a great butt! You make the best macaroni and cheese I've ever had!*

They had done the same for me in the month I'd stayed with Yuki after. Try being sad when people you love yell compliments at you. You can't be.

The teenage girl who only spoke to me about work most of the time, though, grunted. "Boys don't like smart girls though."

From the side, I could see Clara shaking her head. "That's why we're telling you that they're a headache."

"More like a migraine, but sure, a headache works," I chirped up, and then the three of us were cracking up.

And that's when my phone started ringing.

Not actually with a call, I realized after a moment, but with a call through Facebook messenger.

I recognized the face on the screen before I even got a look at the name below it.

I knew that hair. The face with about ten layers of makeup that she never left the house without. Hell, I doubted she left the bathroom without a face full of foundation anymore. Not that there was anything wrong with it, but it was an idea of how important appearances were to her.

HENRIETTA JONES flashed across the screen.

The woman who had been my not-mother-in-law.

Glancing up, I noticed Clara and Jackie were talking about something, and my finger hesitated over the screen. The last thing in the world I wanted to do was ever talk to this woman again. It was half her fault that Kaden and I had split up. The rest of it was all on him. He didn't have to break things off or want more fame or money. I had never cared about that. I would've been happy—

No. I wouldn't have been happy. And none of that mattered anymore and never would again.

And as much as I would have loved to ignore The Mark of the Beast, if I didn't answer, it would just make her think that I was hiding. That I was weak. Worse, she would just keep on calling.

She had run me out, and here she was now. Calling me. A year later.

I snickered and tapped the screen before putting the cell to my face and saying, "Hello?"

She wasn't trying to video-call at least.

"Aurora," the woman whose voice I could have recognized in a packed concert said, sounding just about as stuffy as she had for the last ten years. "It's Henrietta."

Was it petty of me to say "Who?"

It was, but I did it anyway. Because fuck this lady who had canceled my cell phone the day after her son quit on our relationship. Who had told her employees—people who I'd assumed were my friends—she would fire them if she found out they were communicating with me.

"Henrietta, Aurora. Jones." She paused. "Kaden's mother—oh you're just being a pain, aren't you?" she snapped about halfway through, realizing I was fucking with her. "Where are you?"

Where was I?

I snorted again and kept watching Jackie and Clara talk. I couldn't tell what they were saying, but whatever it was, it had to be good from the way their hands were moving. They were cracking up over something.

"In the United States, ma'am. I'm pretty busy and can't stay on the phone long, is this an emergency?"

I knew what she needed. Of course I did. Aunt Carolina had sent me a screenshot this morning of another bad review that Kaden's latest album had gotten. Rolling Stone had used the word "atrocious."

"This isn't an emergency, but Kaden needs to speak with you. Or I can speak with you as well. He's tried emailing you and hasn't gotten a response." There was a pause, and she cleared her throat. "We've been worried."

I couldn't hold back my snort then either. It had been a year since the last time I'd communicated with either one of them. One whole year since I'd been cut cold turkey out of their lives. Out of their *family.*

And now they were worried? Ha. Ha. Ha.

Jackie burst out laughing from the front seat, and Clara gasped, "You're nasty!"

"Aurora? Are you listening?" Mrs. Jones griped.

I rolled my eyes at the same time I caught a whiff of fart and started laughing too. "Damn, Jackie, what did you eat? Demons for breakfast?"

"I'm sorry!" she cried, turning around in the seat with an embarrassed expression.

"She's not sorry," Clara shot back with a shake of her head before rolling the window down.

"Aurora?" Mrs. Jones's voice came over the line again, sharper that time, irritated, I was sure, at not putting my life on hold to speak with her. She was just that kind of person.

And you know what? I had this one life left, and I wasn't going to waste it on this lady. At least not more than I already had. "Mrs. Jones, I'm really busy. I'd tell you to tell Kaden I said hi, but I don't really care—"

She gasped. "You don't mean that."

"I'm pretty sure I do. I don't know what he wants to talk about, but I have no interest in having any more conversations with him. Much less with you."

"You haven't even heard what he wants to talk to you about."

"Because I don't care. Look, I really do have to go. I'm sure he can talk to Tammy Lynn." I didn't need to go there, but it was worth it.

"Aurora! You don't understand. I'm sure, I *know*, you'd like to hear what he has to say."

I rolled down my window too when the smell of Jackie's fart didn't go away fast enough. "No, I don't. I'd say good luck, but you're all going to keep making money off what I did anyway, so I don't need to wish it on you. Please don't bother calling me again." I ended the call and sat there and stared down at the darkened screen, surprised and yet not surprised at all at the same time.

I needed to call Aunt Carolina today and tell her. She'd get a kick out of this. I could picture her rubbing her hands together with glee.

Of course Kaden would have his mom call to break the ice. Did they really think I was that dumb or that easy? That I could, or would, ever, in a million years, forget or forgive what they had done? How they'd hurt me?

Covering my face with my hand, I scrubbed it up and down with a sigh and shake of my head. I folded up all of my thoughts and feelings of the Jones family and set them aside. I wasn't exaggerating. I didn't care that he wanted to talk or that she wanted him to talk to me or any of it.

"You okay back there?" Clara asked.

I peeked up to see her gaze on me through the rearview mirror. "Yeah. Just got a call from evil incarnate."

"Who?"

"My ex-mother-in-law."

Through the rearview mirror, her eyebrows shot up. "She's evil?"

"Let's just say, I'm pretty sure there's a spell somewhere to bind her to another realm."

～

"THAT WAS the best day I've had in a really long time," I said, hours and hours later as we were on the way back into town. It wasn't even full-out dark yet, but I was pretty sure I'd seen my life flash before my eyes at least twenty times. The road from the small, picturesque mountain town was... sketchy was the word.

I thought I'd driven some hair-raising places on the way to Pagosa Springs, but a special section of the road on our trip held no comparison. I hadn't known until we were leaving the shop that Clara was a menace to society behind the wheel. I was beyond relieved to be in the back seat when we'd done the hairpin turns so I could clutch the door and the edge of the seat for dear life without making her nervous.

But it had totally been worth it.

Ouray had been unbelievably busy with tourists, but I'd fallen in love with the small town that reminded me of something straight out of a town in the Alps or a storybook. Not that I'd ever been to the Alps, but I'd seen pictures. I had gotten sick the one Christmas the Joneses had booked a vacation to go...

They'd gone without me, claiming the tickets were nonrefundable, with Kaden insisting it would break his mom's heart if he wasn't there for the holidays. Needless to say, Yuki, being the friend that she was, had sent her bodyguard to pick me up five minutes after they left for the airport and had nursed me back to health over the week at her house.

I should have known then I was never going to be important enough.

They really did deserve that pie of shit.

Anyway.

As cool as the town had been, it had been the company that had made the trip so great.

It had been a long time since I'd laughed so much. Probably since the month I'd spent with Yuki, and we'd been drunk a fourth of the time. A rare thing for both of us.

"Me too," Clara agreed. She'd filled the trip with stories about some of the regulars I was getting to know at the store. One of my favorites being a man named Walter who had apparently found a bag of what he thought were herbs but was really marijuana and had brewed it like tea for months before someone told him it wasn't what he'd thought it was. When she wasn't filling me with gossip, she and Jackie tried to give me all the reasons why I should stay in Pagosa instead of leaving, which had surprised me because I really hadn't been sure the teenager liked me all that much in the first place. They'd made some interesting points, mostly: *you're home.*

Which I was. Home that is.

"I saw you smiling too, Jackie," Clara went on.

I had spotted her smiling a lot too.

Jackie's phone beeped then, and the girl grabbed it, reading whatever was on the screen before saying, "Ugh. I thought it was Grandpa. I texted him when we were in Durango, and he still hasn't texted me back."

Clara went silent, and I caught her glancing at Jackie, her expression thoughtful. Suddenly, she asked, "Do you mind if we make a quick stop before I drop you off, Aurora?"

"Not even a little bit."

"Thanks," she muttered, sounding worried as she turned the wheel to the right. "It's not like my dad to not text back, and he won't answer the home phone. My brother is supposed to be there...."

"Whatever you need to do. I wouldn't mind seeing him either if he's in the mood and it's okay for me to go in," I piped up.

Clara nodded distractedly, putting her blinker on as she drove closer into town. I knew from memory that they lived around one of the lakes. I hadn't been there in forever, but I knew it was closer to everything than where Mr. Rhodes lived. "He's been wanting to see you too. We'll be real quick. We still have to go grocery shopping."

A few minutes later, she pulled up outside of a small one-story home with two cars parked in front of it. A white mini-van... and a restored Bronco. What were the chances of two pristine Brittany blue Broncos in this area *with the same license plate*? I wondered as Clara pulled up alongside the van.

"What's Mr. Rhodes doing here?" Jackie confirmed what I'd processed. "Where is Uncle Carlos's car?"

"I don't know...." Clara trailed off with a frown.

I undid my seat belt just as my phone beeped with a message.

It was my aunt.

Aunt Carolina: Are there coyotes in the area?

I hesitated for a second. That didn't sound like the kind of question I should answer. I didn't need her worrying about coyotes too.

Slipping out of the car, I followed after Jackie and Clara as they headed to the front door. The house was small and older than most in town. The floor was tiled with foot-sized pieces that were either dark brown or green, and the furniture was mostly all antiques. It was just about exactly how I'd remembered it. I used to spend the night here every other weekend. I had a lot of good memories in this house.

"Dad!" Clara yelled. "Where are you?"

"In the living room!" a deep voice hollered back.

"You got pants on?"

I grinned.

"Guess!"

That made me laugh.

Clara turned sharply to the left into a small living room. The first thing I noticed was a flat screen propped on an entertainment table, thirty-something inches wide. The second thing I noticed was the man sitting on a big, comfortable recliner facing the TV. His hair was a mix of gray and white and braided down one shoulder, and on a love seat beside him was my landlord, arms crossed. A football game played on the television.

Clara and Jackie hurried over, kissing both his cheeks. "We brought Aurora, Daddy."

The man's dark eyes moved, then landed on me, and in the time it took me to blink, they had gone wide.

I ignored Mr. Rhodes and hurried over, ducking down and kissing Clara's dad's cheek. "Hi, Mr. Nez. Pants are overrated, huh?"

His big, sudden laugh caught me off guard as he leaned forward and brushed his cheek against mine, two brown hands that looked like leather, landing on my own and squeezing. He pulled back and blinked up at me with his big, dark eyes. "Aurora De La Torre. How the hell are you doing, child?"

His laugh was just the same. Face more lined, and he was much skinnier. But Mr. Nez was still the exact same in every other way that mattered. The sparkle in his eye told me so, even if the trembling in his hands tried to tell a different story.

I stayed where I was right in front of him. "I'm pretty good. How are you?"

"Damn fine." He shook his head and aimed a smile at me that showed he was missing two teeth. He was a handsome man with his dark skin, the whites of his eyes nearly brilliant against his striking face. "Clara said you'd come back, and I couldn't believe it." He gestured toward the seat closest to him, which was the empty spot on the love seat between him and Mr. Rhodes. "Come here, sit down. But first." He gestured toward Rhodes. "Aurora, Tobias. Tobias, this is Aurora. She used to live in my house every weekend and every summer."

I couldn't help but laugh as I glanced at the man I'd just spent time with last night. I smiled at him. "I know him, Mr. Nez."

Mr. Rhodes, on the other hand, grunted.

Mr. Nez frowned. "How?"

"She's renting his garage apartment." It was Clara who answered. "Where's Carlos?"

The old man ignored her question, chuckled and slapped his thigh. "You don't say. You're the one who took Amos to the hospital?"

"That was me," I confirmed, peeking at Mr. Rhodes who was still sitting there with his arms crossed on the love seat... watching me with a really funny expression on his face that made me feel less welcome here than even at his garage apartment.

"You look so much like your mom," the older man said, pulling my attention back toward him. His forehead scrunched, and the surprised expression that had been on his face melted into a troubled one. "I told myself I wouldn't bring it up the first time I saw you, but I have to say—"

I cut him off. "You don't have to say anything."

"No, I do," Mr. Nez insisted, looking more and more upset by the second. "I've been living with this guilt for twenty years. I'm sorry we all lost touch. I'm sorry we didn't see you again after they took you away."

A knot magically appeared in my throat at that exact second.

"Wait, who took who away?" Jackie asked from where she'd taken a seat on the floor by the television screen. Now she was making a face too.

The lack of response to her made the room feel tense, or at least it felt that way to me.

But I didn't want to ignore her, even if I felt Mr. Rhodes's gaze still steady on me.

The knot stayed exactly where it was. "Me, Jackie. Remember Clara said I used to live here? And how I was friends with her? Child services took me. That was the last time I saw your aunt or your grandpa, twenty years ago."

CHAPTER 9

"Okay, someone explain this," Jackie muttered, looking confused.

But Mr. Nez ignored everyone but me as he said, "The last I heard, the state took you into a foster home while they looked for your father."

Well, I didn't really want to talk about this in front of everyone, but it wasn't like I had a choice. He knew. Clara hadn't wanted to bring it up either, but they both deserved to know what had happened, even if it was out of order. "My uncle ended up taking me in," I explained. Trying to go into details about my dad was pointless.

"Uncle? I remember your mother saying she was an only child."

"It was her half-brother. Older. They weren't close, but he and his wife took custody of me. I moved to Florida to be with them. After."

Her eyebrows inched upward with every word out of my mouth, his devastated expression going nowhere.

"I don't know what's happening, and I want to know," Jackie said.

"Jackie," Clara called out from the kitchen where she'd disappeared into. "If you be quiet, you can put it together."

"They wouldn't tell us what happened after child services took you; they said we weren't family, but we were all so worried...," the older man murmured gently. "It was such a relief when you and Clara got back in touch."

"Mr. Rhodes, do you know what's going on?" Jackie asked.

Mr. Nez sighed and eyed his granddaughter for a second before focusing back on me. "Would you mind if I explained?"

"No," I told him honestly.

"Aurora and her mom used to live here in Pagosa, you know that already?"

The teenage girl nodded, glancing in my direction. "And something happened and your uncle and aunt took you in, Ora?"

I nodded. "When I was thirteen, my mom went for a hike and never came back."

It was then Mr. Rhodes happened to lean forward, finally deciding to speak. "Now I know why your last name was familiar. De La Torre. Azalia De La Torre. She went missing."

He knew?

There was more to the story. More to my mom and the mystery, but those were the basics of it. I didn't have the heart to bring up the other parts of it. The parts that some people had whispered about but had never really been confirmed.

How for so long, they had thought that she had abandoned me instead of getting hurt and never making it back out.

How she had struggled with depression and maybe whatever had happened to her hadn't been an accident.

How I was supposed to have gone with her but hadn't, and maybe if I had, she would still be around.

This crushing sense of guilt that I'd thought I'd moved on from weighed my chest down—my very soul down, honestly. I knew my mom would never abandon me. She had loved me. Adored me. She had wanted me.

And something had happened and she hadn't come back.

My mom hadn't been perfect, but she hadn't done the things that they had accused her of.

"That's so sad," Jackie murmured. "They never found her body?"

"Jesus Christ, Jackie," Clara yelled from the kitchen. "Could you ask that any worse?"

"I'm sorry!" the teenager cried. "I didn't mean it like that."

"I know," I assured her. I'd heard the same question stated about a dozen different ways that were genuinely more hurtful. And it was fine. She was curious.

"What made you want to come back here?" Mr. Nez asked, his face thoughtful.

Wasn't that the million-dollar question? I shrugged. "I'm just starting over. It felt right to do it here."

I didn't need to glance at Mr. Rhodes to know he was staring at me intently.

"Well, we're glad you're home. You've got a family with us now, Aurora," Mr. Nez said gently.

And that was just about the nicest thing I'd heard in a really long time.

I HAD JUST GOTTEN out of my car when I heard the crunching of tires on the gravel driveway, and I sighed again, preparing myself for whatever might be potentially on its way.

I knew I hadn't gotten away with anything; I wasn't

trying *to* get away with anything. I had felt the heat of Mr. Rhodes's eyeballs the entire time I'd been at Mr. Nez's house. He hadn't said much after confirming he knew about my mother's case, but I had felt his stare. I'd pretty much been able to hear the gears in his head going as he processed the conversation I'd had with the older man.

I hadn't figured out how exactly he knew Mr. Nez, and I hadn't wanted to just outright ask Clara about it, at least not in front of Jackie. I didn't trust she wouldn't repeat it to Amos and then he'd say something, and the next thing I knew, Mr. Rhodes thought I was stalking him.

What I was, was... curious

I had so many questions. And way too much time.

Anyway, I didn't try and run into the garage apartment as I spotted the Bronco pulling up to the house. I took my time, ducking into the passenger seat to pull out my purse and a small shopping bag I'd gotten from a candy and treat store in Ouray, and had just slammed the door shut with my hip when I heard Mr. Rhodes's "Hey."

I blew out a breath and turned toward the voice, already ready to smile up at him. "Hi, Mr. Rhodes."

My landlord stopped just a few feet away, hands going to his hips. But looking at his face, I noticed he didn't seem irritated or mad that we'd both somehow ended up at the same place. That was a good thing, wasn't it? I still had some time left here.

Part of me was just expecting him to be annoyed that we'd accidentally met up. He hadn't said more than five words to me after Mr. Nez had brought up my mom and he'd asked about where I'd been. I'd skimmed Nashville and settled on my years in Florida lightly, until Clara had come out of the kitchen and asked if I was ready to go.

Now though, Mr. Rhodes's mouth twisted to one side and he pierced me with that gray, nearly purple gaze.

What was he thinking about?

"Did you find somewhere else to stay yet?" he finally asked in his gruff, serious voice.

"Not yet."

Those eyes kept on burning a hole into me before he finally blew out a breath so harsh I wasn't sure if whatever he'd been thinking about was a good thing. Then he surprised me again. Shocked me, really. "If you want it, the garage apartment is yours."

I didn't mean to gasp, but I did. "*Really?*"

He didn't comment on my excitement, but his hands went to that narrow waist hidden beneath the T-shirt and jeans he had on, and Mr. Rhodes dipped his chin. "Rent is half of what you paid. No visitors. You've got to be fine with Amos playing his guitar in the garage."

Yes!

"I won't let him play late, but he likes to go in there after school until the evening," my landlord went on. His face was so no-nonsense I knew that he meant every word and was fully aware that he really hadn't intended to let me stay but he was going against his gut and extending the invitation... for whatever reason.

I knew exactly what it was like when a decision cost you a lot. It wasn't easy.

And that's why I was going to tell myself that I took a step forward and threw my arms around him. Around the top of the elbows that were cocked at his sides, locking his arms against his ribs because I'd surprised him and hadn't given him a chance to brace himself, my palms meeting somewhere on his back. I hugged him. I hugged this man who could barely stand me and said, "Thank you so much. I'd love to stay. I'll pay you every month and not invite anyone over. My only friends here so far are Clara and Mr. Nez anyway."

The whole long length of his body stiffened under my arms.

That was my cue. I instantly jumped back and fist pumped the air twice. "Thank you, Mr. Rhodes!" Yes! "You won't regret it!"

I don't think I was imagining how wide his eyes had gone at some point, but I definitely wasn't imagining how stiff his voice was as he just about stuttered, "You're... welcome?"

"What would you prefer? Check? Cash? Cashier's check?"

His alarmed face didn't go anywhere. Neither did his crisp tone. "Either."

"Thank you so much. I'll pay you the day before this rental period ends and keep paying you the same day." Wait. "How long can I stay for?"

His curly, thick lashes dropped over his eyes. He hadn't talked himself this far into our situation, and I could tell he was thinking. "Until this arrangement stops working out or you break the rules," he seemed to decide.

That wasn't a concrete answer, but I could live with it.

Sure, I'd just hugged him, but I thrust my hand out between us. His eyes bounced from me to my hand and back to my face before he took it. His hold was firm and jerky, his hands dry.

And big.

"Thank you," I told him again, relief pulsing through me.

He dipped that bristled chin of his. "The rent is going to be for Amos."

The idea that I'd had when Amos and I had been in my car on the way to the hospital popped back up, and I hesitated for a second, debating whether or not to make the offer, but doing it anyway because it felt like the right thing to do. "Look, I can probably get him a discount on his guitar depending on who he decides he wants it through. I can't promise, but I can try. Let me know."

His eyebrows crept closer together, and his mouth did that twist again, but he nodded. "Thank you for the offer." He exhaled, a much smaller and normal one this time, and I eyed his full mouth. "I'm still mad at him for going behind my back, and he's going to stay grounded for a few months, but if you're around after that…." He tipped his head to the side.

I grinned. "He told me what he wants. I'll help you, just let me know."

His expression went leery, but he dipped his chin.

I smiled. "Best day ever. Thank you so much for letting me stay, Mr. Rhodes."

He opened his mouth and then closed it again before nodding, then looking away.

Okay. I took a step back. "I'll see you later. Thank you again."

"I heard you the first time," he muttered.

Lord, this guy was grumpy. It made me laugh. "I really mean it. Goodnight."

He turned around to walk away, calling out over his shoulder in what I was pretty sure was a huff, "'Night."

I couldn't even put into words how relieved I was. I was staying. Maybe things were starting to turn around for me.

Maybe just maybe.

THEY WEREN'T.

My eyes popped open in the middle of the night like my bat senses were going off.

Holding my breath, I stared up at the ceiling and waited, listened. Watched. I had convinced myself it had escaped, so I wouldn't worry about it all day.

I heard it. My eyes adjusted just as it started swooping, and I shoved part of the blanket into my mouth.

I wasn't going to scream. I wasn't going to scream....

Maybe it really had left. I'd looked all over the apartment for it that morning and after Mr. Rhodes had extended my stay. And there'd been nothing. Maybe it had—

It swooped right by my face—maybe it wasn't *right* by my face, but it seemed like it—and I squealed.

No way. Pulling the blanket over my face, I rolled off the bed with it and started crawling. Luckily, I'd left my keys in the same place all the time, and my eyes had adjusted enough so that I could see the kitchen counter. I reached up just enough to grab them.

Then I kept on crawling toward the staircase. For the second night in a row. I could never tell my aunt about this. She'd start researching rabies vaccinations.

I wasn't proud of myself, but I took the stairs on my ass, the blanket tucked tight over my head.

I'd shoved my cell down my bra at some point, and at the bottom of the stairs, I slipped my feet into the tennis shoes I'd kicked off down there earlier, keeping as low as possible, and finally headed outside, still wrapped in my blanket.

Small animal noises rustled around as I closed the door behind me and locked it, before basically running toward my car, hoping and praying something wasn't going to come swooping, but I managed to slip inside and slam the door closed.

Reclining the seat and then pushing it back as far as it would go, I settled in, blanket up to my neck, and not for the first time, I wondered—despite how I'd felt earlier when Mr. Rhodes had offered to let me stay—what the hell I was doing here. Hiding in my car.

Maybe I should go back to Florida. We had bugs the size of small bats, sure, but I wasn't scared of them. Well, not really.

It's just a bat, my mom would have told me. I used to be

terrified of spiders, but she'd helped me work the fear out. Everything was a living, breathing being that needed food and water like I did. It had organs and felt pain.

It was okay to be scared. It was good to be scared of things.

Did I really want to go back to Florida? I loved my aunt, uncle, and the rest of the family. But I *had* missed Colorado. I really had. All these years.

That eased the harshest edges of my fear.

If I was going to stay here, I needed to figure this bat situation out, because there was no way, even if I stopped panicking, that I'd be fine with having a bat swooping around while I slept. I couldn't keep doing this, and nobody was going to come and save me. I was a grown woman, and I could handle this.

Tomorrow, I'd start to figure it out.

After another night in my car.

I was going to get that damn bat out of the house some way, somehow, damn it.

I could do this. I could do anything, right?

CHAPTER 10

I didn't need a mirror to know I looked like hell because I sure felt like it the next morning.

My neck hurt from sleeping in every position imaginable in my car for the second night in a row. I was pretty sure I'd probably gotten a solid two hours of sleep on and off. But that was better than zero hours if I'd stayed inside.

I still made myself wait until the sun was totally out before going inside.

And then I immediately stopped when I spotted Amos's face staring out at me from the living room window.

And I knew it wasn't because of my incredible beauty, because fortunately, I'd managed to cover myself with the blanket the same way I'd done the night before, covered from head to toe like it was a rain poncho. Without him saying a word, I knew he was wondering what the hell I'd been up to. There was no way I could pull off looking like I'd gone to the store or a run in the early morning because I was tiptoeing with my shoes barely hanging onto my toes.

"Morning, Amos," I called out, trying to sound cheery even though I felt like I'd gotten run over. I knew he could hear me because they opened the small rectangular windows under the big, main ones to keep the house cool.

"Morning," he replied in a voice that was cracking with sleep. I'd bet he probably hadn't gone to bed yet. "Are you... okay?" Amos asked after a second.

"Yep!"

Yeah, he didn't believe me at all.

"You feeling okay?" I asked him instead, hoping he wouldn't ask what the hell I'd been doing.

He shrugged a bony shoulder, still watching me way too closely. "You're sure you're all right?"

I replied the same way he had, I shrugged. Did I want to tell him about the bat? Yes. But... I was the adult and he was the child, and I didn't want to remind his dad that I was staying in the apartment more than I needed to, so I figured I had to deal with as many things as possible on my own to make this work.

"I need to get dressed for work, but have a good day today," I croaked.

I wasn't fooling anybody.

"Byeee," I called out before hopscotching across the gravel.

"Bye," the kid replied, sounding confused.

I couldn't blame him for being suspicious.

And I hoped he didn't tell his dad, because I didn't want him to change his mind. Oh well.

And like I'd been traumatized, my heart started beating faster as I unlocked the door and slowly climbed the stairs, flipping on all the lights and looking at every wall and every section of ceiling like the damn bat was going to fly out and attack me. My heart raced, and I wasn't proud of that either, but I knew I had to come up with a plan; I just didn't know what.

Part of me had expected to see my arch-nemesis clinging

onto something upside down, but there wasn't a single sign of him.

Oh fuck me, please don't be under the bed, I pleaded before getting to my hands and knees and checking under there too. I hadn't thought about that spot until now.

Nothing.

And even though I had started sweating again, and I was cursing the fact that I hadn't applied deodorant before I'd gone to bed, I checked just about everywhere I could think of where my friend could have hidden. Again.

Under the table.

Under the sink in the bathroom—because I'd been dumb and left the door open when I'd fled for my life.

Under every chair.

In the closet, even though the door was closed.

But he was nowhere.

Because I was paranoid, I looked everywhere again, fingers trembling, heart galloping and everything.

And still nothing.

Son of a bitch.

DESPITE HAVING ONLY SLEPT a solid two hours, when nighttime rolled around, I was on fucking guard.

I'd thought about buying a net, but we'd sold out at the shop and I checked Walmart and they were out too, so I'd grabbed a plastic trash bag, ready.

Ten o'clock hit, and it was all clear.

Damn it.

Even Clara had noted how tired I looked that morning. I'd been too embarrassed to tell her why I'd stayed up. I had to deal with this on my own.

I wasn't even sure when I passed out, but I did, sitting

upright on the mattress with my mom's notebook open, back against the headboard.

What I did know was that when my neck started hurting at some point, the lights still on, I woke up.

And I yelled again because *the son of a bitch was back.*

And he was flying around erratically, like he was drunk; he could've been six feet wide, terrorizing me and the home I was living in.

Actually, it wasn't a he. This one knew what it was doing —raising hell—and only a woman would be that intuitive and ready to fuck with someone for the hell of it.

She swooped, and I screamed, flying off the bed and running down the stairs, screaming again, and out the damn door.

As fate would have it, the moon was bright and high in the sky, illuminating another bat flying around what felt like right over my head but was really more like twenty feet above ground.

And again, I screamed. This time "Fuck!" at the top of my lungs.

I'd left my keys! Upstairs! With her! And my blanket!

Okay, Ora, all right, think.

I could do this. I could—

A loud voice boomed, *"What is going on?"* straight from the darkness.

I kind of knew that voice.

It was Mr. Rhodes, and from the crunching gravel, he was coming over. Probably pissed. I'd woken him up.

Later on, I would be disappointed in myself again for jabbing my finger toward the garage apartment and saying, "Bat!"

I couldn't see him. I wasn't sure if he made a face or rolled his eyes or what, but I knew he was getting closer and closer. But I could hear it in his voice. I could hear him rolling his eyes just from the way he spat, "*What?*" in the same voice he'd used the day I'd shown up.

"There's a bat in the room!"

Finally, I could see the silhouette of his body stopping a couple feet away, and I heard his annoyance as he asked, "*What?* You're bellowing over a *bat?*"

Bellowing over a bat? Did he have to ask it like that? Like it was no big deal?

Was he shitting me?

And like the one outside knew we were talking about its kind, the bat swooped back down toward the light mounted above the garage door, and I pulled my tank top up over my head and ducked, trying to make myself as small as possible so it couldn't get me.

Okay, more like Mr. Rhodes would be bigger, so if one of us was targeted it would be him since he had more mass.

I was pretty sure I heard "Goddamn it" being grumbled right before it sounded like he was walking again.

Leaving me to fend for myself.

Either that or the bat had grown fucking feet, a couple hundred pounds, and was on its way to kill me.

I waited a second and peeked out to see… nothing.

It was gone. At least the one outside was.

Or more like he was sitting somewhere. Waiting to pick on me again.

"Where did it go?" I asked about a split second before I spotted what I was pretty sure was bare feet moving across the ground like that shit didn't hurt like hell.

Where was he going?

"He went back home, to its cave," he muttered, genuinely sounding disgruntled as he walked away.

He was leaving me here. To fend for my life. Because this was no big deal to him.

Then I remembered it was a bat and just about anyone

would scream. It wasn't my fault he was a mutant with no fears.

All right. I needed to calm down and keep my shit together. *Think.*

Or move. Moving was good.

I got up, glancing up at the sky one more time, and then hustled after Rhodes who was... making his way toward his truck?

Fuck it, I was nosey. "There's a cave around here?"

"No."

I frowned, remembering right then that I wasn't wearing pants but then decided I didn't care and kept on following him.

He glanced over his shoulder as he opened the door. "What are you doing?"

"Nothing," I croaked, but really, all I could think about was safety in numbers.

Even with how dark it was, I could tell that he was making a face.

"What are you doing?"

He might have rolled his eyes, but he had his back to me so I would never know for sure. "Going to my truck."

"For what?"

"To get a net so I don't have to hear you hollering at the top of your lungs when I'm trying to get some sleep."

My heart stopped. "You're going to get it out?"

"Are you going to keep screaming if I leave it?" he asked over his shoulder as he rooted around his back seat. A second later, he was out, slamming the door closed and crossing the gravel like it wasn't digging into his feet like glass.

I grimaced but told him the truth. "Yes."

He opened the back of his work truck and started fiddling around in the bed.

"Have you caught them before?"

There was a pause then, "Yeah."

"You did?"

He grunted. "Once or twice."

"*Once or twice?* Where? *Here?*"

Rhodes grunted again. "They come in from time to time."

I almost passed out. "How often?"

"Mostly during the summer and fall."

I didn't mean to choke, but it happened.

"Mice are the real problem during a drought year."

The hairs on the back of my neck stood up, and my whole body went stiff as I stared at him tinkering around the bed of his truck, moving things as he stood there in sleep pants and a white tank top.

"You scared of those too?" he asked in a huff. He was pissed.

Some people got really quiet when they were mad. I was starting to see Mr. Rhodes wasn't one of those people.

"Umm... yes?"

"Yes?"

"How often do you get those?"

"Spring. Summer. Fall." Yeah, he was angry.

Too bad for him, I was always down to talk. I choked again. "Is this a drought year?"

"Yes."

I was never going to sleep again.

I needed to go buy traps.

But then imagining having to pick up the traps made me want to puke.

"Finally," he muttered to himself, standing up straight, holding a medium-sized net in one hand and what looked like thick gloves in another, before slamming the tailgate closed.

I shivered and watched him head toward the door of the garage apartment.

"Want me to wait out here? You know, so I can open the door for you?" I was such a chickenshit and it embarrassed me, but not enough to suck it up and be backup.

I would if he yelled.

I just hoped he didn't.

His stiff, angry body went right by mine. "Do whatever you want."

It was that or lock myself in my car until he was done but screaming my head off had been enough. He was already irritated having to come over and deal with this. Deal with *me*.

And yeah, that was embarrassing too. I needed to get it together. Suck it up.

Do my mom proud.

I'd done some research during the day of how to remove them but hadn't figured out what the best plan of action was yet. I was well aware that bats were wonderful for a whole lot of different reasons. I understood that they weren't trying to attack me even when they swooped. I got that bats were just as scared of me as I was of them. But fear wasn't rational.

I rushed forward, opened the door, and left it cracked after he went in. Then I crouched there and waited. I might have been out there five minutes, or maybe thirty, before I heard him on the stairs.

I opened the door more just as he was a couple steps away from reaching the bottom. He was holding the net in one hand and taking the steps fast on big, bare feet. My God, what were those things? Size twelve? Thirteen?

Tearing my gaze away, I threw the door open as wide as possible, waited for him to cross the doorway, and slammed it closed so the Mistress of the Night couldn't come back in and pay me another visit.

And I tried my best to be quiet as I moved to stand behind Mr. Rhodes. He stopped by a shrub, did something to the net, and stepped away.

I only caught a glimpse of the bat hanging from a branch before she took off, and I let out a squeak that I was going to kick myself in the ass for later. Mr. Rhodes didn't wait or stay to watch where she went, he just started moving toward the main house without another word.

I scrambled after him as he tossed the net in the back of his truck, then made his way up the deck as I stopped and stared up at the sky to make sure another one wasn't dropping out of nowhere.

He was at the door of his house when I yelled after him, "Thank you! You're my hero! I'll give you a ten-star review if you ever want it!"

He didn't say anything as he closed the door behind him, but that didn't mean he wasn't still my hero.

I owed him. I owed him big-time.

CHAPTER 11

I was off a week later, so part of me had expected to get to sleep in, take it easy, maybe go do one of the touristy things in the area. Or maybe do one of my mom's easier hikes. Since I was going to be around for the near future, I wasn't in as big of a rush to get them all done. My lungs needed more conditioning anyway. I figured I had at least until October.

Maybe. What had happened in the middle of the night a week ago might have made Mr. Rhodes change his mind about how long he'd let me stay. I didn't know him, but I knew there was no way he was over that shit yet.

The bat, though, hadn't come back. My brain, on the other hand, was in denial because I still couldn't sleep throughout the night without waking up, paranoid.

That's why I was awake when the sounds outside started up.

Resigned that I wasn't going back to sleep, I rolled up and got out of bed once another glance at my phone confirmed it was seven thirty and instantly peeked out the window.

There was a dull, repetitive sound coming from out there.

It was Mr. Rhodes.

Chopping wood.

Shirtless.

And I mean *shirtless.*

I'd expected something nice beneath his clothes from the way he filled them out, but nothing could have prepared me for the sight of... him. Reality.

If I wasn't already pretty sure that there was dry drool on my face, there would have been five minutes after seeing all.... *That* through the window.

A pile of foot-long logs were tossed around his feet, with another small pile that he'd obviously already chopped, just to the side. But it was the rest of him that really drew my attention. Dark chest hair was sprinkled high over his pectorals. The body hair did nothing to take away from the hard slabs of abdominal muscles he'd been hiding; he was broad up top, narrow at the waist, and covering all that was firm, beautiful skin.

His biceps were big and supple. Shoulders rounded. His forearms were incredible.

And even though his shorts grazed his knees, I could tell the rest of his downtown area was nice and muscular.

He was the DILF to end all DILFs.

My ex had been fit. He'd worked out several times a week at our home gym with a trainer. Being attractive had been part of his job.

Kaden's physique had nothing on Mr. Rhodes though.

My mouth watered a little more.

I whistled.

And I must have done it a lot louder than I'd thought because his head instantly went up and his gaze landed on me through the window almost immediately.

Busted.

I waved.

And inside… inside, I died.

He lifted his chin.

I backed away, trying to play it off.

Maybe he wouldn't think anything of it. Maybe he'd think I'd whistled… to say hi. Sure, yeah.

A girl could dream.

I backed up some more and felt my soul shriveling as I made my breakfast, making sure to stay away from the window the rest of the time. I tried to focus on other stuff. You know, so I wouldn't want to have to move out from shame.

Was I tired? Absolutely. But there were things I wanted to do. Needed to do. Including but not limited to getting away from Mr. Rhodes so my soul could come back to life.

So an hour later, with a plan in mind, a sandwich, a couple bottles of water, and my whistle in my backpack, I headed down the stairs, hoping and praying that Mr. Rhodes was back in his house.

I wasn't that lucky.

He had a shirt on, but that was the only difference.

Darn.

In a faded blue T-shirt with a logo I couldn't place, he was standing off to the side of the pile of wood that he'd stacked at some point under a blue tarp. Beside him was Amos in a bright red T-shirt and jeans, looking an awful lot like he was either begging or arguing with him.

At the sound of the door closing, they both turned.

He'd caught me checking him out. Act cool.

"Morning!" I called out.

I didn't miss the funny face that Amos made or the way he glanced from my backpack to his dad and back. I'd seen that expression before on my nephews' faces. I wasn't sure anything good ever came from those faces either.

But the teenager seemed to make a quick decision

because he jumped right into it. "Hi."

"Morning, Amos. How are you?"

"Fine." He pressed his lips together. "Are you going hiking?"

"Yeah." I smiled at him, realizing just how tired I was. "Why? Do you want to go?" I teased, mostly. Hadn't his dad said he wasn't an outdoorsy person?

The quiet boy perked up in a subtle way. "Can I?"

"Go?"

He nodded.

Oh. "If your dad is fine with it and you want to," I told him with a laugh, surprised.

Amos peeked at his dad, smiled this super sneaky smile, and nodded. "Two minutes!" the teenager yelled ten times the volume he normally spoke at, surprising me even more, before turning on his heel and disappearing up the deck and into his house.

Leaving me standing there blinking.

And his dad standing there blinking too.

"Did he say he's coming with me?" I asked, in almost a daze from pure surprise.

The older man shook his head in disbelief. "I didn't see that coming," he muttered more to himself than to me from the way he was still staring after the door. "I told him he couldn't hang out with his friends since he's still grounded, but if he wanted to be around an adult it was okay."

Oh wow. I got it now.

"Damn, he got you," I laughed.

That had his attention turning toward me, still looking like he'd gotten scammed.

I snorted. "I can tell him no after all if you want me to. I swear I thought you said he didn't like doing outdoor things, that's why I asked." I'd feel terrible retracting the invitation, but I would if it really bothered him. "Unless you want to come too. You know, so he's not totally getting away with it. I don't mind either way, but I don't want you to feel weird with me hanging out with your son. I'm not a creeper or anything, I swear."

Mr. Rhodes's gaze slid toward his front door again and stayed there like he was thinking very deeply about how the hell he was going to get out of the loophole he'd unknowingly given someone who was supposed to be grounded.

Or maybe he was wondering how to tell me that he was absolutely not okay with me taking his child for a hike. I wouldn't blame him.

"It might be torture for him hanging out with me for a couple hours," I told him. "I promise I'm not going to do anything to him. I'd invite Jackie, but I know she and Clara are going shopping in Farmington. I wouldn't mind the company." I paused. "But it's up to you. I promise I'm only attracted to grown men. He reminds me of my nephews."

Those gray eyes moved in my direction, his expression still thoughtful.

The kid burst through the front door, with a stainless-steel bottle looped through one finger and what looked like two granola bars in his other hand.

"You don't care if he goes?" was the quiet question that came at me.

"Not at all," I confirmed. "If you're okay with it."

"You're only going for a hike?"

"Yes."

I saw him hesitate before letting out another one of his deep breaths. Then he murmured, "I need a minute," just as Amos stopped in front of me and said, "I'm ready."

Was... was Mr. Rhodes coming too?

He disappeared into the house even faster than his son had, his movements and strides long and fluid considering how muscular he was.

I needed to stop thinking about his muscles. Like yesterday. I knew better already, didn't I? Subtle, I was not.

"Where's he going?" Amos asked, watching his dad too.

"I don't know. He said to give him a minute. He might be coming too...?"

The kid let out a frustrated sigh that made me side-eye him.

"Change your mind?"

He seemed to think about it for a second before shaking his head. "No. As long as I get out of the house, I don't care."

"Thank you for making me feel so special," I joked.

The teenager looked at me, his quiet voice back, "Sorry."

"It's okay. I'm just messing with you," I told him with a grin.

"He said I couldn't go out with my friends so...."

"You're hanging out with chopped liver?" I could only imagine the kind of relationship he had with his dad if he wasn't used to being picked on. "I'm messing with you, Amos. I promise." I even nudged him with my elbow quickly.

He didn't nudge me back, but he did give me a little shrug before asking quietly and hesitantly, "Is it okay? If I go with you?"

"One hundred percent okay. I like the company," I told him. "Honestly. You're pretty much making my day. I've been pretty lonely lately. I'm not used to doing so many things by myself anymore." The truth was, I'd been surrounded by people almost twenty-four seven for the last chunk of my life. The only alone time I ever really got for just myself was... when I'd go to the bathroom.

The boy seemed to shuffle in place. "You miss your family?"

"Yeah, but I had another family. My... ex-husband's family, and we were always together. This is the longest I've ever gone by myself. So really, you're doing me a favor coming. Thank you. *And* you'll help me stay awake." I thought about it. "Is it safe for you to do physical activity already?"

"Yeah. I had my check-up." The same gray eyes as Mr. Rhodes's roamed my face briefly, and he seemed to have to blink again. "You look tired."

Remind me never to word something in front of a teenager that could be turned into an insult. "I haven't been sleeping that great."

"'Cause of the bat?"

"How do you know about the bat?"

He eyed me. "Dad told me about you screaming like you were gonna die."

First of all, I hadn't been *screaming like I was going to die.* It had just been about five screams. Max.

But before I could argue with him about semantics, the front door opened again and Mr. Rhodes was out, hauling a small backpack in one hand and a thin black jacket in the other.

Wow. He wasn't fucking around. He wanted to tag along.

I eyed the kid next to me as he let out a sigh. "You're sure you want to come?"

His gaze flicked toward me. "I thought you said you'd like the company?"

"I do, I just want to make sure you're not going to regret it." Because his dad was coming too. To spend time with him? To not leave him with me alone? Who knew?

"Anything's better than staying home," he muttered just as his dad made it to us.

All right. I nodded at Mr. Rhodes, and he nodded at me.

I guess I was driving.

We loaded into my car with Mr. Rhodes taking the front passenger seat, and I backed out. I glanced at them both as sneaky as possible, feeling a little bit of pleasure at having them come with me... even if neither one of them talked much. Or I guess really liked me.

But one of them was desperate to get out of the house and the other either wanted to spend time with his kid or keep him safe.

I'd hung out with people who had worse intentions. At least they weren't being fake.

"Where are we going?" the deepest voice in the car asked.

"Surprise," I answered dryly, peeking in the rearview mirror.

Amos had his attention out of the window.

Mr. Rhodes, on the other hand, twisted his head to look at me. If I didn't already know he had been in the Navy, it would have been confirmed in that instant. Because I had zero doubts that he'd mastered the glare he was shooting my way on other people.

A lot of them, more than likely, from how good he was at it.

But I still grinned as I glanced at him.

"Okay, fine," I conceded. "We're going to some falls. You probably should've asked before you got in the car though. Just saying. I could be kidnapping you."

He didn't appreciate my joke apparently. "Which falls?" Mr. Rhodes asked in that stony, level voice.

"Treasure Falls."

"That one sucks," Amos piped up from the back.

"It does? I looked up pictures, and I thought it looked nice."

"We didn't get enough snow. It's gonna be a trinkle," he explained. "Right, Dad?"

"Yes."

I felt my shoulders deflate. "Oh." I thought of the next falls on my list. "I already did Piedra Falls. What about Silver Falls?"

Mr. Rhodes settled into the seat, crossing his arms over his chest. "Is this four-wheel drive?"

"No."

"Then no."

"Damn it," I groaned.

"Your clearance is too low. You won't make it."

My shoulders deflated even more. Well, this sucked.

"What about a longer trail?" the older man asked after a moment.

"That's fine with me." How much longer was long? I didn't want to chicken out, so I just agreed. I couldn't think of one on my mom's list off the top of my head that we could do, but my plans were ruined already and I was going to take advantage of the company. I knew how to be by myself, but I hadn't been lying to Amos about being lonely. Even when Kaden left for a short tour or for an event, someone would be at the house, usually the housekeeper I'd said we didn't need but his mom had insisted on because it was *beneath someone of Kaden's reputation to make his own food or clean his own house.* Ugh, I cringed just thinking about how snobby she'd sounded back then.

"I'll get you directions," my landlord explained, dragging me out of my memories with the Joneses.

"Works for me. Work for you, Amos?" I asked.

"Yeah."

All right then. I drove the car toward the highway, figuring Mr. Rhodes would give me directions once I got there.

"You used to live in Florida?" Amos asked suddenly from the back seat.

I nodded and stuck to the truth. "For ten years, and then I spent the next ten in Nashville, and I was back in Cape Coral —that's in Florida—for the last year before coming here."

"Why'd you leave there to come here?" the teenager

175

scoffed like that was mind-blowing to him.

"Have you been to Florida? It's hot and humid." I knew Mr. Rhodes had lived there, but I wasn't about to drop that knowledge bomb on their asses. They didn't need to know I'd been creeping and stalking.

"Dad used to live in Florida."

I had to pretend like I didn't already know this. But then his word choice sank in. He'd said *his dad* not him. Where had he lived then? "You did, Mr. Rhodes?" I asked slowly, trying to figure it out. "Where?"

"Jacksonville." It was Amos who answered instead. "It sucked."

In the seat next to me, the man scoffed.

"It did," the teenager insisted.

"Did you... live there too, Amos?"

"No. I just visited."

"Oh," I said like it made sense when it didn't.

"We visited every other summer," he went on to say. "We went to Disney. Universal. We were supposed to go to Destin once, but Dad had to cancel the trip."

Out of the corner of my eye, I saw Mr. Rhodes turn in his seat. "I didn't have a choice, Am. It wasn't like I canceled the trip because I wanted to."

"Were you in the military or something?" I asked.

"Yeah" was all he gave me.

But Amos didn't leave me hanging. "In the Navy."

"The Navy," I confirmed but didn't ask more about it because I figured if Mr. Rhodes hadn't even been willing to tell me what branch, he wouldn't want to tell me more. "Well, it's not too far of a drive. Maybe one day you can go."

In the seat behind me, the kid made a noise that sounded an awful lot like a grunt, and I regretted opening the subject again. What if he didn't take him? I needed to shut the hell up.

"Is it true your mom got lost somewhere around here in the mountains?"

I didn't wince, but Mr. Rhodes turned around again. "Am!"

"What?"

"You can't ask stuff like that, man. Come on," Mr. Rhodes snapped, shaking his head incredulously.

"I'm sorry, Aurora," he mumbled.

"I don't mind talking about her. It was a long time ago. I miss her every day, but I don't cry all the time anymore."

Too much information?

"I'm sorry," Amos repeated after a second of silence.

"It's okay. No one ever wants to talk about it," I told him. "But to answer your question, she did. We used to go hiking all the time. I was supposed to go with her, but I didn't." That same pang of guilt that I had never gotten over, that slept in my gut, safe and warm and tremendous, opened an eye. As much as I didn't mind talking about my mom, there were some specific things that were difficult to bring out into the world for everyone to know. "Anyway, she went for her hike and never came back. They found her car, but that was it."

"They found her car, but how could they not find her?"

"Your dad might know more details than I do. But they didn't find her car for a few days. She had told me she was going to do one hike, but Mom would always change her mind last minute and decide to do something that wasn't on a trail if she wasn't in the mood or if there were too many people on the trailheads. That's what they thought happened. Her car wasn't where she had said she would be. Unfortunately, it rained a lot in those days, and it washed out her footprints."

"But I don't get how they didn't find her. Dad, don't you have to do search and rescue a few times a year? You always find people."

Beside me, the big man shifted a bit in his seat, but I kept my gaze forward. "It's harder than it sounds, Am. There are almost two million acres of the San Juan National forest alone." Mr. Rhodes stopped talking for a second like he was watching his words. "If she was a strong hiker, in shape, she could have gone just about anywhere, especially if she wasn't known for staying on trails." He paused again. "I remember the case file said she was a good climber too."

"Mom was a great climber," I confirmed. She had been a fucking daredevil. There was nothing she had been scared of.

We used to go to Utah every chance possible. I could remember sitting off to the side when she did some kind of climb with her friends and being amazed by how strong and agile she was. I used to call her Spiderwoman she was so good.

"She could have gone anywhere," Mr. Rhodes confirmed.

"They looked," I told Amos. "For months. Helicopter. Different search and rescue teams. They did a few more searches for her over the years, but nothing ever came of it." Remains had been found before, but they hadn't been hers.

The silence was thick, and Amos broke it by muttering, "That sucks."

"Yeah, it does," I agreed. "I figure she was doing what she loved to do, but it still sucks."

There was another rush of silence, and I could feel Mr. Rhodes eyeball me.

I looked over and managed to smile a little. I didn't want him to think Amos had upset me—not that he probably genuinely cared.

"Which trail did she do?" Amos asked.

Mr. Rhodes gave him the name, shooting me a side look like he remembered bringing it up during our tutoring session.

There was another pause, and I glanced at the rearview

mirror once more. The boy looked thoughtful and troubled. Part of me was expecting him to drop it before he spoke up again. "Are you doing the hikes to find her?"

Mr. Rhodes mumbled something under his breath that I was pretty positive had a couple curse words in there. Then the meaty palm of his hand scrubbed up and down the center of his forehead.

"No," I answered Amos. "I don't have any interest in going there. She had a journal with her favorites. I'm hiking because she loved to, so I want to do them too. I'm not as athletic or as much of an explorer as she is, but I want to do what I can. That's all. I know we had a lot of fun, but I just want to... remember her. And those were some of the best memories of my life."

Neither one of them said anything for so long, I genuinely started to feel a little awkward. Some people were uncomfortable with the idea of grief. Some people didn't understand love either.

And that was okay.

But I was never going to shy away from how much I'd loved my mom and how much I was willing to do to feel closer to her. I'd been on autopilot for so many years, that it had been easy to... not bury my mourning... but to just keep it on my shoulder and keep going.

For so long, right after her disappearance, it had been hard enough to just force myself out of bed and continue trying to live my new life.

Then after that, there had been school, and Kaden, and just go, go, go.

All this while carrying my mom's memory and legacy with me, covering it up with distractions and life until now. Until I'd dusted all that other stuff off to focus on what I'd buried for so long.

And I was thinking about all this when Mr. Rhodes said in his rough voice, "What's on her list?"

Of hikes? "Probably too many. I want to do them all, but it depends how long I stick around." Which was longer now than I had expected a couple weeks ago since he'd invited me to stay. If I kept being a good guest, then who knew how long he'd rent the garage apartment out to me.

Wishful thinking. Then I'd have to decide whether to rent or buy a place, but all that depended on how things were going here. If I had enough of a reason to stay... or if this would turn out to be another place with no roots to hold me down any longer. "She did all of them when we lived here, but I know for sure she had Crater Lake Trail on there."

"That one's difficult. You can do it in a day though if you pace yourself and start early."

Ooh. He was offering suggestions and information? Maybe he *had* gotten over the incident with the bat.

I threw out another trail in Mom's book.

"Difficult too. You have to be in good shape to do that one in a day, but I'd say spend the night or be prepared to be sore."

I winced.

He must have noticed it because he asked, "You don't want to camp?"

"Honestly, I'm a little scared to camp by myself, but maybe I'll just do it."

He grunted, probably thinking I was an idiot for being scared.

But whatever. I'd watched a movie about an immortal Sasquatch that kidnapped people in the wilderness. And hadn't he said there were millions of acres of national forest? Nobody could *really* know what was out there. When I'd go camping with my mom a million years ago, it had just been fun. I'd never worried about some ax murderer possibly coming up to our tent and getting us. I'd never even worried about bears or Sasquatches or skunks or any of that.

Had she?

I named another one.

"Difficult."

Exactly what I'd read online.

"Devil Mountain?"

"Difficult. I don't know if that one's worth it."

I glanced at him. "She had a couple of funky notes for that one. Maybe I'll put that one at the bottom of the list if I get bored."

"Didn't we take a UTV up that one when you first moved back here?" Amos asked.

When you *first moved back here.* Who the hell had Amos lived with? His mom and stepdad?

"Yes. We got the flat tire," Mr. Rhodes confirmed.

"Oh," the boy said.

I rattled off more names of trails off the top of my head, and fortunately, he said those were intermediate hikes so those seemed more doable. "Have you done any of those?" I asked Amos just to include him.

"No. We don't do anything since Dad works all the time."

At my side, the man seemed to tense.

I was blowing it.

"My aunt and uncle, who raised me, worked all the time. I pretty much only slept at their house. We were always at the restaurant they owned," I tried to soothe, thinking back on all the things that had driven me crazy when I'd been his age. Then again, it didn't help that I'd been so heartbroken over my mom at the same time.

But looking back on it now, I think they had kept me occupied on purpose. Otherwise, I probably would have just stayed in the room I'd shared with my cousin and moped the whole time. And by moped, I really meant cried like a baby.

Okay, I'd still cried like a baby but in bathrooms, in the back seat of whatever car I was in… pretty much anytime I had a second and could get away with it.

"Do you go hiking a lot for work?" I asked Mr. Rhodes.

"For searches and during hunting season."

"When is that?"

"Starting in September. Bow hunting."

Since everyone was asking questions…. "How long have you officially been a game warden?" I asked.

"Only a year," Amos offered up from the back seat.

"And you were in the Navy before that?" Like I didn't already know.

"He retired from it," the boy answered again.

I acted surprised like I hadn't put it together. "Wow. That's impressive."

"Not really," the teenager mumbled.

I laughed.

Teenagers. Seriously. My nephews roasted me all the time.

"It's not. He was always gone," the kid went on. He was looking out the window with another funny expression on his face that I couldn't decipher that time.

Had his mom tagged along with them? Is that why she wasn't around? She got tired of him being gone and left?

"So you moved back here to be with Amos?"

It was Mr. Rhodes that simply said, "Yes."

I nodded, not knowing what to say without asking a million questions that I would more than likely not have answered. "Do you have more family here, Amos?"

"Just Grandpa, Dad, and Johnny. Everybody else is spread out."

Everyone else.

Hmm.

∾

I'D LIKE to think that the ride to the trailhead wasn't the most awkward trip of my life, what with no one saying a word for the majority of the trip.

Well, with the exception of me pretty much "ahhing" over just about everything.

I had no shame. I didn't care. I'd done the same thing on the other hikes I'd done, except I hadn't seen all that many animals on those occasions.

A cow!

A baby calf!

A deer!

Look at that huge tree!

Look at all the trees!

Look at that mountain! (It wasn't a mountain, it was a hill, Amos had said with a look that was almost amused.)

The only comment I'd gotten other than Amos's correction was Mr. Rhodes asking, "Do you always talk this much?"

Rude. But I didn't care. So I told him the truth. "Yeah." Sorry not sorry.

The drive alone was beautiful. Everything got bigger and greener, and I couldn't find it in me to mind or even notice too much that my passengers weren't saying anything. They didn't even complain when I had to stop to pee twice.

After parking, Amos led us over the deceptive looking trail that started from a decent parking lot, giving you the illusion that it would be easy.

Then I saw the name on the sign and my insides paused.

Fourmile Trail.

Some people said there wasn't such a thing as a stupid question, but I knew that wasn't correct because I asked stupid questions all the time. And asking Mr. Rhodes if Four-mile Trail was actually four miles, I knew *was* a stupid question.

And part of me honestly didn't want to actually *know* I was going to hike four times the amount I was used to. I didn't exactly look out of shape, but looks were deceiving. My cardio endurance had gotten better over the last month of jump roping but not enough.

Four miles, f-u-c-k me.

I glanced at Amos to see if he looked alarmed, but he gave one look at the sign and started.

Four miles and four waterfalls, the sign read.

If he could do it, I could do it.

I'd tried to talk twice and had ended up panting so bad both times that I immediately stopped. It wasn't like they were excited to talk to me. As I wound my way behind Amos, with his dad taking up the rear, I was just glad to not be alone. There had been a handful of cars parked in the lot, but you couldn't see or hear anything. It was beautifully quiet.

We were in the middle of nowhere. Away from civilization. Away from... everything.

The air was clean and bright. Pure. And it was... it was spectacular.

I stopped and took a couple of selfies, and when I called out to Amos to stop and turn around so I could take a picture of him, he grudgingly did it. He crossed his arms over his thin chest and angled the brim of his hat up. I snapped it.

"I'll send it to you if you want," I whispered to Mr. Rhodes when the boy had kept on walking.

He nodded at me, and I'd bet it cost him a couple years off his life to grind out a "Thanks."

I smiled and let it go, watching every step as one mile turned into two, and I started to regret doing this long hike so soon. I should've waited. I should've done longer ones to lead up to this.

But if Mom could do it, so could I.

So what if she was way more fit than me? You didn't get in shape unless you busted your ass and made it happen. I just had to suck it up and keep going.

So that's what I did.

And I'd be lying if I said it didn't make me feel better that I could tell when Amos started slowing down too. The distance between us got shorter and shorter.

And just when I thought we were going to the end of the fucking earth and these waterfalls didn't exist, Amos stopped for a second before turning to the left and hiking up.

The rest of the hike went by with me having a huge smile on my face.

We finally walked by other hikers who called out good mornings and how-you-doings that I answered when the other two didn't. I took more pictures. Then even more.

Amos stopped after the second waterfall and said he'd wait there, even though each one was just as epic as the last.

And surprising the shit out of me, Mr. Rhodes followed behind me, still keeping his distance and his words to himself.

I was real glad he did because the path after the last of the four waterfalls got undefined and I turned in the wrong spot, but fortunately he caught sight of the path better than I did and tapped my backpack to get me to follow him.

I did—looking at his hamstrings and calves bunching the whole incline upward.

I wondered again when he got a chance to work out. Before or after work?

I took more selfies because I sure as hell wasn't going to ask Mr. Rhodes. And when I turned as he kept hiking upward, legs stretching as he made his way up the loosely graveled trail, I aimed my camera toward him and called out, "Mr. Rhodes!"

He looked, and I snapped the picture, giving him a thumbs-up afterward.

If he was irritated with me taking a picture, too bad. It wasn't like I would share it with anyone but maybe my aunt and uncle. And Yuki if she scrolled through my pictures one day.

Amos was exactly where we'd left him, shaded by trees and boulders, playing a game on his phone. He looked way too relieved to be leaving. His bottle of water was mostly gone, and I was just about finished with my own, I noticed.

I needed to get a straw, some tablets to purify water, or one of those bottles with a built-in filter. The shop carried all of that.

I was too busy trying to catch my breath on the walk back that none of us said anything then either, and I took the tiniest sips along the way, regretting like a motherfucker that I hadn't brought more.

What felt like an hour later, something tapped my elbow.

I glanced back to find Mr. Rhodes just a few feet behind me, holding his big, stainless steel water bottle toward me.

I blinked.

"I don't want to have to drag you out when you start getting a pounding headache," he explained, eyes locked on mine.

I only hesitated for a second before taking it, my throat was hurting and I *was* beginning to get a headache. I put it to my mouth and drank two big gulps—I wanted more, I wanted all of it, but I couldn't be a greedy asshole—and handed it back. "I thought you finished yours too."

He slid me a look. "I filled it back up at the last waterfall. I have a filter."

I smiled at him a lot more shyly than I would have expected. "Thank you."

He nodded. Then he called out, "Am! You need some water?"

"No."

I looked at his dad, and the man just about rolled his eyes. At some point, he'd put a cap on his head too, just like his son, pulled low so I could barely see them. I hadn't seen his jacket, but I'd bet he'd rolled it into his pack at some point.

"Will you drag him out too or would you carry him?" I joked quietly.

I was surprised when he said, "He'd get dragged too."

I grinned and shook my head.

"He's used to the altitude now. You're not," he said behind me, as if trying to explain why he'd offered me fluids. So I wouldn't get the wrong idea.

I slowed down my walking, so he was closer before I asked, "Mr. Rhodes?"

He grunted, and I took that as my sign to ask my question.

"Does anyone ever call you Toby?"

There was a pause, then he asked, "What do you think?" in the closest thing I'd heard to a pissy tone.

I almost laughed. "No, I guess not." I waited a second. "You definitely look like more of a Tobers," I joked, glancing over my shoulder with a grin, but his attention was down on the ground. I thought I was hilarious. "Would you like a granola bar?"

"No."

I shrugged and turned back forward. "Amos! You want a granola bar?"

He seemed to think about it for a second. "What kind?"

"Chocolate chip!"

He turned and held out his hand.

I tossed it at him.

Then I tipped my head up toward the sun, ignoring how

187

tired my thighs were, and that I was starting to drag my feet because each step was getting harder and harder. I already knew I was going to be hurting tomorrow. Hell, I was already hurting. My boots hadn't been broken in enough for this and my toes and ankles were sore and chafed. Tomorrow, I was more than likely barely going to be able to move.

But it was going to be worth it.

It *was* worth it.

And I said quietly, filling my lungs with the freshest air I'd ever smelled, "Mom, you would have liked this one. It was pretty amazing." I wasn't sure why this one hadn't been in her notebook, but I was so glad I'd done it.

And before I could think twice about it, I jogged forward. Amos glanced over at me as I threw my arms around his shoulders, giving him a quick hug. He tensed but didn't push me away in the one-second embrace. "Thank you for coming, Am."

Just as quickly as I hugged him, I let him go and turned around to go straight for my next victim.

He was big and walking forward, his face serious. Like always. But in the blink of an eye, that rabies-raccoon expression was back.

I got shy.

Then I held up my hand for him in a high five instead of a hug.

He looked at my hand, then looked at my face, then back to my hand.

And like I was ripping out his nails instead of asking for a high five, he lifted his big hand and lightly tapped my palm with his.

And I told him quietly, meaning every word, "Thank you for coming."

His voice was a steady, quiet rumble. "You're welcome."

I smiled the entire way back to the car.

CHAPTER 12

*W*hen Clara's mouth dropped open at the sight of my face a few days later, I knew that the concealer I'd used on my bruises that morning hadn't pulled off a miracle like I'd hoped.

I mean, yesterday I'd *figured* they were going to be awful, but I hadn't anticipated they would be so bad.

Then again, I'd had a bat house fall right on my face so....

At least I hadn't gotten a concussion, right?

"Ora, *who did that to you?*"

I smiled and then instantly winced because it hurt. I'd slapped an ice pack on my cheek and another over my nose after I'd stopped seeing stars—and after I'd been able to finally catch my breath because, let me tell you, falling off a ladder *hurt.* But the ice hadn't done much other than maybe keep the swelling down. Something was better than nothing.

"Me?" I asked, trying to play dumb, as I locked the shop door behind me. We still had fifteen minutes left before opening.

She blinked, set down the money she'd been counting

into the register, and asked, almost cryptically, "It looks like you got punched."

"I didn't. I fell off a ladder and had a bat house fall on me."

"You fell off a ladder?"

"And dropped a bat house on my face."

She winced. "What were you doing putting up a bat house?" she gasped.

It had taken me days, at least five hours of research, and a whole lot of staring at the Rhodes's house and property to set up a plan for battling the damn bats. Then my shipment had gotten delayed before finally arriving.

The problem was, I had never considered myself to be afraid of heights, but... the second I'd climbed up on a ladder leaning against a tree that I'd walked by countless times, I realized why I had felt that way.

I'd never been on anything taller than a kitchen island counter.

Because reality was, as soon as I'd been about three feet off the ground, my knees started shaking and I started to feel kind of ill.

And no amount of telling myself to buck up or reminding myself the worst that would happen would be that I'd break an arm, did... anything.

I'd started sweating, and my knees shook even worse.

And for what I needed, I needed to go as high up as possible—twelve to twenty feet, according to the instructions.

But all it took was the memory of the bat flying over my defenseless head while I slept... and the reality that I hadn't actually slept more than thirty minutes on and off since Mr. Rhodes had saved me because I kept waking up paranoid, to get my ass up that A-frame ladder even though I was shaking so bad it jiggled with me, making it worse.

But it was either climbing up a tree close to the Rhodes's

property—and honestly tucked a little away because I hoped he wouldn't see it because I had a feeling he might complain about it—or having to pull out the even bigger ladder from around the side of the main house and having to go even higher to find where the hell the bat was coming in from.

I was going to go with option A because I would more than likely pass out and break my neck if I fell off the bigger ladder.

But I'd still screwed it up.

And fallen off, screeching like a fucking hyena, nearly blacking out, and had something that weighed less than three pounds but felt like fifty, fall on my damn face while I'd gasped to catch my breath.

My back still hurt.

And now I was at work, with more than a little bit of makeup on, and having Clara stare at me in horror.

"There's been a bat flying around, and I read that a bat house would hopefully attract it so it wouldn't keep flying into the house," I explained, going around the counter and hiding my bag in one of the drawers.

When I stood up straight, she touched my chin and lifted it up, brown eyes focused on my cheek. "Want me to tell you the good news or the bad news first?"

"The bad."

"We've had problems with them at Dad's," she started to explain, wincing at whatever she saw. "But you have to plug up where they're coming in from first, then put the house up."

Son of a bitch.

"Did you put attractant in there?"

"What's that?"

"You need to put some in there to get them to start using it."

I frowned, forgetting I couldn't do that. "I didn't read that online."

"You need it. We might still have some. I'll check." She paused. "How did you fall off?"

"This hawk swooped me, and I freaked out and fell off right when I was trying to nail the house up."

She glanced down before I could make a fist, and she saw the bruise on my hand too.

"I've never used a hammer before."

I had one of the nicest friends in the world because she didn't laugh. "You're better off using a drill."

"A drill?"

"Yeah, with wood screws. It'll hold up longer."

I sighed. "Shit."

Even her nod was sympathetic. "I'm sure you tried your best."

"More like tried my best to bust my ass."

That got her to laugh. "Want me to come over and help?" she offered. "Why didn't Rhodes do it for you?"

I snorted and regretted that shit too. "It's okay. I can do it myself. I should do it myself. And I don't want to ask him; he already got one bat out for me in the middle of the night. I can handle it."

"Even though you fell off a ladder?"

I nodded and gestured to my face. "Yeah, I'm not going to let them win. This isn't going to be in vain."

Clara nodded solemnly. "I'll look for that attractant. I bet if you look in the paper, you can find someone to go and find where the bats are coming in from if you change your mind."

The problem was that it wasn't my house, but... "I'll look," I said, even though I wouldn't. Not unless I absolutely had to.

~

I WANTED to think I was a big girl, but when I kept glancing up at the ceiling even though it was only about six o'clock, I wanted to cry.

I hated being paranoid. Scared. But no matter how much I told myself that a bat was just a sweet little sky puppy…

I wasn't buying it. And it wasn't like I had anywhere else to go to get out of there. I hadn't made enough friends yet.

I got along with most people I met, and most folks were really pretty friendly back, especially my customers at the store. Even the grumpiest people, I could usually win over with time. Back when I'd been with Kaden, I'd met a lot of people, but after a while, everyone wanted something from him, and it had made it impossible to know who wanted to be my friend for me and who wanted it for him.

And that was with them not knowing we were together. We had guarded that secretly tightly. Using NDAs—nondisclosure agreements that pretty much guaranteed that if anyone spoke about our relationship, the Joneses would sue the shit out of them. Not being able to be open with people had just become second nature.

And that was why people like Yuki and even Nori didn't have that many friends either.

Because you never knew what someone really thought about you unless they told you that you had spinach between your teeth and looked dumb.

I picked up my phone and thought about calling my aunt or uncle, and that was when I heard the garage door open, and a moment later, the buzz of an amp come on from downstairs.

Setting my phone back down, I headed toward the top of the staircase and listened as someone, who I could only assume was Amos, strummed a chord and then another. He adjusted the volume and did it all over again.

Planting my butt on the top step, I curled my fingers

around my knees and listened as he tuned his guitar and, after a few minutes, started playing a few blues licks.

And that's when I heard his quiet, soft voice start singing, so low in volume I leaned forward and had to strain.

His voice didn't raise in volume, and I was pretty sure he was singing so low so that I wouldn't hear him, but I could. I had good ears. I'd protected my hearing over the years by wearing top-of-the-line ear protection. I'd left my set of three-thousand-dollar in-ears when I'd left the home I'd shared with Kaden, but I still had a great set of headphones and Hearos that maybe I'd use again someday. To go see Yuki.

Creeping quietly down a few more steps, I stopped and strained some more.

Then I shifted down a couple more steps.

And a couple more.

Before I knew it, I was standing right outside the door that separated the apartment from the actual garage. As quietly as possible, I opened the door that led outside and closed it behind me the same way, moving like a snail to be as quiet as humanly possible.

I stopped.

Because sitting on the top step of his deck was Mr. Rhodes. In dark jeans and a light blue T-shirt, his elbows were propped on his knees. He was listening too.

I hadn't seen him in more than passing since the day we'd gone to see the waterfalls.

He'd spotted me first, I guess.

I put my finger over my mouth to let him know I knew to be quiet and slowly started to sink on top of the mat right outside the door. I didn't want to bother him or intrude.

But his blank face slowly got replaced by a frown.

He gestured to me to come over, even as his frown got deeper by the second.

Standing back up, I tiptoed across the gravel as quietly as possible, relieved when Amos started playing louder, his singing drifting away, wrapping around the notes coming from his guitar.

But the closer I got to Mr. Rhodes, the graver his expression became. The elbows he had resting on his knees slid up his thighs until he was sitting up straight, those pretty gray eyes of his wide, his expression stricken.

And my smile slowly melted off.

What was he—? Oh. Right.

How the hell could I forget when I'd spent the entire day having customers fawn all over my bruised face? One of the customers who I'd met a few times by then, a local man in his sixties named Walter, had left the store and come back with a loaf of homemade bread his wife had made. *To make me feel better.*

I'd just about cried when I'd given him a hug.

"Nothing happened," I started to tell him before he cut me off.

His back couldn't have been any straighter, and I was pretty sure his expression couldn't have been any grimmer. "Who did that to you?" he asked in a slow, slow voice.

"No one," I tried to explain again.

"Someone jump you?" Mr. Rhodes asked, drawing out each word.

"No. I dropped—"

My landlord got up to his feet at the same time one of those big, rough hands went to my shoulder and curled around it. "You can tell me. I'll help you."

I closed my mouth and blinked up at him, fighting the urge to smile. And the urge to tear up.

He might not like me much, but man, was he decent.

"That's really nice of you, but no one hurt me. Well, I hurt me. I dropped a box on my face."

"You dropped a box on your face?"

Could he sound any more disbelieving? "Yes."

"Who did it?"

"No one. I dropped it on myself, I swear."

His gaze narrowed.

"I promise, Mr. Rhodes. I wouldn't lie about something like that, but I appreciate you asking. And offering."

Those pretty eyeballs seemed to take in my features some more, and I was pretty sure the alarm in his eyes faded at least a little. "What kind of box did you drop?"

I'd walked right into that, hadn't I? I plastered a smile on my face even though it hurt. "A bat house...?"

Creases formed across his broad forehead. "Explain."

Bossy. My face went hot. "I read that they help with bat problems. I figured if I got them a new home, they wouldn't keep trying to sneak in to pick on me." I swallowed. "I borrowed your ladder—I'm sorry for not asking—and found a tree with a good, sturdy branch on the edge of your property"—where he wouldn't see it—"and I tried to nail it there."

The branch wasn't as sturdy as I'd hoped, and according to Clara, the nails hadn't been the way to go, and it had fallen... on me. Hence, the black eyes and puffy nose.

The heavy hand on my shoulder fell away, and he blinked. Those short, thick eyelashes swept over his incredible eyes again even slower. There were lines branching out from the corners, but I swear it just made him more attractive. All weathered. How old was he really? Late thirties?

"Sorry I didn't ask for permission," I muttered, busted.

He watched me. "Tell me it wasn't the eight-foot ladder."

"It wasn't the eight-foot ladder," I lied.

A big hand went to his face, and he swept it down over his chin before aiming an eyeball at me as the song inside the garage changed and Amos started playing something different, something I didn't recognize. Slow and moody. Almost dark. I liked it. I liked it a lot.

"Don't worry, I'm not going to give you a one-star review or anything over it. It was my fault," I tried to joke.

Two irises the color of a Weimaraner bore into me.

"I was joking, but really, it was my fault. I didn't know I was scared of heights until I got up there and...."

He tipped his head to look at the sky.

"Mr. Rhodes, you made my whole day being worried, but I'm sorry I was snooping around your property and didn't ask for permission, but I haven't slept a full night in two weeks, and I didn't want my screams to wake you up anymore. But mostly, I don't want to sleep in my car again."

He gave me a side look, and I couldn't help but laugh, pain forcing me to stop almost immediately. Jesus Christ. How did boxers handle this shit?

His look went nowhere.

And that look made me laugh more, even though it hurt.

"I know it's stupid, but I just keep picturing it landing on my face and...." I bared my teeth.

"I get the picture." He dropped his head and his hand. "Where's this bat house at?"

"In the studio."

Those gray eyes were back on me. "When he's done, put it in the garage." That full mouth twisted to the side. "Never mind, I'll bring it down when you're at work, if you're fine with it."

I nodded.

"It'll be too dark today by the time Am is done, but I'll put it up next chance I get," he went on in that serious, level voice.

"Oh you don't need to—"

"I don't need to, but I will. I'll go in there and see what I can caulk too. They can squeeze through the smallest gaps, but I'll try my best."

Hope rose up inside of me again.

My landlord leveled me with an intense gaze. "You won't get back up on that ladder, though. You could've fallen, broken a leg. Your back..."

He was such an overprotective dad. I loved it. It only made him that much more good-looking to me. Even if he did have that scary serious face. And he didn't really like me.

But I still squinted. "Are you asking me not to get back on it or telling me?"

He stared.

"All right, all right. I won't. I was just scared and didn't want to bother you."

"You're paying me rent, aren't you?"

I nodded because, yeah, I was.

"Then it's my responsibility to take care of things like that," he explained steadily. "Am said he thought he saw you sleeping in your car, but I thought he was imagining it and you were drunk."

I scoffed. "I told you, I don't really drink that much."

I wasn't sure he believed me. "I'll get it taken care of. If there's another problem with the studio, tell me. I don't need or want you suing me."

That got me to frown... even though it hurt. "I would never sue you, especially not if it was me being stupid. And no one-stars either."

Nothing.

And here I used to think I was funny. "I'll tell you if I have any more problems with something inside the house though. Pinky swear."

He didn't look all that amused by my offer of a pinky swear, but that was okay. What he did do was nod just as Amos's voice came through the opened garage door and carried outside. The boy crooned, not all that quietly before he seemed to catch himself and lower his volume.

And I couldn't help but whisper, "Does he always sing like that?"

He raised one of those stern, thick eyebrows. "Like he's had his heart broken and is never going to love again?"

Did he just... joke? "Yeah."

He nodded.

"He's got a beautiful voice."

That's when he did it.

He smiled.

Proud and wide, like he knew just how beautiful of a voice his child had and it filled him with joy. I couldn't blame him; I would feel the same way if Am was my kid. He really did have a great voice. There was a ring to it that sounded timeless. The rarest part about it was that it was a lot lower than a boy his age usually had. It was easy to tell he'd had some kind of vocal training because he could project... when he forgot to be quiet.

"He doesn't know it either. He thinks I'm lying when I tell him," my landlord admitted.

I shook my head. "You're not. He gave me goose bumps, see?" I lifted my arm so he could see the little pebbles that had set up shop under my skin. My shirt gave him a clear view of my entire arm. I'd forgotten I was wearing a spaghetti strap tank top that showed off a whole lot of cleavage—all of it. Okay, it was all of it. I hadn't planned on seeing anyone the rest of the day, but Amos's voice had been the pied piper to get me out of the garage apartment.

And I wasn't the only one either since his dad was out here being sneaky and quiet to listen too.

Mr. Rhodes glanced at my arm about a split second before looking away just as quickly. He crouched down and took a seat on the top step again, stretching his long legs out and planting his feet on the stair below. Done with our conversation, I guess. Okay.

I stayed where I was and strained to hear Amos's sweet voice croon about a woman he loved who wouldn't return his calls.

I remembered a man I'd loved once singing about something very similar. But I knew all of those words. Because I'd written them.

That record alone had sold over a million copies. It was what many considered his breakout hit. A song I'd originally penned when I was sixteen and wanted my mom to call me back.

Half of his success had been his own. He had a face women loved... that he'd had absolutely nothing to do with since he hadn't gotten to choose it. He'd made sure to keep his body fit to keep up his "sex appeal" for fans— I'd almost gagged when his mom had used those words. He'd taught himself how to play guitar, sure, but his mom had been the one to egg him into continuing to take lessons. But he'd been a natural performer. His voice a hoarse, gritty thing that he'd also been genetically blessed with.

But as I'd learned over the last two years, you could have a great voice, but if your music wasn't good or catchy, that didn't mean you would sell records.

He had and he hadn't used me. I'd given him everything freely.

Amos's voice rose just a little, his vibrato ringing through the air, and I shook my head as more goose bumps came up on my skin.

Turning my head just a little, I found Mr. Rhodes staring straight ahead, his jaw an absolute perfect line as he listened intently, a faint smile of pure pleasure lingering over his pink mouth.

His eyes happened to move and catch mine. "Wow," I mouthed.

And this gruff, strict man kept that tiny smile on his face and said, "Wow," back.

"Do you sing?" I asked before I could stop myself and remember he didn't really want to talk to me.

"Not like that," he actually answered, surprising me. "He gets it from his mom's side."

Another hint about his mom. I wanted to know. I wanted to know so bad.

But I wasn't going to ask.

Then he spoke again and surprised me even more. "It's the only time he comes out of his shell, and only around some people. It makes him happy."

That was the longest sentence he'd ever shared with me, I was pretty sure, but I figured there was nothing a man could be prouder of than having a talented son.

Neither one of us said a word as the strums of the guitar changed and Amos's voice disappeared as he played and we both kept on listening. It was between him noodling around, messing up and trying again, that I said, "If either of you ever need anything, let me know, okay? I'll let you listen in peace now. I don't want him to catch me and get upset."

Mr. Rhodes glanced at me and nodded, not agreeing but not telling me to go to hell either. I picked my way back across the driveway to a familiar tune that I knew for a fact Nori had produced.

But all I could think about was that I hoped Mr. Rhodes took me up on my offer someday.

And that was probably the reason why I got caught.

Why Amos called out, "Aurora?"

And why I froze.

Busted *again*? "Hi, Amos," I called out, cursing myself for getting sloppy.

There was a pause then, "What are you doing?"

Did he have to sound so suspicious? And did I have to be such a bad liar? I knew what my best bet was: buttering him up. "Listening to the voice of an angel?"

My whole body tensed up in the silence. I was pretty sure I heard him set his guitar down and start walking over. Sure enough, his head peeked out from around the corner of the building.

I lifted my hand and hoped his dad had disappeared. "Hi."

The kid looked at me and froze too. "What happened to your face?"

I kept forgetting I was scaring people. "Nothing bad, no one hurt me. I'm fine, and thank you for worrying."

The same color eyes as his dad's bounced around my face, and I wasn't sure he heard me.

"I'm okay," I tried to assure him. "Promise."

That was good enough for him because his expression finally turned a little anxious. "Did it... bother you?"

I scrunched up my face and then winced. "Are you kidding me? No way."

His dad was right, he didn't believe it. I could *feel* his soul rolling its spiritual eyes.

"I'm serious. You've got such a great voice."

He still wasn't buying it.

I had to go at this at a different angle. "I recognized a couple of the songs you were playing, but there was one in the middle... what was it?"

That got his face to go red.

And my gut went off. "Was it yours? Did you come up with it?"

His face disappeared, and I moved over to look into the garage. Amos had only taken a couple steps back. His attention was focused on the floor.

"If you did, that's amazing, Amos. I..." Shit. I hadn't

planned on saying it, but... I was here. "I... used to be a songwriter."

He wouldn't look at me.

Oh, man. I should have been sneakier. "Hey, I'm serious. I don't like to hurt people's feelings, but if I didn't think you were good—your voice and that song you sang—I wouldn't bring it up. It *is* really good. You're really talented."

Amos lifted the toe of one of his sneakers.

And I felt terrible. "I'm serious." I cleared my throat. "I, uh, a few of my songs have been... on albums."

The toe of his other sneaker went up.

"If you wanted... I could help you. Write, I mean. Give you advice. I'm not the best, but I'm not the worst. But I've got a good ear, and I usually know what works and what doesn't."

That got me a peek of a gray eye.

"If you want. I've sat through some voice lessons before too," I offered. Sat through more than "some" to be honest. I didn't have a naturally great voice, but I wasn't totally tone deaf, and if I sang, cats wouldn't howl and children wouldn't run screaming.

His throat bobbed, and I waited. "You've written songs that other people sang?" he asked in sheer disbelief.

It wouldn't be the first time. "Yes."

Both toes went up, and it took him another second to finally get out, "I had a voice teacher a long time ago"—I tried not to smile at what he might consider to be a long time ago —"but that was the last time I had lessons. I'm in choir at school."

"I can tell."

He slid me a look of total bullshit. "I'm not that good."

"I think you are, but I'm sure Reiner Kulti used to think he had room to improve."

"Who's that?"

It was my turn to slide him a look. "A famous soccer player. My point is... I think you are talented, but someone once told my... friend... that even natural athletes need coaches and training. Your voice—and songwriting—are like instruments, and you have to practice them. If you want. I'm usually bored upstairs, so I really wouldn't mind. But you should ask your dad and mom for permission first."

"Mom would let me do whatever with you. She says she owes you her life."

I smiled, but he didn't see it because he was back to focusing on his shoes. Did that mean that he'd think about it? "Okay, just let me know. You know where I am."

Another gray-eyed gaze met mine, and I swear there was a small, small smile on his face.

There was a smile on mine too.

CHAPTER 13

"What's wrong with that?"

Sitting with one leg crossed over the other in the camping chair of Mr. Rhodes's garage, I eyed his son. He was sitting on the floor with a cushion he'd pulled out of somewhere with his writing notebook propped on a knee. We'd been going at writing advice for the last hour, and I wasn't going to say we were arguing, because Amos was way too conservative around me, but it was about as close as he was capable of. He had yet to roll his eyes too.

This was our fourth session together, and honestly, I was still stunned he'd knocked on the door about two weeks ago and asked if I was busy—I hadn't been—and if I could *check something he'd worked on.*

I couldn't remember ever feeling so honored.

Not even when Yuki had laid on her guest room bed beside me and whispered, "I can't do this, Ora-Bora. Will you help me?" I hadn't been sure I could, but my heart and brain had proved me wrong and we'd written twelve songs together.

Plus… he was a shy kid, and that alone touched me.

Satan couldn't have dragged me away from helping Amos. So that was what I'd done. For two hours that day.

Three hours two days later.

Two hours almost every day after that.

He had been so shy that first time, listening to me rambling mostly, then shoving his notebook in my direction and we'd gone back and forth like that. I took it seriously. I knew exactly what it was like to show someone something you'd worked on and hope they didn't hate it.

Honestly, it humbled me that he had taken such a huge step.

Slowly but surely though, he'd started to open up. We discussed things. He was asking questions! Mostly, he was talking to me.

And I loved talking.

Which was exactly what he was doing then: asking why I thought that him writing a real deep love song was out of his league. It wasn't the first time I'd tried hinting at it, but it was the first time I straight out said maybe not to.

"There's nothing wrong with you wanting to write this song about *love*, but you're fifteen and you don't want to be the next Bieber, am I right?"

Amos pressed his lips together and shook his head a little too rapidly considering the former teen pop star was a bazillionaire.

"I think you should write about something close to you. Why can't it be about love but not romantic love?" I asked.

He scrunched up his face and thought about it. He'd shown me two songs, both of which weren't ready; he'd made that clear about a dozen times. They had been... not dark but not what I'd been expecting at all. "Like about my mom?"

His mom. I lifted a shoulder. "Why not? There's no love more unconditional than that if you're lucky."

Amos's scrunched-up face went nowhere.

"I'm just saying, it's more heartfelt if you feel it, if you experience it. It's kind of like writing a book; show don't tell. Like there's this... producer I used to know who has written a lot of hit love songs... He's been married eight times. He falls in and out of love in the blink of an eye. Is he a scumbag? Yeah. But he's really, really good at what he does."

"A producer?" he asked with way too much doubt in his tone.

I nodded. He still didn't believe me, and it made me want to smile.

But I preferred that than him knowing. Or expecting something.

"Maybe that's why you've been struggling so much trying to write your own music, Stevie Ray Junior."

Yeah, he wasn't biting. But I had learned he got a kick out of me using certain musician's names as nicknames. I missed having people to pick on, and he was such a good kid.

"Okay, tell me, who do you love?"

Amos sneered in this way that made me feel like I was asking him to take a nudie and send it to a girl he liked.

"Okay, your mom, right?"

"Yeah."

"Your dads?"

"Yeah."

"Who else?"

He leaned back on one hand and seemed to think about it. "I love my grandmas."

"All right, who else?"

"Uncle Johnny, I guess."

"I guess?" That made me laugh. "Anyone else?"

He shrugged.

"Well, think about that. About how they make you feel."

His sneer was still there a little bit. "But *my mom*?"

"Yeah, your mom! Don't you love her the most?"

"I don't know. The same as my dads?"

I still hadn't gotten any further with the "dads" thing. "I'm just throwing out ideas."

"Did you ever write songs about your mom?" he asked.

I'd heard one of them playing at the grocery store a week ago. I'd ended up with a headache behind one eye by the time it had finished, but I didn't tell him that. "Only almost all of them." That was an exaggeration. I hadn't written anything new since I'd spent the month with Yuki. There hadn't been all that much to inspire me since, or a need. Personally, writing used to come so easily to me. Too easily according to what Yuki and Kaden used to say. All I ever had to do was sit down and words just... came to me.

My uncle said it was why I talked so much. There were always too many words bouncing around in my head and they had to come out somehow. There were worse things in life.

But I hadn't heard the words that had come to me so randomly for most of my life in forever. I wasn't sure what it said about me or where I was in life now that the absence didn't scare me. Especially not when I knew for sure that at some point, it would have been terrifying.

Looking back on it, the words had tapered off over the years. I wondered now if that should have been a sign.

"I feel like my best songs were the ones I wrote when I was between your age now and twenty-one. It doesn't come as easily to me now anymore." I shrugged, not wanting to tell him more.

Part of it, I thought was that I had been younger and more innocent. My heart had been more... pure. My grief more rabid. I'd felt so, so much back then. And now... now I knew that the world was split about fifty-fifty, if not seventy-thirty with assholes versus good people. My grief, which had been what consumed so much of my life, had tapered with time.

I was pretty good from twenty-one to twenty-eight, when I'd been at my peak in love. When things had been great— not as great now that I thought back on all the things that had been said and done that I had brushed off. But I'd thought for sure I'd found my life partner. It hadn't come as easily, but I'd still felt the words there, lying right under my heart, ready.

Back then, I'd still woken up in the middle of the night with strings of words on my tongue.

Except for the one album I'd written with Yuki, while I'd been grieving the loss of my relationship, with the emptiness of accepting that some things weren't forever so fresh, I'd pulled even more words out of myself. We'd gotten that album done in a month while both of us had broken hearts.

It was some of my favorite work.

Nori had written some of it with us, but she was a machine of music who pushed hits out like she shit out rainbows; she took words and brought them to life. I was the bones, and she was the sinews and pink fingernail beds. It was amazing. A gift from God.

But I couldn't and wouldn't tell Amos any of this. Not yet. It didn't matter anymore.

All I had left anyway was a box full of old notebooks.

"I was thinking about taking a class...," he started to say, and it was hard for me not to scrunch up my nose.

I didn't want to talk him out of doing anything he wanted to do, even if I thought it was pointless. Writing songs wasn't math or science; there wasn't a formula in the world for it. You either had it or you didn't.

And I knew Amos did because the two songs he had shown me, humming them quietly during our last session, were beautiful and had so, so much potential.

"Why not?" I said instead, plastering a smile onto my face so he couldn't read my mind. "Maybe you'll learn something."

He gave me another one of his dubious looks. "Do you think I should?"

"If you really want to."

"Would you?"

I was busy trying to come up with some polite way of saying no when Amos sat up straight and his eyes went wide.

He was looking at something behind me.

"What is it?"

His mouth barely moved. "Don't make any sudden movements."

I wanted to get up and run, his face was that serious. "Why?" Should I turn around? *I should turn around.*

"There's a hawk behind you," he said before I got a chance to.

I sat up even straighter. "A what?"

"A hawk," he kept on whispering. "It's right there. Right behind you."

"A hawk? Like a bird?"

Bless Amos's sweet soul, he didn't make a sarcastic comment. He said, calmly, sounding very much like his dad from how serious he was speaking, "Yes, a hawk like a bird. I don't know them like my dad does." His throat bobbed. "He's huge."

Slowly, I tried to look behind me. Out of the corner of my eye, I saw a small figure just right outside the garage. Even more slowly, I turned the rest of my body—and the chair—around. Like Amos had warned, there was a hawk *right there.* On the ground. Hanging out. He was looking at us. Maybe just at me but probably both of us.

I squinted. "Am, is he bleeding?"

There was a squeaking sound before I felt him crawl over

to sit on the floor beside me. He whispered, "I think so. His eye looks kinda swollen."

One eye did look bigger than the other one. "Yeah. Do you think he's hurt? I mean, he shouldn't be hanging out like that, right? Just standing there?"

"I don't think so."

We sat there quietly together, watching the bird watch us. Minutes passed, and he didn't fly away. He didn't do anything.

"Should we see if we can get it to fly away?" I asked quietly. "So we can tell if it's hurt?"

"I guess."

We both started to get up, and reasoning hit me. I patted him on the shoulder to get him to stay down. "No, let me. Maybe he's a Navy SEAL hawk that doesn't give a fuck, and if we scare him, he'll attack. You can drive me to the hospital if he gets me." I thought about it. "Do you know how to drive?"

"Dad taught me a long time ago."

I eyed him. "Do you have a permit?"

The expression on his face said it all. He didn't.

"Oh well."

I was pretty sure Amos snickered a little bit, and it made me smile.

Not going too fast or too slowly, I got to my feet. I took a step forward, and the bird didn't give a shit.

Another and then another step and still, he refused to do anything.

"He should've flown off by now," Am whispered.

That's what I was worried about. Ready to cover my face if he decided to go crazy on me, I kept going closer and closer to the bird, but he didn't care. His eye was definitely swollen, and I could see the discoloration of blood on his head. "He is hurt."

"Yeah?"

I got two feet away from the hawk. "Yeah, he's got a gash on his head. Aww, poor little baby. Maybe his wing is hurt too since he's not going away."

"He should've by now…," Am whispered.

"We have to help him," I said. "We should call your dad, but my service doesn't work down here."

"Mine neither."

I wanted to ask him what to do, but I was the adult. I had to figure it out. I'd watched a show about game wardens before. What would they do?

Put it in a crate.

"By any chance do you have a crate in your house?"

He thought about it. "I think so."

"Can you go get it?"

"What are you going to do?"

"I'm going to put him in it."

"*How?*"

"I have to grab him, I guess."

"Ora! He'll rip your face off!" he hissed, but I was too busy being focused on him worrying about my safety to focus on anything else.

We *were* becoming friends. "Well, I'd rather have a few stitches than he get hit by a car if he goes off by himself," I said.

He seemed to think about it. "Let's call Dad and have him come and get it. He'll know what to do."

"I know he will, but who knows how far he is, or if he'll even be able to answer the phone anytime soon. Go get the crate, and then we can call and ask, deal?"

"This is stupid, Ora."

"Probably, but I won't be able to sleep tonight if he gets hurt. Please, Am, go grab it."

The teenager cursed under his breath and slowly walked

way around the bird–who still didn't move—before taking off running into his house. I kept on watching the majestic bird as he just waited around, crazy sharp eyes looking from side to side with those insane neck movements of his kind.

Getting a good look at him... he was huge. Like literally massive. Was that normal? Was he on steroids?

"Hey, friend," I said. "Wait here a second, okay? We'll get you some help."

He didn't respond, obviously.

Why my heart started beating faster though, I really didn't get. Never mind, I guess I did. I was going to have to grab this big son of a bitch. If my memory served me correctly—from all the episodes I'd seen of zoo shows and the one game warden show—you just kind of had to... grab them.

Could they smell fear? Like dogs? I eyed my new friend and hoped like hell he couldn't.

Two seconds later, the door to the house burst open and Amos was out, setting a big crate down on the deck before running back inside. He was back out another second later, shoving something into his pockets and then picking up the crate again. He slowed down as he got closer to the garage and walked way around where the bird was still standing. He was breathing hard as he slowly set it down between us, then pulled out some leather gloves from his pockets and handed those over too.

"This is the best I could find," he said, eyes wide and face flushed. "You sure about this?"

I slipped the gloves on and let out a shaky exhale before giving him a nervous smile. "No." I kind of laughed from the nerves. "If I die—"

That got him to roll his eyes. "You're not doing to die."

"Make up some story about how I saved your life, okay?"

He looked at me. "Maybe we should wait for my dad."

"Should we? Yeah, but are we? No, we have to get him. He should have flown off by now, and we both know it."

Amos cursed again under his breath, and I gulped. Might as well get it over with. Five minutes from now wasn't going to change anything.

My mom would've done it.

"Okay, I can do this," I tried to hype myself up. "Just like a chicken, right?"

"You've picked up a chicken before?"

I eyed Am. "No, but I've seen my friend do it. It can't be that hard." I hoped.

I could do this.

Just like a chicken. Just like a chicken.

Opening and closing my hands with the big gloves on, I bounced my shoulders and moved my neck from side to side. "Okay." I inched closer to the bird, willing my heart to slow down. *Please don't let him smell fear. Please don't let him smell fear.* "All right, love, pal, pretty boy. Be nice, okay? Be nice. Please be nice. You're beautiful. I love you. I just want to take care of you. Please be nice—" I swooped down. Then I shouted, "*Ahh!* I got him! Open the crate! Open the crate! Am, open it! Shit, he's heavy!"

Out of the corner of my eye, Amos rushed over with the crate, door open, and set it on the ground. "Hurry, Ora!"

I held my breath as I waddled, holding what I was pretty sure was a steroid-taking bird—who wasn't struggling at all, honestly—and as fast as possible, set him inside, facing away from me, and Amos slammed it shut just as I got my arms out of there without getting murdered.

We both jumped back and then peeked through the metal gate.

He was just hanging out in there. He was fine. At least I was pretty sure he was; it wasn't like he was making faces.

I held up my hand, and Am high-fived it. "We did it!"

The teenager grinned. "I'll call Dad."

We high-fived again, pumped up.

Amos hustled back inside his house, and I crouched down to look at my friend once more. He was a good hawk. "Good job, pretty boy," I praised him.

Most of all though, I'd done it! I got him in there! All by myself.

How about that?

~

AN HOUR LATER, I ran down the stairs at the sound of a car outside. Amos had said that his dad would be by as soon as possible. After relaying the information over, we'd split up, both of us too riled up with adrenaline to get back to writing; he'd gone back in to play video games, and I had gone upstairs. I had planned on going into town and hitting the shops to find something to send to Florida, but I had to know what was going to happen to my new friend.

By the time I opened the door into the garage, Mr. Rhodes was already out and walking over. He was in his uniform, apparently working on the weekend, and I'd be lying if I said that my mouth didn't water a little at the way his pants hugged his muscular thighs. But my favorite part was the way his shirt was tucked in.

He was hot as shit.

"Hi, Mr. Rhodes," I called out.

"Hi," he actually replied, those long legs eating up the distance inside.

I went to stand next to the crate. "Look what we found."

He took his sunglasses off, and his gray eyes settled on me briefly, eyebrows shooting up just a little. "You should've waited," he said, coming to a stop in front of the crate too and then bending over.

He stood up straight almost immediately, looked at me, and then crouched that time, setting the leg of his sunglasses inside of his shirt as he said, in a weird, strained voice that didn't sound pissed off... just strange, "You picked him up?"

"Yeah, I think he's on 'roids. He's pretty heavy."

He cleared his throat and hovered there before Mr. Rhodes's head tipped up toward me. He asked very slowly, "With your bare hands?"

"Am brought me some of your leather gloves."

He peeked into the crate again, staring in there for a long, long time. Actually, probably just a minute, but it felt a lot longer. He only said one thing in that same strange tone, "Aurora...."

"Am said we should wait, okay, but I didn't want my friend here to run off and then wind up on the street and get run over. Or something else. Look how majestic he is. I couldn't let him get hurt," I rambled. "I didn't know hawks got that big. Is that normal?"

He pressed his lips together. "They don't."

Why did he sound so strangled? "Did I do something wrong? Did I hurt him?"

He brought a big hand up to his face and smoothed it down from his forehead to his chin before he shook his head. His voice turned soft as his gaze moved back in my direction; he eyed my arms and face. "He didn't hurt you?"

"Hurt me? No. He didn't even seem to care. He was very polite. I told him we were going to help him, so maybe he could sense it." I'd seen videos all the time of wild animals turning passive when they could sense someone was trying to help them.

It took me a moment to realize what was happening.

His shoulders started shaking. Then his chest. The next thing I knew, he started laughing.

Mr. Rhodes started laughing, and it was rough and

sounded in a way like an engine struggling to come to life, all choked and harsh.

But I was way too disturbed to appreciate it because... because he was laughing at me. "What's so funny?"

He could barely get the words out. "Angel... that's not a hawk. It's a golden eagle."

∾

IT TOOK him forever to stop laughing.

When he finally did, he just started cracking up all over again, these big belly laughs along with what I was sure were a couple of fresh tears his hands scrubbed away as he laughed.

I think I was too stunned to really appreciate that rough, unused sound.

But once he stopped laughing for the second time, he explained—wiping his eyes while he did—that he was going to take my friend to a licensed rehabilitation facility and he'd be back later. I blew my friend a kiss through the grate, and Mr. Rhodes started laughing all over again.

I didn't think it was *that* funny. Hawks were brown. My friend was brown. It was an honest mistake.

Except for the fact that apparently, eagles were several times bigger than their smaller cousins.

I left to go into town then, buying some gifts for my family before circling back to the grocery store. By the time I got home, the Parks and Wildlife truck was back. Most importantly though, there was a long ladder propped against the side of the garage apartment, and at the very top rung was a big man holding a can in one hand and aiming it toward the seam between the roof and the siding.

I parked my car in its usual spot and hopped out, ignoring my bags in the back seat so I could see what was going on. Wandering toward the ladder, I called out, "Whatcha doing?"

Mr. Rhodes was about as high up as he could possibly reach, the arm holding the can extended about as far from the rest of his body as possible. "Filling holes."

"Do you need help?"

He didn't reply before he reached a little over to the side and apparently filled in another hole.

For bats.

He was filling in holes for the bats.

Since I hadn't had another visitor, I'd forgotten all about him filling them in.

"I got one more and I'm done," he said before scooting over just a little toward the side and filling in another. He tucked the can into the back band of his pants and climbed slowly down.

I watched his thighs and butt the whole time. I wasn't proud of myself.

He'd changed from his uniform into jeans and another T-shirt. I wanted to whistle but didn't.

He finally hopped down and turned, taking the can out from where he'd stashed it.

"Thank you for doing that," I told him, eyeing the gray hair mixed in with the brown. It looked so nice on him.

Mr. Rhodes's eyebrows rose a little bit. "Didn't want you to give me that one-star review," he deadpanned. Shocking the shit out of me.

First, he'd laughed earlier; now he was making a joke? Had he gotten kidnapped by aliens? Had he finally figured out that I wasn't some creep?

I wasn't sure, but it wasn't like it mattered. I was going to embrace it. Who knew when the next time he was this friendly was going to be? "It would have been like a three," I told him.

One corner of his mouth went up just a little.

Was that a smile?

"I was about to put up that bat house that almost killed you next," he went on.

He was joking with me. My first changeling. I didn't even know how to respond he surprised me so bad. As I picked my jaw up off the ground, my mom's voice spoke softly into my ear and I pushed my shoulders down. It was my turn to get serious. "Would you mind showing me how to do it instead?" I paused. "I'd really like to know how."

He towered over me, watchfully, like maybe he thought I was joking. But he must have been able to tell I was serious because then he nodded. "All right. Let's get you some gloves and what we'll need."

I brightened up. "Really?"

His eyes bounced from one of mine to the other. "If you want to learn, I'll show you."

"I really do. Just in case I ever have to do it again." I hoped not.

He dipped his chin. "I'll be right back."

While he went inside to get the gloves, I grabbed my bags from the car and took them upstairs. By the time I made it back, Mr. Rhodes had lowered the ladder and moved it back to where it belonged on the other side of the garage apartment. He brought around the ladder that had tried to kill me and dipped back into the house to grab the bat house that he'd brought downstairs at some point.

"Take the house," he said, holding it in his arms.

Take the house, *please?* Ooh.

I smiled and reached to take it. We headed off toward the same tree I had attempted to use the last time. How he'd pinpointed it, I had no idea. Maybe I'd left the imprint of a human body in the dirt around it. "Did you have a busy day?" I asked him instead.

He didn't look at me. "I spent all morning on a trail because a hiker found some remains." He cleared his throat. "After that, I took a golden eagle to a rehabilitator—"

I groaned. "It really was an eagle?"

"One of the biggest ones the rehabber has ever seen. She said she had to weigh close to fifteen pounds."

I stopped walking. "Fifteen pounds?"

"She had a good laugh over you snatching it up and putting it in the crate like it was a parakeet."

"Good thing I like bringing people joy."

I was pretty sure he smiled, or at least did that thing that would only be considered a smile on his face, this mouth-twisting thing. "It's not every day someone grabs a predator and calls it a pretty boy," he said.

"Amos told you that?"

"He told me everything." He stopped. "I'm going to set up the ladder right there."

"Is he going to be okay?"

"*She* is going to be okay. The wing didn't look broken, and the rehabber didn't think her skull was fractured." He moved around me and asked, "Have you used a drill before?"

I'd never even used a hammer until a couple weeks ago. "No."

He nodded. "Hold it steady and press the button." He showed me, holding up the black and green power tool. Mr. Rhodes's eyes met mine. "You know what? Practice right here." He pointed at a spot on the tree before setting up a screw on the tip.

I nodded and took it from him. I did it, screwing it in in about a split second. "Nailed it!" I glanced at him. "Get it?"

He didn't do that partial smile that time, but you couldn't win them all. "It's a screw." He gestured upward. "Get up there. I'll pass you everything and talk you through it. I won't be able to get up there since it'll be over weight capacity," my landlord warned.

I bet it would. He had to weigh over two hundred pounds, easy.

I nodded though and started climbing up before a touch on my ankle made me pause and glance down.

"If you can't hold anything, drop it. Don't fall or let it fall on you, understand?" he asked. "Drop it. Don't save it with your face. Don't break its fall."

That sounded simple enough.

"Get up there and do it."

I could do this.

I smiled and finished climbing up. He carefully handed over the drill and screws before giving me a tube I didn't recognize. Glue? My knees started shaking, and I tried my best to ignore them... and the way the ladder seemed to move a little too even though he was holding it.

"Careful. You got it...," he said as I blew out a breath. "You're doing great."

"I'm doing great," I repeated, wiping my hand on my jeans when I realized it was sweaty before picking the drill back up.

"Set it down. See that tube I handed you? It's open. Put a drop on the screws, just to get them to really stick," he instructed from below.

"Got it." I did what he said, then called down, "If I drop it, run, okay?"

"Don't worry about me, angel. Time for the drill."

"Aurora," I corrected him, blowing out a shaky breath. That wasn't the first time he'd called me the wrong name, I was pretty certain.

"Okay, you only need one screw. It doesn't have to be perfect," he instructed, before handing out more steps that I followed with slippery hands. "You're doing great."

"I'm doing great," I repeated after I'd double-checked that the screw was in well and he'd handed up the bat house. My arms were shaking. Even my neck was tense. But I was doing it.

"Here," he said, holding up a bottle as high as possible. I recognized it as the attractant that Clara had sent me a screenshot of when she'd realized hers was expired.

Aiming my face away, I sprayed it. "Anything else?"

"No, now pass me the drill and glue and get down."

I peeked down. "Please?" I joked.

And his stony, serious face was back.

Much better.

I did what he asked, knees still shaking, and started to climb down. "I'm not that—oh shit." My toes missed a step, but I caught myself. "I'm fine, I meant to do that." I peeked down at him again.

Yeah, his hard face was still there. "I bet you did," he muttered, amusing me way more than he probably meant to.

I finished climbing down the steps and instantly handed over the extra screws. "Thank you for helping me. And doing the foam stuff. And being so patient."

His full lips pressed together as he stood there, watching me again, his gaze moving over my face.

Mr. Rhodes cleared his throat, and all the hints of playfulness I'd seen glimpses of before disappeared. "I did it for me." His serious voice was back even as his gaze flicked to a spot behind me. "Don't want you screaming at the top of your lungs in the middle of the night, waking me up."

My smile faltered before I caught it, and I reminded myself that it wasn't like I wasn't aware he didn't really like me. All this was just... him being a landlord and a decent guy deep down. I'd asked him to show me what to do, and he had. That was it.

But it still hurt even though I knew it was stupid. It took

everything in me to keep my face neutral. "Thanks anyway," I told him, hearing how funny I sounded, but taking a step back. "I don't want to take up more of your time, but thanks again."

Mr. Rhodes's lips parted right as I half-assed waved.

"Bye, Mr. Rhodes."

I headed back into the house before he got anything else out, holding onto my triumphs for the day. That was what I wanted to linger over. Not over his wishy-washy moods.

I'd picked up a fucking eagle and set up my own bat house all by myself. I'd learned how to use a drill. It was a win across the board. And *that* was something. Something big and beautiful.

Next thing I knew, I was going to be catching bats bare-handed. Okay, that was never actually going to happen, but right then, I felt like I could do anything.

Except get my neighbor to like me, but that was okay.

It really was.

CHAPTER 14

I woke up to knocking.

Loud, frantic knocking.

"*Ora!*" an extremely familiar voice called out.

I blinked and sat up. "Amos?" I yelled back, picking up my phone from where I'd left it lying on the floor, plugged in. The screen said it was seven in the morning.

On my day off. Sunday.

What the hell was Am doing awake this early too? He'd literally told me at least three times that he usually stayed up all night playing video games and wouldn't wake up until after one unless his dad was home. It had made me laugh.

Throwing my legs over the side, I called out again, "Amos? You okay?"

He replied then as I grabbed a hoodie from where I'd left it draped over one of the table's chairs and slipped it on. Despite how warm it got during the day, some nights still got cool. "*Oraaaa! Yes! Come here!*"

What the hell was going on? I yawned and pulled on the sleep shorts I'd peeled off last night too, sliding them up my legs at the top of the stairs before I ran down as fast as possible. Amos wasn't a dramatic kid. We'd spent so much time together over the last month, I would have picked up on it. If anything, he was sensitive and shy, even though he was coming out of his bubble around me more and more every day.

At least one of the Rhodes men was.

Unlocking then pulling open the door, I was already squinting at him.

Still in his pajamas—a wrinkled T-shirt from the town's high school and basketball shorts I'd bet he'd inherited from Mr. Rhodes—he stared back at me. There was a drool stain on his cheek, and even his eyelashes looked a little crusty.... But the rest of him was wide awake. Alarmed even.

Why did he look freaked out?

"What happened?" I asked, trying not to worry.

He grabbed my hand, which should have been a sign because he tolerated me on the rare occasions I hugged him but had never initiated one himself, and started pulling me forward, out the door.

"Hold on," I said, stopping to slip on my boots halfway and shuffling after him. "What's going on?"

The kid didn't even glance at me as he kept on leading me toward his house. "Your... your friend is at my house," he basically gasped.

"My friend?" What friend? Clara?

That was when he glanced over, his expression damn near distraught. "Yeah, *your friend.*" His throat bobbed. "You said some things, but I didn't *really* believe you."

"That's rude," I yawned, not knowing what the hell he was talking about but going along with it.

Amos ignored me. "But she's inside. She was banging on the door and calling your name—and she doesn't have her wig on, but it's her."

Wig?

I clomped up the stairs behind him, way too tired to really use my brain yet. One of my boots fell off, and I had to tap his hand to get him to stop so I could put it back on.

"She said she's making us all breakfast, so I ran over here to get you," he kept on rambling a mile a minute, talking faster than ever. More than ever too. He pushed the door open and kept on tugging me after him. "Can I tell Jackie? Dad said she could come over for two hours, remember? She's gonna cry."

"I stayed up last night finishing a book, Am. Who is over here? Clara? Why would Jackie cry?"

He led me straight into the living room before suddenly stopping.

"It's *her*," he whispered, not sounding very reverent but more like... surprised out of his mind.

I narrowed my eyes toward the kitchen with yet another yawn and spotted the jet-black hair and slim body standing in front of the stove, stirring something in a glass bowl.

I couldn't clearly see the woman's features, but all it took was an "*Ora!*" for me to know who she was.

An eight-time Grammy winner.

One of my best friends in the whole world.

One of my favorite people in the whole world.

And one of the absolute last people I would've ever imagined seeing in Mr. Rhodes's house.

"Yuki?" I asked anyway.

I was pretty sure she set down the bowl before rushing over and throwing her arms around me, hugging the shit out of me so hard I couldn't breathe. Still in shock, I hugged her back just as tight.

"What are you doing here?" I asked her in an exhale I was careful to let out above her head since I hadn't brushed my teeth yet.

She hugged me even tighter. "I had the day off, and right after my show last night, I decided to come and see you. I tried calling but it went straight to voice mail. I've missed you so much, cutie pie." Yuki pulled back just a little. "Is this okay? I remember you said you had this Sunday off." Before I could say another word, she went on. "I can leave early if you need me to."

I rolled my eyes and hugged her again. "Yes, it's okay. I have plans but—"

"We can do whatever you need to do!" she offered, pulling back, giving me a rare view of her makeup-less and wigless upper body. Yuki Young, the person I loved and who had painted my nails once a week when I'd stayed with her at her twenty-thousand-square-foot mansion in Nashville.

Looking at her, only a massive fan would recognize her. And it was really, really rare. We could go out in public all the time... with her bodyguard that looked more like a boyfriend.

"I wasn't really going to give you the chance to choose otherwise, Yu." I laughed, feeling so tired but so happy to see her.

Honestly, it filled my heart with so much joy, I might have cried if my eyeballs were capable of it, but they were still so tired.

The only plan I had today had been...

Oh crap. I turned my head to find Amos standing in the exact same spot he'd been in when we'd stopped. His hands were on his belly, his mouth was slightly gaped, and he looked like someone had just told him he was two months pregnant.

"Amos," I said carefully, everything suddenly clicking now. "This is my friend Yuki. Yuki, this is my friend Amos."

He made a wheezing sound.

"Amos, are you sure it's all right that I'm using your mix to make pancakes?" Yuki asked him with an earnest smile, all too familiar with that kind of reaction.

"Uh-huh," the teenage boy whispered.

I, on the other hand, wasn't so sure. Mostly because I knew his dad and how protective he was. "Am, can I borrow the house phone and call your dad real quick?"

He nodded, gaze still stuck on my friend of the last ten years. For someone who wasn't a fan of her music—his words when I'd casually mentioned her during one of our sessions to test out the waters—he sure did seem starstruck. Then again, she was a household name who had magically appeared at his house, in the process of making pancakes while dressed like... well, like normal Yuki. The colored wigs she put on were nowhere in sight and neither were the colorful outfits and even more colorful makeup that so many of her fans tried to replicate.

She was just here, in a small town in Colorado, her sleek black hair cut shorter than it had been in a while, ending right at her chin, in jeans and an old NSYNC shirt... that she'd stolen from me and I hadn't noticed until now.

I loved her. Thief or not.

But first, I needed to call and leave a message. Grabbing the house phone from the dock I found on the counter, I caught a big grin from Yuki, who at another glance looked worn the hell out, and then had Amos recite his dad's number. Half expecting him not to answer—and praying he didn't—I was surprised when Mr. Rhodes picked up.

"Everything all right?" was the first thing he said, sounding alarmed.

It was sevenish in the morning, and he had to be wondering what his kid was doing waking up early when he didn't have school. "Morning, Mr. Rhodes, it's Aurora," I said, cursing in my head that of course he'd answer. "Am is fine."

There was a pause then, "Morning," he greeted me back in a cautious voice. "Is there a problem?"

"No, not at all."

"Are you fine?" he asked slowly in a grumbly voice that had me wondering what time he'd woken up.

We hadn't done much more than wave at each other, which really consisted of me waving and him lifting two fingers or lifting his chin in response, since the day of the bat house. He hadn't been outgoing or kind, but more just... back to putting up with my existence in the peripheral of his life. And that was all right. At least Amos had been keeping me company. I didn't have any illusions.

"We're both fine," I replied, hoping he wouldn't get too mad about having not just me but a stranger in the house too. "I was just calling to tell you that my friend showed up to surprise me and accidentally went to your house first, and we're... here."

"Okay...."

Okay?

Was this the same person who had mentioned at least ten times that I couldn't have visitors over?

"She's making us pancakes," I went on, baring my teeth at myself.

That next "okay" sounded just like the first one had, trailing off and kind of funky.

I walked off toward the hall where Amos's bedroom was so that they wouldn't hear me and dropped my voice. "Please don't get mad at Amos; he was just being polite. I would have let you know in advance or gotten a hotel room, but she surprised me," I tried to explain just to be on the safe side. "I'm sorry we're here."

Did he just sigh in irritation?

"We'll get out of here as soon as possible. My friend is one of the best people in the world, and I'll keep an eye on Amos,

I promise," I whispered, eyeing Amos as he kind of strolled closer to where Yuki was busy trying to pour batter onto a skillet she'd heated up at some point.

There was another sigh. "I...."

Shit.

"I know you would, Buddy. It's fine," he said.

Buddy? Where had that come from? Not that I was complaining, but... I cleared my throat and kept my voice even. "Okay. Thank you."

Silence.

All right then. "Okay, well, I'll see you later maybe."

There was a moment of silence. "I should be home around two."

"Okay." I considered warning him who she was, but decided against it. Based on the few times I'd heard music playing when he had the windows down in his truck or Bronco, he either wouldn't know who Yuki was or wouldn't give a crap.

I heard him breathe. "Bye."

"Have a nice day at work." I hung up then, confused by how weird he was being.

I glanced over to find my old friend staring at me intently from the kitchen, where she had a hip against the counter.

Too intently.

Especially when she seemed to be smiling all sneaky too.

And beside her, Amos was still staring at her.

At least until he asked, "Ora...?"

I made my way over. "Yeah?"

"Jackie's supposed to come over at eleven. To... you know...."

I did know. I was surprised he remembered too, especially when he seemed into a dead-eye stare at Yuki.

For a brief moment, I thought about asking her if she'd

care if his friend came over... but this was his house. And she wasn't that kind of person.

"Of course she can still come over. We might as well take advantage of having Miss One-Hundred-and-Twenty-Seven-Million Albums being here. She can help."

His head snapped over toward me, wide and alarmed.

"She's the one who sent you that crystal in your room."

I swear his coloring changed. Then he choked.

Yuki piped up, "Who needs help? How can I help?"

I grinned at her. "I love you, Yu. You know that?"

"I know," she countered. "I love you too. Who needs help though?"

"We'll talk about it later."

Amos choked again, and his face started to get red at what I was implying, asking Yuki for "help" because we were supposed to work on his performance today. I'd begged him to *try* to sing in front of me. We'd put it off and put it off until he'd finally agreed... as long as Jackie was there too. He'd had to ask his dad for an exception since he was still grounded. I'd learned recently that he'd been supposed to start taking driver's ed over the summer, but because of the apartment rental stunt, he was going to have to wait until he was forgiven.

"Yu." I glanced at her. "How the hell did you get here?"

She turned to flip the pancakes. "Roger"—that was her main bodyguard who had been around for probably a decade; he was in love with her, and we were all pretty sure she had no idea—"drove me straight over after my show last night in Denver. He dropped me off and went to rent a hotel room to get some sleep."

I noted the dark circles under her eyes again before glancing back at Am to make sure he hadn't passed out. He was still standing there, in his own little world, terrified or shocked, probably both. I was pretty positive he wasn't paying either one of us any attention anymore.

"Everything okay?" I asked her quietly, setting the phone back into the cradle and closing the space between us.

The breath she blew out was straight from her soul, and she lifted a shoulder. "You know I shouldn't complain."

"Just because you shouldn't complain doesn't mean you don't have a right to."

She bit her bottom lip, and I knew there was something going on. Or maybe it was just the usual stresses from touring. "I'm tired, Ora. That's all. I'm really tired. The last two months have felt... really long and... you know. *You know.*"

I did know. She was getting burned out. That's why she was here. Possibly to just be... this version of herself. Her normal person. Not the persona she put out for the whole world to see. She was sweet and sensitive, and bad reviews of her albums ruined her month. It made me want to murder people to protect her.

Sometimes you looked at a person and thought that they had everything, but you didn't know how much they still wanted. *What* they were missing. Most of the time, they were things the rest of us took for granted. Like privacy and time.

And she was tired and here.

So the second we were close enough, I hugged her again, and she dropped her forehead into my shoulder and sighed.

I needed to call her mom or her sister tomorrow and tell them to keep an eye on her.

After a minute, Yuki pulled back and braved a tired smile. "Ora, where can I get some Voss water around here?"

I stared at her. Then I kept on staring at her.

She held up the spatula in her hand and muttered, "Okay. Forget I asked. I can drink tap water."

Then sometimes I forgot she was a multimillionaire.

～

NEARLY FOUR HOURS LATER, Yuki and I found ourselves downstairs in the garage in two of Mr. Rhodes's camping chairs while Amos sat on the floor, looking sick. It had only taken a stack of pancakes that were eaten at the table with my young friend not saying a word, a quick talk with the same teenage boy who pleaded with me to take the day off, but I insisted that, no, we shouldn't and arguing about it for a second, which had surprised and amused me, to get to this point. I'd gotten to talk to Yuki in private while I'd gotten dressed about how the tour was going, which was just okay.

Jackie was on her way.

"We can wait another day," the teenage boy insisted, his neck red.

Usually I didn't like to force people to do things they didn't want to do, but this was Yuki and she had the kindest soul in the world. "What if you turn around and pretend neither one of us is here?"

He shook his head.

"Neither one of us would ever say anything mean or bad, and I've heard you already. You've got nothing to be ashamed of, Am, and One-Hundred-and-Twenty-Seven Million Albums over here—"

Yuki grunted from where she was sitting in her chair, legs crossed, holding a cup of tea she'd somehow made in my apartment. Knowing her, she probably kept a couple of packs in her purse. "Would you stop calling me that?"

"Not after you asked for Voss water earlier." I raised my eyebrows. "Would you prefer Eight-Time Grammy Winner?"

"No!"

Amos paled.

"You're making Amos more nervous," she argued.

But there was a method to my madness. "What about... I Puke Before Every Concert?"

She seemed to think about it for a second but nodded cheerily.

And that had Amos snapping out of it and asking quietly, "What?"

"I throw up before every performance," my friend confirmed, seriously. "I get so nervous. I've had to go to the doctor for it."

His dark eyes flicked from side to side like he was processing her comment and having a difficult time doing so. "Still?"

"I can't help it. I've tried therapy. I've tried... everything. Once I'm out there, I'm fine, but getting up there is so hard." She uncrossed her legs and recrossed them. "Have you performed in front of an audience yet?"

"No." He seemed to think about it. "My school has a talent show every February... I was... I was thinking about it."

This was the first time I'd heard about it.

"Getting up there is difficult," she confirmed. "It's really hard. I know some people get used to it, but it's fighting every instinct in my body to go out there every single time."

"How do you do it then?" he asked, gaze wide.

She cradled her cup, looking thoughtful. "I throw up. I tell myself I've done it before and I can do it again, remind myself I love making money, and turn into Lady Yuki. Not normal Yuki, mind you, but Lady Yuki who can do everything that I can't." She shrugged. "My therapist said it's a survival instinct that isn't necessarily healthy, but it gets the job done."

She set her cup down on her thigh. "Most people are too scared to ever put themselves in a position to be criticized. You shouldn't care what they think if they don't have the guts to do what you're doing. You have to remember that too. The only opinion that really matters is your own and other people you respect. Everyone is scared of something, and perfection isn't realistic. We're humans, not robots. Who cares if you're a little sharp or trip in front of national television?"

That had happened to her. Her sister had recorded it and cackled over it for at least a year.

Amos's face was very thoughtful.

"So...." I trailed off to give him some time to think about her advice. "Have you written anything new?"

"Are you writing a song?" Yuki interrupted.

"Yeah," I answered for him. "We're still trying to figure out long-term what story he wants to tell with his music."

She understood and puckered her lips together. "Yes. You absolutely have to figure that out. Amos, you've got the best person in the world right here to help you. You have no idea how lucky you are."

I gritted my teeth, hoping she wouldn't say much more, but the boy made a face.

"Who? *Ora?*"

That got me to snicker. "Dang, Am, don't make it seem like it sounds that wild. I told you I've written a few songs." He just didn't know that some of them had done... well.

It was Yuki's turn to make a crazy face. "A few?"

I had told her while we were upstairs that they had no idea about Kaden, that they only knew about her, at least Amos had been warned in a backward way with little hints. All they knew was about my... "divorce."

"Hers? You wrote *her* songs?" my young friend wheezed, acting like he was floored.

Yuki nodded way too enthusiastically. I just bared my teeth at him in a noncommittal smile and threw in a shrug for the hell of it.

The confusion—and surprise—on his face didn't go

anywhere, and just as he seemed to think about what to respond with, a car started coming down the driveway, and we all turned as a familiar SUV drove by and did a three-point turn, a teenage girl coming out while it was still in motion. The window rolled down, and Clara's familiar face appeared behind the driver's seat. "Hi! Bye! I'm late!" And then she was gone as Jackie carried her backpack in one hand and headed toward where we were.

It was Am who held up his hand in a stopping motion and said, "Jackie, don't freak out—"

And that's when she stopped walking, the smile she'd had on her face dropping like a damn fly as her gaze landed on the person sitting next to me.

She fell over like a fucking tree.

So hard it was a miracle her skull didn't smack against the concrete foundation as she passed out.

"Told you," Am muttered as we all rushed over, crouching beside her just as her eyes shot open and she screeched.

"I'm fine! I'm fine!"

"Are you all right?" Yuki asked, kneeling beside her.

Jackie's eyes went wide again, and her face went just as pale as Amos's had earlier when I'd told him that we were going to recruit Yuki into helping today. "Oh my *God*, it's you!" she shouted with another gasp.

"Hi."

Hi. I almost burst out laughing. "Jackie, are you okay?"

Jackie's eyes filled with tears, and I realized Amos and I were invisible now. "Oh my God, it's *you*."

My friend didn't even hesitate; she scooted forward on her knees. "Would you like a hug?"

Jackie's eyes were full of tears as she nodded frantically.

"I didn't look like that, did I?" Amos whispered at my side as the woman and the teenager hugged and even more tears spilled out of Jackie's eyes.

She was sobbing. Jackie was flat-out sobbing.

"Almost." I met his eyes and grinned.

He gave me a flat look that reminded me way too much of his dad. I laughed.

But as I turned back, I happened to catch Jackie's eyes as she pulled away from Yuki's hug and saw something an awful lot that looked like guilt in them.

What was up with that?

~

EVENTUALLY, after Jackie had calmed down and quit crying—which ended up taking close to an hour because the second she would start to get herself under control, she'd burst into tears again—we all managed to take a seat in the garage. Amos and Jackie let us keep the seats while they sat on the floor, one of them looking nauseous and disgruntled at the same time, and the other... if my life were an anime, Jackie would have had hearts in her eyes.

"So...," I said, eyeing Amos especially.

He looked up at the ceiling, but I'd caught him peeking at me a second ago.

I wasn't going to put him on the spot if he was really against it. He either wanted to perform, which we hadn't really talked about much yet, or he liked to write. He could just write for himself.

Amos had a beautiful voice, but it was his decision what he wanted to do with his gifts. Keep them to himself or share them with the world—it was his choice.

But I wanted Yuki to hear what he'd written, at least one song. Because maybe he didn't admire her work, but without a doubt, I had a feeling that any praise she had for him would be good for his soul.

And if that meant me having to do it, so be it.

"Am, do you mind if I show Yu a little bit of your other song? The darker one?"

He peeked at me again, pink taking over his neck. "You're not gonna make me do it?"

"I'd like it if you did because you know how I feel about your voice, but it's 100 percent up to you. I just want her to hear it. Only if it's okay with you."

He lowered his head then, and I could tell he was thinking about it.

He nodded.

As he handed over his notebook, I pointed at the acoustic guitar he had propped up on a guitar boat at his side, and he passed that over too, along with a guitar pick. I ignored the raised eyebrow he was shooting at me. This child never believed.

Beside me, Yuki threaded her fingers together. "Oh, I love it when you sing!"

I groaned, propping the lightweight guitar across my lap and sighed. "I'm not that great at singing and playing at the same time," I warned the two teenagers, one of whom was staring at me intently and the other who I was pretty sure hadn't heard a single word out of my mouth because she was too busy still staring at Yuki. "So it's just an idea," I said, even though we'd worked together enough to know that everything was just an idea until it had been tweaked to the second.

"You're gonna sing?" Amos asked slowly.

I wiggled my eyebrows. "Unless you want to?"

That got him to stop talking, but it didn't get him to look any less dubious.

"What about you, Jackie? You want to?" I asked my coworker.

That got her to snap out of it. She looked at me too and shook her head. "In front of Yuki? No."

With the notebook propped on my knee, I closed an eye and whispered the words under my breath to get the timing of them okay. Clearing my throat, I heard the distinct sound of tires on the driveway.

I remembered the chords he played along with the lyrics the day his dad and I had overheard him and was going to stick to them. They were simple enough for me to follow since I wasn't specifically talented enough to play difficult things and sing at the same time; it had to be one or the other. Figuring it was as good as it was going to get, I started. There wasn't a nervous bone in my body. Yuki knew I wasn't Whitney or Christina. Then again, no one was Whitney or Christina. I wasn't Lady Yuki either.

I found a book yesterday
with stories I cannot speak
empty and hollow
the words are nothing but bleak

Okay, this was going well. I smiled a little at Am, whose mouth was slightly gaped, before I kept going. There wasn't much left.

Maybe there is a map
To find the happiness in me
Don't let me be
Left to sink into the debris

I dipped straight into the chorus because it was what he had written since I hadn't convinced him to save it for a little later.

We rise and fall with the tide
I cannot be led
Nowhere left to hide
The fire must be fed

Yuki caught on to the rhythm and started tapping her foot, smiling wide. "Do it again!" she cheered.

I smiled back at her and nodded, doing the chorus once

more and then starting from the beginning, doing it a little easier, tapping my foot to keep the time. My friend gestured me to sing it once more, but this time, her sweet voice joined in, clearer, higher, and more piercing than mine.

Some people in life just had it, this talent embedded into their DNAs that made them extra special, and Yuki Young was one of them.

And it was the same vibe I'd gotten from Amos. This ability to make me break out in goose bumps.

So I smiled as she sang along the parts she'd memorized and eyed the two teenagers sitting on the floor, staring at us. And when I got to the end of the chorus, I grinned at my friend and said, "Good, right?"

Yuki was already nodding and smiling so wide, I couldn't have loved her more for being so sweet to my new friend. "He wrote that? You wrote that, Amos?"

He nodded quickly, gaze going from her to me.

"Great job, teddy bear. Just great, great job. That line about being left to sink into the debris..." She nodded again. "That was really good. Memorable. I loved it."

Amos's eyes swept to me, and just as he opened his mouth, another much deeper voice spoke up from behind me.

"Wow."

I turned to look over my shoulder to find Mr. Rhodes standing just inside the garage. Dressed in that incredible uniform with his arms crossed over his chest, feet wide apart, he was smiling. Faintly, but it was definitely there.

Probably because of Yuki's beautiful voice.

But it was me he was looking at. Me that he was focusing that slim smile on.

I smiled right back at him.

"I didn't know you sang!" Jackie shouted out of nowhere.

I turned my attention back to her. "I've sat through a lot of voice lessons. I'm not bad, but I'm not good."

Beside me, Yuki snorted. I didn't even spare her a glance. "What? I wish my voice was as husky as yours."

That got me to blink at her. "Don't you have a four-octave range?"

She blinked back. "Just accept the compliment, Ora."

Standing up, I handed the guitar back over to Amos, who was watching me still pretty sneaky and then set his notebook down beside the pillow he'd been sitting on. My old friend had gotten up too, and I tapped her shoulder before gesturing to my landlord.

"Yuki, this is Mr. Rhodes, Amos's dad and the man who owns the house. Mr. Rhodes, this is my friend, Yuki."

She instantly thrust her hand out. "Pleasure to meet you, Officer."

Mr. Rhodes's eyebrows rose up from beneath the sunglasses. "I'm a game warden, but nice to meet you too." I hadn't noticed until then that he was carrying bags in each hand. He shifted the one in his right hand over to the left and shook hers quickly, so quickly it wouldn't hit me until later how quickly he moved on, before he turned his attention back... to me. "Not sure if you want to come over, but I brought the kids lunch. I've got plenty."

What kind of weird game was he playing? Did he take some kind of happy pill every once in a while? My little heart gave a tight, confused squeeze. "Um, well—"

Yuki's phone started ringing obnoxiously loud, and she cursed before walking away, answering with a "Yes, Roger?"

"I'll ask her," I explained, tilting my head in the direction she had gone. I threw out the first thing I thought of. "How was work today?"

"Fine. I wrote out too many tickets."

He'd actually answered. Huh. "Did a lot of people play the dumb card and say they didn't know something?" I asked, not expecting much more of a response.

"Half of them."

I snorted, and the corners of his soft mouth went up just a little bit.

"I'll take the kids," he said. "You decide you want to eat, you know where we are."

He was serious about inviting us over. I wanted to wonder why he was being so friendly but wasn't positive I should find out. Instead, it was probably best to just accept it. "Okay, thank you."

But Mr. Rhodes didn't walk away. He stayed right where he was, just being all big and muscular. No big deal. "How'd it go today?"

"Really good. They know my friend."

"The kids?" He didn't ask how or why they recognized her though.

"Yeah."

He nodded, but there was something very casual about the way he did it that didn't sit right in my head, but I wasn't sure why.

"Is your friend staying the night?"

"I have no idea, probably not." She had a show tomorrow in Utah, so I highly doubted it. I just hadn't wanted to ask.

His next nod, again, was a little too casual.

"Dad, can we eat now?" Amos called out from where he was lingering right outside the garage.

The older man replied just as I turned a little to catch Jackie by him, but this time, she was looking at me. Again. That funny, funny expression on her face. Little Rhodes and Mr. Rhodes headed out of the garage, not saying a word to each other, and it made me snicker.

Jackie wasn't following after them though.

"You okay?" I asked her, hearing just a hint of Yuki's voice from around the house, still talking on the phone.

"Umm, no?" she croaked.

I took a step closer to her. "What's wrong?"

"I need to tell you something," she said very seriously.

She was starting to scare me, but I didn't want to put her off. "Okay. Tell me."

"Please don't be mad."

I hated when people said that. "I'll try my best to think about what you're saying and try to take it with an open heart, Jackie."

"Promise you won't be mad," she insisted, her slim fingers tap-dancing at her sides.

"Okay, all right, I promise not to get mad, but maybe I'll get frustrated or have my feelings hurt."

She thought about it for a second and nodded.

I waited for her to tell me... whatever it was she was scared to say.

And then she did. "I *know* who you are." The words were rushed and so fast I almost couldn't take them apart, so I squinted at her.

"I know you do, Jackie."

"No, Aurora, *I know who you are* like I KNOW WHO YOU ARE."

I had no idea what the hell she was trying to say.

She must have sensed that because she dropped her head back, squeezed her eyes shut, and said, "I know you were Kaden Jones's girlfriend... or wife... or whatever you were."

My eyes went wide.

She kept going. "I didn't want to say anything! I... I saw your messages with Clara a long time ago... so, I... I looked you up. Your hair isn't blonde anymore, but I recognized you

243

the first time I saw you. There was like a whole page dedicated to women he was seen with, and there were pictures of you two together, like old pictures, I saw one or two of them before they got deleted—"

"Oraaa," Yuki called out suddenly. "Roger's being a party pooper, and he's on his way to pick me up."

I was going to need to ask Yuki if there was a crystal for mental clarity I could get.

"I'm not going to tell anyone, okay? I just... I wanted you to know. Please don't be mad."

"I'm not," I told her, stunned. Just as I opened my mouth to say something else, Yuki came around the corner, huffing.

"I wanted to hang out with you for longer," she said, sounding exasperated.

Jackie hesitated. She took a single step back, braced herself and spat out in a quick stream, "I love you so much. Today has been like, the highlight of my entire life. I'll never forget it." Then, in the time it took me to blink, Jackie came forward, kissed her on the cheek and took off running before suddenly stopping and turning around. "I'm sorry, Aurora!" she shouted before taking off again. Yuki watched her part of the way, a faint smile on her face.

"Is she okay?" she asked.

I swallowed. "She just admitted that she knows about me and Kaden and she isn't going to tell anyone."

Yuki's head basically spun. "What? How?"

"Some fan page."

She grimaced. "Want me to pay her off?"

Of all the things that could have made me burst out laughing, that was going to be it. "No! I'll talk to her more about it later. What were you saying? Roger is coming to get you?"

She explained about her manager pitching a fit and wanting her to get to Utah tonight, so she had chartered her a flight that was scheduled to leave in an hour from the local airport. "He said he'll be here in fifteen."

"That sucks," I told her. "But I'm glad you at least came and we got to see each other for a little while."

She nodded, but her expression slowly turned funny. "Before I forget, why didn't you tell me about Tall, Silver, and Handsome?"

I burst out laughing. "He is handsome, huh?"

She whispered, "How old is he?"

"I think early forties."

Yuki whistled. "What is he? Six-four? Two-forty?"

"Why are you so creepy? You're always measuring people."

"I have to when we're hiring bodyguards. Bigger isn't always better... but most of the time it is."

It was my turn to wiggle my eyebrows at her. "I wish. I mess with him all the time, and I don't think he likes me much unless he's in a good mood."

My friend frowned. "How could he not like you? If I was sexually attracted to women, I would be attracted to you."

"You say the nicest things, Yu."

She lifted her eyebrows. "It's true. It's his loss if he doesn't, but I swear I saw him staring at you the way I look at cupcakes when I see them in catering—like I really want one but my costumes say otherwise."

"You're perfect, and you can have a cupcake if you want one," I assured her.

She giggled, and the next few minutes went by in a blur. The next thing I knew, a small SUV was pulling into the driveway and parking, and a man just a little bigger than Mr. Rhodes came out. Roger, Yuki's bodyguard, gave me a hug, said he missed seeing me, and pretty much shoved Yuki toward the front seat of the SUV. It wasn't until then that I realized she had gone upstairs to get her purse... and how the hell had she gotten service, now that I thought about it? I needed to switch providers.

She rolled down the window as the big, ex-Marine went around the front. "Ora-Bora."

"Yeah?" I called out.

She set her forearm across the frame of the window and propped her chin on it. "You know you can always come on tour with me, don't you?"

I had to press my lips together before I nodded and smiled at her. "I didn't, but thanks, Yu."

"Will you think about it?" she asked as her bodyguard set the car into drive.

"I will, but I'm pretty happy here for now," I told her honestly.

I didn't want to live out of hotels anymore. That was the truth. The idea of living on a tour bus with my best friend didn't bring me much joy or excitement anymore, even if she was the only thing that would make it bearable and fun.

I wanted roots. But that was something cruel to bring up to her when I knew that with each time she left home, she was more and more miserable. It was hard being away for months and months at a time, far from loved ones and peace and privacy.

And the little smile she gave me as Roger hollered, "Bye, Ora!" told me that she knew exactly what I was thinking.

If I could leave again for anybody, it would be her.

But I wouldn't.

"Love you," she called out, sounding way too wistful. "Buy a new car before winter! You're going to need it!"

I was going to text her mom and sister ASAP, I decided as I yelled back, "Love you too! And I will!"

And she was gone. In a trail of dust. Off to fly high and nurture a career made from tears and guts.

And suddenly, I didn't really want to be by myself.

Hadn't Mr. Rhodes invited me anyway?

My feet took me to the house as I nursed the bittersweet visit that had lifted my spirits and made my day. I knocked on the door and spotted a figure through the glass making its way over. From the size, I knew it was Amos.

So when it opened and he gestured me inside, I managed a little smile for him.

"Did she leave?" he asked quietly as we walked side by side toward the living area.

"Yeah, she told me to tell you bye," I said.

I could sense him looking at me out of the corner of his eye. "Are you okay?"

Sure enough, Mr. Rhodes and Jackie were sitting at the small kitchen table, demolishing plates loaded with Chinese food. They both sat up at Am's and my voices. "Yeah, I just miss her already," I told him honestly. "I'm glad she came. It's hard not knowing when I'll see her again."

The chair beside Mr. Rhodes was pulled out, and it took me a second to realize he'd pushed it with his knee and it hadn't been magic. He was chewing as he gestured to a stack of plates on the counter beside the containers of food. I picked one up, feeling a little shy all of a sudden, and loaded it up with a little bit of everything—not really that hungry for some reason but wanting to eat anyway.

"How do you know her?" Amos asked as I served myself.

My hand stilled for a moment, but I went for the truth. "We met at a big music festival in Portland about... eleven years ago. We both got heatstroke backstage and were in the infirmary tent at the same time, and we hit it off."

I hoped they didn't ask how I got backstage and was ready to explain... but neither one of them did.

"Should I know who she is?" Mr. Rhodes asked out of nowhere, sitting there eating quickly and neatly.

It was Amos who covered his face with his palm and

groaned, and Jackie who launched into an explanation that I was sure made Mr. Rhodes regret asking.

I wasn't sure why he'd decided to be so nice to invite me for lunch, but I really appreciated it.

He really was a decent man.

And I could not have asked for a friend better than Yuki.

CHAPTER 15

"*W*ait a second, wait a second…."

Clara grinned as she handed the customer she had just finished ringing up his receipt.

Tidying up the stack of flyers on the counter for hunting excursions, I made a face at them. "Why do people catch bass if they don't eat them?"

Walter, one of my favorite customers because he was so sweet and one who came in when he was bored, which seemed to be very often because he was newly retired, picked up the small plastic container of flies he'd bought from Clara just a moment ago. "Bass don't taste good, Aurora. Not good at all. But they don't fight much when you reel them in, and there's plenty in the reservoirs around here. The game wardens restock them."

I wondered who.

The older man winked in his friendly way. "It's about time I get going. Have a nice day, young ladies."

"Bye, Walter," Clara and I both called out as he headed toward the door.

He threw us a wave over his shoulder.

"We should go one day," Clara said when the door shut behind him.

"Fishing?"

"Yeah. Dad was talking about wanting to take his boat out. It's been a while since he has, and the weather has been nice. He's been feeling good lately and hasn't had any accidents getting around."

I didn't even need to think about it. "All right, let's do it."

"We can launch—"

She stopped talking at the same time I spotted the man at the door, holding his cell to his face.

It was Johnny, Amos's uncle.

"Go help him," I whispered to Clara.

She scoffed. "You do it."

"Why?"

"*Because* he dated my cousin, and I was serious, I'm not ready to date, and I like him but not like that," she explained. Clara gestured to where he was kind of wandering around. "Go help him. You're single too."

I huffed. "I'll just see if he needs help."

I'd made it about halfway to where he'd stopped, at a rack holding a waterproof shell, when his eyes flicked to me. It took a second, but a smile crept across his mouth. "I know you."

"You do. Hi, Johnny. Need some help?"

"Hi, Aurora." He set the jacket back on the shelf and eyed me from my face down to my shoes and back up. I ignored it like I had when two other guys had done the same earlier.

"How are you? Can I help you find something?" I'd found that it was a lot easier to delegate work if I asked first if they needed to find something. Stuff in the store, I could find, easy-peasy. Answering complicated and specific questions, I was still not a professional at, even though I'd gotten a hell of a lot more informed about all outdoor things. The time I'd spent with Mr. Rhodes had helped, but I'd been doing research and bugging Clara now that business had calmed down a bit. The bulk of tourist season was over.

"I came in for some leaded weights," he started to say.

I knew now that was used for fishing.

"Then I got sidetracked with this jacket here." He eyed me down again, and the sides of his mouth curled up even more.

"We have leaded weights over there in the back where you see that display, but if we don't carry what you're looking for, I'm sure we could order it."

Johnny nodded, that goofy-pleased smile still on his mouth. "All right, I'll wander over there in a minute." He paused. "You really work here?"

"No, I just steal Clara's shirt and come hang out with her when I have free time."

He grinned. "That was a stupid question, wasn't it?"

I shrugged. "I feel like stupid is a very strong word."

He laughed, and it made me smile. "You just don't... I can't see you working here. That's rude. I'm sorry."

"It's all right. I'm learning as I go." I shrugged again. "If you need more help, let me know. I'll be standing around."

He nodded, and I took that as my sign to walk away. I headed back toward Clara who was looking at her phone, but I was pretty sure it was just a façade and she was really eyeballing the shit out of us.

I wasn't mistaken.

"What did he say? Does he want to bear your children?"

The loudest fucking laugh burst out of me, and I had to lean forward and press my forehead against the counter between us so that I wouldn't fall to the ground.

"Hold on. Men don't bear children."

"Not that I know," I cracked up, still facing the floor.

We both started laughing our asses off. The next time I managed to peek up, she had disappeared behind the counter. She might have been lying on the ground because I could hear her laughing but couldn't see her.

I wiggled my eyebrows at her. "I need to bring some of my romance books over to teach you some things."

"I know things."

"At your age, you should know more."

"We're the same age!"

"Exactly."

Clara laughed, and I could see the top of her head starting to peek back up before it suddenly disappeared again about a split second before I heard, "Would you mind ringing me up?"

It was Johnny.

I turned toward him, wiping the tears from under my eyes from laughing, and said, "Of course." I went around the counter where the register was and unlocked it. Johnny handed over the two small packages that I scanned quickly.

"So... Aurora...."

I raised my eyebrow at him. "Yes?"

"You got big plans tonight?"

I'd forgotten it was Friday. "Big plans with my iPad and some sangria I was planning on making."

His laugh was bright, and it made me grin as I gave him his total just as the door to the shop opened and Jackie slipped inside.

We made eye contact, and I smiled at her. She gave me a little one back. Things had been... I wouldn't want to say awkward, but a little strained since she'd admitted she knew I had been with Kaden. I hadn't been mad at her, not even a tiny bit. Neither one of us had made an effort to talk about it again since Yuki had interrupted our conversation to say that she was getting picked up because they had to start their trip to Utah.

I wasn't upset or mad or worried. I just figured that...

well, if she had wanted to tell Amos and Mr. Rhodes, she would have already. My secret was safe with her.

But eventually, I would need to talk to her.

And at least tell Amos.

Johnny greeted the girl as she passed him and dug into his back pocket, pulling out his wallet and handing over a card.

"Would you like a receipt?"

"No." He cleared his throat, picking up the two packages of weights and hesitating. "Would you like to ditch your iPad and go to dinner with me? There's a Mexican place I like that I bet has sangria."

That wasn't what I was expecting. And his offer surprised me so much I didn't know what to say.

Go out on a date?

"Unless you're seeing somebody," he added quickly.

"I'm not," I admitted just as fast, thinking about his offer.

His smile turned flirty. "I'd ask about Rhodes, but he's weird around beautiful women."

I groaned and made a face, but….

What the hell did I have to lose? Clara had said she wasn't interested in him like that, hadn't she? I could always double check with her.

And it sure wasn't like I'd sleep with him.

Sure, I thought Mr. Rhodes was hotter than hell, but it wasn't like that meant anything. He barely talked to me, still. From the way he looked at me more often than not, I was pretty sure sometimes he regretted inviting me to stay longer. He could be so nice one minute and not so much the next. I didn't get it, and I didn't want to overthink it.

I had moved here to… move on with my life, and part of that included… dating. I didn't want to be alone. I liked stability. I wanted someone around to care about me and vice versa.

This wasn't the first time I'd gotten asked out since I'd

started working here, but it was the first time I was considering it.

Screw it. "All right. Sure. At least you'll talk back to me unlike my iPad, right?"

His smile grew even wider, and I could tell he was pleased. It made me feel nice. "I'll talk back. Promise." He smiled just a little more. "Want me to pick you up?"

"I'll meet you there? Wherever we're eating?"

The man nodded. "All right. Seven work?"

"Deal."

He gave me the name of a restaurant I recognized on the river that wound its way through part of the town. "I'll meet you upfront."

I knew this was a step, like Clara had said. It was something. And something was better than nothing, especially when you had that to begin with.

"I'll see you later then," Johnny said with that big grin still on his face. "Thanks."

"No problem, see you," I said.

And it was only because the store was empty that Clara let out a whoop. "Did you just get asked out on a date?"

"Hell yeah, I did," I called back. "Is that okay with you? I won't go if you do like him."

She shook her head, and I could tell from the easy way she did it she was telling the truth. "Go. I'm really not interested in him like that." She paused. "Do you have anything to wear?" I must have thought about it too long because she made a face. "I guess I know what I'm doing during my lunch break."

I raised my eyebrows at her. "What?"

Clara just smiled.

WITH ONE FINAL look in the mirror of the bathroom of my apartment, I figured I wasn't going to spontaneously get better looking.

I was as good as I usually got.

I hadn't gone heavy with my makeup, but I hadn't gone ultra-light either. Just right, I figured, for a date. Good enough to hide the scratches and dents in the used goods that I was, but not hiding so much that I looked like a different person.

A few times in the past, I'd gotten my makeup profession-ally done and ended up washing it off afterward because I didn't like the way it felt. I didn't have much to complain about without foundation. And if someone could see a hint of the pimple I'd popped that morning, too bad.

Fortunately, Clara had gone home during her break and brought back a skirt that she said was a size too small and a cute blouse she told me I could have. I didn't have heels, my feet were a full size and a half bigger than her size seven and a halves, so I'd had to settle for some sandals that fortunately did match the skirt and emerald green shirt.

I thought I looked pretty. I felt pretty at least.

I didn't expect anything from tonight except hopefully some pleasant company. I'd even pay for my own food, just in case.

Snatching up my purse—and for some reason randomly remembering the twenty purses and clutches that I'd left behind at Kaden's, gifts from over the years—I grabbed my keys too and headed down the stairs and out the garage, only to stop short.

I hadn't heard the garage door open, but it was a wide and gaping maw. Amos and Mr. Rhodes stood in the center, looking up at the mechanism that was the garage door opener.

I guess they hadn't heard me either because when I said,

"Hey, fellas," Amos jumped and I was pretty sure that Mr. Rhodes's shoulder might have jerked a bit too.

What I was sure of was that Mr. Rhodes's eyes narrowed a little.

I think he might have glanced at my legs.

"Everything okay?"

"Hi, Ora. The garage door opener isn't working anymore. Dad's fixing it," Amos answered.

Part of me was surprised he wasn't bringing Yuki up again. He'd demanded to know why I hadn't told him that I knew her. That I was *friends* with her. *Good friends*.

Personally, I was still butthurt he'd been so surprised to hear her say I was a good songwriter.

We'd been side-eyeing each other a lot since.

"Good luck." I grinned at my teenage friend. "If you need anything from up there, go for it. I'll be back later."

"Where are you going?" my landlord asked out of nowhere.

I looked at Mr. Rhodes in surprise.

Was he… frowning?

I told him the name of the restaurant. Then I wondered if I should tell him I was meeting Amos's uncle there.

But before I could decide, the teenager asked, "Are you going on a date?"

"Sort of." I let out a breath. "Do I look okay, you think? It's been a long time since I've been on one." Kaden and I hadn't been able to go out unless it was to a family thing and a private room had been booked.

I cringed thinking about it now.

I'd been so stupid for putting up with that for so long. Man, if only I could go back in time and tell a younger Aurora not to be stupid and settle.

I wanted to think I'd loved him so much that's why I'd put up with it, with the secrets and the subterfuge. Now, some part of me thought I'd just been desperate to be loved, to have someone, even if it cost me.

And maybe love always had a price, but it shouldn't have been that high.

"No." Amos's throat bobbed, bringing me back to the present. "I mean, you look really, uh, pretty," he stammered.

"Aww, Amos, thank you. You made my day. I hope your uncle thinks so too, otherwise, tough shit for him."

Mr. Rhodes scowled. "You're going out with Johnny?"

Why did he have to sound like I was doing something wrong? "Yes, he went by the shop today and invited me. He asked if I wanted him to come pick me up, but I didn't want to make it weird. I promised no one would come over and didn't want to cross the line," I rambled quickly, his facial expression staying exactly the way it was. "Is that okay with you? It's only dinner."

Those purple-gray eyes raked over me again.

Did his jaw just go tight?

Was he... mad?

"It's none of our business," he said very slowly.

His tone disagreed.

Even Amos glanced at him.

"We might have to turn off the power, but I'll have it back on by the time you get back," Mr. Rhodes went on, his voice tight.

Okay...? Someone must have forgotten to take his chill pill. "Whatever you need to do. Good luck again. See you later. Have a good night."

"Bye," Amos said in what had become his normal voice now. More comfortable, not so quiet.

Mr. Rhodes though said nothing.

Well, if he was annoyed with me going out with his relative or whatever he was... too bad. I wasn't bringing him back here. It was only dinner. Just a nice date with nice company.

And I was looking forward to it.

One small step for Aurora De La Torre, one giant leap for the rest of my life.

I wasn't going to let anyone ruin it. Not even Game Warden Moody.

~

"So," Johnny asked, sipping on the one and only beer he'd said he was drinking that night, "how are you still single?"

I snickered as I set my glass of sangria down and shrugged. "Probably the same reason as you. My addiction to creepy dolls gets in the way."

My date, my *first* first date in forever, laughed. Johnny had already been waiting for me inside the restaurant when I'd gotten there. So far, he'd been polite and curious, asking all kinds of questions about my job at the shop so far mostly.

And asking about my age. He was forty-one. He owned his own radon mitigation company and seemed to really like his job.

He was very cute too.

But it had taken about fifteen minutes in to decide that, as easy as he was to talk to and joke around with, at least so far, I didn't get that... that feeling, I guess. I knew the clear difference between when I liked someone and when I *liked* someone.

From the way he'd checked out our waitress's ass and the hostess', I figured he wasn't feeling the chemistry either. That or he expected me to be blind. Either way... it was a bust.

I wasn't heartbroken.

And I was going to pay for my half of the food.

Pulling into the driveway not too long afterward, I was

surprised to see that the garage door was still wide open. I had just barely closed my door when a shadow covered the gravel right in front of the opening. By the length and mass of it, I knew it was Mr. Rhodes.

"Hey," I said.

"Hi," he replied, stopping right on the edge of the concrete floor.

I stepped closer, my toes just on the other side of where the foundation was and peeked in and up. "Did you get the opener fixed?"

"We have to order a new one," he replied, staying right where he was. "The motor burned out."

"That sucks." I looked at him. He'd shoved his hands into his dark jeans.

"It was as old as this apartment is," my landlord explained.

I smiled faintly. "Did Amos bail on you?"

"He went back inside about half an hour ago, saying he had to use the bathroom."

I grinned.

"You're back home early," Mr. Rhodes added out of nowhere in that serious voice of his.

"We only had dinner."

Even though it was dark, I could sense the heavy weight of his gaze as he said, "I'm surprised Johnny didn't ask you to go out for drinks after."

"No. I mean, he did, but I told him I'd been up since five thirty."

The hands came back out of his pockets as he crossed his arms over that swimming-pool-sized chest. "Going out again?"

Someone was chatty tonight. "No."

I was pretty positive the lines across his forehead deepened.

"He checked out the waitress's ass every time she walked

by," I explained. "I told him he needs to work on that next time he goes on a date."

Mr. Rhodes shifted just enough under the light that I saw him blink. "You said that?"

"Uh-huh. I messed with him about it nonstop for the last half hour. I even offered to ask her for her number for him," I said.

His mouth twitched, and for one split second, I caught a hint of what might be a stunning smile.

"I didn't know you were best friends growing up." That was really all I'd freely gotten out of Johnny about Rhodes and Amos. I hadn't pressed. That information alone had been interesting enough.

Rhodes tipped his head to the side.

"What about you? Do you go on dates?"

The way he said "No" was like I'd asked him if he'd ever considered cutting off his penis.

I must have flinched at his tone because he softened it when he kept talking, looking right into my eyes all intense when he did. "I don't have time for that."

I nodded. That wasn't the first time I'd heard someone say that. And as someone who had… not even been second best… it was fair. It was the right thing to say and do. For the other person. Better to know and accept what your priorities were in life than waste someone else's time.

He worked long hours. I saw how late he came in some days and how early he left on others. He wasn't exaggerating about not having time. And with Amos… that was an even higher priority. When he was off work, he was home. With his son. As it should be.

At least I had no ideas in my head about this hot guy. Look but don't touch.

With that in mind… "Well, I don't want to keep you. Have a good night, Mr. Rhodes."

His chin dipped, and I thought that was all I was getting, so I started moving toward the door, but I only managed to take about two steps when his rough voice spoke up again. "Aurora."

I looked at him over my shoulder.

His jaw was tight again. The lines across his forehead were back too. "You look beautiful," Mr. Rhodes said in that careful, somber voice a heartbeat later. "He's an idiot for looking at anyone else."

I swear to God my heart just totally stopped beating for a second. Or three.

My whole body froze as I felt his words burrow deep in my heart, stunning the hell out of me.

He moved toward the middle of the garage on the outside, those big hands grabbing hold of the door's lip.

"That's really, really nice of you to say," I told him, hearing how weird and breathy my voice came out. "Thank you."

"Just speaking the truth. 'Night," he called out, hopefully oblivious to the destruction the verbal grenade he'd just launched at me had caused.

"Goodnight, Mr. Rhodes," I croaked.

He was already pulling the door when he said, "Just Rhodes is good from now on."

I stayed frozen there for way too long after the door had closed, soaking in every word he'd spoken as he headed to the main house. Then I started moving, and I realized three things as I went up the stairs.

I was pretty sure he'd checked me out again.

He'd told me to call him Rhodes, not Mr. Rhodes.

And he'd waited for me on his deck until I'd unlocked the door and gone in.

I wasn't even going to try and analyze, much less overanalyze, that he'd called me the b-word earlier.

I didn't know what to think about anything anymore.

CHAPTER 16

I was excited about my hike that morning, even though I'd had to wake up at the crack of dawn to do it.

I'd still been squeezing in jumping rope a few days a week, longer every day it seemed like, and I'd even gone as far as wearing a light backpack sometimes while I did it. Was I anywhere near ready to do Mt. Everest? Not in this lifetime or the next unless I developed a lot more self-control and stopped being scared of heights, but I had finally convinced myself I could handle a difficult hike. The four-mile one we'd done had been rated as intermediate, and I'd survived it. All right, barely, but who was keeping track?

Mom had a little star and a wave-like symbol next to it. I hoped it meant something good since her information had literally been pretty direct with no other notes on it.

Every day I could feel my heart growing. Could feel myself growing here in this place.

The truth was, I loved the smell of the air. I loved the customers at the shop who were all so nice. I loved Clara and Amos, and even Jackie was back to making eye contact with me… even though we didn't talk much. And Mr. Nez made me so happy during the few times I'd gotten to see him.

I was doing a lot better at work. I'd put up a bat house. I'd gone on a date. I was owning all of this. I was settling in.

And finally, I was going to do this hard-ass hike.

Today.

For not just my mom but for me too.

I was so motivated I even sang a little bit louder than normal while I got ready, telling someone about what I really, really wanted.

Making sure I had all of my things—a life straw, a bottle with a built-in water filter, two extra gallons to start with, a turkey and cheddar sandwich with nothing else in it so that it didn't get soggy, way too many nuts, an apple, a bag of gummies, and an extra pair of socks—I walked out, double-checking my mental list to make sure I hadn't forgotten anything.

I didn't think so.

Glancing up as I made it to my car, I spotted Amos trudging back to the house, shoulders slumped and looking exhausted. I bet he'd forgotten to roll the trash can to the street and his dad had woken him up to do it. It wouldn't be the first time. He'd complained to me about it before.

I lifted my hand and waved. "Morning, Amos."

He lifted his hand back, lazily. But I could tell he noticed what I was wearing; he'd seen me leave the house enough to go for hikes to recognize the signs: my dark UPF pants, long-sleeved UPF white shirt I'd bought at the store layered over a tank top, my jacket in one hand, hiking boots on, and a cap barely resting on the top of my head.

"Where are you going?" he asked, pausing on his journey back to bed.

I gave him the name of the trail. "Wish me luck."

He didn't, but he did nod at me.

One more wave and I ducked into my car just as Rhodes came out of his house, dressed and ready for work. Someone was running later than usual.

We'd barely seen each other over the last couple of weeks, but every once in a while, his words the day of my date with Johnny came back to me. Kaden used to call me beautiful all the time. But out of Rhodes's mouth... it just felt different, even if he'd said it casually, like it was just a word with no meaning behind it.

That's why I honked, just to be a pest, and noticed his eyes narrow before he lifted a hand.

Good enough.

I was out of there.

~

I'D HOPED in fucking vain, I realized hours later when my foot slipped on a patch of loose gravel on a downhill part.

Mom had put the star around the name of it to symbolize the stars she'd seen after getting a concussion crossing the main ridge of the trail.

Or maybe a star to mean you had to be an alien to finish it because I wasn't ready. I wasn't ready at all.

Fifteen minutes in, I should have known I wasn't in good enough shape to do this in a day. It was five miles in, five out. Maybe I should've listened to Rhodes's advice way back when he'd suggested I camp, but I still hadn't been able to talk myself into doing it by myself yet.

I'd sent Uncle Mario a text to let him know where I was hiking and approximately what time I would get back. I'd promised to text him again when I was done, so that someone knew. Clara wouldn't worry unless I didn't show up at the shop the next day, and Amos might not notice I wasn't around until he hadn't seen my car for too long, and who knew what he'd consider to be too long.

You didn't know what it was like to be alone until you didn't have people who could or would notice if you went missing.

Besides being out of breath, my calves cramping, and having to stop every ten minutes to take a five-minute break, everything had been going okay. I was regretting it, sure, but I hadn't given up hope that I could actually finish the hike.

At least until I got to that damn ridge.

I really had tried to catch my balance on the way down, but I'd hit the ground hard anyway.

Knees first.

Hands second.

Elbows third when my hands gave up on me and I'd gone face-first.

Into gravel.

Because there was gravel everywhere. My hands hurt, my elbows hurt, I thought there might be a chance my knee might've been broken.

Could you break a knee?

Rolling onto my butt, careful not to slide farther off the trail and toward the jagged rocks below, I blew out a breath.

Then I looked down and squeaked.

The gravel had scraped my palms raw. There were little pebbles *buried in my skin*. Beads of blood were starting to pop up on my poor hands.

Bending my arms, I tried to glance at my elbows... only to see enough to imagine that they looked the same as my palms.

Only then did I finally take in my knees.

The material covering one of them was totally torn. It was scraped raw too. The material over my other knee was intact, but it burned like hell, and I knew that knee was fucked up too.

"Oww," I moaned to myself, looking at my hands, then my elbows—ignoring the pain that shot through my shoulders as I chicken-winged my arm—and finally back at my knees.

It hurt. Everything fucking hurt.

And I hadn't brought anything with me as first aid. How could I be so dumb?

Slipping my backpack off, I dropped it on the ground beside me and peeked at my hands once more.

"Owwie." I sniffled and swallowed hard before looking back the way I'd come.

Everything really did hurt. I'd liked these pants too.

There was a tiny stream of blood going down my shin from my knee, and the urge to cry got worse. I would've punched the gravel if I could close my fist, but I couldn't even do that. I sniffled again, and not for the first time since moving out here, to basically the middle of nowhere, but for the first time in a while, I wondered what the fuck I was doing.

What *was* I doing with my life?

Why was I here? What was I doing, doing this? I was doing hikes by myself with the exception of the one time. Everyone had their own lives. No one would even know I'd hurt myself. I had nothing to clean my wounds with. I was probably going to die from some weird infection now. Or I'd bleed out.

Squeezing my eyes closed, I felt one little tear pop up, and I wiped it away with the back of my hand, wincing as I did it.

Pure frustration mixed with throbbing pain formed a ball in my chest.

Maybe I should go back to Florida, or go back to Nashville, it wasn't like there were any chances I'd ever see Mr. Golden Boy there. He rarely left the house. He was too hot shit to hang out with normal people after all. *What the hell was I doing?*

Whining, that's what.

And my mom never whined, some small part of my brain reminded the rest of me in that moment.

Opening up my eyes, I reminded myself that I was *here.* That I didn't *want* to live in Nashville, Yuki or no Yuki. I'd liked Florida, but it had never really felt like home because it seemed more of just a reminder of what I had lost, of a life I'd had to live because of the things that had happened. In a way, it was a bigger reminder of a tragedy than even Pagosa Springs.

And I didn't *want* to fucking move from Pagosa. Even if all I had were just a couple friends, but hey, some people had no friends.

Just earlier, when I hadn't been feeling so pathetic, I'd thought that everything was working out. That I was getting somewhere. I was settling in.

And now all it took was one little thing to go wrong and I wanted to quit? Who was I?

Taking in a long, deep breath, I accepted that I was going to have to go back. I had nothing for my hands, my knees ached like fucking hell, and my shoulder was hurting more and more by the second. I was pretty sure I'd be in unbelievable pain if I'd dislocated it, but I'd probably just hurt it a little.

I had to take care of myself, and I had to do it now. I could always come back and do this hike again. I wasn't quitting. I *wasn't.*

Picking the hand that looked the worst, I set it palm up on top of my thigh, gritted my teeth, and started picking out the gravel that had decided to make a home in my skin, hissing and groaning and flinching and saying, "Oh my God, fuck you," over and over again when a particular piece hurt like extra hell… which was every piece of gravel.

I cried.

And when I finished that hand and even more blood pooled in the tiny wounds and my palm throbbed even worse, I started on the other.

I was taking care of myself.

There was a small first aid kit in my emergency roadside bag, I remembered when I was nearly done with my other hand. I'd bought it when I got my bear spray. It didn't have a whole lot, but it had something. Band-Aids to help me survive the entire two-and-a-half-hour drive home, on top of the time it would take to hike back out.

Oh my God, I was going to cry again.

But I could do it while I dug out rocks from my elbows, I figured, and that was what I did.

THREE AND A HALF hours and a lot of curse words and tears later, my hands still ached, my elbows did too, and every step I took hurt the joints in my knees and the painfully stretched skin covering them. If I didn't have black pants on, I was sure I'd look like I'd gotten into a fight with a bear cub and lost. Bad.

Feeling defeated but trying my best not to, I sucked in one breath after another, forcing my feet to keep fucking going until I made it to the stupid-ass parking lot.

I'd gone through periods of pure rage toward everything on the way down. Over the trail in the first place. Over doing this. Over the sun being out. At my mom for bamboozling me. I'd even been pissed off at my boots and would have taken them off and thrown them into the trees, but that was considered littering and there were too many rocks.

It was the boots' fault for being slippery, the sons of bitches. I was donating them the first chance I got, I'd decided at least ten times. Maybe I'd burn them.

Okay, I wouldn't because it was bad for the environment and there was still a fire ban in effect, but whatever.

Pieces of shit.

I growled just as I turned on a switchback and came to a sudden stop.

Because coming toward me, head down, backpack straps clinging to broad shoulders, breathing steadily in through his nose and out through his mouth, was a body I recognized for about ten different reasons.

I knew the silver hair peeking out from under a red ball cap.

That tan skin.

The *uniform*.

The man looked up then, blinked once, and stopped too. A frown took over a face that solidified I knew the man on his way up. And I definitely recognized the raspy voice that asked, "Are you *crying?*"

I swallowed and croaked, "A little bit."

Those gray eyes widened just a little and Rhodes stood up even straighter. "Why?" he asked very, very slowly as his gaze swept over me from my face down to my toes before going back up. Then those eyes flicked down to my knees and stayed there as he asked, "What happened? How bad are you hurt?"

I took a step that was more like a limp forward and said, "I fell." I sniffled. "The only thing broken is my spirit." I wiped at my face with my sweaty forearms and tried to smile but failed at that too. "Fancy seeing you here."

His gaze went back to my knees. "Tell me what happened."

"I slipped along the ridge and thought I was going to die,

lost half my pride along the way too," I told him, wiping at my face again. I was so fed up. *Beyond* fed up. I just wanted to get home.

His shoulders seemed to relax a little with every word out of my mouth, and then he was moving again, setting down two trekking poles I hadn't noticed he'd been holding along the side of the trail and slipping his backpack off too before he stopped in front of me and kneeled. His palm went around the back of the knee with the ripped pant leg, and he gently lifted it. I let him, too surprised to do anything other than stand there trying to balance as he whistled under his breath, inspecting the skin there.

Rhodes glanced up from under those thick, curly lashes. He set my leg back down and touched the back of my other calf. "This one too?" he asked.

"Yeah," I answered, hearing the sulkiness I was trying to hide in my voice. "And my hands." I sniffled again. "And my elbows."

Rhodes kept kneeling as he reached for one of my hands and flipped it, instantly wincing. "Jesus Christ, how far did you fall?"

"Not that far," I said, letting him look at my palms. His eyebrows knit together in a pained expression before he took my other hand and inspected it too.

"You didn't clean it?" he asked as he lifted that arm up a bit, grimacing again. I'd taken my UPF shirt off not even thirty minutes before falling. My skin might have been more protected if I'd left it on. Too late now.

"No," I replied. "That's why I turned around. I don't have anything on me. Ouch, that hurt."

He lowered my arm slowly and took the other, lifting it high up to check out that elbow too and earning him another "Oww" from me when it made my shoulder ache.

"I think I hurt my shoulder when I tried to break my fall."

His gaze met mine. "You know that's the worst thing you can do when you fall?"

I gave him a flat look. "I'll keep that in mind next time I fall on my face," I grumbled.

I was pretty sure his mouth might have twisted a little as he stood up. Rhodes gave me a single nod for sure though. "Let's go, I'll walk you down and get you cleaned up."

"You will?"

He slanted me a look before picking up his trekking poles and backpack, slipping the straps on, then maneuvering the two sticks through crisscrossing cords on his back, leaving his arms free. Finally aiming his body back up the trail toward me, he held out his hand.

I hesitated but set my forearm into his open palm, and I watched as some emotion I didn't initially recognize slid over his face.

"I meant your backpack, angel. I'll take it for you. The trail's not wide enough for both of us to go down at the same time," he said, his voice sounding oddly hoarse.

Maybe if I hadn't been in so much pain, and been so damn cranky, I would've been embarrassed. But I wasn't, so I nodded, shrugged, and gingerly tried to take my backpack off. Luckily, I just started to shimmy a strap off when I felt the weight leave my shoulders as he tugged it away.

"Are you sure?"

"Positive" was all he replied with. "Come on. We've got half an hour to get back to the trailhead."

My whole body slumped. "Half an hour?" I'd thought I had... ten minutes max.

My landlord pressed his lips together and nodded.

Was he trying not to laugh? I wasn't sure because he turned around and started heading down the path ahead of me. But I was pretty sure I saw his shoulders shaking a little.

"Let me know when you want water" was one of the only two things he said on the way down.

The other being, "Are you humming what I think you're humming?"

And me replying with "Yes."

"Big Girls Don't Cry." I had no shame.

I tripped twice, and he turned around both times, but I gave him a tight smile and acted like nothing had happened.

Like he predicted, thirty minutes later, when I was basically wheezing and he was acting like this was a stroll down a paved path, I spotted the parking lot and almost cried.

We'd made it.

I'd made it.

And my hands hurt even worse from how dry the cuts were, and my elbows felt the same way, and I was sure my knees would too, but their joints were so bad, they didn't have room to wonder about any other pain.

But just as I started heading toward my car, Rhodes slipped his fingers around my biceps and steered me toward his work truck. He didn't say another word as he unlocked it and dropped the tailgate, shooting me a look over his shoulder as he patted it briefly before heading around to the passenger door.

I went straight for the tailgate and eyed it, trying to figure out how to sit on it without using my hands to boost myself up.

That was how he found me: staring at it and trying to decide if I went face-first and shimmied up on my stomach, I could wiggle around and sit up on my butt eventually.

"I'm trying to figure out how to—*okay*."

He scooped me up, one arm under the backs of my knees, the other around my lower back, and planted me on the truck. In a sitting position. Like it was no big deal. I smiled at him.

"Thanks." I would've figured it out, but it was the thought that counted.

It didn't change the fact he was confusing, but I wasn't going to pick at that thought any longer. I still hadn't moved past him calling me beautiful. I probably wouldn't.

From under his arm though, he set a red kit beside my hip. Wordlessly, those big hands went straight for my foot, and I watched as he undid the lace and tugged the boot off by the heel as I said, "Hold your breath. I've been sweating, and I'd like to think my feet don't smell, but they might."

That gaze flicked up for a second, and he lowered it again before doing the same to my other boot.

I sighed in relief. Man, did that feel good. I wiggled my poor, tormented toes and sighed again just as he started rolling my pant legs up, stopping the folds just above my knee. His hands were gentle as they did the same to the knee that hadn't totally torn.

And I watched, silently, as his palm cupped my calf and he extended my leg, the side of it pressing against his hip. He tilted his head and examined it some more before doing the same to the other. He had just started digging through his case when I asked, "Whatcha doing here?"

He didn't look over as he pulled a couple packets out and set them on top of my thigh.

Not the tailgate. My thigh.

"Someone reported illegal hunting; I was coming to see if I heard anything," he answered, setting out a small clear bottle too.

I watched him put on some gloves, then take the top off the bottle and give it a swirl. "I thought hunting season hadn't started yet?"

He still didn't look at me as he lifted my leg again at an angle and squirted the clear fluid over my knee. It was cold and it stung just a little, but mostly because the skin was broken. I hoped. "It hasn't, but that doesn't matter to some people," he explained, focused below.

I guess that made sense.

But what were the chances…?

Had Amos told him I was here?

He did the same to the other knee, which was scraped up but not as bad.

"Are you going to get in trouble for not going up there?" I asked him with a hiss as it stung too.

He shook his head, setting the bottle aside and nabbing some precut strips of gauze that he used to dab under the wounds, drying them. Rhodes worked on me some more before grabbing a couple more gauze pads and putting them over the treated wounds, taping them down.

"Thank you," I told him quietly.

"You're welcome," he replied, meeting my gaze briefly. "Hands or elbows first?"

"Elbows are good. I need to work up to my hands; I think those will hurt the most."

He nodded again, taking my arm and starting the whole process over again with the solution. He was drying it off as he asked quietly, "Why are you by yourself?"

"Because I don't have anyone else to come with me." With his head ducked, I got a really great view of his incredible hair. The silver and brown mixed together perfectly. One could only hope to gray that nicely. At least I did.

Those almost purple eyes flicked to me again as he applied something to my elbow. "You know it's not safe to go hiking alone."

Here was the inner Dad and game warden. "I know." Because I did. Better than anyone, probably. "But I don't really have a choice. I texted my uncle and told him where I was. Clara knows too." I watched his face. "Amos asked when I was leaving this morning. He knew too."

His features didn't shift in the slightest. Amos had definitely told him. Right?

But what? He drove all this way... to check on me? Drive two and half hours away... for me?

Yeah, *right*.

"You turned around at the ridge then?" he asked as he covered my elbow with a big Band-Aid.

"Yeah," I told him sheepishly. "It was a lot harder than I expected."

He grunted. "Told you it was difficult."

He remembered? "Yeah, I know you did, but I thought you were exaggerating."

He made a soft sound that might have been a snort... coming from anyone else... and I smiled. He didn't see it though. Fortunately.

"I need to train harder before I try this again," I told him.

Rhodes took my other elbow. His hands were nice and warm even through the gloves. "Probably a good idea."

"Yeah—oww."

His thumb brushed right below the wound of my elbow, and his eyes flicked up. "Okay?"

"Yeah, just being a baby. It hurts."

"Mm-hmm. You scraped them up pretty bad."

"It feels like—*owwie*."

He snorted really softly again. It was definitely a snort.

What the hell was going on? Did he take his chill pill again?

"Thank you for doing this," I said once he'd tenderly—and I mean *tenderly*—put another Band-Aid on my other elbow.

Rhodes took my hand then, flipping the palm up and setting it on top of my leg. "How were you planning on driving home?" he asked softly.

"With my hands," I joked and grimaced when the pad of his index finger grazed one of the puncture-like wounds. "I don't really have another choice. I figured I'd just cry and bleed all the way home."

Those gray eyes moved toward my face again.

I smiled at him as he took ahold of the solution again, working it over my hands. His thumb grazing over the tiny wounds there like he was making sure there was nothing else embedded in my skin; then he poured some more. I gritted my teeth and tried to get my mind off what he was doing. So I did what came second nature. I kept on talking.

"Do you like your job?" I asked, making a face he didn't see.

His eyebrows knit together as he kept on working. "Sure. More now."

That distracted me. "Why now?"

"I'm on my own now," he actually answered.

"You weren't before?"

One gray eye peeked at me. "No, I was a cadet." He didn't say anything for so long, I didn't expect him to say more. "I didn't like starting over and having people tell me what to do again."

"They really treated you like a rookie? At your age?"

That had his head jerking up, the funniest expression on his handsome face. "At my age?"

I pressed my lips together and lifted my shoulders. "You're not twenty-four."

Rhodes's mouth twisted before he lowered his gaze once more. "They still call me Rookie Rhodes."

I watched his fingers on my palm. "Were you… in charge of a lot of people? In the military?"

"Yes," he answered.

"How many?"

He seemed to think about it. "A lot. I retired a Master Chief Petty Officer."

I didn't know what that was, but it sounded pretty important. "Do you miss it?"

He thought about it as he again, gently, put a big Band-Aid over my wound, his fingers slicking the edges down so that they adhered well. "I do." The corners of his mouth whitened as he took my other hand. His were a lot bigger than mine, his fingers long and blunt as they stretched the material of the gloves. I could tell they were nice, strong hands. Very capable-looking.

It wasn't any of my business, but I couldn't help myself. This was the most he'd talked to me in... ever. "So why did you retire then?"

His full mouth pinched. "Did Amos tell you his mom is a doctor?"

He hadn't told me much of anything. "No." I'd just settled for imagining a beautiful woman that Rhodes had once loved.

"She's wanted to do this Doctors Without Borders-type program for years and got accepted. Billy wouldn't want her to go by herself, but Am didn't want to go, so he asked if he could stay with me." He glanced at me. "I'd missed so much of his life because of my career. How could I tell him no?"

"You couldn't." So not only was his ex more than likely stunning, but she was smart too. No surprise there.

"Right," he agreed easily. "I didn't want to be gone if he needed me. I was up for reenlistment and decided to retire instead," he explained. "I know I'm gone a lot, but it's less than it could have been."

"You can't stay at home with him all day with any job." I tried to make him feel better. "And you'd probably drive him nuts if you were hovering around constantly."

He made a soft sound.

"I'm sorry you miss it though."

"It was my entire life for more than twenty years. It'll get better with time," he tried to say. "If I was going to be some-where, I'm glad he's here. It's the best place to grow up in."

"You wouldn't go back after he starts college? If he goes?"

"No, I want him to know I'm here for him. Not out in the middle of the ocean or thousands of miles away."

Something tugged at me then. How much he was trying. How deeply he had to love his child to give up on something he loved and missed so much.

I touched his forearm with the back of my other hand, just a quick brush against the soft, dark hairs. "He's lucky you love him so much."

Rhodes didn't say anything though, but I felt his body loosen a bit as he worked on my palm quietly, taping me up.

"He's really lucky to have his mom and other dad too."

"He is," he agreed, almost thoughtfully.

When he finished with me and was putting all of his things back into his bag, his hip right against my knee, I went for it. I leaned forward, put my arms around him loosely, and hugged him. "Thanks, Rhodes. I really appreciate it." Just as quickly, I let go of him.

His cheeks were flushed, and all he got out in a quiet voice was "You're welcome." He took a step back then and met my eyes. The lines on his forehead were in full effect. If I didn't know him better, I'd think he was scowling. "Come on. I'll follow you home."

I DIDN'T SULK ALL the way home, but I maybe pouted a quarter of the distance there.

My hands still stung. My knees—the insides as well as the outsides—felt battered too, and I'd accidentally hit my elbow against the center console and cursed half the members of the Jones family to hell... because there was no one else really that I had any beef with.

I didn't even bother putting my shoes fully back on either. I'd just slipped them on enough to hobble to my car and get in. Rhodes had closed the door after me, knocking once on the top while I'd kicked them off and set them in the passenger seat.

I stopped once to pee at a gas station, with Rhodes pulling in too and waiting in his truck until I got back.

Frustration pulsed deep inside of my chest, but I tried not to focus on it too much. I'd tried to do the hike. And failed. But at least I'd tried.

Okay, that was a lie. I hated failing more than anything. All right, just about more than anything.

So when I spotted the turnoff for the driveway to the property, I sighed in relief. There was a semi-familiar hatchback parked in front of the main house that I vaguely remembered belonged to Johnny. I hadn't seen him again since our failed date. Rhodes went for his usual spot, and so did I. Leaving everything in my car that I absolutely didn't need, which was all of my stuff minus my cell phone and boots that I casually slipped on, I got out to see my landlord already shutting his truck door, attention on the ground as I closed mine.

"Rhodes," I called out.

"Want to come in for some pizza?"

He was inviting me over? *Really? Again?*

My heart skipped a beat. "Sure. If you don't mind."

"I got an icepack you can put on your shoulder," he called out.

He watched me as I staggered over, muttering, "Fuck," to myself because every step hurt.

"Are you sure you're not going to get in trouble for leaving work early?" I asked as we went up the deck stairs.

He opened the door and gestured me to follow. "No, but if anybody asks, I did help an injured hiker out."

"Tell them I was very injured. Because I am. I had to drive back with my wrists. If I could give you a review, it would be ten stars easy."

He stopped in the middle of closing the door and looked at me. "Why didn't you say something when we were at the gas station? You could've left your car there."

"Because I didn't think about it." I shrugged. "And because I didn't want to be more of a baby. You already saw me cry enough."

The lines across his forehead crinkled.

"Thank you for making me feel better." I paused. "And for helping me. And following me back."

That got him to start moving again, but I kept on yapping.

"You know, you keep on being nice to me, and I'm going to think you like me."

That big body stopped right where he was and one gray eye was on me over his shoulder as he asked in that rough, serious voice, "Who says I don't like you?"

Excuse me?

Did he just say...?

But just as quickly as he stopped, he started moving again, leaving me there. Processing. I snapped out of it.

I hadn't realized until then that the television was on, and I heard Rhodes say, "Is the pizza ready?" It wasn't until I was in the living room too that I spotted Amos's head over the back of the couch.

"Hey, mini John Mayer," I called out, hoping I didn't sound weird and winded from what Rhodes had said. Or was it more like what he'd implied? I'd have to think about it later.

That tiny little pleased expression he tried his best to hide crossed his features as he said, "Hi, Ora." Then he frowned. "Were you crying?"

He could tell too? "Earlier," I told him, making my way over and holding out a loose fist since it was the only thing that wasn't injured.

He fist-bumped me back but must have seen the bandages on my palms because his head jerked a little. "What happened?"

I showed him my hands, elbows, and lifted up the knee with the torn pant leg. "Almost fell off the ridge. Living my best life."

There was a snicker from the kitchen area that I refused to take too seriously.

The teenager didn't look amused or impressed.

"I know, right?" I joked weakly.

"What happened?" another voice asked. It was Johnny coming from the hall, wiping his hands on starched khaki pants. He stopped walking when he spotted me. The good-looking man flat-out grinned. "Oh, hi."

"Hi, Johnny."

"She's eating with us," Rhodes called out from where he was in the kitchen, rooting around in the freezer.

Johnny grinned, flashing bright white teeth that reminded me of why we had gone on a date in the first place, and then started moving again. He held out his hand, and I showed him my palm briefly before flipping it back into a half-assed fist. He bumped it.

"You fall?"

"Yeah."

"You didn't make it to the lake then, Ora?" Amos asked.

"No. It happened right at that sketchy ridge of death crossing, and I had to turn around." I told him the truth. "I'm not in good enough shape yet to do it in a day, apparently. I threw up twice on the way up."

The kid made a disgusted face that made me laugh.

"I'll brush my teeth later, don't worry."

That disgusted expression went exactly nowhere, and I was pretty sure he leaned away from me. We had come so far. I loved it.

"Are you okay?" Johnny asked.

"I'll live."

A blue ice pack was shoved into my face, and I tilted my head back to find Rhodes holding it, the cleft in his chin looking extra adorable right then. "Put this on your shoulder for ten minutes."

I took it and smiled at him. "Thank you."

I was pretty sure he muttered, "You're welcome," under his breath.

Amos moved the pillow beside him, giving me a pointed look, and I took the spot, setting the ice pack between my collarbone and shoulder with a wince at how cold it was. Johnny took one of the two recliners.

"Pizza should be ready in about ten," he said to who I figured was Rhodes who didn't verbally respond. From the sound of it, he was doing something in the kitchen. "What hike did you try and do?"

I told him the name.

Johnny's smile was flashy. "I haven't done that one."

"I thought you said you don't really like hiking."

"I don't." Was he trying to flirt again?

"Hold that ice pack closer on your back."

I peeked over my shoulder to find the man who'd spoken in the kitchen, putting up dishes from the dishwasher. I watched his pants stretch across his thighs and butt as he bent over.

Suddenly my hands didn't hurt so bad.

"Am, don't forget it's your dad's birthday tomorrow.

Make sure to call him so he doesn't cry," Johnny said, drawing my attention back to them.

"It's Rhodes's birthday?" I asked.

"No, Billy's," Johnny answered.

"Oh, your stepdad?"

Amos frowned this face that reminded me exactly of Rhodes. "No, he's my real dad too." I tried not to make a face, but it must have been obvious I had no idea what he was talking about when Am said, "I have two dads."

I pursed my lips together and kept on trying to think about it. "But one's not a step?"

He nodded.

"Okay." This was none of my business. I knew it. I didn't need to ask for clarification. But I wanted to. "And you're his uncle on his... mom's side?" I asked Johnny.

"Yes."

Had they been... in a polyamorous relationship? An open relationship? So they didn't know who the birth father was? Johnny had been fine with his best friend being with his sister?

"Billy's our other best friend," Rhodes spoke up from the kitchen. "We've all known each other since we were kids."

Both of his friends had been with his sister? That made no sense. I glanced at Am and Johnny, but neither one of them had an expression that gave me any clues about how this worked out. "So... you were all... together?"

Amos choked, and Johnny busted a gut, but it was Rhodes again who spoke up. "Neither one of you is helping. Billy and Sofie, Am's mom, wanted to have kids, but Billy had... trauma—"

"He couldn't have kids," Am finally supplied. "So he asked Dad. Rhodes. Dad Rhodes. Instead of them using a donor."

Things finally started clicking.

"Dad Rhodes said yeah, but he wanted to be a dad too and

didn't want to just... donate. Everybody said okay. Now I'm here. Make sense?" Am asked casually.

I nodded. I hadn't seen *that* coming.

And suddenly, my little heart swelled. Rhodes's best friend and his wife wanted to have a child but couldn't, and he'd agreed, but insisted on being a part of the baby's life. He'd wanted to be a dad too. Did he think he'd never have kids on his own? With someone else?

It was... it was beautiful.

And my period must have been really close because my eyes filled up with tears and I said, "That's one of the nicest things I've ever heard."

Two horrified faces looked at me, but it was Rhodes who spoke up sounding the same way. "Are you crying again?"

How could he tell? "Maybe." I sniffled and turned my attention to Amos who looked like he wasn't sure whether to comfort me or move away. "That's the kind of love you have to write about."

That got him to give me the same skeptical face he'd given me when I'd initially brought up him writing a song about his mom. "You don't think it's weird?"

"Are you kidding me? No. What could be weird about it? You had two dads who wanted you but couldn't have you. You have three people who love you to death, not including your uncle and who knows who else. The rest of us are missing out."

"Dad's last girlfriend thought it was weird."

His last girlfriend? So he did date. I kept my face even.

But it was Rhodes who grumbled, "Am, give me a break. That was ten years ago. I didn't know how religious she was, how she didn't even believe in divorce." I heard the sound of dishes moving around. "I broke up with her right after that. I said I was sorry."

Amos rolled his eyes. "It was *eight* years ago. And she was annoying too."

I pinched my lips together, sucking this interaction and information up.

"You haven't met any other women I've seen since, Am."

"Yeah, because Mom says you need to dye your hair to get a girlfriend, and you won't."

"You're talking a whole lot of shit considering you might turn out like me and start finding some grays when you're in your twenties, man," Rhodes responded, sounding pretty incredulous.

Amos snorted.

And before I could tell myself not to butt in, I did. "I don't know about that, Am. I like all the silver in your dad's hair. It's really nice." Which I did. Even though I shouldn't have said it, so I backtracked to cover my steps by throwing out. "And I don't know about anybody else, but I think it's beautiful what your parents did. There's nothing ugly about selflessness and love."

He took my bait even though he still didn't believe me. "Where's your dad?" the teenager suddenly asked, trying to change the subject, I guess. "You never talk about him."

He got me. "I see him every few years. We talk every few months. He lives in Puerto Rico. He and my mom weren't together for long, and he wasn't ready to settle down when they had me. They barely knew each other actually. He loves me, I think, but not like your dads love you."

Amos still scrunched up his nose. "Why didn't you go live with him after your mom…?"

"He's not on my birth certificate, and I was already with my uncle and aunt when he found out what had happened. It was better for me to stay with them."

"That's messed up."

"I've had so many other sad things happen, that it isn't even in the top ten, Am," I told him with a shrug.

And I knew I'd made it awkward when imaginary crickets chirped afterward.

So I was beyond surprised when a hand reached over and patted my forearm.

It was Amos.

I smiled at him and happened to glance over into the kitchen to see another pair of eyes looking in our direction.

The faintest smile was on Rhodes's face.

$\mathcal{I}$ knew that Jackie had something on her mind when I'd caught her—for the third time—peeking at me and then immediately looking away when she realized she'd been caught.

We still hadn't talked about the Kaden situation. We just kept on pretending like everything was the same, which it technically should be. She had already known from the beginning.

Now that I'd had time to think about it, I had a feeling that she hadn't said anything to anyone because then Clara would find out that she'd snooped through her account. And I wasn't willing to throw her under the bus and get her in trouble either. It really wasn't that big of a deal to me.

So I was a little surprised when she eventually wandered over and asked slowly and very sweetly, "Aurora?"

"What's going on?" I asked as I flipped through one of the fishing magazines that we sold in the store. There was an article about rainbow trout that I wanted to check out. The more I learned about them, the more I realized fish were pretty interesting, honestly.

"Amos's birthday is coming up."

What? "Really? When?"

"On Wednesday."

"How old is he turning? Sixteen?"

"Yeah... and I was wondering...."

I looked at her and smiled, hopefully encouraging her.

She smiled back. "Could I use your oven to make him a birthday cake? I want to surprise him. He says he doesn't like or want one, but it's his first one without his mom, and I don't want him to be sad. Or get mad at me. And I'd order one from the bakery but they're expensive," she shot off, wringing her hands. "I thought I could make it the day before and then give it to him after I get there, so he's not expecting it."

I didn't even have to think about it. "Sure, Jackie. That sounds nice." I thought about offering to buy him a cake, but she seemed kind of excited to make it and I didn't want to ruin it.

"Yeah?"

"Yeah," I agreed. "Come over Tuesday. I'll put it in the fridge until you're ready to get it."

She squealed. "Yes! Thanks, Aurora!"

"You're welcome."

She smiled briefly before glancing away.

I figured I was going to have to get this over with once and for all. Clara was in the back. "You know we're good, right?"

Her eyes drifted back over, her smile staying small and tight too.

I touched her arm. "It's okay that you know. It used to be a secret, but it's not anymore. I just don't like telling people unless I have to. I'm not mad at all. We're fine, Jackie. Okay?"

She nodded quickly, then hesitated before asking, "Are you going to tell Amos?"

"I will one day, but I'd like to be the one to tell him. But if you do accidentally, or if you don't feel comfortable keeping it a secret, I understand that too."

She seemed to think about it. "No, it's your business. I'm just sorry I didn't tell you."

"It's okay."

It looked like she had something on her mind still, so I waited.

I knew I was right. "Can I ask you something?"

I nodded.

She seemed shy all of a sudden. "Did you really write his songs for him?" she whispered.

And that wasn't what I'd thought she would pull out. I thought maybe she'd ask if he was cute in person or why we'd broken up or anything else. Not... that.

But I told her the truth. "Most of them. Not the last two albums." I wasn't taking credit for those hot messes.

Her eyes went wide. "But those you wrote were his best albums!"

I shrugged but inside... well, it was nice.

"I wondered what happened with the last two, but now it makes *so much* sense," she claimed. "They sucked."

Maybe I cared less and less every day about him and his career and his mom. I hadn't even thought about them in weeks. But...

I still got a real kick out of it.

Suckers.

JACKIE STUCK TO HER PLAN. Since school had just gotten back in session, she walked over to the shop afterward and rode home with me, so that we wouldn't alert Amos that she was there. I snuck her in and out of the house. And we baked the two layers of cakes on pans she'd brought over from Clara's, let them sit out and cool for an hour while she helped me work on a new puzzle. Then we'd decorated the cake to look like a massive Oreo with thick vanilla frosting between the layers and sprinkled cookie crumbs over it.

It looked *amazing.*

Jackie took about a thousand pictures of it.

And when the time came, she asked me quietly if I could carry it down the stairs for her the next day, and I agreed.

The next evening, I stood at the corner of the building and peeked as she walked over to the main house so slowly balancing that cake, you'd figure she was carrying something priceless. I only went back inside when Rhodes opened the door for her, smiling to myself. Hoping Amos loved it because Jackie had made it with so much effort and excitement.

He was a good kid. I was sure he would.

Speaking of...

We'd seen each other a few days ago, and he hadn't said a word about his birthday coming up, but I'd stopped and got him a card anyway. I'd sneak it to him the next time we talked.

I was just beginning to sign it when someone knocked.

"Come in!" I hollered, figuring it was Jackie.

But the sound of heavier than normal footsteps had me freezing, and when I heard them on the landing, I turned around to find Rhodes there. Not Jackie or Amos.

We *had* seen each other since the day he'd found me at the trail. In passing. I'd waved at him from upstairs, he'd come in the other day while Amos and I had been in the garage and he'd checked out my elbows and hands, then sat through another half hour of his child singing. Very, very shyly but singing *in front of us*, which was a miracle in itself. I guessed he had been serious about the talent show he'd brought up around Yuki. Things had been... good.

And I had tried not to be confused over the little comments he'd dropped along the way.

Specifically him calling me the b-word.

And saying that thing about *"who said I don't like you?"*

Now, he was standing there mere feet away from me in jeans, another T-shirt, and black slippers. But it was his wide eyes that interested me the most. "What the hell happened in here?" he asked, eyeing the clothes I had thrown all over the place and the shoes I had kicked off at opposite ends of the room. I was pretty sure he was standing about a foot away from a pair of panties too, to top it off.

I hadn't cleaned up in... a while.

I grimaced when his gaze met mine. "The wind blew everything around?" I offered.

Rhodes blinked. The edges of his mouth tightened for a second before they were back to normal and he glanced up at the ceiling then looked back at me and said, in that dry, bossy voice, "Come on."

"Where?"

"To the house," he answered calmly, watching me with those intense gray eyes.

"Why?"

His eyebrows went up. "Do you always ask this many questions when someone's trying to invite you somewhere?"

I thought about it and smiled. "No."

The man tipped his head to the side, and his full mouth went flat. Was he trying to hide a smile behind that? His hands went to his hips. "Come to the house to get some pizza and cake, Buddy."

I hesitated for a second. "Are you sure?"

His tightened mouth melted away, and he just looked at

me. For a second. For two. Then he murmured, almost softly, "Yes, Aurora. I'm sure."

I smiled. Maybe I should've asked if he was *really* sure, but I didn't want him to take back the offer. So I held up a finger and said, "One minute. I was actually just in the middle of signing his birthday card."

Rhodes dipped that cute, cleft chin before shifting his attention back to the disaster that was the garage apartment. It wasn't *that* bad, but I'd been in his house enough to know our interpretations of "clean" were pretty different. I didn't have a sink full of dishes or overflowing trash cans, but my clothes had slowly stopped finding their way to my suitcase at some point....

But I focused back on the card and scribbled my friend a little message.

HAPPY BIRTHDAY, AMOS!

I'm so happy we're friends. Your talent is only overshadowed by your good heart.

Hugs,

Ora

P.S. Diarrhea

Might as well take it back to the moment that started it all, or at least the second moment.

I cackled a little before stuffing bills between the folded card. Then I glanced back at my landlord, who hadn't moved an inch, and said, "I'm ready. Thank you for inviting me."

He just looked at me as we walked side by side toward his house.

"Did you have a good day today?" I asked him, taking a peek at his silhouette.

His attention was forward, but his eyebrows were knitted together like he was worried about something. "No." He let out a heavy sigh before shaking his head. "There was an accident with a little girl and her dad while I was on my way to the office."

"Was it really bad?"

Rhodes nodded, his attention forward, eyes glassy. "They had to LifeFlight both of them to Denver."

"That's terrible. I'm sorry," I said, lightly touching his elbow.

His throat bobbed, and I had a feeling he hadn't even registered my touch.

"That's so rough. I hope they're okay. I hope you're okay too. I'm sure that's hard to witness."

He wrung his hands almost subconsciously, picturing or thinking about who knows what, before finally shaking his head and saying in a troubled voice that pierced at my heart, telling me exactly how deeply the accident had gotten under his skin, "It's hard not to picture it being Am."

"I'm sure."

He finally glanced at me, and that glassy gaze was still there, so were the lines on his forehead. "It probably doesn't help that it's his birthday."

I just nodded, unsure of what to say to reassure or comfort him. So I waited a second until I went with the first thing that came to mind. "When is your birthday?"

If he was surprised by my question, his face didn't register it. "March."

"March what?"

"Fourth."

"How old are you turning?"

"Forty-three."

Forty-three. I raised my eyebrows. Then processed the number again.

If it weren't for all the silver in his hair, he might look a lot younger. Then again, he looked exactly like the hottest forty-two-year-old I'd ever seen, and that was not a bad thing. Not by far.

"What are you?" he asked out of nowhere. "Twenty-six?"

I grinned at the same time he happened to glance down. "Thirty-three."

That amazing silver head jerked. "No, you're not."

I winked. "Promise I am. Your kid has a copy of my driver's license."

Those gray eyes roamed my face for a moment before flicking even lower. The lines on his forehead were back. "You're thirty-three?" he asked in what sounded like total disbelief.

"Thirty-four in May," I confirmed.

He looked at me again, and I was pretty certain his gaze hung on my chest for a second longer than before. A very long extra second. Huh.

We were both quiet as we went up the deck and into the house. Johnny was standing in the kitchen, holding a can of beer with his eyes glued to the TV. On the couch, Amos and Jackie were sitting together, watching TV too. Some action movie was playing. There were three boxes of pizza sitting on the kitchen island.

And all three heads swiveled to look at me—and Rhodes by default—the second we stopped between the kitchen and the living room.

"Hi, birthday boy," I called out, a little more shyly than I would've expected. "Hi, Jackie. Hi, Johnny."

"Hi, Ora," the teenager called out as Jackie hopped off the couch and came over to hug me, Johnny's greeting ringing out too.

We were good together, but she had never really hugged me before, probably because of the awkwardness. Secrets and lies could do that to people.

Out of the corner of my eye, I noticed Amos got to his

feet and headed over too, looking like he wasn't totally onboard with the idea but resigned. I was winning this kid over slowly but surely. Just as Jackie pulled away, he gave me one of those little half smiles that I could only guess he'd learned from his dad and said, "Thanks for helping with the cake."

"You're welcome," I told him. "Want a birthday hug?"

He hunched his shoulders, and I stepped forward and wrapped my arms around him, feeling his thin ones go up too, patting me on the back gently and awkwardly.

He was too precious.

When he stepped back, I thrust the card at him. "This was the best I could do on short notice, but happy birthday."

He didn't even really look at the card before taking it after glancing at Jackie. He opened it, his gaze moved across the inside of it, and his gray eyes flicked up to me. Then he surprised the shit out of me.

He smiled.

And I knew in that moment that the second he hit his next growth spurt, this kid was going to have the same effect his father did on humanity.

Someone was going to need to protect him from the sexual vultures.

Then again, if he developed his dad's scowl, maybe not.

He was just a sweet kid for now.

And that smile stayed on his face as he pulled out the wad of fives and ones. Then he said, "Hold on," went to his room and came back empty-handed. His lips were pinched, but his words were clear, "Thanks, Aurora."

"You're welcome."

"What? I don't get to see it?" his uncle asked.

"No," Amos replied.

I snickered and another glance at Rhodes showed me his mouth was twisting.

"Why?" the uncle asked.

"Because it's mine."

"Can I see it?" Jackie asked, bouncing on her tiptoes.

"Later."

Johnny snickered. "Rude."

"Now that Ora's here, can we eat?" the birthday boy asked.

Apparently, the answer was yes. There was a stack of plates on the counter waiting already. I took one and moved, going to stand next to Johnny who looked down at me and smiled.

"Hey," he greeted.

"Hey," I answered. "How are you?"

"Great, you?"

"Pretty great too. Did you go out with that waitress after all?"

He chuckled. "No. She never called me back."

"Did you check out someone else's butt on your date or...?"

He started laughing.

"If you two are done flirting, what kind of pizza do you want, Buddy?" Rhodes's voice came sharp.

We were flirting? Was he serious? I was just joking. Johnny made his eyes go wide, and I lifted my shoulders, helplessly. *Okay.*

And it wouldn't hit me until much later that no one else had reacted to the "Buddy." Only me.

Grabbing two slices of supreme pizza, I sprinkled some parmesan on it before heading to the table where the kids were. I sat next to Jackie, and then Johnny sat on my other side with Rhodes taking a seat beside his son.

Where the extra chairs had come from, I didn't know.

Jackie was in the middle of asking Amos if his grandpa was coming over this weekend or next, and the next thing I knew, the birthday boy focused on me and asked, "Are you doing any more hikes before it snows?"

I had just stuck a huge slice of pizza into my mouth and had to chew through it fast before I got out, "Yeah, but I need to start checking the weather."

"What are your options?" that was Rhodes who asked.

I told them the names of the two easy trails that were less than two miles roundtrip. Honestly, I was still a little traumatized. I had scars on my palms and knees, damn it. "Why? You want to go again? I was probably going to go on Saturday. Clara's closing the shop at noon to get the carpets cleaned."

"I want to go," Jackie piped up.

Three sets of heads turned to look at her.

She frowned. "What?"

"You get winded walking to the garage apartment," Amos muttered.

"No, I don't."

"We went to do Piedra River, and you stopped half a mile in and refused to hike any more," he kept going.

"Yeah, so?"

"One of the hikes is one mile round trip and the other is two," Rhodes explained to her, carefully but firmly.

The girl grimaced, and I tried my best to bite back a smile. "I'll let you know when I do a shorter one. If I do a shorter one. I guess if I'm still here next year."

I was smiling when I made eye contact with Rhodes.

His jaw was tight. And out of the corner of my eye, I saw Amos was making a weird face. Why were they looking at me like that?

Before I could think about it too much, Jackie started talking about how unfair they were being because she used to hike all the time, and I focused on that for a while, at least until the urge to pee came at my bladder like a bomb.

"I'll be right back, I need to use the bathroom," I told them, pushing the chair back.

I headed straight for the half-bathroom I remembered seeing on my other visits over. I peed and started washing my hands, and it was when I reached for a towel that I happened to look down and saw something small and brown run across the floorboard. I froze.

Leaning over just a little, I peeked around the toilet and saw it again.

Two little eyes.

One bare tail.

About two inches long.

It darted off, disappearing around the trash can.

I wasn't proud of myself... but I screamed. Not loud, but it was still a scream.

And then I got the hell out of there.

Honestly, I wasn't sure I'd ever moved so fast going down the hall, thankful I'd seen him *after* I'd pulled my pants on and zipped them up, going as far away from the bathroom as possible.

Which ended up being the kitchen.

Rhodes was standing by the island, tearing paper towels off when he noticed me coming. A frown came over his face. "What's—"

"There's a mouse in the bathroom!" I squeaked and went past him, pretty much leaping onto the stool beside the counter, then jumping from there to the back of the couch with a frantic look toward the floor to make sure I hadn't been followed.

Out of the corner of my eye, I noticed Amos stood up so fast the chair he was in fell backward, and the next thing I knew, he'd leaped onto the couch and ended up beside me, his butt propped up on the back of it, legs dangling inches off the floor in the air. Johnny and Jackie either didn't care or were so stunned by Amos and me, that they hadn't moved a single inch from the table.

"A rat?" Rhodes asked from the exact same spot he'd been in.

I shook my head at him, exhaling hard to try and bring my heart rate down. "No, a mouse."

His eyebrows crept up about a half-inch, but I noticed it. "You're screaming because of a mouse?" Did he have to ask so slowly?

I swallowed. "Yes!"

He blinked. Beside me, Amos suddenly snorted deep in his throat like he hadn't knocked his chair over. Then I noticed that Rhodes's chest was shaking.

"What?" I asked, eyeing the floor again.

His chest was shaking even more, and he barely managed to wheeze out, both eyes squeezing closed, "I… I didn't know you were into parkour."

Amos snorted again, lowering his legs and planting his feet.

"You backflipped onto the table…," Rhodes choked out.

He was wheezing. The son of a bitch was wheezing.

"No, I did not!" I argued, starting to feel just a little bit… foolish. I *hadn't*. I didn't know how to backflip.

"You jumped from the island to the couch," Rhodes kept going, raising a fist to hold it right in front of his nose.

He could barely talk.

"Your face… Ora, it was so white," Am started, bottom lip starting to tremble.

I pressed my lips together and stared at my favorite traitor. "My soul left my body for a second, Am. And you didn't exactly walk over here either, okay."

Rhodes, who decided that *this* was what he was going to find hilarious, barely choked out, "You looked like you saw a ghost."

Amos burst out laughing.

Then Rhodes burst out laughing.

One quick glance confirmed that Johnny was chuckling too, Jackie was the only one giving me a smile. I was glad someone had a heart.

They were cracking up, totally and completely cracking up.

"You know, I hope it crawls into one of your mouths for being so mean to me," I muttered, joking. Mostly.

Rhodes grinned so wide, he came over and slapped his son on the back while they both kept laughing.

At me.

But together.

And maybe I wasn't going to be able to sleep tonight now, worried there might be a mouse next door, but it would be worth it.

CHAPTER 18

I was sitting at the table reading when I heard the familiar crunch of tires on the driveway.

I perked up.

Amos had mentioned last night while we'd discussed how many rhyming words were too many rhyming words in a song, that his grandfather, Rhodes's dad, was coming over to spend the weekend. I'd forgotten all about Jackie bringing it up at his birthday dinner. The brand-new sixteen-year-old had claimed he was thinking about acting sick so he could have an excuse to hide in his room.

The thing was, I hadn't realized until then that no one really brought up Rhodes's parents. Amos mentioned his other four grandparents in bits and pieces from time to time, but that was it. I doubted that my own nephews ever talked about me, so I tried not to think it was too strange... but it was strange.

Or at least I had a feeling there was something there, especially after Am told me that Rhodes's dad lived in Durango, which was only about an hour away. I'd been with them for months now. Shouldn't he have come over already?

Rhodes and Am both rarely left the house together. Maybe part of it was because he was still grounded, but the strictest part of it was over, I was pretty sure. But it was still off to me.

I stayed where I was, telling myself not to be nosey and stand by the window.

But if I could hear them from all the way over here, that was different. I wasn't *really* eavesdropping if they just happened to talk so loud I could overhear their conversation, right?

So that's how I reasoned out what I did. I kept my gaze on the words of the book in front of me. But also kept an ear out. I had already spent enough time looking out my window at my brand-new car. I'd gone and traded it in after work the day before. The SUV was bigger than I'd planned on getting, but it had been love at first sight. Amos and Rhodes had both checked her out yesterday and approved of my purchase. Winter was coming, and all signs were pointing toward me being here for it.

I was thinking about that when I was pretty sure I heard a door being shut, followed by Amos's mutter of, "Why does he have to stay here?"

"It's only for the weekend," his dad replied, not exactly sounding like he thought two days was that short of time either but trying to convince himself.

"All he's gonna do is complain and bring up everything you've done wrong, Dad, like he always does."

That made me frown.

"He doesn't even really like us. He could come over for the day."

"We don't take his words to heart, man. In one ear, out the other," Rhodes said.

I perked up at that and let my eyes stray toward the window. What the hell was up Granddaddy Rhodes's ass? For Rhodes to tell Am not to let his words bother him....

"It doesn't make sense why he gives you so much shit for not getting married when he literally married someone that used to attack him?"

"That's enough, Am. We know how he is, and luckily, he only comes over a couple times a year—"

"Even though we live an hour away?"

The kid had a point there.

"I know, Am," Rhodes pacified gently. "He comes from a different time. And I told you before, he's got a lot of regrets, and it took me a long time to accept that the way he is, is his own way of caring."

The kid grunted. "Can we invite Ora over? To distract him?"

I snorted and hoped like hell they couldn't hear me.

"No, we're not doing that to her." There was a pause, and I think he might have snickered. "It would've been a good idea though. Then it wouldn't be awkward silence… and it would be pretty funny to see his face."

"Yeah, I bet she'd get him to tell her why it took him so long to divorce your mom."

The car door slammed shut, and a split second later, a voice I didn't recognize said, "I have a company who can come re-gravel the driveway for you, Tobias. I got a headache just from doing this stretch."

I blinked.

"The driveway is fine, sir," Rhodes replied in a voice I hadn't heard from him in months. His Navy Voice, as Amos called it once when we'd brought up that first day we'd met and how pissed off Rhodes had been.

And who the hell called their dad "sir"?

"Welcome," Rhodes kept going.

Welcome?

I had to slap my hand over my mouth to keep from laughing; I could only imagine what Amos's face must look like. I wondered if he was turning red.

I was pretty sure I heard feet on the driveway. "Amos," the unfamiliar voice said, "how is your mother? And Billy?"

"Fine."

"You haven't managed to gain any weight? Still not playing any sports?"

The silence was *piercing*. Overwhelming. I was pretty sure my ears were ringing.

"He's perfect the way he is," Rhodes spoke up in that same crisp, careful Navy Voice that reeked of whatever careful control he'd built up over the twenty years he spent in the military.

My sixth sense told me this wasn't going to go well.

Like... really not going to go well.

Mostly because I was going to go beat the shit out of a grandfather for talking about my Amos like that. My sweet, shy friend had to be dying inside now. I knew he was self-conscious about his slim build, and here this fucker went and—

"Maybe he would be if you'd enrolled him in some when he was younger," the old man replied. "He could use a cheese-burger or two."

I growled and slowly closed my book.

"He was enrolled in the things that interested him," Rhodes replied, his voice sounding grittier and grittier with each syllable. "He eats more than enough."

The mean "Hmph" had me setting it down.

My God, this man reminded me... of Mrs. Jones.

"A little muscle would be nice if he ever wants to get a girlfriend. You don't want to be single your entire life like your father, do you?" the old asshole asked.

I shot to my feet so fast, I was surprised I didn't knock the table over.

These two were going to set the house on fire if I didn't do something. I wasn't sure I'd ever witnessed a conversation go downhill that fast, and I'd heard some things.

Amos and Rhodes were rookies.

Luckily for them, I had a doctorate in passive-aggressive and straight-up aggressive family figures. And this man wasn't the woman who I'd thought of as my mother-in-law. I knew I didn't have to spend the rest of my life kissing this man's ass to be happy.

I owed them. I could do this.

I took the stairs as fast as I could and had just strode outside when I heard Rhodes's strained, strained voice, spitting out, "—can look however he wants to look, *sir*."

Yep, the house was going to get burned down.

And my garage apartment would go up with it.

I would tell myself later on I was doing it for me just as much as I was doing it for them, and that's why I shouted, sounding like an out of breath maniac from taking the stairs so fast, "Rhodes, can you help me—oh, sorry. Hi."

Amos's eyes were wide, and I could tell he was trying to process what I was doing while being so surprised.

Standing beside a Mercedes G-Wagen, the older Mr. Rhodes was shorter than his son, but the resemblance was there in different ways. The same cleft chin. The shape of his cheeks. The beefy build. Especially the shape of that severe mouth.

And he was staring at me.

I had to use my powers for good.

Focusing on Rhodes, I saw the pensive expression on his face… the slight confusion there. The lines were there across his forehead. His mouth was pressed flat, but I doubted it was from me.

I was still looking at Rhodes when he asked, "What do you need, angel?"

"Nothing that can't wait, sorry," I said, hoping I actually sounded apologetic and not full of shit and winging everything. He'd called me the wrong name again, but it was fine. "Is this your dad?" I asked, trying to sound sweet so he wouldn't get the wrong idea.

"Yes. This is Randall. Dad, this is Aurora... our friend," Rhodes said softly.

His *friend*?

That might be more epic than being his girlfriend, honestly. Screw it, I'd even go as far as to say this might be more of an honor than being someone's wife. *What!*

A big, effortless smile took over my mouth and, honestly, probably my entire face too as I decided right then that I hadn't made a mistake coming over.

I was about to smooth shit over as much as possible for them. As long as Rhodes didn't give me a dirty look that said beat it. I recognized that face on him.

"Nice to meet you, Randall," I said, coming to a stop in front of the man who was standing at the bottom of the deck.

Then I went for it, laying it on real thick because killing people with kindness was so satisfying. I threw my arms around his shoulders and hugged him.

I was pretty positive I heard Amos choke, but I wasn't sure.

Randall Rhodes stiffened under my arms, and I squeezed him tighter before taking a step back and thrusting my hand out.

The older man's eyes flicked toward his son's in surprise or maybe even disgruntlement for being touched by a stranger before he slowly extended his own hand and took mine. His wasn't too firm or too soft, but I'd learned not to be the weaker party unless it was in my best interest, so I gave him a solid shake back.

"Nice to meet you," I told him brightly.

The older man gazed at me like he didn't know what to think before flicking his gaze back to Rhodes. "You didn't tell me you were seeing someone."

"We're not together," I corrected him, imagining for a second a world in which Rhodes wouldn't kill me if I pretended to be his girlfriend.

Because I would.

But he would kill me, I was pretty sure, so we were going to stick to the truth. "But I wish, you know what I mean, Mr. Randall?" I snickered playfully.

The older man blinked, and I didn't miss the long, inspection-like look he gave me. Not an old perv, but curious. Not dead. Maybe a little confused on top of everything.

Meeting Amos's gaze, he gave me this bug-eyed expression that told me he might be having the time of his life.

"I apologize," Randall Rhodes said, sounding cryptic and still confused. "My son doesn't tell me anything."

Shots fired.

I smiled about as sweetly at him as possible. "You're both so busy, you don't call each other much period, I'm sure. It happens." He wasn't going to put all the blame on his son.

The very good-looking older man's face went carefully blank. Or maybe it was cautious.

Yeah, pal. I know your game.

"Let me put your bag in the house, and then we can leave for dinner," Rhodes kept going, before angling his body toward me.

They were going to a dinner I hadn't been invited to. I could read a cue. "In that case, it was nice meeting you, Mr. Randall. I will—"

Rhodes's hand landed on my shoulder, the side of his pinky landing on my bare collarbone just a little bit. "Come with us."

I jerked my head up to meet his gray eyes. He had his

serious face on, and I was pretty sure he'd used his Navy Voice, but I hadn't been paying enough attention because I'd been distracted by his finger. "I'm sure you three want to spend some quality time together…." I trailed off, cautiously, not sure if he wanted me to go or… not?

"Come with us, Ora." It was Amos who piped up. But he wasn't the one I was worried about.

Rhodes's big hand gave my shoulder a gentle squeeze, and I was fairly certain his gaze softened, because his voice definitely did. "Come with us."

"Are you asking me or telling me?" I whispered. "Because you're whispering, but you're still using your bossy voice."

His mouth twisted, and he lowered his voice to reply, "Both?"

I grinned. I mean, okay. I wasn't at a good part in my book yet, and I hadn't eaten dinner either. "Okay then. Sure, if none of you care."

"Nope," Am muttered.

"Not at all," Mr. Randall answered, still eyeballing me speculatively.

"I'll wait out here then while you put his things up," I said.

"I'll come along. I'd like to wash my hands before we leave," Randall said with a sniff.

Rhodes gave me another squeeze before he stepped aside and headed toward the back of his father's Mercedes. In no time at all, he had pulled a suitcase out of the back, and he and his dad were heading inside the house. Amos stayed outside with me, and the second that door closed, I said, "I'm so sorry, Am. I just heard him being so rude, and you guys were trying to be polite, and I could tell your dad was about to lose his shit, and I just wanted to help."

The kid stepped forward and wrapped his arms around me, hesitated for a second, then patted me on the back awkwardly. "Thanks, Ora."

He hugged me. He'd fucking hugged me. It felt like my birthday.

I hugged him back real tight and tried not to let him see the tear in my eye so I wouldn't ruin it. "Thanks for what? Your dad is going to kill me."

I felt him laugh against me before he dropped his arms and took a big step back, his cheeks a little flushed. But he was smiling that sweet, shy smile he rarely shared. "He's not."

"I'm 50 percent sure it might happen," I claimed. "He's going to bury me somewhere no one will ever find me, and I know he could do it because I'm sure he has a bunch of spots picked out where, if it ever came down to it, he could pull it off. Why is your grandpa so mean anyway?"

Amos smiled a little. "Dad says it's because his parents were really mean to him; then he married my grandma who was just as mean and crazy, but he didn't know that until it was too late, and he's spent his whole life trying to make more and more money because he didn't have anything growing up."

That would do it. For sure. And I wanted to ask about the crazy mother/grandma, but I figured we didn't have time to get into it.

"It's okay," he tried to assure me. "You're doing Dad a favor."

I eyed him. "How?"

"Because he doesn't talk, but you do, and you'll save him from his dad."

I grimaced. "Are you sure I should come to dinner? I don't want to—"

The kid groaned and rolled his eyes.

I laughed and then rolled my eyes back at him. "If you're sure. If he tries to drive me anywhere to dump my body, I want you to at least give me a nice burial, Am. I need my purse."

"I'll go get it," he offered a second before he said, "Be right back." He stopped suddenly and said, "Thanks, Ora."

Then he took off. Running. Amos was running.

I hoped this went okay.

IF I HADN'T LIVED through the tension of the day Amos, Rhodes, and I had done the four-mile hike to see the waterfalls, I would've been in for a real shock at the level of awkwardness that dinner with the two of them and Mr. Randall reached.

But my entire relationship with Kaden—having to deal with the Antichrist—had been preparation for this. And in another lifetime, I would've considered my relationship with that woman to have been training to deal with not just Mr. Randall, but every difficult person I'd ever encounter.

No fucking wonder why Amos and Rhodes hadn't told me to leave when I'd come running over.

The complaining and criticizing started before we even got into Rhodes's Bronco with Mr. Randall sniffing and suggesting, "We can take my Mercedes to be more comfortable."

I had kept my mouth shut, but Rhodes—who I'd bet later on had heard this argument before—said, "The Bronco is fine."

It was only the beginning.

I'd watched Mr. Randall out of the corner of my eye as he got into the front seat, and I climbed into the back with Amos. Five minutes later, it started up again with him saying, "I don't think any of us would complain if you drove over the speed limit some."

Rhodes didn't even glance over. "I'm not speeding. I'm a peace officer. What would it look like if I got a ticket?"

"A peace officer?" he scoffed in this way that said he didn't think very highly of his son's occupation. "You're a game warden."

In my mind, it was time to tag myself in, so I piped up from the back, "A great game warden. One time, Amos and I were in the garage, and you would never guess what came up to us."

Silence. And that silence continued even after I slapped my hand over my mouth and made a face at Amos who glanced up at the ceiling and pressed his lips together to keep from cracking up.

"Okay, you don't need to guess. I'll tell you. We thought it was a hawk, but it was not." And then I rambled on for a good five minutes, telling him about the golden eagle and Rhodes laughing at me and how the eagle was still in rehabilitation but would hopefully get released soon.

I'd just asked about my majestic friend, and he had found out for me.

Eventually, Rhodes parallel parked off the main street and we got out, following him into the Mexican restaurant overlooking the river that I'd met Johnny at. Randall Rhodes sighed when we had to wait two whole minutes to get a table, while I asked Amos about school—careful not to bring up his music because I didn't want the old man to criticize him about it. I might be the one to bury his body somewhere if that was the case. The two men just stood there, each purposely looking around and not speaking to each other, the tension suffocating.

On the way to the table, I spotted a few customers from the shop and greeted them, Amos hanging back with me. By the time we made it, Rhodes and his dad were standing there, and I knew for a fact I didn't imagine Am pushing me toward his dad before grudgingly sliding into the seat closest to his grandpa and earning a "The lady sits first, Amos. How did Billy not teach you that?"

"My cousins would say I'm not really a lady," I tried to joke as I stopped beside Rhodes since that's where his son had aimed me. I smiled up at him, not sure if I'd done the right thing.

He pulled my chair out.

All right then. I took it.

None of them said a word as we looked at the menu. I snuck a glance at Rhodes, and he must have sensed it because his eyes flicked toward me. His mouth twisted just a little.

I took it as a sign. The more I talked, the less chances Mr. Randall had to be rude.

And that's what I did for the next hour.

I told them one story after another about something that had happened at the shop. Amos was the only one who chuckled, but I did catch Rhodes's mouth twitching a time or two. His dad, on the other hand, settled for focusing on the chips and salsa and looking at me like he wasn't totally sure what to think. I didn't think he meant for me to catch him, but his gaze bounced back and forth between his son and me way too often as well, like he wasn't sure about us.

Mr. Randall got up to "find the facilities," but I caught him actually paying the bill when I got up to go too. To avoid arguing with Rhodes? I didn't know, but I thanked him on the walk to the car, and he simply nodded.

The ride back to the house was quiet, and I felt talked out, so I didn't say anything. Amos was on his phone the whole time, and I took the opportunity, since there was cell service off the main highway, to finally check mine for the first time all evening. There were messages from Nori and my aunt waiting. I opened my friend's first.

Nori: Nailed it [picture of *arroz con gandules*]

Me: [drooling face emoji] Please come cook for me.

She texted me back immediately.

Nori: Come visit me first. Yu's still talking about how much fun she had.

That made me smile, and I opened the messages from my aunt.

Aunt Carolina: The antichrist just emailed me to ask for your phone number. She offered to pay for it!

Aunt Carolina: [picture image attachment of a screenshot of her email]

I blew it up and read it. And yes, Mrs. Jones had lost her shit. She was offering to pay my aunt for my phone number. Wow. That woman literally hadn't heard the word "no" in years. It was kind of nice to know she was desperate since I'd blocked her on Facebook too.

Me: I've never felt so honored. A whole $500! WOWEE.

Mrs. Jones spent five hundred dollars on *dinner*. *Really?* That was nothing for her anymore.

I thought about that the entire ride back. About how one person could throw someone else away and then decide they wanted them back after all. For selfish purposes. Not because she was so fond of me or thought that I could make her son happy.

How could they think that I would ever forgive and forget? This wasn't *50 First Dates*. I wouldn't forget what they'd done.

And they really thought so little of me? Of my *family*? That they would rat me out for five-hundy? For ten thousand, they totally would.

But then they'd take me to get my number changed and we'd go out to eat afterward and have a good laugh.

I stewed on that shit for way too long as Rhodes steered the SUV, which was really nicely restored now that I'd finally seen the inside of it, down the driveway. We all got out, and Am ambled toward their front door, pretty much

313

dragging his feet. Rhodes hovered by the car, and Mr. Randall headed toward his SUV, muttering about something he'd left in it.

And I just stood there before saying, "Bye, Amos. Bye, Rhodes. See you guys tomorrow. Thank you for inviting me!" I wasn't sure what their plans were, and I could only wish them the best.

Rhodes, though, turned and nailed me with his serious face, all angles and harsh bones. He was so close, and he dropped his voice so only I could hear him. "Thanks for coming with us." I could feel the heat coming off his body.

"You're welcome." I beamed at him.

"I owe you one."

I shook my head. "You don't, but if you want to give me any skiing or snowshoeing tips, I'll take them."

Those incredible gray eyes swept over my face, and it was his turn to nod. "You got it."

We both stood there watching one another, the silence between us thick and heavy.

Lowering my gaze, I noticed his fisted hands at his sides.

I forced myself a step back. "'Night. Good luck." Then I took another step. "Goodnight, Mr. Randall. Thank you again for dinner."

The older man was already at his car with the driver-side door open. He seemed to stand up straight, but didn't turn around before he replied, "You're welcome. Goodnight."

Rhodes and Am disappeared into the house just as I was halfway to the garage apartment when Mr. Randall spoke up again.

"Do they hate me?"

I stopped and found him standing between the opened door and the seat. The faint glow of the dome light illuminated him from the back, telling me he was looking in my direction. I hesitated. I hesitated big-time.

"You can tell me the truth; I can handle it," Mr. Randall went on, his voice like steel.

And still, I hesitated. Then I pressed my lips together for a second before telling him, "I don't think that they do. I didn't even know up until about a week ago that you... were around."

"They do hate me."

"If that's what you think, Mr. Randall, I don't understand why you're asking me. I told you the truth. I don't think they do, but...."

"Should I leave?" he asked suddenly.

"Look, I know very, very little about your situation with them. Like I said, I didn't know until a week ago that Rhodes —Tobias—whatever you call him, even had a dad. I've lived here since June, and I've never seen you before."

Like his son and grandson, he fell back into silence.

"Do you *want* them to hate you?" I asked.

"What do you think?" he snapped.

"That you're asking me a question, and now you're being kind of rude," I told him. "And that you were being rude to Am and to Rhodes—Tobias—and now you're trying to turn this around and seem like the victim."

"*Pardon me?*"

Oh man, it really was so much easier when I didn't have to care about my future with someone when they were being jerks. "You criticized Amos. You talked down to your son. My uncle has three sons, and they all think he's the absolute greatest. I think he's the greatest. My dad wasn't around hardly at all while I was growing up, and sometimes I wish he would have been. But he seems like a pretty decent man.

"Like I told you, I don't know what your situation is, what your background is, but I know Amos and I kind of know Rhodes. And Rhodes adores his kid, like a good father would. I know Am knows it but not the extent, because he doesn't see the way his dad looks at him, but Rhodes keeps on trying even though they're pretty much complete opposites except for having the exact glare and quietness.

"All I'm saying is, if you're worried enough about what they think of you to ask *me*, I think you care. And if you care, then maybe you should put in some positive effort. You're a grown man, you wouldn't be here if you didn't want to be, right?"

He said nothing.

He said nothing for a long, long time as we stood there looking at each other. Or at least trying to look at each other considering it was getting pretty dark outside and his dome light had finally turned off.

And when it had been so long, and he still got nothing else out, I figured—and more like hoped—he was thinking about what I'd said. But I still added, "We don't get to choose who the people we love become or are, but you do get to pick if you want to stick around. If we want them to know that too, that they're worth sticking around for. Anyway, I'll see you around, Mr. Randall. Your son and grandson are pretty awesome. 'Night."

It wasn't until I was back upstairs, that I realized what I had noticed but hadn't been paying enough attention to.

I'd never actually heard the front door close when Amos and his dad had gone inside.

Rhodes had been standing at the doorway the whole time.

CHAPTER 19

"Thank you so much. I'll be there in a little while," I said into my cell before hanging up.

Pure excitement shimmered through my veins as I started collecting my water and food for the day. I'd just finished slapping two sandwiches together when the sound of a car leaving drifted into the apartment, making me pause for a second. I wondered where they were going. Last night hadn't been the worst time I'd ever spent, but it hadn't been the best either.

Good luck to them.

I had just finished putting my things into my backpack when a loud knock came at the door followed by an "Ora!"

It was Am. "Come in!" I hollered back a split second before the door creaked open and the sound of his footsteps warned me he was coming up.

Sure enough, I'd just finished with the zipper when he huffed out, "Can I hang out here?"

I was already grinning when I looked up to find him clearing the landing, stomping over to the table. "Of course you can." I paused and thought about it. "I thought you were supposed to be doing things with your grandpa today though."

Amos blew out a breath before dropping into one of the chairs around the little table. "He left a second ago after he and Dad got into it." He leaned forward and picked up one of the pieces to a puzzle I had barely begun putting together. "Dad's all pissed off now, and I don't wanna be around him."

Ooh. What happened? I didn't ask as I picked up my backpack and put it over my shoulder. "That's sucks, Am. I'm sorry. I'm leaving, but do you want to come with me? If your dad will let you."

He was still leaning over the puzzle. "Where are you going?"

"I'm renting a UTV."

The teenager shook his head. "Nah."

I shrugged. "All right then. Finish that puzzle if you want."

Amos didn't even glance up as he nodded, and I snickered on the way out, wondering what the hell had gone down with Rhodes and his dad. I had just opened the door outside when I spotted the figure rooting through the back seat of his work truck.

Would he...?

"Hi, Rhodes!" I yelled.

The muscles in his back bunched before he stood up and leveled his gaze at me.

Yeah, Amos hadn't been joking. He was in a bad mood.

Something that had to be affection nipped at my chest, and I couldn't help but smile at him even as he scowled. Rhodes was pretty cute even while he was mad.

"Hi," he replied, not moving an inch.

"I saw your dad left," I said, approaching him.

He grunted.

What the hell had happened? "Am's in the apartment...."
He was *so grumpy* and maybe this wouldn't be a good idea,

but maybe it would. He'd pretty much hinted that he didn't *dislike* me, so…. "I was going to invite you to come with me, but I think I'm just going to tell you to come."

Those thick eyelashes dropped over his purple-gray eyes.

I smiled, then tipped my head toward my car.

"I don't think I'd be good company today," he muttered.

"That's subjective, but you should come anyway," I told him. "You don't even have to talk if you don't want to. Maybe you'll let some steam off though."

The man grunted and started shaking his head. "No, it's not a good idea."

I knew what I could handle, and him in a pissy mood was nothing. "Okay then. I'll be back this afternoon." I took a step back. "Wish me luck."

He had started turning back toward his truck when he suddenly stopped and looked at me again, suspicion bubbling beneath the grumpiness his features were formed into.

"Bye—"

"Where are you going?"

I told him the name of the location where I was renting the UTV from.

"You're going for a hike?" he asked slowly.

"Nope." I extended both my hands forward and made a driving gesture. "I rented a Razorback UTV." I lifted a hand at him before he could ask another question. "All right, see you later!"

"Do you know what you're doing?"

"Does *anyone* really know what they're doing?" I joked.

There wasn't even a second of hesitation before he tilted his head back toward the sky, let out a huff, then grumbled, "Give me a second."

I stopped and tried to keep my features even. "You want to come after all?"

He was already moving toward the house after slamming the car door closed. "Wait for me."

I couldn't help but grin as I glanced up toward the apartment to find Amos at the window. I gave him a thumbs-up. I was pretty sure he smiled.

True to his word, Rhodes was back out with his backpack and what looked like two jackets in his hand, maybe a minute or two later.

He still looked pretty pissy, but I didn't take it to heart. Maybe he'd tell me what happened that had his dad leaving early and possibly ruining his mood, but maybe he wouldn't. Hopefully though, maybe, just maybe, I could help turn his day around a little. That was my goal at least. Even if he didn't talk, that was okay.

His mouth was a flat line as he headed straight toward my passenger door, pausing right as he got there before bellowing, "I'm going with Aurora, Am. Don't leave the house. We'll be back later."

Which got him a hollered, "K!"

That boy sounded way too excited to be left home alone. I bit back a smile as I got into the car and watched as Rhodes did the same. It wasn't until we were way down the road, turning onto the main highway, that Rhodes asked, "You were going to do this by yourself?"

I kept my attention forward. "Yeah, I've been wanting to do it for a few weeks."

He muttered something under his breath as he shifted his weight around in my front seat.

Someone was really in a mood. "I would've invited Clara and Jackie, but I know they had plans with her brothers, and I asked Amos, but he said no, and I don't really have any customers from the store that I know well enough yet to invite," I explained. "I think we're getting there, but not yet."

Rhodes's "Hmph" had me biting back another smile.

Maybe he was coming because he didn't have anything else to do now—which I doubted—but I had a feeling he'd come to make sure I didn't do anything stupid.

I waited until I knew we were getting close to the campground before offering, "You know, if you want to talk about whatever is bothering you, I'm a pretty good listener. I don't always run my mouth off."

His arms were crossed over his chest, and his knees were spread as wide as they could get in my passenger seat. I could still feel the tension coming off his body, so I wasn't totally surprised when he grunted, "I think coming might have been a bad idea."

"Maybe, but I'm not taking you back home now, so try your best if you want. Or don't," I told him.

I didn't miss the look he sent me, part surprised at the message and maybe even a little annoyed.

It wasn't even a little surprising when he kept quiet the rest of the way, me humming a Yuki song under my breath until I'd parked the car, and we both got out. There was a big truck with an even bigger trailer parked at the start of the UTV trail, and I waved at the customer I'd met who had told me all about his UTV business.

"Hi, Ora," the man called out, already holding a clipboard with the papers he'd warned me would need to be signed.

"Hi, Andy," I greeted him, shaking his hand when he extended it. Rhodes stopped right beside me, the side of his arm brushing mine. "This is Rhodes. Rhodes, this is Andy."

It was Andy who extended his hand out first. "You're the game warden in the area, aren't you?"

My landlord nodded, giving him a solid shake. "I've worked with your partner before," he told him, his tone still pretty pissy.

Andy made a funny face, I wasn't sure what it might have meant before focusing back on me and saying, "Let's get this paperwork done so you can get started, what do you say?"

"I say let's do it," I told him with a smile.

The arm at my side brushed it again, and I flashed Rhodes a smile too, earning a pinch of that mouth. But I didn't miss the way his gaze went from my eyes to my mouth and back, and I didn't imagine the soft sigh that he slowly let out before I turned back to the man renting out the UTV.

It didn't take more than ten minutes to fill out all the consent forms and disclosures and for him to briefly explain how to use the UTV. I'd given him my credit card information over the phone, so the payment was already made. Andy paused to think for a second before pulling out two helmets from the back of his truck and throwing out a suggestion we wear sunglasses. Then he handed the keys over, and I finally looked back at Rhodes and asked, "Want to drive first?"

"You can go first," he said in that grumpy voice.

He didn't have to tell me twice. What he did do though was hand over one of the jackets he'd brought. I tugged it on, zipped it up, and then strapped my backpack down in the back before hopping into the driver's seat. Rhodes got in too, his face still stony, and buckled himself in. It was then that he finally turned just a little and asked, seriously, "Do you know where you're going?"

I started the UTV and smiled. "No, but we'll figure it out."

And then I hit the gas pedal and we were off.

∼

WHAT WAS MAYBE HALF an hour later, Rhodes slammed his hands down on the console in front of his seat and turned to look at me with the widest eyes—in shock? Alarm? Panic? All of the above maybe?

To give him credit, he wasn't pale. His cheeks were pink

under silver and brown facial hair, but he didn't look scared. Honestly, his expression was closer to the rabid raccoon one than anything else.

I smiled at him. "Fun, huh?"

His mouth opened a little, but no words came out.

I'd had fun at least. The UTV had incredible suspension, so I was pretty sure I wouldn't have a bruised tailbone or anything—been there, done that before, and it was *not* fun—but even if I did end up with one, it would have been totally worth it. That had been *awesome.*

At one point, Rhodes's hands had been formed into tight fists on his lap... when he hadn't been gripping the closest rails at my super sharp turns.

And when I hit the gas and accelerated fast.

And when I didn't tap the brakes and kept on going at the same speed I'd been at.

"What... the... fuck... was... that?" he asked slowly, every word coming out his mouth about two seconds apart from the previous one.

I unbuckled the seat belt and turned off the vehicle, deciding a water break would be pretty great about now. The windshield had kept a lot of dust from coming in, but just enough had—more than likely while I'd been laughing—to dry my mouth and throat out.

"Having fun?" I answered him. "Want some water?"

Rhodes shook his head slowly, his eyes still wide, fingers still gripping the console. "I do want some water, but first I want to know, *what in the hell was that?*"

"Did I scare you?" I asked him, feeling concerned all of a sudden. "I asked if you were okay a few times, but you didn't say anything, and I told you to trust me right after we took off. I'm sorry if I worried you."

"You just drove like a... like a...."

"Rally car driver?" I suggested.

I'm pretty sure the forty-two-year-old gave me the stink eye. "Yes. I thought you were going to drive, five, maybe ten miles an hour, and I saw... I saw the speedometer," he accused.

I winced. So had I.

"Where did you learn how to drive like that?" he finally managed to ask, mouth still slightly open.

I leaned against the back of the seat and gave him a subdued smile. "From a rally car driver."

He stared at me for a moment; then his mouth twisted to the side. Those gray eyes flicked up toward the ceiling of the vehicle at the same time his expression went from irritated to straight thoughtful. Then and only then did Rhodes's mouth twist before saying, with his attention still upward, "I should be surprised, but somehow I'm not."

Was that a compliment, or was that a compliment? I smiled again, not that he saw it though. "My friend Yuki, remember her? My friend that came to visit? Anyway, she has this farm, and one of her sisters was dating a rally car driver that she brought over that weekend. Long story short, he showed us some things." I snorted to myself before I cracked up. "Yuki rolled the UTV, but other than that, it was a lot of fun. He said I had a natural talent."

His gaze flicked to me then, and his mouth twisted even more a moment before he lowered his chin and pressed his lips together. "A natural talent?"

I shrugged. "I'm scared of animals that carry diseases, heights, and disappointing people. I'm not scared of dying."

"Oh" was what he said. The twist of his mouth fell apart as he stared at me. He really was too handsome for his own good.

And I needed to stop staring at his face. "Vroom, vroom, want to go again?" I asked.

This attractive man ran a hand through his brownish

silver hair and nodded after a moment. But there was something in his eyes... amusement? Maybe? "You're a menace to
society, but I'm off the clock," he said. "Show me what you
got."

We got a drink of water and took off again.

⁓

A WHILE LATER, after we switched off and he took over
behind the wheel, we stopped again at a small clearing. I
handed Rhodes one of the two sandwiches I'd packed, and
we sat on a patch of grass in the sun. We'd barely spoken to
each other, both of us too busy gritting our teeth and going
faster than what was suggested or safe, but it was off-season
and there hadn't been any other trailers parked, so we went
for it. At least that's what I'd assumed when he didn't say
anything about slowing down.

Two or three times, I heard Rhodes laugh, and I couldn't
help but smile each time he did.

Slowly, most of his tension had eased from his shoulders
and chest. It was when he'd stretched his legs out in front of
him, one hand behind his back, the other holding the sandwich up to his mouth as he ate the ham and cheese in neat
bites, that he said, "Thank you for bringing me."

I had to wait to answer because my mouth was full.
"You're welcome. Thank you for coming with me."

Neither one of us said a word for a while, eating a little
more, soaking up the warm rays of the sun. It was a beautiful
day after all. The sky was my favorite shade of blue, a color I
wouldn't have imagined was real unless I'd seen it with my
own eyes. The silence was comfortable. Comforting. The
small sounds of the birds in the trees were a reminder that
there was more than just us. That life carried on in ways that
had nothing to do with our human lives.

More than I would ever admit to him, so that I wouldn't make him feel weird, I liked that I wasn't alone. That this big, stoic man was here with me, and I was, hopefully, turning his day around at least a little bit. It was the least I could do after so many people throughout my life had done the same for me, trying to cheer me up when things weren't great.

"My dad and I got into an argument before he left," he said suddenly, holding what was left of his sandwich loosely.

I waited, taking another bite.

"I forgot how much he pisses me off."

I kept on waiting for him to say something else, and it took him a couple more bites to continue.

"I know Am doesn't care if he stays or he goes, but I do. Business has always been more important to him than anything," Rhodes kept talking, his voice calm. "I think he genuinely felt guilty for once in his life, but...."

I didn't know how he felt. Not really. And that's why I think I set my hand on his. Because I understood what it was like to have people disappoint you.

His eyes caught mine and stayed there. There was still frustration in his gaze, but it was less. Mostly because there was something else in them. Something I wasn't totally sure I understood or recognized.

I moved my thumb a little, the pad brushing over a raised scar. Peeking down at it, I saw the puckered line was pale and about two inches long. I touched it again, and sensing that he might want an out from talking about his dad—about something personal to him—I asked, "What's this from?"

"I was... processing a bull—"

I must have made a face because one corner of his mouth hitched up a tiny bit.

"An elk. A male elk, and my knife slipped."

"Ouch. Did you have to get stitches?"

His other hand came over, hovering just above mine—

and *oh*, was it a warm palm—before his index finger swept over the scar too, brushing the side of my finger in the process. "No. I should have, but I didn't. Probably why it healed so bad."

I didn't want to move my hand, so I stretched my pinky finger and touched a tiny scar on his knuckle. "And this one?"

Rhodes didn't move his hand either. "Fight."

"You got into a fight?" I squawked, surprised.

Yeah, the side of his mouth went a little tighter, just a little higher. "I was young."

"You're still young now."

He huffed. "Younger then. Johnny got into a fight when we were in high school, and Billy and I jumped in. I don't even remember what it was over. All I remember was splitting my knuckles and bleeding all over the place. It took forever to stop," he told me, moving his finger just a little, brushing mine again as he did it.

I still didn't move. "Did you get into a lot of fights when you were younger?"

"A few, but not since. I had a lot of anger back then. I don't anymore."

I lifted my eyes and caught those gray ones already intent on me. His features were smooth and even, almost carefully blank, and I wondered what he was thinking. I smiled at him, but he didn't smile back.

Instead, Rhodes asked, "You? Did you get into fights when you were younger?"

"No. No way. I hate confrontations. I have to be really mad to raise my voice. Most stuff doesn't bother me anyway. My feelings don't get hurt that easily," I told him. "You can fix a lot of things by just listening to someone and giving them a hug." I pointed at a couple spots on my face and arms. "All my scars are from being accident-prone."

His snort caught me off guard. From his facial expression,

I think it did him too.

"Are you laughing at me?" I asked, grinning.

His mouth twitched, but his eyes were bright for the first time. "Not at you. At me."

I narrowed my eyes, playing with him.

His finger brushed mine as his mouth formed a full-on smile that could have made me fall in love on the spot if it had lasted any longer than the blink it did. "I've never met anybody like you."

"I hope that's a good thing?"

"I've met people who don't know what it's like to be sad. I've met resilient people. But you...." He shook his head, his gaze watching me closely in that rabid raccoon way. "You got this spark of life that nothing and no one has taken away despite the things that have happened to you, and I don't understand how you still manage to... be you."

My chest ached for a moment in not a bad way. "I'm not always happy. I'm sad sometimes. I told you, not a lot hurts my feelings, but when something gets under there, it really gets under there." I let his words settle deep inside of me, this soothing, warm balm I didn't know I needed. "But thank you. That's one of the nicest things anyone has ever said about me."

Those gray eyes moved over my face again, something troubled flashing across his eyes for a moment so brief I thought I might have imagined it. Because the next thing he said was normal. More than normal. "Thank you for bringing me out here." He paused. "And giving me a few more gray hairs from the way you were driving."

He was joking. Hold the presses. I smiled at him sweetly, trying to act normal. "I like your silver hair, but if you want to drive back, you can."

His huff made me smile, but the way his finger grazed my hand made me smile even more.

CHAPTER 20

"**W**hat are you doing?"

I popped up from where I'd been down on one knee, padded against the gravel by my jacket. I smiled at Rhodes, who had snuck so quietly out of his house that I hadn't heard the door open or close. It was Thursday evening, and he'd not just gotten home early, but he'd changed out of his uniform and into thin sweatpants—*Don't look at his crotch, Ora*—and another T-shirt that I'd seen before. Something about the Navy was washed out on it.

Rhodes really was the hottest forty-two-year-old on the planet. He had to be. At least, I thought so.

Something had changed between us since the day we'd spent on our UTV adventure. We'd even *finally* exchanged phone numbers once we'd gotten back. Whatever it was, was small and more than likely only noticeable to me, but it felt significant. We hadn't spent a whole lot of time together since—he'd been working extra-long hours lately—but the two times I had seen him when he'd gotten home early enough and Amos was in the garage with me, he'd given me these long, watchful looks that were less rabid raccoon and more... something else.

Whatever it was had the little hairs on the nape of my neck coming to attention. I really didn't think I was making something out of nothing either. It was an awareness, like when you're washing your hair and you've held your breath for too long and suddenly there it is, that breath you needed that tells you that you aren't drowning.

But I was trying not to think about it too much. He liked me well enough to be around me and not have a terrible time, I knew now. In his own way. He worried about my safety, I was pretty sure. Rhodes had called me his friend that day his father had been over.

And I had a bone-deep feeling that this decent, quiet man didn't use the word "friend" very often or lightly. And he didn't freely give away his time either. He had with me though.

So it was with that knowledge, with that something in my heart toward him that was definitely affection for someone so private, that I held up the thin fabric in my hand. "Trying to do a dummy run with my new tent," I told him, "and failing."

Coming to a stop on the other side of where all my supplies were laid out, Rhodes leaned over and inspected the equipment. Blues and blacks overlapped each other in a mess.

"It's not labeled right... I spilled water on the booklet, and I haven't figured out what goes into what and where," I explained. "I haven't felt this dumb since I started working at the shop."

"You're not dumb for not knowing things," he said before crouching. "Do you have the box or a picture of it?"

He said the nicest things sometimes.

I went around the side of the house where I'd left the box

by the trash cans that Amos dragged out once a week and brought it back, setting it beside him.

Rhodes glanced up and caught my eyes briefly as he took it. A notch appeared between his eyebrows at the image on the cardboard box, his lips twisting to one side before he nodded. "Do you have a Sharpie?"

"Yeah."

Those gray eyes flicked up to mine again. "Get it. We can mark off each piece so you know what meets up with what."

I wasn't taking this opportunity for granted. Back upstairs, I grabbed a silver Sharpie from my purse and took it to him. Rhodes had already started piling the poles of the tent together, his face thoughtful.

I crouched down next to him and handed the permanent marker over.

His callused fingertips brushed mine as he took it, plucking off the top with his opposite hand and making a thoughtful sound in his throat as he held up a piece. "This is clearly one of the pieces that goes over the top, see?"

I didn't.

"This one looks just like that one," he explained patiently, picking up another pole and setting it with the first.

All right, I could see that. "Oh, yeah."

After a moment, he lifted up the box to look again, scratching the top of his head, then swapping things around. Then he did it again and hummed in his throat.

I took in the blurred pieces on the instructions that I'd accidentally given a bath to. I squinted. I guess it sort of looked right.

Eventually, he started connecting pieces together, and when he stood back—half of them used—he nodded to himself. "Where are you going camping?"

I stood up straight. "Gunnison."

He scratched at his head, still focusing on the pieces of the tent he'd constructed. "Alone?"

"No." I moved the booklet around a little bit to see if that made more sense. It didn't. "Clara invited me to go with her to Gunnison this weekend. It's going to be me, her, Jackie, and one of her sisters-in-law. Her brother is staying with Mr. Nez. She offered to let me borrow one of her tents, but I wanted to be a big girl and buy my own so I have it for the future, in case I go camping again. I know I used to like going, but that was a long time ago."

"Yeah, that piece goes there," he said after I'd connected one of the poles I'd picked up. "A long time ago? When you lived here?"

"Yeah, my mom and I used to go," I answered, watching him hook up another pole. "I'm pretty excited, actually. I remember we used to have a lot of fun. Making s'mores—"

"There's a fire ban."

"I know. We're using her stove." I squinted at some of the poles and flipped it around. "Maybe I'll hate sleeping on the ground, but I won't know unless I try."

Without looking at me, he took that same pole and moved it where it actually looked right.

"You're good," I told him after he'd done a couple more and it really started to look like it should. "You don't do a whole lot of camping then? Since Amos isn't about it?"

Rhodes was taking the Sharpie out of his pocket as he answered, "Not often. When I've gone hunting or for training, but that's about it." He paused, and I thought that was the end of it as he put the marker between his teeth and finished connecting the last few pieces, but he surprised me when he kept talking. "My older brother used to take us all the time. That's the most fun I remember having back then."

His brief story perked me up as he started moving along

the rods, marking them with the silver color. "Do you have more than one brother?"

"Three. Two older, one younger. It got us out of the house and out of trouble," he said in a strange tone that told me there was more to it than that.

"Where do they all live?"

"Colorado Springs, Juneau, and Boulder," he answered.

Yet none of them, including his dad, ever came over. Colorado Springs and Boulder weren't exactly down the street, but they weren't *that* far either. The one in Alaska was the only exception, at least I thought.

Like he could read my mind, he kept talking. "They don't come down here much. No reason to. We meet up a couple times a year, or they used to come visit when I was in Florida. Everybody liked visiting when I was there, mostly for the theme parks."

No reason to? Even though his not-exactly-dad-of-the-year father was only an hour away? And where was his mom? "Why didn't you take Amos and move up closer to where one of them lives?"

He kept on marking away. "Amos grew up here. Living on base wasn't for me when I had to, and I don't miss living in big cities. And when I applied to become a game warden, they opened the office in Durango. I don't believe in fate, but it seemed like it to me."

To me too. "Is your mom in the picture?" I asked before I could stop myself.

The Sharpie stopped moving, and I knew I didn't imagine the gruffness in his voice when he said, "No. Last I heard she passed away a few years ago."

Last he heard. That wasn't loaded. "I'm really sorry."

Even though Rhodes was looking down, he still shook his head. "There's nothing to be sorry about. I don't lose sleep over her."

If that wasn't some deep fury, I didn't know what was.

And he must have surprised himself because he glanced up and frowned. "We didn't have a good relationship."

"I'm sorry, Rhodes. I'm sorry for asking."

That handsome face went rigid. "Don't. You didn't do anything wrong." Rhodes's attention moved back to the tent a little too quickly, and he seemed to take another steeling breath before saying, "Let's take it apart and do it again with the canopy, just to make sure all the numbers match up and you've got it."

Someone was done talking about his parents. I already knew better than to ask people such personal questions, but I could never seem to stop myself. "Thank you," I blurted out. "For helping me."

"Sure" was all he replied with. His tone said it all though.

Two days later, I was sitting on the edge of the bed, shaking my foot and trying my best not to feel disappointed.

But mostly failing at that.

I had been really, *really* looking forward to going camping.

But I knew that shit happens, and that's exactly what had been the case. Clara had gotten a call while we'd still been at the store, just about getting ready to shut down. Her nephew had broken his arm, and he and her brother were on their way to the hospital.

I could tell Clara had been disappointed as hell in the first place from the way her shoulders had dropped and the way she'd sighed.

And on such short notice, she wouldn't find anyone else to stay. Her dad's daytime caretaker had plans. Her other brothers... I wasn't sure, but I'd bet if they could have done it, she would have asked.

Then again, knowing Clara, she would rather not.

So, we made plans to make camping happen some other time. I'd offered to stay with her dad the next day if she wanted to get out of the house, but one thing led to another, and Jackie offered to stay home. We'd agreed to go on a hike tomorrow instead, even though I knew she wasn't much of a hiker. She swore up and down she could handle it, and I wasn't going to tell her what she could and couldn't do. If we had to turn around, it wouldn't be the end of the world.

And that was why I found myself on a Saturday night at home, feeling just a *little* disappointed.

I could go camping by myself some other day....

No, I couldn't.

A knock on the door though had me sitting up.

"Aurora?" through the window, a voice called out from downstairs.

I knew who it was and got up. "Rhodes?" I replied before taking the steps as fast as I could in my socked feet.

"It's me," he said just as I reached the bottom, flipping the lock and pulling the door wide.

I gave him the friendliest smile I could muster. "Hey."

I knew he'd just gotten home not too long ago, I'd heard his truck. He'd already changed out of his uniform, settling for dark jeans and a formfitting T-shirt that I would have eyeballed him in if I could have done it sneakily. "Getting a little late to be leaving, isn't it?" he asked.

It took me a second to blink at what he was asking. "Oh, we're not going after all."

"You're leaving tomorrow?"

"No, not this weekend. Clara's brother had an emergency, and he couldn't come down to stay with their dad, and his usual caretaker had a funeral," I explained, watching him watching me. His eyes moved over my face as I talked, like he was measuring my words.

His smooth right cheek flexed.

"Another time, I guess," I told him. "What are you two doing this weekend?"

His "Nothing" took a moment to come out of his mouth. "Johnny picked up Am, and they're doing something tonight." His cheek twitched again. "I saw your light on and wanted to make sure you were all right since you said you were leaving right after work."

"Oh. Yeah. No, I'm here, and I'm good. Clara and I are going to try and do that hike you saved me on, when half my skin ate gravel."

He nodded as he narrowed his eyes a little, thoughtful.

I thought about it. "I was thinking about making a pizza right now, do you want half?"

"Half?" he asked slowly.

"I can make you your own if you want…." I trailed off. "I'm hungry actually. I can eat a whole one, but I have two."

For some reason, that made the corners of his mouth tighten.

"What?"

"Nothing, I wouldn't be able to picture you eating a whole pizza if I hadn't seen you nearly do it on Am's birthday."

I almost winced at the memory of the shit show that day had been. I'd never asked what happened with the mouse, and I wasn't going to ask now. I shrugged and smiled. "I had a big salad for lunch. It balances out, I think."

"Make two pizzas. I'll get you another one next time I go to the store," he said after a moment of looking at my face again.

Did he have to be so handsome?

"Yeah?" I asked, sounding way too excited.

He nodded soberly, but there was still something in his

eyes that seemed very, very thoughtful. "What do you think? Thirty minutes?"

"Maybe? By the time I heat up the oven and both pizzas cook, closer to forty?"

Rhodes took a step back. "I'll be back then."

"Okay," I said as he took another step. I waited to close the door until he'd turned and jogged back to his house.

Why he jogged back, I had no idea, but okay. Maybe he had to take a poop. Or he hadn't exercised. Amos had confirmed one day that his dad got up early to go to the twenty-four-hour gym in town a few days a week. Sometimes he did push-ups at home. He'd volunteered the information randomly, but I hadn't complained.

Back upstairs, I preheated the oven and wondered if he was planning on eating with me or taking the pizza back to his house.

I wondered for a second if he'd planned on going on a date tonight and that's why he asked if I was sticking around, but no.

Unless he was planning on sharing his pizza....

No, that didn't seem like him either.

Well, whatever, if he wanted to eat with me, awesome. If he didn't, I could watch a movie. I had a new book. I could call Yuki to check on her. Or my aunt.

But forty-five minutes later, Rhodes still hadn't come back and the pizzas were overcooking in the cooling oven.

I guess I could just cut it up, put it on a plate and take it over?

I had just started cutting up one of them with a steak knife, because I didn't have a pizza cutter, when another knock came from the door, and before I could answer, it creaked open and I heard, "Angel?"

Lord, I didn't understand this man and how he sometimes screwed up my name.

"Yes?"

"Pizzas done?"

"Yeah! Want me to bring yours down?" I yelled.

"Bring them both."

He wanted to eat together? "Okay!" I hollered back.

The door closed, and I finished slicing up both supreme masterpieces, stacking them onto plates, and wrapping them with some of the beeswax covers that Yuki had sent randomly to my PO box. Then I went down.

I managed about two steps outside before I stopped.

There was a sleek tent pitched in the area between the garage apartment and the main house.

Beside it were two camping chairs with a lantern between them. Rhodes was sitting in one of them. There was a small bundle on the other.

"It's not Gunnison, but we can't have a fire here either because the ban is statewide," he said, sitting up.

Something beneath my breastbone stirred.

"I looked for your tent in the garage and in your car, but it wasn't there. If you want to bring it down, we can set it up in a minute. But mine is a two-person." He stopped suddenly, talking that was, and leaned forward, squinting at me in the dark. "Are you crying?"

I tried to clear my throat and went with the truth. "I'm about to."

"Why?" he asked softly in surprise.

That thing moved around some more, sliding awfully close to my heart, and I tried to will it to stop moving.

It didn't listen.

He'd pitched a tent.

Set up chairs.

So that I could go camping.

I squeezed my lips together, telling myself, *Don't do it. Don't do it. Don't do it, Ora.*

I better not cry. I better not cry.

I even cleared my damn throat.

And it didn't matter.

I started to cry. Just these tiny, pitiful streams that came out of me silently once the choke was out. I didn't make a sound, but the tears kept coming out of my eyeballs. Seasonal little streams of salt at an act of kindness I would have never in a million years expected.

Rhodes stood up, alarmed, and I tried to say, "I'm fine," but it didn't exactly come out.

It didn't come out at all. Because I was trying so hard not to cry harder.

"Buddy?" Rhodes said cautiously, concern all over his tone.

I pinched my lips together.

He took another step forward and then another, and then I did the same.

I went straight toward him, still pressing my lips together, still clinging to my small amount of pride.

And when he stopped about a foot or two away, I set the plates on the ground and kept going. Straight into him. My cheek going into the space between his shoulder and collarbone, tucking myself in right there, and wrapping both arms around his waist like I had a right to. Like he would want me to.

Like he liked me and this was fine.

But he didn't push my arms away once they were there. Once I was basically totally pressed against him, not crying-crying but tearing up into his shirt. "This is the nicest thing anyone's ever done for me," I whispered into his chest with a sniff.

What had to be his hand landed right smack in the center of my back.

"I'm sorry," I pretty much whispered before attempting to

keep myself together and trying to take a step back, but I couldn't. Because the hand covering my bra strap didn't let me. "I don't mean to get all mopey or cry all over you. I don't want to make you uncomfortable."

Another hand landed low on my back, right above the band of my jeans.

And I stopped trying to move away.

"You're not making me uncomfortable. I don't mind," he said, his voice as gentle as I'd ever heard it.

He was hugging me back.

He was hugging me back.

And son of a bitch, I wanted it. So I hugged this man more, my arms going low on his waist. He was warm, and his body was solid.

And my God, he smelled like the good laundry detergent.

I could wrap him around myself and live there forever. Cologne be damned. There was nothing better than good detergent.

Especially when it was molded to a body like Rhodes's. Big and firm. All comforting.

A man who I had thought up until not too long ago couldn't stand me.

And now... well, now I was second-guessing everything.

Why would he do this? Because of Amos's appendicitis? Because I'd saved him when his dad had come over? Or possibly because of our UTV adventure?

"You okay?" he asked as his hand hesitated on the middle of my spine before giving it another pat.

He was patting my back, like he was trying to burp me.

Affection surged through my bloodstream. Rhodes was attempting to comfort me, and I didn't think I'd ever been so confused, not even when Kaden had told me he loved me but said we couldn't let anyone find out about it.

"Yeah," I said. "You're being so nice. I really thought you didn't like me for the longest."

Rhodes pulled back just enough for him to tip his chin down. His eyebrows were knitted together, and his eyes bounced from one of mine to the other, and he must have realized I was serious because his features slowly softened. His serious face took over, and so did his Navy Voice. "It had nothing to do with you before, are we clear? You reminded me of someone, and I thought you were like her. It took me too long to figure out that you're not. I'm sorry I did that."

"Oh," I told him with another sniff and then a nod. "I get it."

He kept on looking straight into my eyes before dipping his chin a little. "Do you want to go back in?"

"No! I'm sorry I got emotional. Thank you so much. This means the world to me."

He nodded, his hands briefly moving over my spine before he took a step away. Then he seemed to think twice about it because he was back and dabbing at my face with the sleeve of the sweater I hadn't realized he'd thrown on at some point.

And before I could think twice about it, I dove forward again and hugged him tight again, so tight he went "oof" for a second before I let him go just as quickly, sniffled and gave him a big, watery smile. Picking the plates of pizza back off the ground where I'd set them, I held one out to him. "Well, let's eat, if you're hungry," I nearly croaked.

He was watching me way too closely, the lines across his forehead prominent. "You're still crying."

"I know, and it's your fault," I said, clearing my throat and trying to keep it together. "This really is the nicest thing anyone has ever done for me. Thank you, Rhodes."

His eyes flicked up toward the night sky as he said in that hoarse voice, "You're welcome."

We each took a seat, quietly, taking the wrapper off, going straight into eating our pizzas, the light of the lantern illuminating us both enough so we could see each other pretty clearly.

We finished up our pizzas in silence, and he reached over to take the plate from me, setting it down and then saying, "I found a pack of Chips Ahoy and some marshmallows I don't remember buying, but they aren't expired."

My bottom lip started quivering, and in that moment, I hated that I thought of Kaden, and I hated even more that I hated him for not understanding me a fraction of as much as I thought he understood me.

He hadn't. I saw that now. Saw it in a complete picture. Years ago, I would have killed for something like this. Not for the things he bought that took him three minutes to find online and even faster to order because he had his account information saved on his phone. I could remember the times I'd brought up just visiting Pagosa and how he'd change the subject, not listening. Not caring. Everything had always been about what *he* wanted. All that time I'd wasted....

"You good with the cookies and marshmallows?" Rhodes asked, oblivious.

My "yes" was the smallest yes in the world. But it got the point across because Rhodes shot me a long look before getting up and ducking into the tent, bringing out a plastic grocery bag. He pulled out what looked like a half-full container of chocolate chip cookies, a nearly demolished bag of marshmallows, a couple of the kind of things used for kebabs, an oven mitt and a full-sized lighter.

I went over and we split the things up; he handed me the pokers and a marshmallow at a time and I loaded them. I put the mitt on, shooting him a smile as I did, and then held out the marshmallow sticks toward him, where he lit the flame and I slowly turned the marshmallows once before flipping them upside down and letting the flame swallow the rest of them. We did it twice for four total.

"Have you ever done this before?" I asked as I blew out the flame on the last set.

His face was even more handsome under the moonlight and the lantern; his bone structure was absolutely something else. "No, but I hoped it'd make sense—careful, don't burn yourself."

What a dad.

I loved it.

I was careful as we slowly dragged the marshmallows across their sticks and onto a cookie each, using the rods to smash them down as they cracked open with gooey goodness. He took two, and I kept the other two, unable to stop smiling and not caring.

"Okay?"

I wasn't sure what he was referring to specifically, so I took it in general. "More than okay, this is awesome," I admitted.

"Yeah?"

"Yeah," I confirmed. "The pizza, outside, the moon, the cookies."

"Am's got a couple movies downloaded on his tablet. I got it just in case you wanted to watch it in there," he said, gesturing to the tent.

He was serious. *What else was in the tent?*

"Should I grab my sleeping bag since the ground is hard?"

"There's a couple in there. They're clean. We washed them after our last failed trip."

"What happened?"

"Am got stung three times by a yellow jacket on the second day. He wasn't very happy."

I grimaced. "Did you leave?"

He snickered. "Second and last time we ever went."

"That sucks. Hopefully there's other things you both enjoy doing together."

Those broad shoulders moved in agreement. "I'm here for Amos, not to do things without him."

That made me smile. He really was such a good dad. A good man.

"We don't have to watch anything if you don't want to," he said when I guess I took too long to say anything else.

I didn't even hesitate a little bit. "I'm game if you are."

"I brought it out here, angel," he replied.

He totally had. "Yes, I want to. Give me five minutes to grab a drink—"

"I've got a couple bottles of water and a soda in the tent, the kind you like," he cut me off.

I didn't want to think that everyone had an ulterior motive. I didn't feel that way at all. But... *he had my favorite soda?* What kind of witchcraft was going on here?

I pinched myself as subtly as possible, and when I figured I should have woken up because this was a dream and didn't, I realized this was real.

And I was going to take advantage of this handsome man being so nice to me for whatever reason he had.

"I want to change my pants and grab a sweater. These jeans weren't meant to be worn all day."

He gave me that serious nod.

I took a step back then stopped again. I wanted to make sure... "Did you... want to camp out all night?"

"Only if you want to."

I hesitated, eyeing the two-person tent. The proximity. The intimacy.

A tent propped between his house and mine—technically his, but whatever—and this tiny thrill filled my whole chest cavity.

He was just being nice, I told myself. *Don't fly too high, little heart*, I pleaded, surprised suddenly by the words that had come out of nowhere.

But just as quickly as they appeared, they were gone. A figment of my imagination.

"We can play it by ear. You change your mind, you walk the fifteen steps home," he amended after a moment.

That wasn't what I was thinking at all, but I nodded, not willing to say what I was hesitating over. I couldn't forget I was, hopefully, going hiking with Clara tomorrow and I'd need to wake up early, but being tired would be worth it for this. "Okay. I'll be right back."

And I was right back. I changed into some loose flannel pajama pants that someone had bought me, peed, and headed back out. I made it to the opening of the tent and started to unzip it, finding Rhodes sprawled on top of a sleeping bag, all long and physically perfect, and on top of the kind of foam pad we sold at the store all the time. He had the tablet propped against his knees, head pillowed by his real pillow and his forearm that he had tucked back there.

I didn't need to witness it to know he watched me as I undid the rest of the zipper and ducked inside, closing it back after me.

I wasn't sure what I'd imagined when I'd pictured a two-person tent, but it hadn't been this cozy.

I liked it.

And I sure wasn't going to complain.

"I'm back," I said, Captain Obvious.

He gestured toward the sleeping bag on top of another pad directly beside him. "I saved you a spot from the raccoon that tried to get in a minute ago."

I froze. "Are you serious?"

He was messing with me.

I started to unzip the tent again as he chuckled, and I guess, dipped a finger into the band of my pants and tugged me back, surprising me yet again with this change in him. His voice was warm. "Come on."

"All right," I muttered, crawling across the floor and lying right beside him. There was a pillow on my side too, and it was a house one, not an inflatable one. This was so, so nice.

The nicest.

I didn't understand it.

"We've got three choices: the 1990s *Twilight Zone*, *Fire in the Sky*, or a documentary about Bigfoot hunters now that I see it. What do you think?"

I didn't even need to think about it. "If I watch the Bigfoot movie, I'll never go camping again. We're out in the open, and unless you want me crying myself to sleep, *Fire in the Sky* is out—"

His laugh surprised me, all deep and hoarse and perfect.

"Let's do *The Twilight Zone*."

"Is that what you want?" he asked.

"We can watch *Fire in the Sky* if you're fine with me peeing myself and having to smell it later."

He only said one word, but there was definitely amusement in it. "No."

"That's what I thought."

He rolled his head to the side to eye me.

But something in me eased as I scooted over, so close his upper arm brushed my boobs. I was totally on my side, with a hand between my head and the pillow propping it up enough to get a good look at the screen.

He didn't start the movie right away though, and when I glanced at him, I could tell his gaze was trained on a spot along the tent wall.

I didn't want to ask what he was looking at.

And I didn't have to because his gray eyes flicked to me, and the smile that had just been lingering there a moment ago was gone, and he said, voice steady, "You reminded me of my mom."

The mom he didn't like? I winced. "I'm sorry."

Rhodes shook his head. "No, I'm sorry. You don't look alike or act alike, angel. She was just... She was beautiful like you are. You-can't-look-away gorgeous, my uncle used to say," he explained softly, like he was still trying to process whatever it was he was thinking exactly.

"Looking back on it, I'm pretty sure she was bipolar. People, including my father, let her get away with a lot because she looked the way she did. And it was a shitty instinct that made me think you could be like that too." His Adam's apple bobbed. "I'm sorry."

Something really heavy churned in my chest, and I nodded at him. "It's okay. I understand. You weren't that mean."

His eyebrows went up a little. "That mean?"

"That's not what I meant. You weren't mean. I just... thought you didn't like me. But I promise, I'm not that bad of a person. And I don't like hurting most people's feelings. I still think about the time when I was in third grade and hid my Halloween candy instead of sharing it with Clara when she came over to my house."

The softest little snort went through his nose.

"Mental illness is hard. With a parent especially, I think. My mom battled depression when I was growing up, and it was hard for me too. It still is, I guess. She was really good at hiding it, but when it got to be too much, she would pretty much be catatonic. I thought I could fix it, but that's not the way it works, you know? Stuff like that sticks with you. I wondered... what had happened. With her, I mean. Your mom."

The way he shook his head, like he was reliving some of the things he'd gone through with her, hurt my heart. I couldn't imagine what she had done to make a man like Rhodes look the way he did right then. Maybe this was why his relationship with his dad was so strained. I didn't want to ask. Didn't want to rehash more hurt when he was being so kind. So I settled for touching his arm. "But thank you for apologizing."

His gaze went straight to the place where my fingers were. That thick, muscular throat worked, and slowly, oh so slowly, he lifted his gaze to mine and just watched me.

I didn't know what to say for once, so I didn't say anything at all. What I wanted to do was hug him, to tell him that there were some things you could never truly get over. What I actually did was pull my hand back and wait. And what was only a deep breath and a few moments later, he started talking again, his voice only sounding a little bit different, huskier, if anything. "Thanks for what you did with my dad. For what you said."

He *had* heard me. I waved him off. "Not even a big deal, and it was only the truth."

"It is a big deal," he argued gently. "He called to ask when he could visit again. I know what he's like… thank you."

"I'm glad he took it to heart, and seriously, it's nothing. You should meet my ex's mom. I've got a lot of experience."

That gray gaze swept down to my mouth, and his voice was low. "And thanks for how much you do for Am."

"Meh. I love that kid. But not in a weird way. He's just a good, sweet kid, and I'm a lonely old lady that he doesn't totally hate. Honestly, I think he just misses his mom, and I guess I'm old enough to be kind of a weird mom figure, so he puts up with me."

"That's not it," he claimed, a hint of a smile flashing around the corners of his mouth.

A question bubbled up into my brain. Maybe because he seemed to be in a good mood and I wasn't sure when the next chance I'd get to ask this would be. Or possibly just because I was nosey and figured I had nothing left to lose except possibly getting a stare in return. So I did it. "Can I ask you something personal?"

He thought about it for a moment before nodding.

All right then. "If you don't want to answer, you don't have to, but... were you planning on never getting married?"

The face he made said he hadn't been expecting that question.

I tried to rush on. "Because you had Amos so... unconventionally. So young. You were what? Twenty-six when your friend and his wife asked you to be a donor? Or did you just want to be a dad then?"

Realization dawned on him, and he didn't have to think about it. "We were twenty, I think, when Billy got into a bad mountain biking accident. He had trauma to his..."

"Testicles?" I offered.

He nodded. "Billy's wife is older than us by eight or nine years—yeah, that face was the same one everyone made back then. It took Johnny a while to get over his friend and his big sister getting together. But, that's why they were insistent on having a baby then, if they could. I stayed over at his house a lot growing up... because I didn't want to be home," he explained, matter-of-factly. "To answer your question, I didn't see myself ever getting married. There's a lot of things I can commit to, but most people will disappoint you."

I heard that. But I knew not everyone was like that.

Rhodes's eyes swept over my face as he kept talking. "Besides one girlfriend in high school who dumped me after two years, and a few women I dated but not seriously, I haven't been in a long-term relationship. I had to choose between focusing on my career or trying to get to know someone, and I chose my career instead. At least until Amos came along, and he became the only thing more important than that."

More important than his career. It took everything in me not to sniff.

"I always liked kids. I thought I'd be a good dad someday, and when they asked, I thought that might be my one shot at having a real family in case I never met anyone. My only chance at knowing I could be a better parent than mine were. That I could be what I wished they had been." Rhodes shrugged, but it was a heavy one that pulled at my heart.

So I said the only thing that I could think of. "I understand." Because I did.

Since my mom, all I had ever wanted was stability. To be loved. To love. I needed an outlet. And unlike him, at least in one way, I'd looked in the wrong place. Held on for the wrong reasons.

There were some things in life that you had to prove to yourself. I had come here for that exact reason. I got it.

Rhodes shifted in front of me and asked, out of nowhere, "Did your ex cheat on you?"

It didn't feel like a punch to the face this time. This question. When I'd spent a week with an old roadie of Kaden's when I'd gone through Utah, he had asked me the same thing... and it had felt exactly like it. Mostly, I think, because I guess some part of me wished it had been that simple. That easy to explain. Kaden had had women throwing themselves at him forever, and that would have surprised no one.

Luckily, I'd been born with what my uncle called more self-esteem than a group of people combined, but my aunt said that I'd just been so confident in how he felt about me. That I knew better. That Kaden knew better than to cheat on me because he had loved me—in his own easy way. I had never been jealous even when I'd had to stand at the sidelines and people touched his butt and his arm and put spectacular boobs in his face.

I wished, at more than one point, that he had cheated on me. Because I could've excused the end of our relationship more easily. People understood adultery and its impact on most relationships.

But that wasn't what happened.

"No, he didn't. We took a break once, and I know he kissed someone, but that was it."

More like his mom had come up with a stupid-ass idea that he'd tried to sell me on. *Mom thinks it would be a good idea to be seen with someone else. Out. There's been posts about me, you know... being into guys. She thinks I should go out with someone— just as friends! I would never do that to you. For publicity, beautiful. That's all.*

That's all.

Instead, that had been the first piece of my heart he'd broken. One thing led to another, me asking if he would be fine if I pretended to go out with someone, him getting red-faced and saying it was different. Blah, blah, blah, I didn't care anymore. And it had ended with me saying he could do whatever the hell he wanted, but I wasn't going to stick around. He kept insisting it wasn't going to be like that, but at the end of the day....

He did exactly what he wanted. He went on that date, thinking I was bluffing. So I left.

I spent three weeks with Yuki before he came around and begged and pleaded for me to come back. That he would never do something like that again. That he was so sorry.

That he had kissed Tammy Lynn Singer and he felt terrible.

I didn't imagine that Rhodes's voice got deeper as he asked, "Then why did you get divorced?"

The urge not to lie to him was so strong in my heart, I

had to think about how to word this without giving more than I was ready to. "It's pretty complicated...."

"Most breakups are."

I smiled at him. He was so close, I had the best view of those full lips. "There were a lot of reasons. One of the biggest was that I wanted to have kids, and he kept putting it off and off, and I finally figured out that he was going to keep making excuses forever. It was important to me, and it wasn't like I hadn't made that clear to him from the beginning of our relationship. I probably should have known he was never going to fully commit to our future when he kept insisting on condoms even after being together for fourteen years, right? Too much information, I'm sorry. And there was his career. I'm not really the clingy type or need a lot of attention, but his job was number one through ten on the list of priorities in his life, and I was... going to be number eleven forever when I would've been happy being three or four. I'd prefer number two, but I could settle."

The lines across his forehead made another appearance.

"And it was just a bunch of other stuff that compounded over the years. His mom is the Antichrist, and he was a momma's boy. She hated me with a passion unless I could do something for her or him. We just ended up growing into totally different people who wanted totally different things... and now that I think about it, I guess it really isn't that complicated. I guess I just wanted someone to be my best friend, someone good and honest who doesn't make me second-guess being important. And he would never give up his job or even try and compromise." I felt like it was always me that had to give and give and give, while he took and took and took.

I made a farting sound with my lips and shrugged at Rhodes. "I guess I am a little clingy."

His gray eyes roamed my face, and after a moment, he

raised his eyebrows and dropped them back down with a shake of his head.

"What?" I asked.

He snickered. "He sounds like a fucking moron."

I smiled faintly. "I like to think so, but I'm sure there are some people who would think he was too good for me."

"Doubt it."

That got me to full-on smile at him. "I used to want him to regret the end of our relationship for the rest of his life, but you know what? I just don't care anymore, and that makes me pretty damn happy."

It was him that touched my arm that time. His thumb a two hundred degree point on my wrist. The gray pools of his eyes this close were deep and hypnotizing. Rhodes was so handsome in that moment—so much more than usual—all partially scowling and so focused on me, it was easy to forget we weren't in the middle of the woods, just the two of us alone. "He was an idiot. Only somebody that's never talked to you or seen you, would think you were the lucky one." Rhodes's gaze flicked to my mouth, and he let out a soft sigh through his nose, his words a hoarse whisper. "Nobody in their right mind would let you walk away from them. Not once and no way in hell twice, angel."

My heart.

My limbs went numb.

We looked at one another for so long, the only thing I could hear was our steady breaths. But eventually, with this loaded moment strung so tightly between us, he looked away first. Mouth parted, eyes going to the top of the tent before he picked up the tablet and tapped the screen all while clearing his throat. "Ready to watch the movie?"

No, no, I wasn't, but somehow I managed to say, "Yes."

And that was what we did.

CHAPTER 21

I scrubbed my hand over the back of my neck as I filled the last of my water bottles. Through the window overlooking the sink, the sun was barely beginning to peek out. If I'd had just about any other plans, I would have still been in the tent from last night.

Only my mom could get me to roll out of bed this early. I'd had a dream about her the night before. It wasn't that I could remember what had happened in it, because I couldn't, but there was a certain feel to my dreams when she was in them. I woke up happier. The happiness usually tapered into sadness, but not the bad kind.

I figured the dream had to be some kind of omen for the hike I was doing today.

I was here because of her, after all.

But, some part of me couldn't help but wish that I'd stayed in the tent last night with Rhodes.

Lying on the sleeping bags, me in my pajamas, and basically lined up along that incredible body, we had watched one movie and started another. The night had been quiet and comfortable, with only the slight sounds of the occasional car driving down the county road, interrupting the voices of the actors coming from the tablet.

Honestly, it had been the most romantic night of my life.

Not that Rhodes had known that.

And as we'd rolled up the sleeping bags and torn down the tent, he had asked me what I was taking with me to do the hike I was going to knock out today. Rhodes had given me some quiet warnings, and sitting in the camp chairs afterward, we'd checked the weather on his phone.

And that was exactly why I'd drug myself out of bed at five thirty in the morning. I needed to get an early start. This might be my last shot at doing the Hike From Hell, unless I wanted to wait until next year. Snow was going to be hitting the highest peaks soon.

And I probably would have waited, but... I needed to do it.

I had to.

The reminder of how short life was had blossomed in my head and stayed there, and I knew I had to at least try and knock another hike out of the way since I actually had the time. Might as well. Go big or go home, and my mom had been a supernova of guts and fearlessness. I had to do it for her.

I'd pumped myself up to try and make this hike my bitch once and for all. The forecast was good. There had been a post I'd found on a forum from someone who said they'd done the trail two days ago and it had been great.

So why not? I'd gotten my things mostly together, and I was going to do this. To prove to myself that I could.

For my mom and for all the years she hadn't gotten. For all the experiences she had missed. For the path that her life's course had paved for me.

I was here, in this place, with hope in my heart because of her. It was the least I could do.

And that was probably why I was so caught up in my head, as I finished lugging my supplies downstairs to my car, that I didn't notice the figure approaching from across the driveway until Rhodes asked quietly, "Are you good?"

Over my shoulder, I caught a glance of his silvery hair and smiled at the handsome face looking at me. "Yeah. I'm great, just thinking about my mom," I answered before dropping my backpack into the back seat.

"Good thoughts or bad thoughts?" he asked softly before covering his mouth for a yawn. He was already in his uniform, but the top buttons were undone and he hadn't put his belt on.

Had he come out here just because he saw me through the window?

Turning around slowly, I took in his heavy features, those slashes of cheekbones, the subtle cleft in his chin. He was pretty awake even though he couldn't have been up for long.

"Both," I answered him. "Good as in I'm here because of her and I'm really happy that I came back and things are going good, but bad because...."

He watched me closely, so good-looking it made my chest ache a little.

I had never really spoken the words out loud. I'd heard them from other people's mouths but never mine. But I found that I wanted to. "Did you ever hear that there were some people who didn't believe she got hurt and couldn't make it out?"

Rhodes's eyes bounced from one of mine to the other, but he didn't bullshit me. He took a small step forward and dipped his chin, still watching. "There were a few trains of thought that she—" He sucked in a breath like he wasn't sure he wanted to say the words either, but he did. "—harmed herself."

I nodded.

"Or that she walked away to start a new life," he finished quietly.

That one specifically had stung the worst. That people would think she would leave everything behind, leave *me* behind, to start over fresh.

"Yeah," I agreed. "I wasn't sure how much you'd heard. I never thought she would leave like that, not even because of all the financial issues she was having that I didn't know about. How she was going to have to declare bankruptcy, how we were about to get evicted... or how she might have...." The words bubbled in my throat like they were acid, and I couldn't say the S-word. "Not come back on purpose," I settled for. "I know the police knew about how she was on medication for depression."

Rhodes nodded.

"I was just thinking about that, I guess. How her going on her hike and all those things and how that one decision of hers changed my life completely. How I wouldn't have moved to Florida and gotten to know my aunt and uncle. How I wouldn't have gone to Tennessee, and then I wouldn't have lived that life there... and then eventually ended up back here. Life is just weird, I guess, is what I was thinking about. How one decision that you don't even make can affect another person's life so dramatically.

"I just miss her extra today, I guess, and I wish I had answers. I wish I knew what really happened," I finished telling him, adding a shrug to hopefully make it seem like it was all casual and fine. It wasn't the first time I had mornings or days like this, and it wouldn't be the last.

You didn't survive someone taking a wrecking ball to your existence and not have thousands of fractures to live with the rest of your life.

The hand he had over mine lifted and Rhodes set it on my shoulder, his fingers curling around, lying flat against me. "It was a strange case, and maybe if I didn't know you, I could see why people would think that. But now that I do—know you, Buddy—I don't believe she left intentionally. I told you, I don't know how anybody could let you walk away. Or how anyone could be the one to do the walking. I'm sure she loved you very much."

"She did," I told him before pressing my lips together for a second and blinking. "I think so at least." I swallowed and eyed him. "Can I have a good-morning hug? Is that all right? If not, don't worry about it."

He didn't even use his words.

His answer was to open his arms before coaxing me into them after the first step I took.

And I thought to myself that I fit in them pretty damn well.

His palm skipped over the patting thing he'd done before and went straight into stroking up and down my back once. What was minutes later, when my heart was beating nice and slow and the scent of his laundry detergent clung to my nostrils in a way that I hoped lasted all day, he asked, "Are you going for your hike still?"

"Yeah. Clara hasn't texted me yet, but we're going to meet at the trailhead."

He pulled back just enough for our gazes to meet. The fingers on my back brushed the strap of my bra. "If you change your mind and want to wait, I'm off next Sunday."

He was offering to go on a hike with me. Why did it feel like a marriage proposal? I knew for a fact he'd already done the trail a couple of times before—as I'd learned the first time I'd tried it—and he knew that I knew that. "I'd rather do a new one another day so you aren't bored like when we did Four-Mile. If you want to."

"If you want to," he agreed. "And I wasn't bored."

That made me smile up at him. "And here I thought you

were miserable the whole time."

"No." His nostrils flared just a little. "If you change your mind, I'm hanging around here today," he said quietly. "I've got a couple of poaching issues I need to check on."

"I'm going to try and do it; I've got everything packed. The faster I get it over with, the faster I can do another one. Maybe with you... if you're free. Maybe we can get Am to come too. Maybe we can bribe him with food."

It was his turn to nod before he eyed my collection of water, food, and emergency supplies of a tiny blanket, tarp, flashlight, and first aid kit. I'd gotten pretty decent at figuring out what I needed and how much. It was too long and hard of a trail to go crazy and over pack, but I didn't want to starve either. I got way too cranky for that. My choices must have been approved by him because he looked back at me and nodded.

His arms let me go, and in the next blink of an eye, he held out a ball of dark blue. "Take my jacket with you. It's wind and waterproof. It's lighter than yours, and it'll be easier to pack." He gestured for me to take it. "Take your sun protective pants too. There's a lot of brush on the trail the way you're taking today. You've got trekking poles?"

Something inside of me eased, and I nodded at him.

His gray eyes were steady and somber on me. "Call me when you get there and when you finish." He paused, thinking about his words before adding, "Please."

I HAD JUST PARKED at the trailhead when my phone happened to ring. It was honestly a miracle that I even got service in the first place, but as I'd learned over the last few months of living in the mountains, sometimes you randomly hit a sweet spot in the perfect place if the elevation was just right.

Maybe it helped that I'd switched my cell provider to the same one as Yuki. And based on the altitude my watch was registering, I was way up there.

Rhodes had warned me about just how sketchy the drive up was since I was going to try to hike to the lake from a different starting point, but I should've known he didn't blow things out of proportion or exaggerate. The road had been s-k-e-t-c-h-y. I'd been gripping the steering wheel for dear life for part of the route, the road was so rutted and littered with sharp rocks. I'd told myself to ask him when was the last time he'd been up because, even though I figured he trusted my driving skills enough to send me this way instead of the route I'd gone the last time, my gut said Mr. Overprotective would have been pushier about me not driving up alone if he'd known it was this level of shitty.

That or he really believed in me.

I'd only regretted being stubborn about doing this every thirty seconds.

I had a bad feeling in my stomach when my phone rang and "CLARA CALLING" flashed across the screen.

According to the text she'd sent me as I was leaving Rhodes's, she had been about to leave her house. She should've been somewhere close by, behind me, if not already here. And I knew that wasn't the case because there were two vehicles in the clearing that doubled as parking for the start of the hike, and neither of them were hers.

"Hey," I greeted, leaning my head back against the head-rest and sensing the unease pool in my stomach again.

"Aurora," Clara answered. "Where are you?"

"I'm at the trailhead," I confirmed, eyeing the very blue skies. "Where you at?"

She cursed.

"What happened?"

"I've been trying to call you, but it wasn't going through.

My car won't start. I called my brother, but he's still not here yet." She cursed again. "You know what? Let me call the tow truck service and—"

I didn't want her to spend money on a tow truck service. She'd been stressing enough about money when she thought I wasn't looking or paying attention, but at-home care for her dad ate up a massive chunk of the store's earnings.

Plus, we both also knew this was my last chance to do this hike this year, more than likely. October was knocking on the door. The drought had kept the summer warm and the start of fall warmer than normal, but Mother Nature was getting bored. The temperatures were going to start dropping soon and snow was going to start being a real thing in higher elevations. If I didn't do it now, it'd be eight months before I could even think about doing this again. Maybe next week would still be fine, but it was a hard maybe.

"No, don't do that," I told her, trying to figure out what to say. "Wait for your brother. The drive here was rough anyway."

"Really?"

"Yeah, the washboard"—that was crazy horizontal ruts that resembled a washboard on the road—"is unreal." I paused and tried to think; it would easily be three hours before she got here, if she was even able to. By that point, it'd be late morning and we'd be cutting it too close to dark. And that damn drive back....

I wasn't scared to do the hike alone. I worried more about other people than I did encountering animals. Plus, I was more prepared this time. I could handle it.

"I'm sorry. Damn it. I can't believe this happened."

"It's okay. Don't worry about it. I hope your brother gets there soon and it's not anything serious."

"Me too." She paused and said something away from the phone before coming back. "I'll do it with you next week."

I knew what I was going to do. I had to. This was why I'd come.

I had to do it for Mom. And for me. To know I could.

It was just a hike—a hard one, sure, but plenty of people did difficult ones. I wasn't camping. And there were two cars parked here.

"It's okay. I know you were just going to do it to keep me company, and I'm already here."

I heard the caution in her tone. "Aurora—"

"The weather is good. The drive was shit. I'm early enough to knock this out in about seven hours. There are two cars here. I'm in peak condition to get this shit done. I might as well get it over with, Clara. I'll be okay."

"It's a difficult hike."

"And you told me that you have a friend that runs it by himself," I reminded her. "I'll be fine. I'll be out of here while I still have hours of sunshine left. I got this."

There was a pause. "Are you sure? I'm sorry. I feel bad I'm always bailing on you."

"Don't feel bad. It's okay. You've got a life and so many responsibilities, Clara. I get it, I swear. And I've done other ones by myself. Start doing some jumping jacks or something so we can do an eleven-mile one-way hike next year."

"*Eleven miles one way?*" She made a sound that sounded almost like a laugh but mostly like she thought I was fucking nuts.

"Yeah, suck it up. I can do this. You know where I'm at; I'll be fine. I'm not doing what my mom did and doing a different hike without telling anyone. I'll leave my phone on; the battery is fully charged. I've got my whistle and my pepper spray. I'm good."

Clara made another hesitating sound. "You're sure?"

"Yes."

She sighed deeply, still hesitating.

"Don't feel bad. But also don't laugh at me if I can't walk tomorrow, deal?"

"I wouldn't laugh at you…."

I knew she wouldn't. "I'll text you if I get service and when I'm done, all right?"

"Will you tell Rhodes too?"

That made me smile. "He already knows."

"All right then. I'm sorry, Aurora. I promise I didn't know this was going to happen."

"Stop apologizing. It's okay."

She groaned. "Okay. I'm sorry. I feel like a piece of shit."

I paused. "You should." We both laughed. "I'm kidding! Let me call him real quick and then get started."

She wished me good luck, and we hung up right after that. I waited a second and then called Rhodes. It rang and rang, and after a moment, his voice mail picked up.

I left him a quick message. "Hi. I'm at the trailhead. Clara's having car trouble and won't be able to make it for at least another three hours, so I'm going to do the hike alone after all. There are two cars parked in the lot. Their license plates are…" I peeked at them and rolled off the letters and numbers. "The skies are bright blue. The road was *really* sketchy, but I got it done. I'm going to do this as fast as I can but still try and pace myself because I know the way out might kill me. I'll see you later. Have a good day at work and good luck with those poaching assholes. Bye!"

I started the hike with a smile on my face even though my soul felt a little heavier than normal, but not for bad reasons. Missing my mom made me sad, but that wasn't a bad thing. I just hoped she knew I still missed her and thought of her.

I put my phone on airplane mode so it wouldn't start roaming and drain the battery in no time. I'd learned that shit the hard way months ago. I could check it again once I got started going up.

Despite the cool temperature, the sun *was* bright and beautiful, the sky the bluest thing I'd ever seen. I couldn't have asked for a better day to do this, I knew. Maybe Mom had worked it out to cheer me up.

That thought lifted me up even higher.

Despite losing my breath after the first fifteen minutes and having to stop a lot more often than I would have wanted, I kept going. I took my time, had to peel my jacket off after a little bit, and kept an eye on my watch but tried not to stress about all my stops. The entire back of my shirt ended up soaked with sweat where the backpack rested, and that too was no big deal. I checked my phone every other pit stop and didn't find service. I just kept on going. One step in front of another, enjoying the incredible scent of the wilderness because that's exactly what this was.

I was in the middle of millions of acres of national forest all by myself, and as much as I would have enjoyed company, on today of all days, doing this gave me chills.

I imagined my mom taking this very same trail thirty-something years ago, and it made me smile. Her notes didn't specify which way she'd started the hike—there were two ways to get to the lake, one of which was the path I was on now and the other was the one I'd taken last time—but regardless, she was here. These trees had given her some sort of peace, I'd like to think.

I was pretty sure she'd done it by herself too, and that made me smile wider. It'd be even better to have Clara here... even better to have Rhodes with me or Am, but maybe it was meant to be for me to tackle this alone. To do this one last trip by myself like I'd started. I had wanted this move to Colorado to be me reconnecting with my mom, and nothing could have prepared me for the changes I'd made in the months since. They had made me stronger. Better.

Happier.

Sure, I'd still scream if a bat snuck back into the house or if I saw another mouse, but I knew I'd be able to figure out a solution if it happened. Maybe you didn't have to get over your fears completely to conquer them. Maybe if you just faced them in general that counted. Or at least that's what I wanted to believe.

And maybe... this was my goodbye to at least part of the past. Closing all the opened chapters that hadn't been completed. I had so much going for me. So much joy just waiting around. Like with the end of my relationship, I had so much I was leaving behind to start over with all these new possibilities. I had people who cared about me again, who worried for me, and they didn't care about who I knew or how much money I had or what I could do for them.

So maybe it could be like I'd thought before. You could start over any day of the week, at any time of the year, at any point in your life, and it was fine.

And I kept that thought in my head as I kept climbing, another hour after hour went by; my calves cramped, and I stopped briefly again to take some magnesium capsules I'd brought along. For all I tried to jump rope, my thighs burned like a son of a bitch too, and I was going through my water faster than I'd expected, but I'd planned for that too and could refill at a stream or the lake, even though the water would taste like butthole. I didn't want to get altitude sickness more than I disliked the taste of filtered water, so tough shit.

The scenery changed and changed, and I marveled at the beauty and greenery around. And maybe it was because I was too busy admiring everything and thinking that life was going to be okay that I didn't notice the sky. Didn't see the dark clouds that had started rolling in until a flash of lightning and a boom of thunder cracked across what had been clear skies, scaring the shit out of me.

I literally yelped and ran toward the closest collection of trees, crouching down a second before the rain started. Luckily, Clara had warned me to take a tarp with me on long hikes, and I covered myself with it, pulling Rhodes's rain jacket on too for extra protection. I was still sitting there when hail started pelting everything.

But I stayed optimistic. I knew this was just part of it. I'd gotten hailed on once or twice before. It never lasted long, and this time was no exception.

I started again, kept pushing, getting tired, but no big deal. It didn't rain long enough for it to be muddy, but simply damp.

I crossed a sketchy section and the ridge that had tried to assassinate me last time, that I pretty much had to scramble over, and that's when I knew I didn't have much further left. I was almost there. An hour maximum. I checked my phone, saw I had service, and sent out a couple of texts.

The first was to Rhodes.

Me: Made it to the ridge. Everything is good. I'll text you on the way back.

Then I sent one to Clara that was basically the same.

That's when an incoming message came through from Amos.

Amos: Did you go do the hike by yourself?

Me: Yessss. I made it to the ridge. Everything is good.

I didn't even get a chance to put my phone on airplane mode again when another message came through from him.

Amos: Are you nuts?

Well, I guess I might as well sit here another minute. I could use the break. So I texted him back, propped my butt on the nearest rock, and figured five more minutes wouldn't kill me.

Me: Not yet

Amos: I could've gone with you

Me: Do you remember how miserable you were when we did four miles?

I took out a precious granola bar and ate half in a bite, peeking at the skies. Where the hell had these clouds come from? I knew they rolled in uncalled for, but....

Another message came through while I was chewing.

Amos: You're not supposed to do it by yourself!!!

He was using *exclamation marks.*

He loved me.

Amos: Does dad know????

Me: He knows. I called him, but he didn't answer. I promise I'm okay.

I finished off the rest of my bar in another bite, slipped the wrapper into a grocery store bag I was using for trash, and when I hadn't gotten a response from Amos again or Clara, or anyone, I got up—my lower body crying in frustration from how tired it already was—and kept on going.

The next hour fucking sucked ass. I thought I was fit, thought I could handle this shit.

But I was exhausted.

Just thinking about the hike back made my enthusiasm disappear.

But I was doing this for Mom, and I was *here* and fuck if I wasn't going to finish this. This lake better be the greatest thing I'd ever seen.

I kept going and going.

At one point, I caught a flicker of what I figured had to be the lake in the distance, shiny and mirrorlike.

But with each step I took, the clouds got darker and darker.

It started pouring again, and I took out my wet tarp and hunkered under a tree with it.

But this time, it didn't clear up after five minutes.

Or ten.

Twenty or thirty.

It poured. Then it hailed. Then it poured some more.

Thunder shook the trees, my teeth, and my soul. I pulled my phone out of my pocket and checked to see if I had service. I didn't. I ate most of the snacks I'd planned on treating myself to when I got to the lake to save time. I was going to have to get there and pretty much turn around and start heading back.

The rain finally turned into a sprinkle after nearly an hour, and the quarter mile I had left felt like ten.

Especially when the bullshit lake was the most under-whelming thing I'd ever seen.

I mean, it was nice, but it wasn't... it wasn't what I'd expected. It didn't glow. It wasn't crystal blue. It was just... a regular lake.

I started laughing; then I started laughing like an idiot, tears bubbling up in my eyes as I cracked up some more.

"Oh, Mom, now I get what the wave was for." So-so. It was for so-so. It had to be.

I'd expected to find some people around, but there was nobody. Had they kept on hiking? The Continental Divide was miles out, branching off from a different trail attached to this one.

I laughed even more, again.

Then I sat down on a wet log, toed my boots off as I ate my apple, enjoying the crunch and the sweetness. My fucking treat. Whipping my phone out, I took a selfie with the dumbass lake and laughed again.

Never again.

I took my socks off and wiggled my toes, keeping my ears open for animals and people, but there was nothing.

Ten minutes later, I got up, put my socks and shoes back on, zipped my jacket because the rain had seriously cooled everything down and the sun wasn't out, and started the damn hike back.

Everything hurt. It felt like every one of my leg muscles was shredded. My calves were on the verge of dying. My toes were never going to forgive or forget this.

I'd lost my momentum having to stop for the rain, and another glance at my watch told me I'd lost two hours because of the weather and my breaks. What had seemed hard on the way to the lake was about a hundred times harder on the way back.

Fuck, shit, fucking shit, motherfucking fucker all came out of my mouth. How the hell anybody *ran this* was beyond me. I stopped what felt like every ten minutes, I was so tired, but still, I kept on going.

Two hours later, not knowing how I was going to survive the next three hours and eyeballing the damn clouds that were back again, I pulled out my phone and waited, hoping for service.

There wasn't any.

I had to try to send a few messages out.

The first was to Rhodes.

Me: Running late. I'm okay. Heading back.

Then I sent Clara another with basically the same message.

And finally Amos got my third one.

Me: On my way back. I'm good. The weather turned bad.

I left my signal on, hoping it would eventually reconnect with a tower. The battery was at 80 percent, so I figured it would be good enough. I hoped.

The ground was slippery, the gravel dangerous under my boots, and that slowed me down even more. There was no one around. I couldn't risk hurting myself.

I knew I was going to have to go even slower than I'd planned.

And the clouds opened up more, and I gave myself the middle finger for being a stubborn idiot.

I had to be careful. I had to be slow.

I couldn't even call out for rescue because there wasn't any service, and I wasn't going to shame Rhodes by being that person who had to get saved. I could do this. My mom could do this. But...

If I made it out of here, I was never doing this shit alone again. Didn't I know better? Of course I fucking did.

This was stupid.

I should've stayed home.

I wished I had more water.

I wasn't going to hike at all next year.

I wasn't going to walk anywhere ever again.

Oh God, I still had to drive home.

Fuck, fuck, fuck.

I wasn't giving up. I could do this. I was going to make it.

I was never doing a difficult hike again. At least not in a day. Fuck that shit.

One foot after another took me down. I stopped. I hid under my tarp. The temperature started to drop, and I couldn't believe I hadn't brought my thicker jacket. I knew better.

I layered Rhodes's jacket over my pullover when I started to shiver.

My water was getting low even though I'd filled it up with water from a creek, and I started having to take the tiniest sips every time I stopped because there weren't any more water sources.

My legs hurt worse and worse.

I couldn't catch my breath.

I just wanted a nap.

And a helicopter to come save me.

My phone still wasn't connecting.

I was so stupid.

I hiked and hiked. Down and down, slipping sometimes on the wet gravel and trying my best not to fall.

I did. I busted my ass twice and scraped my palms.

Two hours turned into three, I was going so slow. It was getting too dark.

I was cold.

I cried.

Then I cried more.

Genuine fear settled in. Had my mom been scared? Had she known she was screwed? I hoped not. God, I hoped not. I was scared already; I couldn't imagine....

Half a mile to go, but it felt like thirty.

I took out my flashlight and put it in my mouth, clutching to my trekking poles for dear life because I would have probably died without them.

Big, fat, sloppy tears of frustration and fear ran down my cheeks, and I took out the flashlight to scream "fuck" a couple of times.

No one saw me. No one heard me. There was no one here.

I wanted to get *home*.

"Fuck!" I yelled again.

I was finishing this motherfucker, and I was never doing this so-so hike again. This was bullshit. What did I have to prove? Mom had loved this. I liked six-mile hikes. Easy and intermediate ones.

I was just kidding; I could do this. I was doing it. I was finishing it. It was okay to be scared, but I was getting out of here. *I was.*

A tenth of a mile left that switchbacked and rounded and dipped, and I was cold, wet, and muddy.

This sucked.

I glanced at my watch and groaned when I saw the time. *It was six.* I should've been done hours ago. I was going to be driving in the dark, and I mean, the pitch-black shit. I could barely see anything now.

All right. It was all right. I'd just have to go really slow. Take my time. *I could do it.* I had a spare. I had a Fix-a-Flat. I knew how to change a tire.

I was going to make it home.

Everything hurt. I was pretty sure my toes were bleeding. The cartilage in my knees was shot.

This sucked.

I could do it.

It was fucking cold.

This sucked.

A couple more tears spilled out of my eyes. I was an idiot for doing this by myself, but I'd *done it.* Hail, some snow, rain, thunder, eating shit. I'd made it. I'd done this bitch-ass hike.

I was tired and a couple more tears came out of my eyes, and I wondered if I'd taken a wrong turn and was on a game trail instead of on the real trail because nothing looked familiar, but then again it was dark and I could barely see anything that was out of the beam of my flashlight.

Fuck, fuck, fuck.

Then I saw it, the big, low-hanging tree that I'd had to duck under right at the beginning of the hike.

I'd made it! I'd made it! I shivered so hard my teeth chattered, but I had an emergency blanket in my bag and in my car, and I had a thick, old jacket of Amos's that had found its way in there somehow.

I made it.

More tears filled my eyes, and I stopped, tipping my head up. Part of me wished there were stars out that I could talk to, but there weren't. It was too cloudy. But it didn't stop me.

My voice was hoarse from the screaming and the lack of water, but it didn't matter. I still said the words. Still felt them. "I love you, Mom. This sucked ass, but I love you and I miss you and I'm going to try my best," I said out loud, knowing she could hear me. Because she always did.

And in a burst of energy I didn't think I had in me, I took off running to my car, my toes crying, my knees giving up on my life, and my thighs shot for the rest of my existence—at least it felt like that in the moment. It was there.

The only one.

I didn't know where the hell those other people had gone, but I had no energy left to wonder how I hadn't run into them.

Fuckers.

As exhausted as I felt, I chugged down a quarter of my gallon bottle of water, stripped off Rhodes's rain jacket and my damp one, and pulled Amos's on. I took my shoes off and almost tossed them in the back seat but didn't just in case I needed to get out of the car; instead, I propped them on the floor of the passenger seat. I wanted to look at my toes and see what the damage was, but I'd worry about it later.

I checked my service, but it was still nonexistent. I shot off a message to Rhodes and Amos anyway.

Me: Finally done, it's a long story. I'm okay. Didn't have service. I think the tower is down. On my way out, but I have to go slow.

Then I backed out and started the trip home. It was going to take about an hour to get there once I got off this sketchy part. Best-case scenario, it would be two hours to get to the highway.

And it was just as shit as I remembered. Worse even. But I didn't care. I gripped the steering wheel for dear life, trying to remember what path I'd taken on the way up, but the rain had cleared my tracks.

I got this. I can do it, I told myself, driving literally two miles an hour and squinting like never before and hopefully never again.

My hands cramped, but I ignored them and the weird feeling of driving with no shoes on, but I wasn't putting those boots back on anytime soon.

I drove, not turning on the radio because I had to concentrate.

I made it maybe a quarter of a mile down the road when two headlights flashed through the trees around a bend.

Who the hell was driving up here this late?

It was my turn to curse because the best path was straight down the middle, and it wasn't like the road was wide to begin with. What were the chances? "Fuck," I muttered just as the lights disappeared for a moment and then reappeared on the straightaway, coming toward me.

It was an SUV or a truck for sure. A big one. And it was going a hell of a lot faster than I was.

With a sigh, I pulled off to the side, zipping up Amos's jacket to my chin, and then pulled off even more. With my luck today, I was going to get stuck.

No, I wasn't. I was going to get home. I was going to—

I squinted at the approaching car.

The SUV slammed to a stop, and the driver's side door opened. I watched as a big figure jumped out and stopped in place for a second before starting to move again. Forward.

I locked my doors, then squinted again and realized... I knew that body. I recognized those shoulders. That chest. The cap on what was definitely a man's head.

It was Rhodes.

I wouldn't remember throwing my own door open, then reaching to grab my shoes and slipping them halfway on before sliding out of my car. But I'd remember hobbling forward with my boots barely hanging on by my toes and watching Rhodes make his way toward me too.

His face was... he looked furious. Why did that make me want to cry?

"Hi," I called out weakly. Relief shot straight through me. My voice broke in half, and I said the last thing I would have wanted to. "I was so scared—"

Those big, muscular arms wrapped around me, the only thing holding me up, one hand going to palm the back of my head. My hair was wet with sweat—that shit wasn't rain—but the entire length of his body pressed against mine. There and comforting, and everything I needed then and more.

That entire beefy, hunky body trembled lightly, I faintly noticed. "No more hiking by yourself," he whispered roughly, so hoarse it scared me. "No more."

"No more," I agreed weakly. I shivered once in his arms, supported nearly completely by his frame. "It rained so much, and I don't know where the fuck those clouds came from, but they were shitheads, and I had to hunker down."

"I know. I thought something happened." I was pretty sure he stroked the curve of my head. "I thought you got hurt."

"I'm okay. Everything hurts, but just because I'm tired and these boots suck. I'm sorry."

I felt him nod against me. "I came up here as fast as I could when your text came through. I had to go to Aztec and didn't get service. Amos called me flipping out. He wanted to come, but I made him stay, and now he's pissed off. I got here as fast as I could." The hand on the back of my head swept down my spine, palming the small of my back, and there was no way I was imagining the fact he hugged me tight. "Don't ever do that again, Aurora. Do you hear me? I know you can do this all by yourself, but don't."

At this point, I was never going hiking again. Ever.

Another shiver shook through my body. "I'm so happy to see you, you have no idea. It was so dark, and I got really scared there for a while," I admitted, feeling my own body start to tremble.

The hand on my head stroked down, pulling me in so close, I felt like if he could have put me inside of him, he would have.

"You're fine though? You're not hurt?" he asked.

"Nothing I won't get over. Not like last time." I pressed my cheek against his chest, savoring his warmth. His steadiness. I was fine. I was safe. "Thank you for coming." I pulled back a little and gave him a small, sheepish smile. "Even though it'd be you they'd send in if I didn't make it back, huh?"

Rhodes's face was serious, his pupils wide, as he stared down at me, taking in my features with dark eyes. "I didn't come because it's my job."

Then, before I could react, those arms were around me again, swallowing me up completely. A human cocoon I could have lived in for the rest of my life.

I didn't imagine the faint tremble that shot through those hard muscles.

And I definitely didn't imagine the fierce expression he shot me when he pulled back again. His hands moved to settle low on my back. "Are you fine to drive?"

I nodded.

One of those hands moved to squeeze my hip in a way I wasn't even sure he knew he was doing it as his gaze roamed my face. "Buddy?"

"Hmm?"

"I want you to know... Amos is going to want to kill you."

That was probably the only thing that could have made me laugh then, and I did. Then I told him the absolute truth. "That's okay. I'm kind of looking forward to it."

CHAPTER 22

*E*verything hurt.

Literally, every single part of my body ached in some way. From my poor toes that felt like they were bleeding, to my calves that were traumatized, to my exhausted thighs and butt cheeks. If I focused hard enough, my nipples probably hurt too. But it was my hands and forearms that suffered the most on the drive home.

Those one hundred and twenty minutes were spent with me clutching the steering wheel for dear life, holding my breath more often than not.

If I hadn't just spent the last few hours terrified, my body might have been capable of summing up genuine fear at the rocks and ruts that I drove over. It was only because I was so focused on following Rhodes and not driving over anything sharp, that I didn't lose my shit as we drove painstakingly slow. And if I hadn't been so tired, I might have cheered when we finally made it to the highway.

It was then that I finally managed to exhale, deeply and completely, from the bottom, bottom of my gut.

I'd made it.

I really had made it.

It had to be the relief that kept me from shaking on the rest of the drive. But the moment after I turned off my car, that was when it hit me. It was a backhand to my face when I wasn't expecting it.

I blew out a breath a split second before my entire body started shaking. In shock, in fear.

Leaning forward, I pressed my forehead against the steering wheel and shook hard from my neck down to my calves.

I was fine, and that was all that mattered.

I was *fine*.

The door to my left opened, and before I could turn my head to the side, a big hand landed on my back and Rhodes's gruff voice spoke inside the car. "I'm here. I've got you. You're going to be okay, angel."

I nodded, my forehead still there even as another harsh shiver racked my body.

His hand stroked farther down my spine. "Come on. Let's get inside. You need food, water, rest, and a shower."

I nodded again, a knot forming in my throat.

Rhodes reached behind me, and a moment later my seat belt loosened. Rhodes guided me to sit back, letting the seat belt snap back into place. I glanced toward him right as he leaned forward, and before I knew what was happening, his arms slipped beneath me, under the backs of my knees, the other under my shoulder blades, and he hoisted me up. Against his chest I went, cradled.

And I said, "Oh" and "Rhodes, what are you doing?"

And he said, "Taking you upstairs." He closed the door with his hip before beginning to move, carrying me like it was no big deal as we made our way to the garage apartment. The door was unlocked, so all it took was a quick flip of his wrist to open it before we were going up.

"If you help me, I can do the stairs myself," I told him, taking in the silver-brown facial hair covering his jaw and chin.

His gray eyes flicked to me as he took one step after another up. "You can, and I would, but I can do it." And like he was proving a point, he squeezed me tighter to him, closer to that broad chest that had been the biggest relief of my life when I'd spotted him coming out of his car.

He'd come for me. I pressed my lips together and glanced down at my hands, which I was holding against my chest, and felt more tears spring up in my eyes. That same familiar fear that I'd suppressed the entire drive home flared up inside of me again.

Another shiver raced through me, strong and potent, coaxing a few more tears into my eyes.

I could feel Rhodes's gaze on my face as he kept on climbing the stairs, but he didn't say a word. His arms held me even closer somehow, his mouth dipping closer too, and if I hadn't closed my eyes, I was pretty sure I would have seen him brush his mouth against my temple. Instead, all I did was feel it, light and more than likely an accident.

I sucked in my breath and held back a choke as he lowered me to the bed and said, quietly, "Take a shower."

Opening my eyes, I found him standing almost directly in front of me. A frown took over his mouth as I nodded.

"I reek, I'm sorry," I apologized, barely able to get the words out.

His frown got even more severe.

I pressed my lips together.

Rhodes's head cocked to the side at the same time his gaze moved over my face and he said very carefully, "You had a scare, angel."

I nodded, holding my breath and trying to swallow the

emotion clogging my throat. "I was just thinking...." I sniffled, my words a croak.

Rhodes kept on looking at me.

I curled my fingers in my lap, felt my knee shaking, and whispered, "You know that time I told you I wasn't scared of dying?" I scrunched up my face and felt a tear slip out of my eye and stream down my cheek. "I was lying. I am scared." A few more tears escaped, hitting my jawline. "I know I wouldn't have died, but I still thought I was going to once or twice—"

A big, big hand swept over half of my face before doing the same to the other side, and in the time it took me to realize what he was doing, I was up again, his arms around me once more. Then I was on top of him, seated across his thighs with my shoulder to his chest, and it was me that pressed my face to his throat as another shiver ran through me.

"I was so scared, Rhodes," I whispered into his skin as his arm curled low around my back.

"You're okay now," he said hoarsely.

"All I could think about, when I could, was that I had so much still left to live for. There's so much I want to do, and I know it's dumb. I know I'm fine. I know the worst that could have happened was that I'd have to hide under a tree with my tarp and an emergency blanket to rest for a while, but then I pictured myself falling down and getting hurt and no one knowing where I was, or not being able to help me, and I was alone. And why did I go alone? What the hell do I have to prove to anybody? My mom wouldn't have wanted me to feel like that, right?"

He shook his head against me, and I buried my face even deeper into the softest skin of his throat.

"I'm sorry. I know I stink and I'm sticky and gross, but I was so happy to see you. And I'm so glad you went. Otherwise...." I sniffled, and a couple more tears spilled between us. I could feel them stream between my cheeks and his skin.

Rhodes hugged me even closer to him, and his voice was steady when he said, "You're fine. You're totally fine, angel face. Nothing's going to happen. I'm here, and Am is next door, and you're not alone. Not anymore. It's all right. Take a breather."

I took the deep breath he'd mentioned and then took another one. I wasn't alone. I was out of there. And I was never going hiking again... though I might change my mind eventually, but that was beside the point. My shoulders slowly loosened, and I felt my stomach begin to unclench; I hadn't even realized I was sucking it in.

The hand on my back stroked my side down to my hip, and Rhodes kept on holding me.

Digging deep into my gut, I said, "I'm sorry."

"There's nothing for you to be sorry about."

"I'm probably overreacting—"

He petted me again. "You're not."

"It feels that way though. It's been a long time since I've felt that scared, and it really just got under my skin."

"Most people are scared of dying. There's nothing wrong about it."

"Are you?" I pressed my forehead closer to the warm, smooth skin of his throat.

"I think I'm more scared of the people I care about dying than I am of myself."

"Oh," I said.

Rhodes's sigh was soft. "I'm a little scared of not doing all the things I want to do, I guess."

"Like what?" I asked him, my forehead still to his neck. I could feel the steady beat of his heart, and it soothed me.

"Well, seeing Am grow up."

I nodded.

His palm settled on top of my thigh. "I hadn't thought about it in a long time, and I don't think I have too much time left, but I think I'd like to have another kid." His chest rose and fell against me. "Not I *think*. I'm sure."

Something inside of me stilled. "You would?"

He nodded, the bristles of facial hair tickling my skin. "Yeah. I told you how much I regret all the things I missed with Am. I like kids. I just wasn't sure I ever would be able to have one in the first place, but back then I didn't think I'd be back in Colorado, not in the Navy, not...."

"Not what?" I asked him, holding my breath.

The hand on my thigh slid up to my hip, lingering there. "Not... here. "

I didn't know what he meant. Or maybe I was just too tired to think about it too much because I nodded like I understood when I didn't, feeling a small pang in my chest at the idea of him wanting another child, considering how that child would need to be conceived.... How he would need a woman in his life to have one because Amos's mom couldn't have another. I asked, "What would you want? If you could choose. Another boy or a girl?"

The arms around me tightened just a little. "I'd be grateful for either." His breath drifted over my cheek, and I realized then just how much I liked his voice. The steady roughness of it. It was such a treat to my ears. "But I only have brothers, and I only have nephews, so maybe a girl would be kind of fun. Break the cycle."

"Girls *are* fun," I agreed with a shaky exhale. "And I'm sure you still have time. If you wanted. I've heard of men having kids in their fifties and sixties."

I felt his "mm-hmm" through his chest as his hand moved down my thigh again. "You?" he asked.

"I don't care either. I'd love them anyway." I sniffled. "I might have to settle for a puppy though at the rate I'm going."

His laugh was a soft puff, his words damn near a whisper, "No. I don't think you'll have to do that."

I lifted my head and looked at his handsome face. This close, the color of his eyes was even more incredible. His lashes were thick, his bone structure perfectly pronounced. Even the lines at his eyes and alongside his mouth were shallow but added so much to his features, I'd bet he was even more handsome now than he'd been in his twenties. Even though my cheeks felt tight from the tears, I managed to smile at him a little. "At this point, I think I'd be happy to have someone to grow old with so I'm not alone. It might have to be Yuki."

Rhodes's face softened as his gaze, which I felt to the tips of my toes, roamed mine and his hand slipped back down my leg to rest on my thigh. He gave it a squeeze. "I don't think you have to worry about that either, Buddy." His gaze settled on mine, and the next thing I knew, he hugged me again.

He hugged me for a long time.

And after a while, he eventually pulled back and said, "I got news today. I have to leave for a few weeks."

"Is everything okay?"

Rhodes's nod was grave. "Another warden in the Colorado Springs district was in an accident, and he won't be able to get back to work for a while, so they're sending me there." The hand on my thigh flexed. "They said two weeks, but I wouldn't be surprised if it was longer. I've got a few days to get things sorted. I need to call Johnny and see about Amos."

"Anything I can do to help, let me know," I threw in.

His mouth twisted, and I had to fight the urge to hug him. "You sure?"

"*Yes.*"

His mouth twisted a little more. "I'll talk to Am and get back to you."

I nodded and thought about something. "Is he still grounded?"

"Technically. I still tell him 'no' to a few things, so he doesn't think everything has been forgiven and forgotten, but I'm letting him off the hook a little. He barely complained about his punishment, so I don't see a point being too hard on him."

I smiled.

But the twist of his mouth dropped off, and Rhodes said, seriously, "You'll be fine here."

"I know."

"I might let Am stay, but I might not. I haven't thought about it enough, but I'll tell you as soon as I do."

I nodded.

"You're welcome over at the house any time you want," he said, his eyes careful. "Might save you some hassle to do your laundry there from now on."

From now on? That got me to smile. "Thanks."

"Colorado Springs is only a few hours away. You need help, call Am or Johnny."

"If you or Am need anything, tell me. I mean it. Anything. I owe you big-time after today."

"You don't owe me anything." His hand moved back up to my hip. "I'll only be away for a little while."

"I'm not planning on going anywhere. I'll be here," I told him, setting my hand down on his forearm. "Whatever you, Johnny, or Am need, I've got you three." I owed him for today and yesterday—for so much, really, regardless of what he thought. I wouldn't forget, not any of it.

He looked right into my eyes as he said it. "I know, Aurora."

CHAPTER 23

*T*he next three weeks went by in basically a blur.

With the changing colors of the leaves, something inside of me changed right along with them. Maybe it was the sheer fear I'd experienced on the Hike from Hell that had been the catalyst, or maybe it was just something in the cool air, but I felt some part of myself growing. Settling too. This place that I had come back to, where I had spent some of my best times and the single worst moment of my life, embedded itself into my skin even deeper with each passing day.

I wanted to live. It wasn't like that was a new thought, but there was a difference between living and *living*, and I wanted the latter. I wanted the latter more than anything. An entire life could change in a single moment, with one action, and in a way, I had forgotten that.

Maybe every day wouldn't be perfect and it was naïve to expect that, but every day could be good.

This place was where I wanted to be, and I found myself embracing everything even closer than before. I absorbed even more of my relationship with Clara and my friendship with customers who sure started to feel more like friends. I appreciated my teenage friends even more too.

In fact, the only thing I hadn't embraced had been Rhodes.

It had been two weeks by that point since he'd left, and he hadn't managed to come visit yet. Supposedly, he'd been on his way to visit for the day when he'd gotten called back to Colorado Springs—a four-hour drive away—with an emergency. I still saw Amos just about every day between getting dropped off by the school bus and picked up by his uncle. He told me all about his dad calling him every day and had even —not so subtly—mentioned how Rhodes asked about me too.

But Rhodes didn't call me or text me, and I knew he had my number.

I thought that everything that had happened with us before had been some kind of turning point, I was *sure* it was, but... maybe he was extra busy. And I tried not to wallow in worrying about things I couldn't control. And how someone felt about you was one of those.

I was just trying to keep on living my life and settling in even more in the meantime, and that was exactly why that morning, three weeks after the Hike from Hell, I found myself getting a dubious look from Amos as I clutched my helmet, trying to give him a reassuring smile.

"Are you sure?" he asked, putting on the wrist guards that I was sure Rhodes had insisted he wear when he'd given him permission to go to the ski resort with me. I had mentioned to him two days before that I wanted to go. I had never been snowboarding. I knew for sure I'd gone skiing with my mom back when I'd been younger, but that was it. It hadn't snowed in town yet, but a couple of nights had dropped enough snow this high in the mountains to open some parts of the resort.

I focused back on the teenager in front of me in a

matching green jacket and helmet he'd explained that his mom and other dad had bought him last season. "Yes, I'm sure. Go with your friends. I'm sure I can figure it out."

He didn't believe me, and he wasn't even trying to pretend otherwise. "Do you remember what I told you? About using your toes and heels?"

I nodded.

"Keeping your knees bent?"

I nodded again, but his features stayed reluctant. "I promise. It's fine. Go. See? Your friends are waving at you."

"I can go down with you once to make sure. Getting off the lift is kind of tricky—"

This was exactly why I loved this kid. He could be so quiet, stubborn and surly—just like his dad—but he had a heart of gold too. "I just saw a little four or five-year-old do it. It can't be that hard."

Amos opened his mouth, but I beat him to it again.

"Look, if it's going really bad, I'll text you, deal? Go with your friends. I got this."

"K." He looked like he wanted to keep arguing but barely stopped himself from it. Amos turned around to grab his snowboard from the rack he'd propped it on and muttered in a way that made me feel like he genuinely thought he would never see me again, "Bye."

Well, that didn't sound foreboding.

I snapped my helmet on, tugged my gloves on over the wrist guards I'd put on while waiting for Amos to buy his season pass, and trudged over to the lift that would lead up to the top of the bunny hill after grabbing my own rented snowboard from the rack. I'd rented it from the shop at an extremely discounted rate. I'd spent the night before looking up videos for how to snowboard, and it didn't look that hard. I had decent balance. I'd taken a couple of surfing lessons with Yuki before, and they had gone pretty well... at least until the surfboard had clipped me in the face and my nose had started bleeding the last time.

I'd put up a bat house and grabbed a fucking eagle. I'd hiked up a mountain under the shittiest conditions. I could do this.

~

I couldn't do this.

And that was exactly what I told Octavio, the nine-year-old little boy who had helped me up four times now.

"It's okay," he tried to assure me as he pulled me up to standing position again. "You only fell on your face four times now."

I had to hold back a snort as I brushed the snow off my jacket and pants. I liked kids so much. Especially friendly ones like this one who had come over to me on my second time down the hill and helped me after I'd eaten at least a cup of snow. I had already told his mom, who was never too far away with another little girl that she was teaching how to snowboard—and doing a better job than I was—that he was such a nice boy.

Because he really was. My own nine-year-old white knight.

"Tavio!" his mom called out.

My little friend turned to me and blinked up with pretty brown eyes. "I gotta go. Bye!"

"Bye," I replied, watching as he made it over to her effortlessly.

Shit.

Taking a deep breath, I eyed the packed snow covering the gentle hill and sighed.

I *could* do this.

Bend my knees, keep my weight balanced, toes up, toes down—

I sensed the presence coming up behind me before I saw it. As it came to a stop just a couple feet away, I took in the big figure in a dark blue coat and black pants. Goggles covered half his face, a helmet covering all of his hair... but I knew that jaw. That mouth.

"Rhodes?" I gasped as the man lifted the goggles over his head and onto his helmet.

"Hi, Buddy," he said with a small smile, his hands going to his hips, his gaze roaming my face.

I beamed, and my soul might have as well. "What are you doing here?"

"Came to find you and Am," he said, like we were meeting at a restaurant instead of at the ski resort.

"Amos took one of the other lifts since they just opened it and he actually knows what he's doing," I told him, taking in the rough stubble covering his cheeks. He looked tired.

But happy.

I'd missed his moody butt.

"I know. I saw him already. He's the one who told me you were down here." His small smile lifted into a bigger one that tickled my chest. "I thought you would have taken snow-boarding lessons with a pro."

He was messing with me again. I groaned and shook my head. "I had a nine-year-old helping me, does that count?"

His laugh was pure, surprising me even more.

Someone was in a good mood.

Or maybe he was just really happy to be home.

"It's harder than I thought it would be, and I can't figure out what I'm doing wrong."

"I'll help you," he said, not giving me a choice, not that I would have said no in the first place.

I nodded at him way too enthusiastically, so happy to see him and not bothering to hide it. He might not have called me his friend again, but we *were* friends. I knew that at least for sure.

Rhodes waddled over, oblivious to how he made me feel, stopping right at my shoulder. "Let me see your stance, angel face. We'll go from there."

~

IT TOOK three runs down the hill before I finally managed to make it without busting my ass more than once. From the way I pumped my fist in the air, you would have figured I'd won a gold medal, but I didn't care.

And from the way Rhodes smiled at me, he didn't care either.

I'd been surprised by how patient of a teacher he'd been. He'd never raised his voice or rolled his eyes, other than the one time he used his Navy Voice on a teenage boy who knocked me over. But he had laughed a couple times when I'd lost control, freaked out, and bailed, which had then resulted in me busting my ass. But he'd also been the one to tug me up to sitting, wiped my goggles off with his gloved hand, and then helped me to stand.

"I need a break," I told him, rubbing my hip with my glove. "I have to pee."

Rhodes nodded before bending over to release his boots from the snowboard.

I bent over and did the same.

Finished, I picked up my board and followed after him. There was a small building I'd seen when we'd arrived with a sign for restrooms and concessions. Leaving our boards in one of the racks, I headed toward the bathrooms, used it, and by the time I got done, I found Rhodes sitting at one of the tables on the small deck surrounding the concession stand with two cups in front of him. Music played softly through small speakers.

But it was the woman sitting in the chair opposite of him that had me pausing.

She was pretty, about my age if not younger... and from the smile on her face, flirting her ass off.

Jealousy—pure-blooded jealousy—sprung out of nowhere inside of my stomach, and honestly, it surprised the shit out of me. My chest went tight. Even my throat felt a little funny. I could probably count on one hand the number of times I'd ever been jealous while I'd been with Kaden. One of those times had been when he'd gone on his fake date; the other time had been right after we'd split up and he'd gone on a date a month later. And the other two occasions had been when his high school girlfriend had shown up at his shows, and that was only because Mrs. Jones had liked her, I'd determined one day.

But right then, as I took in the woman talking to my landlord, that sensation came at me like a damn hurricane.

He wasn't smiling at her. It didn't even look like he was talking to her by the way his lips were pressed together, but... none of that changed anything.

I was jealous.

Aunt Carolina and Yuki would be shocked because I sure as hell was.

He wasn't my boyfriend. We weren't even dating. He could—

She touched his arm, and my throat muscles had to work extra hard to get me to swallow.

Holding my breath a little, I put one foot in front of the other and got myself to move toward them just as the woman smiled brighter and touched Rhodes once more. I was only a few feet away when those gray eyes I knew too well moved in my direction, and then, *then*, a small smile came over his mouth. And as I kept making my way over, I watched as he pulled out the chair beside him, a little at an angle and closer to his.

I could hear the woman talking in a nice, clear voice even as her gaze flicked over her shoulder to try and figure out who Rhodes was looking at. "...if you have time," she said at just about the same time her smile wilted a little.

I smiled at her and carefully took the seat that he'd pulled out, my gaze going from him to her and then the steaming cup on the table.

He pushed it toward me as he said, "Thank you for the invitation, Ms. Maldonado, but I'm going to be in Colorado Springs at the time."

I picked up the cup and brought it to my mouth, peeking at the woman as discreetly as possible. She was looking back and forth between Rhodes and me, trying to figure out... what? If we were together or not? "I can possibly work some things around if you have time once you get back," she offered, apparently deciding that we weren't. Maybe because I wasn't shooting her eye daggers.

I couldn't exactly blame her.

I'd be hitting on him too.

That thought alone made me feel petty. Of course women flirted with him. He was gorgeous, and his crabby little attitude just made him more attractive to some people more than likely. I was probably the only sucker who had been drawn in by how good of a dad he was.

Or maybe not.

"I appreciate the offer," Rhodes replied in that tight voice that reminded me of what our relationship had been like months ago. "I won't have time then either, but I'll make sure to tell Amos you asked about him, and if you have any questions, you can call the office, and someone should be able to help you out."

To give her credit, she wasn't giving up even as she pushed her chair back and shot me a smile that wasn't totally friendly or unfriendly. "If you change your mind, my number is in the school directory then." She got to her feet. "Hopefully I'll see you around school, Mr. Rhodes."

I was the only one who watched her walk off, and I knew that because I felt his intense gaze on my face as I did it. It was confirmed too when I glanced back toward him and found him looking at me.

He'd shot her down. Politely, but he had.

"Hi, sneaky," I told him, holding the cup of hot chocolate a little higher. "Sorry to interrupt you and your friend." Did that sound sarcastic, or was I blowing it out of proportion?

"She's not a friend, and you didn't interrupt anything," he replied, picking up his own cup and taking a small sip. "She was Amos's English teacher last year."

I nodded before taking another sip. So she'd waited to make her move. It all made sense now.

Rhodes's eyes narrowed a little as he took another drink, the cup looking small in his hand. "I had a feeling she had been interested, but I hadn't known for sure until today."

I raised both my eyebrows and nodded. "She'll probably ask you out again real subtle the next time she sees you."

He got a funny look on his face. "I'm sure she got a clue now that I don't feel the same way." He leaned forward in his chair, propping his elbows on the table. His gaze was steady on my face as he whispered, "She talks too much."

I reeled back and laughed. "I talk too much! Remember when you asked me, 'do you always talk this much?' You do, don't you?"

A big smile came over his full mouth, and I swear he was more handsome than ever. "I changed my mind, and the difference is that I like hearing you talk."

My heart skipped a damn beat or ten before he managed

to keep going.

"I don't like talking either, but you get me to somehow."

I didn't even try and suppress the elation that had blossomed in my chest. I was sure it was on my face too as I grinned at him, pleased. So pleased. "It's a gift. My aunt says I've got a friendly face."

"I don't think that's it," he argued softly.

I shrugged, still beaming from the inside out. "So...," I started to say, not wanting to talk about Amos's flirty former teacher.

Those gray eyes caught and held mine, inviting my question.

"How are you? How's Colorado Springs treating you?"

"Fine," he said, lowering the cup to sit on top of the thigh furthest from me. "It's keeping me busier than I was expecting. I'm glad I didn't take the position when it became available."

"Busier than our little stretch of the woods?"

He tilted his head to the side. "It's more driving here, a lot more, but it's still less. Less people. Less bullshit."

"Any idea how much longer you'll be there?"

"No. Nothing has been finalized yet," he replied before taking another sip. "They told me no longer than two more weeks, but I'm not holding my breath."

I moved my leg until it tapped against his. "I hope it goes fast, but we're holding down the fort. Amos is doing okay, at least from what he tells me. He's eaten dinner with me a few times when his uncle is running late, and I make sure to get him to eat some vegetables. I asked Johnny about him the other day when he picked him up, and he said he was doing fine."

"I think he's doing all right," he agreed. "He doesn't seem too heartbroken to be alone so much."

I grinned at him, and his mouth hitched up in that

familiar way I liked.

"You? You're okay?"

We had barely seen each other in that week between the Hike from Hell and him leaving, and we hadn't really gotten a chance to talk about what happened that night. Me almost losing it. Me sitting on his lap while he comforted me. Him stroking my back and holding me close. There were all these signs... all these things I picked up from him and... I wasn't sure what to think about any of them. I knew a man didn't act that way for nothing. I wanted to ask... but I was too much of a chicken.

But I still told him the truth. "Yeah, I'm good. Business has picked up a lot with so many hunters in town, so we've been busy at the shop."

His purple-gray eyes were on me as the side of his leg nudged mine beneath the table. "And when you're not at the shop?" Rhodes asked slowly.

Was he asking me...? I kept my face neutral. "I've been hanging out with Clara at their house. I went horseback riding with one of my customers and his wife last week. Other than that...."

He took another sip, attention still totally on me.

"Hanging out at home after work with your boy. Same old. I like my quiet life."

He pressed his lips together and nodded slowly.

"What about you?" I asked, ignoring the strange feeling in my stomach that was way too similar to the one I'd experienced coming out to see the woman talking to Rhodes. "What are you doing when you're not working?"

The leg beside me shifted, rubbing against my own through my pants. "Sleeping. They got me a rental house that's too quiet, but there's a gym close by I can go to easily. I've gotten to see my brother and his family a couple of times. That's about it."

"How long are you staying today?"

"I have to leave tonight," he said just as the music I'd been ignoring changed.

A song I recognized too well came on. I let it go in one ear and out the other, keeping my face about as even as possible. "Some time is better than no time," I told him, feeling the strain in my cheeks before I managed to push the faint resentment away.

"But I've got another seven, eight hours before I have to head back." His thigh brushed mine again, and his expression went thoughtful. "You don't like this song? I don't know if I've ever heard it."

I should tell him. I really should. But I didn't want to. Not yet. "I like the song, but I'm not a fan of the guy singing it."

His mouth made a funny shape, and his voice was dry as he said, "It's only 90s pop groups you like then?"

I blinked. "What makes you say that?"

"You forget the windows are open and we hear you shouting Spice Girls lyrics."

I dropped my voice. "How do you know it's Spice Girls?"

Rhodes's smile was so quick I almost missed it. "We looked up the lyrics."

I couldn't help but laugh and blurt out the first thing I thought of. "You know... I've kind of missed you."

I hadn't seen that coming. Was it the truth? Yes, but I was still surprised by how sensitive saying the words out loud made me feel.

But that sensation only lasted for about a second.

Because he hadn't seen that coming either from the slow way his eyebrows rose in sheer surprise even as his facial features simultaneously softened. And he said quietly, looking right at me in what felt like pleased shock, "Kind of missed you too."

CHAPTER 24

"*O*ra, are you sure you don't want to come with us?"

I finished marking off the jackets I'd been inventorying and glanced over at Clara who was on the other side of the rental counter with Jackie beside her. It was the day before Thanksgiving, and honestly, it had snuck right up on me. I'd never been big on the holiday. Until I'd moved in with my aunt and uncle, I had never actually celebrated it.

"No, it's okay," I insisted for the second time since she'd brought up me accompanying them to Montrose to spend the night with her dad's sister.

Honestly, if they had decided to stay in Pagosa, I would have gone over to their house, but I didn't want to intrude on the whole family.

I wasn't heartbroken at all over the idea of staying in the garage apartment all nice and toasty. I had hot cocoa, marshmallows, movies, snacks, a new puzzle, and a couple books. Maybe if one day I ended up with a family of my own, I'd go all out and ask my mom for forgiveness for celebrating a holiday she had raised me to boycott, but... I'd worry about that some other day.

Jackie leaned over the counter. "Are you going with Mr. Rhodes and Am to his aunt's house?" she asked.

They were going to his aunt's house? I had no idea. I had just seen them both last night when we'd had dinner together, and neither one of them had mentioned anything. Rhodes had just gotten back from Colorado Springs for good a week ago, and I'd spent every night except for two of them eating dinner at their house. Those two nights I hadn't were because Rhodes had worked late. "No, I wasn't invited," I told her honestly. "But I'm good. I don't even like turkey all that much anyway."

Jackie frowned. "They didn't invite you? Am said he did."

I shook my head and then glanced down to make sure the rest of the inventory form was done. It was. This was my fourth time doing it, and I was glad it was done right.

"Aurora, you want to come over to my house for Thanksgiving?" Walter, a regular customer and friend, asked from across the shop where he was going through some fly-making materials that Clara had put on sale just that morning. "We always have plenty of food, and I have this nephew who could use a good woman in his life to straighten him out."

"Your wife hasn't straightened you out, and it's been forty years," I muttered, smiling at him slyly. This whole conversation was a perfect example of part of the reason why I'd been so happy lately. I had *friends* again.

"Listen here, child... my Betsy had no idea what she had in store for her. I'm a life project," Walter shot back.

We all laughed.

Honestly, it wasn't just Thanksgiving that had snuck up on me; October and most of November had too. Since the Hike from Hell that I'd overcome, time had blown by, especially the last three weeks.

Clara, her sister-in-law, Jackie, and I had gone camping

once, even though it had been freezing. Amos tagged along with me to do random things, like going grocery shopping and playing putt-putt with Jackie one time, when his dad let him off the hook from being grounded. I'd gone snowboarding once more too, and I'd only busted my ass a few times. I hadn't moved on from the bunny hill yet, but maybe next time I would.

Every day was just... good.

"You know I have almost zero experience driving in snow," I reminded them.

"This isn't really snow, Ora," Jackie argued. "There's only about an inch out there."

That wasn't the first time I'd heard that. But to me, who had only seen significant snow from the windows of a tour bus, a quarter of an inch was snow. Kaden avoided going on tour during the winter, after all. We had usually gone to Florida or California the minute the weather started to get cool. Some flurries had fallen in town over the last few weeks, but most of it had been focused in the mountains, leaving them capped and beautiful. "I know, I know. Either way, I'm putting people's lives at risk just driving home, I feel like, but if I change my mind, I'll give you a call for your address, deal?" I asked Walter right as the door opened.

"No, no, no, just come on over. I want you to meet—"

I glanced back toward the door to see a familiar figure in a thick dark jacket coming in, stomping his feet on the rug I shook out every hour if I had time.

And I smiled.

It was Rhodes.

Or as my heart recognized him as: one of the main reasons I'd been so happy over the last two months, even though I'd only seen him a total of seven times, including the two visits he'd squeezed in while he'd been working in Colorado Springs.

"—my nephew. Oh, how's it going, Rhodes?" Walter asked as he caught sight of our new visitor.

Rhodes dipped his cute chin down, a little notch forming between his brows. "Well. How are you, Walt?" he greeted him.

How he knew people when he said about twenty words a day, depending on his mood, was beyond me.

"I'm doing just fine, apart from trying to convince Aurora here to come over to my house for Thanksgiving."

My landlord's hands went to his hips, and I was pretty sure his lips pressed together before he said, "Hmm."

"Hi, Rhodes," I called out.

Things were good between us. Since getting back, that something that I'd thought before had changed, *had* changed even more. It was like he'd gotten back and decided... something.

Some part of me knew that he wouldn't have done everything he had for me and with me if he was indifferent, landlord or not. Friend or not. Finding people attractive was one thing. But liking other things about a person, their personalities, was something else entirely.

I wasn't sure what exactly was going on, it felt different than friendship somehow, but I could see it in the way that he had accepted my hug that first day he'd gotten home and squeezed me back tightly. It was in the way he would touch my shoulders and my hand randomly. But mostly it was in the way that he talked to me. In the weight of that purple-gray gaze. I ate up every single word out of his mouth after dinner when we sat around the table, and he told me a lot of things.

Why he'd chosen the Navy—because he thought he loved the ocean. He didn't anymore; he'd seen more of it than most people would in a lifetime.

That he'd had that Bronco since he was seventeen and had spent the last twenty-five years working on it.

That he'd lived in Italy, Washington, Hawaii, and all over the East Coast.

I found out his favorite vegetable was brussels sprouts, and that he hated sweet potatoes and eggplant.

He was generous and kind. He cleaned my windshield off in the mornings if there was ice on it. He'd become a district wildlife manager—his official title—because he had always loved animals and someone had to protect them.

And in that moment, this man who loved scary movies, looked so, so tired.

So I wasn't totally sure what to think about the scowl he made at the possibility of me going over to Walter's house, especially if he'd heard the part about the older man's nephew.

"Hi, sweetheart," he replied before tipping his head to Walter and starting to come over.

You could have heard someone fart from all the way in the employee bathroom after that.

He'd called me sweetheart.

In front of all of three people.

It took me a second to swallow, this bright little rush going through my chest, and I had to fight to keep my smile normal instead of this massive one that more than likely would make me look like a lunatic. "Whatcha doing?" I asked, staying where I was until he stopped about a foot away, willing myself to act cool.

He looked exhausted. He'd been gone by the time I left that morning, just like most days. Gone before I was and not back until I was already toasty in bed. He worked endlessly and tirelessly, never complaining. It was one of the many things I liked about him.

"I came so I could follow you home before I have to get

back out there," he answered quietly, that serious look in his eyes.

Clara turned around and so did Jackie, like they were giving us privacy, but I knew they were just pretending and were really eavesdropping. We'd already gotten just about everything done that needed to be finished in preparation for having tomorrow off for the holiday. We had ten minutes left before closing time.

Since there were no customers around and Walter didn't count because he was becoming my friend... I took a step forward and hugged him. His jacket was cool against my cheek and hands. That big chest rose and fell once, and then he hugged me back.

Look how far we'd come.

"It's starting to come down outside," he said against my hair.

He'd come to follow me home because it was snowing. If my heart could grow a size or two, it would have right then.

"That's really nice of you, thank you," I said, pulling back after a moment, not wanting to be a total clinger.

"Do you need to finish anything before you close up?"

I shook my head. "No, I finished inventory right before you walked in. Now we just have to wait until three."

He nodded, casting a quick look toward Walter before glancing back at me. "You never texted me back."

"You messaged me?" Rhodes hadn't texted me at all while he'd been gone, but since getting back, he'd messaged me twice, and it had been both days he wasn't going to get home until late. According to him, he didn't like talking, and he wasn't much for texting either. It was pretty adorable. I wondered if it was because his fingers were so big.

"Last night."

"I didn't get it."

"It was late. I asked Am if you had given him an answer

about Thanksgiving, and he said he forgot to ask you about it," Rhodes explained.

I didn't want to presume. "What about Thanksgiving?"

"You coming with us. He always spends it with Billy's family, and his mom and dad got here this morning as a surprise."

My eyes widened. "His mom's here?"

"And Billy. They picked him up on the way home from the airport, he's spending the week with them until they fly back," Rhodes explained, watching me carefully. "Am wants you to come over and meet them."

"He does?" I asked quietly.

One side of his mouth tipped up. "Yeah, he does. I do too. Billy said I can't come over if you aren't with me. They've heard too much about you."

"From Am?"

He gave me one of his rare, small smiles. "And me."

My knees went like jelly, and it took everything in me to stay upright. It was a miracle in itself that I managed to even smile back at him—so big it made my cheeks hurt.

"Do you... want me to?" I asked. "I was just planning on staying in the studio and hanging out."

Those purple-gray eyes bounced around my face. "We were wondering since you didn't say anything about going back to Florida or seeing your friends," Rhodes replied, sounding cryptic and not answering my question about whether he wanted me to come over or not.

"Yeah, I don't really care about Thanksgiving all that much. My mom never made a big deal about it. She used to say that the Pilgrims were a bunch of colonizing pieces of shit and we shouldn't celebrate the start of a people's geno- cide." I paused. "Pretty sure those were her exact words."

Rhodes blinked. "That makes sense, but... you still get the time off anyway, and why can't you just make the holiday about being thankful for the blessings that you have? The people that you have?"

I smiled. "That sounds pretty nice."

"You'll come then?"

"If you want me to."

His mouth twisted into that not-officially-a-smile smile, and his voice was gruff. "Get ready to leave by noon."

"You're using your bossy voice again."

He sighed and looked at the ceiling, his tone lightening. "Please come over for Thanksgiving?"

I brightened up. "Are you positive?"

That got him to dip his face a little, his breath touching my lips, his eyebrows up. My heart swelled within my chest. "Even if it didn't make you smile like that, I'm positive."

I DIDN'T WANT to think that I was nervous, but... I was nervous the next day.

Just a little bit.

I'd stuck my hands between my thighs to keep from rubbing them against the leggings I'd pulled on under my dress to wipe off the sweat that kept accumulating on them.

"Why are you squirming so much?" Rhodes asked from his spot behind the steering wheel as he navigated us down the highway, closer and closer to Amos's aunt's house. She lived two hours away. I wasn't proud to admit that we'd had to stop for me to pee twice.

"I'm nervous," I admitted. I'd spent way too long doing my makeup earlier, putting on bronzer and brow gel for the first time in months. I'd even ironed my dress. Rhodes had smiled at me when I'd walked into his house and asked if I could use his iron, but he hadn't made a comment as he stood by me while I did my dress... and then he redid it because he was better at ironing than I was.

A lot better.

And honestly, the image of him ironing my clothes was going to be burned into my brain for the rest of my life. Watching him... this weird little tinkle had built up in my chest. I was going to pick that apart later. In private.

"What do you have to be nervous about?" he asked, like he thought I was nuts.

"I'm meeting Amos's mom! Your best friend! I don't know, I'm just nervous. What if they don't like me?"

His nostrils flared a little, eyes still glued to the road. "How often do you meet people who don't like you?"

"Not that often, but it happens." I held my breath. "You didn't like me that much when we first met."

That got him to glance at me. "I thought we talked about this already? I didn't like what Amos had done, and I took it out on you." He cleared his throat. "And the other thing." Oh, about me reminding him of his mom. We hadn't brought her up anymore, and I had a feeling it would be a long time before we did again.

I glanced out the window. "That too, but you still didn't want to like me."

"Fine. I didn't," he agreed, glancing at me real quick with not a smile but just about the most fond expression I could ever have dreamed of on his features. "But I lost that battle."

The tinkling in my chest was back, and I braved a smile at him.

The fond expression was still there, trying its best to short circuit my brain and heart.

I wiped my hands again, and I gulped. "His mom is just so accomplished, and so is his other dad, and I'm just over here... not knowing what I want to do with my life at thirty-three."

He slid me a look that was way too close to the rabid raccoon one. "What? You think they're better than you because they're doctors?"

I scoffed. "No!"

His mouth twitched just a little bit. "Sure sounds like it, angel."

"No, I like working with Clara. I like working at the shop. But I keep thinking that I'm... I don't know, that I should try to do something more? But I don't want to, and I don't even know what I would want to do. I know it's not a competition, and I'm sure I'm overthinking things because my ex's mom scarred me. And like I said, I really do like working there a lot more than I would have ever imagined. I can actually help most people out now without having to bother Clara. Can you believe it?"

He nodded, his mouth twitching even more. "I can believe it." Then he peeked at me. "Are you happy?" Rhodes asked seriously.

I didn't have to think about it. "Happier than I've been... ever, honestly."

The lines across his forehead were back. "You mean that?"

"Yeah. I don't remember the last time I got mad over anything that wasn't a customer being annoying, and even then, I forget about it five minutes later. I don't remember the last time I felt... small. Or bad. Everyone is so nice. Some people ask for me now. That matters to me so much, you have no idea."

He was silent before grunting. "Kind of pisses me off imagining you feeling small and bad."

I reached over and squeezed his forearm.

His mouth did that twisty thing as he let go of the steering wheel with his free hand and covered mine. His palm was warm. "We're here," he claimed.

I held my breath as he pulled into a very full driveway. I'd kept a vague eye on the neighborhood when he'd turned in, and it seemed to be spaced out with at least five-acre lots for each home.

"I'm glad you're good here," Rhodes said quietly right after he'd parked.

My cheekbones started to tingle.

He undid his seat belt and angled his body to look at me from across the dark cab. He dropped his hands into his lap and leveled me with a stare that nearly took my breath away. "If it matters any, you make Am and me both happy. And you help Clara out a lot." His throat bobbed. "We're all grateful you're in our lives."

My heart squished, and my voice definitely came out funny. "Thanks, Rhodes. I'm grateful for you all too."

Then he threw a verbal grenade. "You deserve to be happy."

All I could do was smile at him.

I swear his expression went tender before he blew out a breath. "All right, let's get in there before—there he is." He gestured through the windshield.

Standing in the doorway of the adobe-style home was Amos, waving big, in a button-down shirt that surprised me more than anything. I waved back, and he started gesturing for us to come in. Beside me, Rhodes chuckled lightly.

We got out, smiling at each other one last time before he met me on my side, taking my elbow while his other hand held the multiple bottles of wine he'd picked up at some point yesterday.

"About time!" Am called out from where he'd kept on standing at the doorway, waiting. "Uncle Johnny is on his way too."

"Hey, Am," I greeted him as we went up the stairs. "Happy Thanksgiving."

"Happy Thanksgiving. Hi, Dad," he said. "Come on, Ora, I

want you to meet my mom and dad." He paused and eyeballed me for a second. "You look...." He trailed off and shook his head.

"I look what?" I asked as I wiped my feet on the mat and then the rug before going inside the house. Rhodes had let go of my arm, but the second he was in, his hand landed at the small of my back.

"Nothing, come on, come on," he said, but I didn't miss the way his cheeks went red.

The house was huge, I could tell as we went through the foyer.

"I didn't know they were coming, but Mom called when their flight landed, so I couldn't tell you I was going to go with them, but—Mom!" he yelled suddenly as the foyer opened into a kitchen on the left-hand side. I could hear voices, but I only spotted three women in the kitchen. One had hair so white it was nearly blue who was stirring something and oblivious to us, another was an older woman who might be in her fifties, and the last was a woman who appeared to be a few years younger. She was the one who looked up at the "Mom."

She smiled.

"Dad Rhodes is here, and this is Ora," Am said, looking at me and patting my shoulder once.

It was basically a hug coming from him, and I would've cried if Amos's mom hadn't circled around the island and come straight toward us. She ignored Rhodes as she passed by him, and the second she was close enough, she thrust her hand out toward me.

But her eyes glittered.

I took out my own hand and grabbed hers.

Her smile was tight but genuine. And I knew I didn't imagine the tears in her voice when she said, "It's so nice to finally meet you, Ora. I've heard everything about you."

I know I heard tears in my voice when I replied, "I hope it was only the good stuff."

"All good stuff," she assured me before appearing to fight back a smile. "I even heard about the bat and the eagle."

I couldn't stop the snicker or the glance toward the sheepish-looking teenager still beside me. "Of course you did."

A grin took over the woman's face at the same time I laughed. She shook her head. "When he wants to, he has a big mouth like his dad."

I must have made some kind of face at the idea of Rhodes having a big mouth because she smiled even wider.

"Billy. Most of the time though, he takes after Rhodes with his one-word answers," Amos's mom explained. "When they're not in the mood, getting them to talk is like..."

"Getting wisdom teeth removed wide-awake?"

Rhodes grunted from where he was standing, and we both turned to look at him. Then Amos's mom's gaze and mine met again. Yeah, we both knew that was exactly it. She grinned at me, and I grinned right back.

"Remind me to give you my number or email before we leave, and I'll give you the real scoop any time you want," I offered with a wink, feeling a sense of ease come over me.

Rhodes had been right about Thanksgiving and Amos's other parents. I didn't have anything to worry about.

$\mathcal{I}$ was at the table in the garage apartment, trying to finish this son of a bitch of a puzzle. How many different shades of red *were there?* I had never really considered that I might be color-blind, but I kept putting the wrong shades of red together and the pieces still weren't matching up.

This was what I got for buying a used puzzle that had to be at least twenty years old. Maybe it was faded or the color had yellowed with time. Whatever it was, it was making this a whole lot more complicated than it needed to be. And I was cursing at myself over this puzzle that I shouldn't have bought on clearance *at a resale store* when I heard the garage door rolling up downstairs.

I had just picked up another piece when I heard Amos yell from downstairs—not this panicky thing of terror but just frantic enough to make me sit up straight. Just in time for him to shout again.

"Am?" I yelled, dropping the puzzle piece to the table and heading straight downstairs. I opened the garage door and peeked my head out. "Am? You okay?"

"No!" the kid pretty much shrieked. "Help!"

I threw the door wide. Amos stood in the center of the garage, head tipped back as he stared at the ceiling with a look of pure helplessness on his face. "Look! What do we do?"

"What the hell," I muttered, finally taking in what he was freaking out over.

There was a massive stain on the ceiling. Dark, dark gray patches were formed along the sheetrock. A few drops of water dripped onto the floor at Amos's feet, just short of where most of his music equipment was.

There was a leak. "Do you know where the water shutoff is?"

"The what?" he asked, still staring at the ceiling like his vision alone was going to be enough to prevent the sheetrock from crumbling and have water come flooding down.

"The water shutoff," I explained, already whipping around to find what I was pretty sure I knew what to look for. When the Antichrist's child and I had found the home that he eventually bought—and like a dumbass I had been fine with them not putting me on the deed because *someone could look up the records and ask questions*—I remembered the realtor pointing at something along the wall in the garage and specifically mentioning a water shutoff in case of a leak. "It's a lever thing in the wall. Usually. I think."

There was no way Rhodes would have let him cover it with padding or mattresses. I knew that. I spotted what I thought could be it and ran over, moving the lever down and shutting off the water into the garage apartment. At least I was pretty sure. One more peek at the bulging ceiling had me focusing.

"Let's get your stuff out of here before something bad happens," I told him, snapping my fingers when he focused back up. "Let's do it, Am, before your stuff gets ruined. Then we can make sure it did get turned off."

That did it.

Between the two of us, we carried the heavier equipment into the tiny bottom landing that flowed into the stairs that led to the second floor. We pushed the big cab up against the door to the outside to leave room and took turns taking the drum set apart and walking it up to my studio. It took us about six trips each to take all the equipment upstairs; we couldn't put anything outside because of frost and the risk of snow. It was way too cold now.

By the time we finished moving the most valuable stuff out from the garage—even though it was all valuable to Am because it was his—we were both back downstairs and staring up at the awful-looking ceiling.

"What do you think happened?"

"I think it might be a burst pipe, but I don't know," I told him, eyeing the damage. "Have you called your dad?"

He shook his head, eyes still glued to the disaster. "I yelled for you as soon as I saw it."

I whistled. "Call him. See what he wants to do. I think we should call a plumber, but I don't know. We should call him first."

Amos nodded, unable to do anything but stare in horror at the damage.

It hit me then that the water was turned off; I'd checked before coming back down. But *the water was off*, as in I wouldn't get water to shower or even fill my water filter to drink. I'd figure it out.

The overhead light started flickering suddenly, a flash-flash-flash of light before it went off completely.

"The breaker box!" I yelled at him before sprinting for the gray frame on the wall. *That* I knew exactly where it was. I flipped it open and literally flipped every switch.

"Did that mess up the electricity?"

"I don't know." I turned to him with a wince. A wince for him. For the amount of money it would cost to get this fixed. Because even I knew that electricity and plumbing issues were going to be a nightmare. "All right. Okay. Let's go call your dad and tell him."

Amos nodded and led the way out through the main garage door, heading to his house. I patted him on the shoulder. "It's okay. We moved all of your things in time, and nothing was plugged in. Don't worry."

The teenager let out a deep, deep sigh, like he'd been holding it in for hours. "Dad's gonna be so pissed."

"Yeah, but not at you," I reassured him.

The look he sent me was one that told me he wasn't totally convinced that was going to be the case, but I knew it would.

And I'd be nosey and eavesdrop.

We headed into the house. I went to the table in the kitchen, picking up a hunting and fishing magazine stacked neatly in the middle as Amos went for the house phone and punched in some numbers. His face was gloomy as hell. I pretended not to look at him as he held the receiver and let out a deep breath.

He winced right before saying, "Hey, Dad... uh, Ora and I think there's a leak in the garage apartment... The ceiling has, like, pockets of water, and there's drops—what? I don't know how... I just went in there and saw it... Ora turned off the water. Then she turned off the power when the lights started flickering... Hold on." The boy held the phone out. "He wants to talk to you."

I took it. "Hi, Rhodes, how's your day going? How many people have you busted for not having a permit?" I flashed a grimace-like smile at Amos, who suddenly didn't look *so* sick.

Rhodes didn't say anything for a heartbeat before coming on the line with "It's going good now." Excuse me? Was that *flirting*? "And only two hunters. How's yours?"

He was really asking me about my day. Who was this man and how could I buy him? "Pretty good. A customer brought me a Bundt cake. I gave Clara half when she gave me the stink eye. I'll give Am half of my half so you can try it. It's good."

Amos was giving me the funniest look, and I winked at him. We were in this together.

"Thanks, Buddy," he said almost softly. "You mind telling me what happened over there?"

I leaned my hip against the counter and watched as Am slowly moved toward the fridge, still giving me that funny-ass look before ducking in there to root around. He pulled out a can of strawberry soda before pulling out another one and turning to hold it up for me.

I nodded, processing the drink for a second before answering. "What Am said. There's a huge stain on the ceiling of the garage. There's water dripping. We moved everything we could out and into the studio upstairs. We turned off the water and the electricity off at the breaker box."

His exhale was deep, but it didn't shake.

"I'm sorry, Rhodes. Want me to call a plumber?"

"No, I know one. I'll give him a call. Sounds like it might be a burst pipe. I was just in the garage this morning and didn't notice anything, so I don't think it's a leak."

"Yeah, I'm sorry. I promise I didn't flood it or do anything weird." I paused. "I'll leave everything off for now."

"Put your groceries in our fridge. I'll tell Am to sleep on the sofa and you can take his room. It shouldn't get below freezing tonight, so the pipes should be fine today, but it'll be too cold for you to stay over there."

I blinked. Stay in Amos's room? In their house?

Did I want to go stay in a hotel? I could, of course, I could.

But stay in the same house as Rhodes? Mr. Flirty McFlirterson now?

Some part of my body perked up, and I wasn't going to think twice about which part it was.

"Are you sure?" I asked. "About me staying with you two?"

His voice suddenly went low. "You think I'd invite you to stay if I didn't want you to?"

Yeah, my body parts were *awake.* And out of control. "No."

"Okay."

"But I can sleep on the couch. Or, seriously, I can stay at a hotel or ask Clara—"

"You don't need to go stay at a hotel, and they don't have much room at their house."

"Then I'll sleep on the couch."

"We'll argue over it later," he said. "I've got a few more spots I want to check out, and then I'll be heading home. Take your stuff over and everything in your fridge so it doesn't go bad. You got anything heavy, leave it and I'll grab it when I get home."

I swallowed. "You're sure?"

"Yeah, angel, I'm sure. I'll be home soon."

I hung up the phone, feeling... jittery? Staying in the house was no big deal, okay. But it kind of felt like it at the same time.

I liked Rhodes way too much. In small, subtle ways that got under my skin. I liked how good of a father he was, how much he loved his son. And even though I'd loved someone once who had adored a family member more than he would ever care about me, in this case, that love was for very different reasons and in very different ways. He loved him enough to be tough but at the same time let him be his own person.

Rhodes was no Mrs. Jones.

I'd liked him even when he gave me the stink eye. And I had no idea what his plans were. Plans with me. I knew what I wouldn't mind them looking like but….

I happened to look over and found Amos leaning against the counter, looking way too introspective.

"What?" I asked him, popping the tab on my own soda and taking a sip.

The boy shook his head.

"You can tell me anything, Little Sting, and I can tell you want to."

That seemed to be enough for him. "Are you flirting with my dad?" he straight-up asked.

I almost spit the soda out. "No…?"

He blinked. "No?"

"Maybe?"

Amos raised an eyebrow.

It was my turn to blink. "Yes, okay. Yes. But I flirt with everyone. Men and women. Children. You should see me around pets. I used to have a fish, and I sweet-talked her too. Her name was Gretchen Wiener. I miss her." She had passed away a few years ago, but I still thought about her from time to time. She'd been a good travel companion. Not fussy at all.

That had the teenager's cheeks going puffy for a second.

He fucking liked me. I knew it.

"Does it bother you if I flirt with your dad?" I paused. "Would it bother you if I liked him?" That wasn't the best word to describe it, but it was the simplest.

That got him to scoff. "No! I'm sixteen not five."

"But you're still his wittle baby, Am. And my feelings won't be hurt"—that was a lie, they would be—"if you weren't okay with it. You're my friend too. Just like your dad. I don't want to make things weird."

The kid gave me a disgusted expression that made me laugh. "I don't care. We already talked about it anyway."

"You did?"

He nodded but didn't clear up what they'd talked about. Instead, he got a funny look on his face, and I'd bet a finger it was his version of a protective expression. "He's been alone a long time. Like, a *long* time. My whole life, he's had some girlfriends, and none of them lasted that long. With my dad Billy not here and my uncles moving away, he doesn't have that many friends, not like when he was in the Navy; he knew everybody then."

I wasn't sure where he was going with this so I stayed quiet, sensing there was more on his mind.

"My mom told me to tell you that it takes him a while to trust people."

"Your mom said that?"

"Yeah, she asked me."

"About your dad... and me?"

Amos nodded and took another sip. "Don't tell him I told you, but you make him smile a lot."

There went my heart again.

"You look... you know, like that, and... whatever. I don't care if you like him, and I don't care if he likes you. I want him... you know... to be happy. I don't want him to regret being here," he said in a way that told me he meant it, but still felt kind of loaded. Like he was giving me his blessing to follow what my heart was asking for. Not that I even really knew what that was.

"In that case, thank you, Am. I'm positive your dad doesn't regret anything when it comes to you." The urge to talk to him about how confusing his father was, was right there, but I wouldn't do it. Refused to, more like it.

"Changing the topic, I guess, I'm staying over tonight and sleeping on the couch since everything is shut off over there. Will you help me bring some of my groceries over, please? I can make dinner, and maybe we can watch a movie or you can let me listen to that song you've been working on—"

"Nope."

I laughed. "It was worth a shot."

Amos did that tiny smile as he rolled his eyes, and it just made me laugh more.

~

It was the gentle squeeze on my ankle that had me prying an eyelid open.

The room was dark, but the high ceilings reminded me of where I was, where I'd fallen asleep. On Rhodes's couch.

The last thing I remembered was watching a movie with Amos.

Opening my other eye, I yawned and spotted a big, familiar figure hunched over the other end of the couch. Amos was slowly sitting up, his dad's hand on his shoulder as he muttered, "Go to bed."

The kid yawned huge, barely opening his eyes as he nodded, more than half asleep, and stood up. I'd bet he had no idea where he was or even that he was on the couch with me. Sitting up too, I stretched my arms up over my head and croaked, "'Night, Am."

My friend let out a grunt as he stumbled away, and I smiled at Rhodes who was back to standing. He was in his uniform, his belt off, and he had the gentlest expression on his face.

"Hi," I grumbled, dropping my arms. "What time is it?"

Rhodes looked tired but okay, I thought, yawning again. "Three in the morning. Fell asleep watching TV?"

418

I nodded, muttering, "Mm-hmm," and closing one eye as I did it. Oh man, all I needed was a blanket and I'd pass right back out. "Everything okay?"

"Some hunters got lost. I didn't get service out to call and warn you two," he explained quietly. "Come on then. You're not sleeping down here."

Oh. I nodded again, too sleepy to be hurt he'd changed his mind. "Will you watch me walk back to the garage apartment then? Make sure the coyotes don't get me?"

Rhodes suddenly frowned. "No."

"But you said—"

He was fast, coming over, his hands going to my elbows and guiding me up to standing. Then his hand slipped into mine, like he'd done it before a million times, his palm cool and rough and big, and he started pulling me to follow him.

Where were we going?

"Rhodes?"

He glanced at me over his shoulder; his facial hair was thick over his jaw and cheeks. I wondered, not for the first time, if it was soft or kind of bristly. I'd bet it tickled.

And just like that, I realized he was leading me toward the stairs. The stairs up. To his room. Someone had hinted once where it was at.

"I can sleep down here," I whispered, not alarmed but... something.

"You want to sleep down here with the bat?"

I stopped walking.

His laugh was so soft I didn't know whether that surprised me more than the fact he was getting me to go upstairs... with him? "Didn't think so. My bed's big enough for both of us." He let out a soft breath. "Or I can take the floor."

My feet moved, but the rest of me didn't.

Did he just say his bed was big enough for both of us?

And there was a bat in here?

Or that he could take the floor in his room?

"Whoa, whoa, whoa, pal," I whispered. "I don't even know your middle name."

His hand tensed in mine, and he glanced over his shoulder. "John."

He wasn't trying to... get me to go up there to have sex with him, was he? I didn't think so—as in *really* didn't think so but.... "Not that I wouldn't mind having sex with you eventually—"

Rhodes made this terrible choking sound in his throat.

"—but I barely learned your middle name, and I don't know what you wanted to be when you were growing up, and this is going really fast if you want to do more than just sleep in the same bed together," I rambled out in a rush, so I had no clue what the hell I was even saying.

Apparently, he barely understood it too because he made another choking sound—not as aggressive—and just looked at me for a long second. "Sometimes I think I know exactly what you're going to say... and then the exact opposite comes out of your mouth," he whispered back.

Was he laughing?

"No sex, Buddy, just sleep. I'm too tired, and I do know your middle name, but I'm not real big on rushing things, Valeria," he finally got out. Definitely laughing and trying not to. "But I wanted to be a biologist. It took me a long time, but I got my degree in it. I'm using it better now than I'd dreamed of back then." He took a deep breath. "What did you want to be?"

"A doctor, but I couldn't even get through dissecting a frog in high school without throwing up."

His chuckle sounded rusty.

And I liked it.

"Okay," I agreed, "just sleep."

He shook his head and, after a minute, started the journey again. My feet hit the stairs one after another, and even though I was mostly thinking about what it would be like *to* have sex with him, I still glanced up at the ceiling to make sure there was no bat there. There wasn't.

Not yet at least.

Were we really going to sleep in the same bed? Or was I going to tell him I could sleep on the floor? Or was he going to sleep on the floor?

I was way too exhausted to think this over so closely. It didn't help that I had no idea what went on in the dating game anymore. My friends weren't good examples of real-life dating because their lives were so complicated.

But my thoughts just circled back around to one thing: sex with Rhodes.

I mean, I was all for it eventually. It scared me, made me nervous too.

I'd seen him without a shirt on. He was all brawny and big, and I'd bet he wasn't lazy at all. I bet he liked being on top.

Whoa, whoa, whoa, I needed not to think about that.

"Rhodes," I whispered.

"Hmm?"

"In the same bed?"

"I'd rather not sleep on the floor, angel, but I will if you're not good with it."

I blinked, and my heart thumped in response.

"Don't think you want to either. There might be mice running around still. They are nocturnal."

I was still taking turns looking up at the ceiling and down at the floor when he led us into his bedroom. He didn't flip on the light, but the moon through his window was huge and bright, illuminating everything with just the right amount to not wake me up too much more than talking about mice and bats had.

Fuck. I was relieved when he closed the door behind him and moved toward the bed, still holding my hand. He pulled the bedspread aside and murmured, "Take this side."

I did, plopping down on the edge and watching him as he unbuttoned his shirt. When he was almost done, he jerked it out from where it had been stuffed into his pants, finished with the buttons, and shrugged it off. Right in front of me.

I sat there. My mouth went a little dry at the way his undershirt clung to the thick muscles of his upper body. "Are you showering?" I asked without even meaning to.

"Too tired," he replied softly, folding the shirt and setting it into a hamper I hadn't spotted in the corner of his room. I wanted to look around... but he was stripping.

Rhodes went for his pants then, undoing the tab, then the zipper, and pulling it down...

That's when I glanced up to meet his eyes. He was looking right at me. Busted. I smiled just as he started tugging his pants down his long legs.

"Did you find the hunters?" I asked, hoping my throat sounded husky from sleep and not for another reason.

I was weak and I flicked my gaze down.

He was a boxers guy.

Part of me had expected him to be a tighty-whities type of man, but he wasn't.

His boxers were dark and short. His thighs were everything I had expected them to be. Someone didn't skip leg day and hadn't. Ever.

I swallowed to make sure my mouth was shut.

"Yes. They wandered too far from their campsite, but we found them," he answered.

He bent down and pulled off his socks, and I swore there

was something about his bare feet just visible that seemed more intimate than if he'd been standing there buck naked.

Drawing my legs up, I snuck them under the sheet and the heavy comforter, drawing it up as he pulled his other sock off, still watching me. I was doing this. Sleeping in his bed. Still not sure what any of this meant or where it was going but… going along with it.

He had been so nice to me lately for a reason, I understood now. Maybe he'd been distant because of his mom, maybe he'd finally just decided I was decent. I had no clue what drove him to this point now, of leading me to his room.

Yet it didn't matter.

My mom used to say that most of the time, when you're on a trail, you get to a point where another one branches off from it, and you have to choose which way you want to go. What you want to see. And I knew in that moment, that I had to make another decision.

For a tiny, brief moment, I wondered if this was fast. I'd been with someone for fourteen years, and it had been almost a year and a half since we'd split up. Should I give myself more time?

But in another tiny, brief moment, I came to my decision.

When you lose enough, you learn to take happiness where you can find it. You don't wait for it to be handed to you. You don't expect it in big firework-like displays.

You take it in small moments, and sometimes those come shaped in a two-hundred-and-fortyish pound man going above and beyond. I wanted to understand what was happening. I needed to.

So before I could think twice about what I was doing, what I was setting myself up for, I asked him, "Rhodes?"

"Yes?"

"Why didn't you call or text me while you were gone?"

I was pretty sure I could hear my heart beating it was so

loud in the silence that came right after my question. Just this thud, thud, thud that rang between my ears as he stood there, looking in my direction. Part of me didn't expect him to answer until he finally repeated in surprise, "Why?"

Maybe I should've saved the question for when it wasn't three in the morning, but we were here, and I might as well get it out. "Yeah. Why? I thought... I thought there was something going on with us, but then I didn't hear from you." I pressed my lips together. "Now I'm in your bed and I'm confused with what's going on. If it means anything."

He didn't say a word.

I cleared my throat though, figuring I might as well keep going. "I thought maybe you liked me. As in liked me-liked me. It's okay if you don't, if you changed your mind. If you're just being this nice to me because you're a good man, but I'd like to know if that's the case. I'd still like to be your friend anyway." I swallowed. "It just... kind of felt sometimes like we were dating, you know? Minus the physical stuff.... I'm fucking this up, aren't I?"

I heard him suck in a breath before saying, seriously, "We're not dating."

I wanted the floor to eat me up. I wanted to get up and walk out, or at least sleep in the living room and take my chances with the bat—

"I'm too old to be anybody's boyfriend," Rhodes said in that hoarse, solemn voice that carried so much weight on it. "But I do like you more than I should. More than you might feel comfortable with."

He didn't move, and neither did I. My heart felt like it was going to jump out of my chest at his implications. Even my skin prickled.

"I wanted to call you, but I was trying to give you room."

"Why?" I asked like he'd just said he liked eating mayonnaise straight from the jar.

His answer was a sigh followed by, "Because... I've been watching you grow for months. I don't want to be something you grow around. You were with someone who gave you too much shade before, right? I'd rather us take our time than me stunt where you're going, who you're becoming."

I could hear my heartbeat again.

"I know how I want you to feel, but I'm not rushing you. I know how I feel. I haven't changed my mind about anything, especially not you. I only want you to be sure of what *you* want."

I was breathing through my mouth loudly.

"Don't mistake me giving you space as me not being interested. It's not every woman I let into my bed, much less into my life, and even more into Amos's life. Before you, it'd been nobody. So just because I don't know what your mouth tastes like yet doesn't mean I haven't thought about it. Doesn't mean I'm not going to. But Sofie would tell you I've got a big, fragile heart, and I think I do, so I need you to know what you want for my sake too, Buddy. Does that make it clear?"

I was having a heart attack. Maybe even melting. As tired as I was, I wasn't sure how I was supposed to sleep next to *that* all night. He might as well have pinned me down and licked down my body, because I'd never heard anything more erotic or amazing in my life.

And I was sure he knew something was going on within me because I was panting and all I could get out was a breathy "Okay." Real eloquent. Me who couldn't shut up ever, who had basically asked for this, had no idea what to say other than "okay."

Because... I knew how I felt too. And I might be more than a little halfway in love with him, I was pretty sure, but... he was right. It didn't feel right yet. Some part of it. Maybe it was all just the physical aspect, but maybe I needed to be certain too. A part of me needed to tread with some caution. I didn't want to get my heart broken again.

The truth was, I liked him even more for saying those words. For thinking that deeply. I liked him so much in so many ways.

And if we were both on the same page, then that was more important than anything else.

One day I'd know how his lips felt, but it didn't have to be right at that moment, and *that* filled me with so much joy and playfulness I couldn't help but smile, inside and outside. It renewed a need inside of me to win him over. To make him more than my friend.

I wasn't sure if he could see my face or not, but I still raised my eyebrows and told him in a voice that was way too cheery for how tired I was—and turned on, "Well, if you want to sleep naked, I'm okay with it."

The burst of his laughter surprised the shit out of me, and I couldn't help but laugh too.

This was so right, there was no reason to rush anything.

"No thanks," he said once his laugh slowed.

I'd made a lot of people laugh in my life, but I wasn't sure I'd ever felt this triumphant. "If you change your mind, go for it," I told him, totally serious. "My body is too tired, but my eyeballs aren't."

He laughed some more, the sounds slow and subtle and raspy. If I could've bottled it up, I would have, because all I could do when I heard it was smile.

"I don't sleep naked either, if you're wondering," I told him, wanting to lighten the mood.

He laughed again, but it was totally different. Husky. Loaded. Nice.

Take it easy. We were both tired, and we were going to sleep. Right.

I pulled the sheets up to my chin and rolled over, facing

the door as Rhodes headed into the bathroom, flipping on the light but leaving the door open. The tap ran briefly; then I heard him brushing his teeth. The water ran again, there was some splashing, and just as I started to get sleepy once more, tucking the pillow in close under my neck, I made sure I wasn't too far over in either direction.

The light flipped off, and I didn't bother pretending like I was asleep, but I tried to steady my breathing, thinking of just how sexy my tank top and baggy pajama pants with reindeers on them were.

The bed dipped and there were more sounds of something heavy being set on the nightstand before the familiar beep of his phone being plugged in.

"'Night, Rhodes," I said.

The bed dipped a little more as the covers were pulled taut at my back, and after a moment, I felt him settle in.

He stretched. He sighed so deeply, I felt bad for how tired he had to be. He'd been gone a lot longer than I'd bet he'd expected.

"Goodnight, Aurora," I muttered to myself when he didn't reply.

His chuckle made me smile right before he whispered right back, "Goodnight."

I rolled over.

He was lying facing me. I strained to see his features. His eyes were already drooping, but there was the faintest little hint of a smile on his incredible mouth.

"Can I ask you something and you won't get mad?"

His "yes" came a lot faster than I would have expected.

But I braced myself anyway. "It's kind of personal."

"Ask."

"Why doesn't anyone call you Tobias other than your dad?"

He let out a soft, soft breath. "My mom called me that."

Could I have asked a worse question? I doubted it. "I'm sorry I brought it up. I was just curious. It's a nice name."

"It's all right," he replied softly.

I had to fix this. "Just so you know... I really like you. More than I probably should too."

He said one thing and one thing only, "Good."

I bit my lip again. "Hey, can I ask you one last thing?"

I was pretty sure I hadn't ruined the night when I heard a lazy grunt. "Yes."

"Were you being serious about there being a bat or...?"

His sleepy chuckle made me smile. "'Night, angel face."

CHAPTER 26

I woke up warm.

Very, very warm.

Mostly because I was cuddled up against Rhodes's back. My arms were crossed, my forehead was tucked between his shoulder blades, and my toes were hiding under his calves. Rhodes, thankfully, was oblivious.

The memory of our conversation last night had me eyeing the smooth skin in front of my eyes. The urge to stroke those sleek muscles was right there. But I kept my hands to myself. Because he was right. I wanted more time. For all my big talk last night, I didn't want to rush into anything *yet*. I wasn't going anywhere, and from what he had said, he wasn't either.

Not that I wouldn't mind seeing him naked. Because I would sign up for that in a heartbeat.

Carefully, so that I wouldn't wake him, I scooted away slowly and exhaled. Then I rolled out of bed and peeked at the sleeping figure some more. On his side, that smooth skin of his peeked out from where the heavy comforter lay tucked right beneath his armpits. He was breathing deeply.

You know… I was pretty sure I was in love with him.

And I was pretty sure he might be a little in love with me too.

I opened the door as quietly as possible and snuck out of the room, closing it behind me with the softest click. Creeping down the stairs, I stopped right at the bottom.

Amos was in his pajamas, sitting at the table eating a bowl of cereal. He gave me a sleepy look. I lifted my hand and tipped up my head.

"Your dad told me to sleep up there," I muttered as I made my way to get a glass for some water.

The kid gave me a sleepy but funny look as he muttered, "Uh-huh," just as my phone started vibrating. "It's done that like three times in the last ten minutes." He sighed, sounding disgruntled.

Picking it up from where I'd left it charging on the counter last night, I peeked at the unknown number calling. It was seven in the morning. Who could it be? Only about twenty people had my number, and I had every person's contact information stored on it. The area code was local too.

I answered. "Hello?"

"Aurora?" the familiar voice replied.

My whole body jerked in place. "Mrs. Jones?"

The Antichrist barreled on like she went through everything in her life: with no regard for anyone but herself and her children. "Look here, I know how stubborn you're being about all this—"

"*What?*" It was too early for this shit. It was way too early. What was she doing contacting me? "How the hell did you get my number? Why are you calling?" I spat in sheer disbelief this was happening.

Her pause was too short. "I really need to speak to you if you won't respond to Kaden."

I remembered then. I remembered right in that moment that I didn't need to take her bullshit anymore. So I hung up.

And I smirked.

And Amos asked in his sleepy voice, "Why do you look like that?"

"I forgot how much I like hanging up on people," I answered him, feeling pretty damn pleased with myself as I processed what I'd done. Damn, did that feel good.

He frowned like he thought I was nuts just as my phone started vibrating again. The same number flashed on the screen. I hit ignore.

"Who is that?"

"Did you know the devil is really a woman?" I asked.

My phone started vibrating *again*, and I cursed. She wasn't going to let this go. Why would I expect otherwise from someone who thought we were all around to serve her? The urge to keep playing this game—ignoring her calls—pulsed deeply in my chest... but the urge to never have this shit happen again was even stronger once I thought about it. That surprised me a lot.

I didn't actually want to keep doing this with her. With any of them, really. I didn't even want to waste my time thinking about them anymore.

I knew damn well I needed to end this once and for all, and there was only one way to do that.

I answered the call and went right into it. "Mrs. Jones, it's seven in the morning, and this is—"

"I'm in town, Aurora. Please meet me."

And *that's why* the number was local. Son of a bitch. I was still tired enough I hadn't put two and two together. I was lucky I didn't have anything in my mouth because I would've spit it out. "You're in town where?" I pretty much demanded.

"In this... town. At the resort with the springs," she replied, sounding totally put out by the nicest hotel in town.

"I need to speak to you. Clear some things up that I think may have gotten... out of hand," she said way too carefully compared to how she used to speak to me.

I glanced at Amos to find him staring blearily at his phone, but I knew this sneaky kid was listening.

"Please," the older woman said, "for old times' sake."

"The 'old times' sake' thing won't work on me, ma'am," I told her honestly.

Yeah, I knew that was going to go down real well with her. She was probably shooting me the middle finger in her head because she thought she was way too classy to actually do it. And to me, that just made it a hell of a lot worse.

"Please," she insisted. "I will never contact you again if you don't want me to."

Liar.

The urge to hang up was still there, pulsing and pounding and telling me to move on with my life. There was nothing I wanted to hear from her mouth. But... there were things I wanted to tell her. Specific things that needed to be said so I would never have to go through this again. Speaking to them, I meant. Because ultimately, that was what I needed more than anything now. To fucking move on. To not have the Joneses hanging over my head anymore.

What I wanted was my current life. The man in bed upstairs. And I couldn't have those things with these damn ghosts still haunting me when they felt like it.

I thought about what I knew about this woman, which was just about everything, and cursed. "Fine. There's a restaurant on the main street that's in walking distance. I'll meet you there in an hour."

"Which restaurant?"

"There's only one open this early. The front desk can give you directions." And it was usually busy with tourists and retired locals, so I figured it was the best place for us to meet so that she wouldn't throw a fit. I hadn't eaten breakfast there yet, but I drove by it every morning and knew what kind of traffic they got. It would be perfect.

"I'll meet you there," she said after a moment, her voice strained, and I knew this was costing her.

I rolled my eyes so well, Amos would have been proud. And the fact that he snickered cheered me up even though I didn't look at him. He didn't need to know I knew what he was doing.

"See you in an hour," I said before hanging up, not bothering to wait for her to make another comment. I let out a deep breath to release the tension in my stomach. *Once and for all*, I told myself.

"You okay?" Amos asked.

"Yeah," I told him. "My old mother-in-law is in town and wants to meet up."

He yawned.

"I'm going to get ready in your bathroom and then head out," I said. "Need anything? Why are you awake this early?"

"After Dad woke us up, I stayed up and haven't gone to sleep yet." He paused. "What does she want?"

"The Antichrist? I'm not sure. Either to get me to go back to work for them or…." I shrugged, not willing to say it out loud, not even thinking about what I'd admitted. That I had worked for my ex. Of all the things we'd talked about, neither father nor son had asked about what I used to do for a living. I'd told them I'd been an assistant when we'd first met, but they'd never asked for more information.

And he either didn't care or was too tired to notice or pay attention because all he did was nod, his gaze bleary.

I cursed under my breath at what the hell I was about to do. "I won't take too long in the bathroom, Mini Eric Clapton. If you fall asleep before I get out, I'll see you later. Tell your dad I'll be back."

~

I GOT to the diner early. It was a cute, very small restaurant wedged between a retail store that had been around for over a hundred years and a real estate company. It was tourist central, even though the only people visiting this time of year were hunters from Texas and California mostly.

But I knew that everything with Mrs. Jones was a power play, and that would include getting to the diner ahead of time and picking out her seat.

Fortunately, I managed to snag a table—waving at a couple I recognized who frequented The Outdoor Experience—and picked my seat facing the door. Sure enough, five minutes after sitting down and ten minutes before we were supposed to meet, I spotted her by the door—thin, tan, and slimmer than ever. Then I noticed the way she was clinging to her thirty-five-thousand-dollar purse like if it brushed against something in the diner, she'd get cooties.

I knew for a fact she'd worked at a Waffle House back in the day.

God, help me with this family.

The best thing I ever did was get kicked out of it. And *that* knowledge made me straighten my spine. I was happy. Healthy. I had my whole future ahead of me. I had friends and loved ones. Maybe I still had no clue what I was going to be doing a year from now, much less five or ten, but I *was* happy. Happier and more secure than I'd been in a long, long time.

And that was why I was smiling as I stood up and caught Mrs. Jones's attention. She frowned, upset at being got, and made her way over as I sat back down. Just as she took the seat across from me, I held my hand out to her.

Did I want to be the bigger person? No. Would it irritate her if I was? Yes. And that's why I did it.

She looked at it with surprise. She sniffed as she shook it, her hand cool and almost clammy. Either somebody was nervous or irritated. I hoped both.

"Hello, Aurora," she said.

"Hi, Mrs. Jones." I felt some more of that lingering bitterness slip away. I opened my menu, regretting leaving my overnight oatmeal in the fridge at Rhodes's so I'd have time to get ready.

I had thought about not putting makeup on or doing my hair but decided against it. I wanted her to see with her own eyes that I was kicking ass and taking names. Kind of.

You know what? I *was* kicking ass. I was fine. Better than ever, and that was the absolute truth. My hair was healthy since it was totally grown out after a decade of frying it to get it the pale blonde it had been. I was tan from all the time I still managed to spend outside, and I was better mentally and physically than I had been in forever.

And I felt like I wore my sense of peace over me like a cloak.

Life didn't have to be perfect for you to be happy. Because what was perfect really, anyway?

"How are you?" I asked her, my attention still on the menu.

Ooh, French toast. I hadn't had that in... months, not since before I'd gotten here.

"Well, I'd be doing better if I was home, Aurora," the older woman bitched.

I let it go in one ear and out the other. Maybe I'd just have coffee, actually, and go back to Rhodes's and eat breakfast with them. This honestly wouldn't last too long by the way it was looking. And I only had enough cash to pay for a coffee and leave a tip, so that I wouldn't have to be awkward and wait around for a waitress to take my debit card if I decided to bounce quickly.

Actually, that sounded like a plan. Breakfast with people who made me happy or with a demon? Like that was even a choice.

With that settled, I closed my menu and focused back on the woman who hadn't even opened hers, confirming maybe this wasn't going to be a long conversation. Perfect. Well, that and Mrs. Jones wouldn't lower herself to eating *at a diner.* My God. *No eggs benedict? A mango power smoothie?* God forbid. That shit was delicious, but the way she demanded things made them obnoxious.

With a deep breath, I leaned back and watched her sitting there, her beautiful green purse sitting on her lap, manicured fingers resting on the strap.

"You look well," I told her honestly.

"You look... tan" was the nicest thing she managed to get out of her mouth.

I laughed and shrugged. Like that was an insult.

"What are you doing here?" she asked, pinching her lips together.

I didn't know what to do with my hands, so I set them on top of the table, tapping the plastic-covered menu with my fingernails. "I live here," I told her, hopefully with a "duh" tone in my voice.

Her nostrils flared a little. "It took us a long time to find you. We had to hire a few private investigators."

I lifted a shoulder. "I wasn't hiding, and it wasn't like Kaden didn't know I grew up here." He'd just forgotten or never processed it enough in the first place.

What a fucker, now that I thought about it.

Mrs. Jones's nostrils flared again, and I could tell it was taking everything in her not to make a smart-ass comment. "You know how busy he is; he always has so many things going on in his head."

I wasn't going to make excuses or believe that same line I'd told myself over and over again during the length of our relationship. Poor wittle Kaden. So busy. So many things to do.

No, he didn't. His mom did everything for him. I'd done everything for him. He had other people who did everything for him. I bet he had no idea how much money he paid in taxes or how much his mortgage was.

"Is that why he's not here?" I asked her, barely repressing smiling sarcastically. "Because he's so busy?"

I didn't miss the way the corners of her mouth went white before she collected herself and said, "Yes." Mrs. Jones cleared her throat lightly, just barely. "Aurora...."

"Look, Mrs. Jones, I'm sure you have better things to do than hang around Pagosa trying to catch up with me, because I know I do. What do you want?"

She gasped. "That's incredibly rude."

"It's not rude if it's the truth, because I really do have things to do." It was my day off. I had breakfast to eat. A life to keep living.

She huffed in her seat, that thin, pink mouth pressing tight before she set her shoulders in a way that reminded me of all the times she'd had to be the bad guy with someone in honor of her son. "Fine." She sat up straighter than she'd been before, collecting her words and possibly even bracing herself. "Kaden made a mistake."

Maybe they would end up with that shit pie eventually, after all. "He's made a lot of mistakes."

Bless her heart, she tried not to sneer, but I knew her too well to fall for it. "I'd like to know what all these 'a lot' of mistakes are," she snapped before she could stop herself.

I kept my mouth closed and gave her a look that I'd learned from the best, the man whose bed I'd left that morning. That was what I would have rather been thinking about.

What was happening *there*. What could happen there. It sent a thrill through me.

"With you, Aurora. I'm talking about the mistake he made... leaving you."

Bingo. I bet that cost her to say. "Oh, that. Okay. A) He didn't *leave me*. You two kicked me out. B) I knew he'd regret it someday, so that's nothing new, Mrs. Jones. But what does that have to do with me?" I had to coax her into saying what I was already totally aware of.

She couldn't think I was so stupid to not *know*, right?

Then again, she probably did.

She let out an exasperated sound, her dark brown eyes moving across the diner quickly before returning to me. I knew what she saw. People in T-shirts and flannels, camouflaged coveralls, old jackets, and pullover Columbia sweaters. Nothing fancy or flashy.

"It has everything to do with you," she whispered, stressing her words. "He never should have ended the relationship. You know he was under a lot of pressure with the way the Trivium album went, and you were making all these demands."

Demands. Me asking him when we could get married. *Really* married because it mattered to me. When we could have kids because I had always wanted them and he knew it, and I wasn't getting any younger.

I'd been his most faithful friend for fourteen years, and I had made *demands*.

But I kept the comments to myself and kept my face even. I let her keep going.

"He was in a bad place."

In his ten-million-dollar house, traveling around in a two-million-dollar tour bus, flying around in a private jet that his record label owned.

He hadn't been in a "bad place." I knew Kaden better than

anyone and knew that, apart from a time after his grandfather had died, he had never been devastated a day in his life. He had been bummed and disappointed after his Trivium album had gotten reamed by music reviewers, but he'd shrugged it off and said he was lucky it had taken him six albums to finally have a flop. *It happens to everybody*, he'd insisted. His mom on the other hand had been furious... but it had been her idea to stop using my songs so....

He slept soundly every night, fueled by the countless people who brushed off the failure and kept reaming him with butter-covered words that would go up his butt easier. He had lived in a fantasy world of love. Part of it was my fault but not all of it.

"And you'd been together so long, he needed to get his head straight. Make sure."

Make sure?

I almost choked, but she didn't deserve that.

Make sure. Wowee wowsers.

I wanted to laugh too but held that back as well. Just... wow. She was digging herself into a deeper and deeper hole, and she had no idea. I should've been insulted by how dumb and desperate she assumed I would be to fall for this.

But I could play this game. I was good at it. I'd had fourteen years to perfect this with her. I'd even practiced on Randall Rhodes. I should've invited him over and unleashed him on her.

"He had so many options. Wouldn't you rather he be totally confident than question everything later on?" she asked.

I nodded seriously.

She bared her teeth in something that tried to resemble a smile but actually made her look like she was being tortured. Which this probably was for her. "He misses you, Aurora. Very much. He wants you *back*."

She emphasized that "back" like it was some sort of fucking Christmas miracle—no, not a Christmas miracle, an immaculate conception. Like I should fall to my knees and be *grateful.*

Instead, I just nodded seriously some more.

"He's tried calling everyone he knows to get them to give him your new number. He's begged Yuki and that sister of hers."

They might have gotten along while we'd been together, but *I* was their friend. A real friend who cared about them and worried about them and loved them for no reason other than they were great people. Not because they could do something for me.

"One of the private investigators we hired had to get creative to get your phone number once he located you. He has tried getting back in contact with you. I know he's emailed you and you haven't had the decency to respond."

And that's when I snapped.

Decency.

Decency was a strong word that usually people the furthest away from being decent would use. Because *decent* people didn't use the word as a weapon. Decent people understood that there were reasons for everything and that there were two sides to every story.

And I *was* a decent person. Fuck it. I was a *good* person. These motherfuckers were the ones who wouldn't know what decent meant if it backhanded them.

And I wasn't going to get dragged through the mud more than I already had. So that's when I stopped her.

I leaned forward across the table, reached toward the woman who I had never really loved but had cared about because someone I'd loved adored her, and set my hand on top of hers, the hand she had sitting on top of her Hermès purse. And I smiled at her, even though I absolutely didn't feel like smiling at all.

My smile was the only weapon I needed then.

"I didn't respond, not because I wasn't decent, because I am, and the next time you approach someone to try and get them to listen to you, maybe don't disrespect them. There is literally nothing I want from Kaden. Not six months ago, not a year ago, and definitely not today. I told him, Mrs. Jones, when he showed up at our house after spending the night at yours, that he didn't mean what he said. That he would regret ending our relationship. And I was right."

I exhaled through my nose and pulled my hand back, aiming another one of those deadly smiles at her so she would know her time for talking was done. *She* was done. "I don't give a shit if he actually misses me or if he misses what I did for him and that's why he wants me back. I know he loved me, at least he did genuinely for a while, and I hope he knows I loved him. But that's the thing, I don't anymore, and I haven't in a long time. He killed every inch of the love I felt for him. *You* helped kill every inch of the love I felt for him too."

I met her gaze and asked her as seriously as possible, "That's why you're here, isn't it? Because he regrets ending our relationship? More like he regrets letting you talk him into it, right? Is he mad at you now? Are you here trying to clean up his mess because he blames you for this happening instead of being an adult and taking responsibility for his actions? I bet that's exactly what it is. That should tell you everything though. Why your spoiled kid won't get what he suddenly decided he wants again. Why I will never, ever go back.

"You all shunned me. Embarrassed me. You turned people against me, and that's on them too, but it's on you two for putting them into that position in the first place. At this point, I don't wish bad things on either of you, but if you're looking for a blood transfusion or an organ donor, don't bother looking in my direction. I've moved on. I'm happy, and I'm not letting you or Kaden or any of your lackeys take that away from me."

I was glad the waitress still hadn't come. I was glad I could leave. I started to get up, taking in the furious but astonished expression that had taken over her entire face.

"Please don't bother me anymore. And I'm only saying please to be polite because I really want to tell you to leave me the fuck alone. You always saw me as some worthless piece of crap that should kiss your son's feet, but you forget what his career was like before I came around. Before I gave him all of my best songs. Before he took advantage of how much I had loved him. I will never go back. There isn't enough money in the world that you could pay me to do so."

I stood up straight and kept on going just as she opened her mouth to tell me I was a useless bitch, like she had once before when she'd been drunk after an awards show I hadn't been allowed to go to.

"I wish that I could tell you that I hope you'll both find peace and happiness in your lives, but I'm not that good of a person. What I hope for is that you'll leave me alone. That's what I hope. Those ten million you transferred into my account was enough to get me to shut up, and I'm going to take advantage of them. I'm going to put my kids through college with them, kids I'm going to have with someone that isn't your son and will never be your son. You don't have to worry about me running after Kaden begging for scraps, ma'am. Find someone else who doesn't mind being in eleventh place, because it sure as hell isn't going to be me."

There were two last things left that needed to be said, and I knew my time was up, so I told her the words carefully, looking right into her soulless eyes as I did. "I can't write anymore. I haven't in over a year. Maybe one day the words will come back to me, but they're not here now, and part of me hopes they don't return. But even without my notebooks and without my songs, I was worth a lot. Worth more than all that money you paid me. So, please, leave me alone. All of you. If I see you or Kaden again, I'll make sure you regret it."

I leaned forward so she wouldn't mistake how dead serious I was. "If any of you contact me, and I mean *any of you*, I will tell everyone about that lie we were all part of. I know people, and you know that. After that, I'll spend every dollar of those millions you sent me, taking you to court, Mrs. Jones. Every single penny. I've got nothing better to do. I would rather spend it on people that make me happy, but I won't lose sleep using it on other things. So I want you to think long and hard about knowing where I live, knowing what my phone number is, if your little baby ever decides he wants to get in contact with me again."

Her neck had started to turn pink, and I could see her fingers shaking, but before she could collect herself, I dipped my head at her, and said what I hoped would be the last thing I ever told her.

"Goodbye, Mrs. Jones."

And I walked out of there.

I HAD a low-level headache on the drive home, just this faint buzzing thing from the tension of being around the Antichrist. She had that effect on people. A small part of me still couldn't believe the bullshit she'd tried to spill.

Decent people.

Make sure.

That was the way to win someone over.

Yeah, right.

I snorted and shook my head at least ten times, rewinding her words and then speeding through them again. I wanted to call Aunt Carolina and tell her. I wanted to call Yuki. Or Clara.

But more than all of that, I just wanted to get back to the life I knew now. The one that had built me back up from the place of indecision and confusion and fear that I had once been in. To the people who mattered.

I didn't even realize there were a couple of tears popping out of the corners of my eyes until I sniffed back a watery nose and realized it wasn't actually coming from there. Wiping at them with the back of my hand, I just wanted a hug.

I was done with that life. So fucking done it felt like a hundred pounds had fallen off my chest. The second I turned into the driveway, I was ready.

I didn't know for what exactly, but for something.

For the future more than ever. For everything, maybe.

A whoosh of air left my lungs as I turned the car into Rhodes's driveway. Determination reinforced my spine as I drove onward, ready to park, to get out, and to continue appreciating everything I had. Because of the Joneses in part. But still, always and forever, mostly thanks to my mom. I had no idea where I'd be or how I'd feel if I didn't have this place.

But as I approached the garage apartment, I spotted Rhodes himself coming out of his house, this tight expression on his face that lasted about a second before he focused on my car. Then and only then did some of the tension ease off his features. Like relief. Was he relieved?

His flannel shirt was buttoned halfway up, his undershirt, as always, clinging to his chest. There were keys in his hand too, I realized as I parked my car in the usual spot and got out.

He was coming down the deck stairs as I circled around

the front. That purple-gray gaze was on me. "You all right?" he called out, a frown coming over his mouth again.

But it didn't stay there for long.

Because I said, "I'm great," about a split second before I went for him the moment he was within reaching distance. Going up to the tips of my toes, my arms went around the back of his neck, my chest plastering itself against his, and I went for it.

I pressed my lips against Rhodes's.

His body went rock solid for all of a second before his upper body relaxed and one of his arms wrapped around the middle of my back, the other forearm settling just above my butt. Rhodes crushed me against him, tilting his head to the side, a warm kiss his reply to mine.

And it was only a freaking miracle that I didn't try to scale him like a wall and wrap my legs around his waist because his mouth was warm, his lips firm and soft at the same time, it was sweet and gentle... it was everything I had ever wanted and more.

His breath washed over my mouth, eyebrows knitting together. He licked his lips, looked right into my eyes for a single moment and then dipped for another kiss before he pulled back and focused down on me some more with his intense face. "And here I was worried you were coming back and telling me you were moving out."

I shook my head, taking in the fine lines at his eyes, the ones across his forehead, the sharp color of his eyes, and all that incredible silver hair.

"Are you all right?" he murmured, kneading my hip with his big hand, still staring at me like if he looked away I would suddenly disappear.

"Yeah," I answered. "I met up with my ex's mom."

"Am told me," he breathed. "I was debating whether to go be your backup or let you handle it alone."

I couldn't help but smile at him, taking in his care and tucking it in deeply along my heart. "I'm fine," I told him quietly. "She just riled me up, and all I wanted was to come back here." I swallowed. "I want no part of them anymore. Not even a little bit."

"I hope not," he said, watching me carefully. "You sure you're all right?"

"Yeah, but I'm even better now," I admitted, because it was 100 percent the truth. And that was exactly when I realized what I'd done. What I'd started and where we were. "I'm sorry I jumped you like that. I know we just talked about taking our time and being sure, but all I could think about was how lucky I am to have you guys, and you're so handsome, and you make me feel safe, and you always believe in me and—"

That full mouth cracked into the slowest smile I'd ever seen, his eyebrows going up at the same time. But it wasn't words that cut me off. It was the sweet press of his lips against mine once more. Slow and tender, his lips only lingered over mine for a moment, but it might have been the greatest moment of my life.

If I liked kissing him this much with my mouth closed, how much would I like his tongue?

I needed to calm the hell down, that was what I needed to do.

Rhodes pulled back, that lingering soft smile still taking over his mouth as he said, "Whenever you're ready, you'll tell me?"

I nodded, and that was when I whispered, "I don't kiss just anybody."

The way he said "good" was probably going to be etched into my soul for the rest of my life.

"Ora!" a yell came from the house, surprising us both.

I peeked over Rhodes's shoulder to find Amos standing at

the doorway, still in his pajamas and looking even more sleepy.

"You okay?" he asked, confirming exactly why I'd come here.

Because it was a place where a sixteen-year-old and a forty-two-year-old who I'd only known for about six months worried about me more than people I had known for over a decade.

It was my place of comfort. The place where my mom had wanted me to be. Somewhere that lifted me up and kept me up, even on the crappy days.

"I'm good!" I yelled back. "Are you?"

"Scarred for life watching you grab Dad's butt like that, but I'll get over it. Thanks for wondering!" he hollered sarcastically before shaking his head and closing the door.

Rhodes and I both froze. Our eyes met, and we both started cracking up.

Yeah, I was right where I wanted to be. Where I was happy. *Thank you, Mom.*

$\mathcal{T}$he next couple of weeks went by in an absolute blur. Mostly because we were so busy at the shop. Summer had been hectic, fall had been slow until hunting season had started, but everything had gotten kicked into high gear once the snow came and schools started closing down for holiday break.

We were slammed with rentals and sales, and Clara had given me a crash course in helping customers select skis and snowboards the day I'd gotten my own rental. Everything else I needed to know—questions that customers could or would ask—I made a list of and asked some of the locals I'd gotten to know since working at the shop. Amos, surprisingly, answered a lot of them on the nights we had dinner together. Fortunately, there was only one resort close by, so there weren't too many things people could ask, except where they could take the tubes they rented for sledding.

With work being so busy, I was grateful that I'd bought all my Christmas presents in advance on my lunch breaks, shipping most of them straight to my aunt and uncle's, and having a few sent to my PO box in town. If it hadn't been for those presents I had sent to my box, I might have totally forgotten about the plane ticket I'd booked back in October to go to Florida for Christmas.

Even back then, I hadn't wanted to leave Clara alone for too long, so I'd reserved my ticket to leave early in the morning on Christmas Eve and come back the 26th.

When everyone started talking about a big storm that was supposed to roll in the day before Christmas, I didn't think much of it. We had been getting steady snowfall every few days for a while. I'd gotten more confident driving in it, even though any time he could, Rhodes came to the shop and followed me back home.

Just thinking about Rhodes made the funniest feeling fill up my chest.

I wasn't sure if it was because I had been raised by people who believed in me too much or just weren't the helicopter-parenting type, but his overprotectiveness just did something to me. Big-time. I swear it lit me up from the inside out like one of those Lite-Brites I used to have when I'd been a kid.

We hadn't gotten to spend any time together by ourselves again, and there hadn't been any more *real* kisses since the day I'd basically thrown myself at him after Mrs. Jones's visit, but that was mostly because of how often he'd been working late. There were all kinds of issues he had to deal with that I had no idea were even a thing. From problems with snow-mobilers, to ice-fishing issues, and illegal hunting. He'd explained to me one night when he'd gotten home early enough and brought pizza with him, that after summer, winter was the busiest season he had.

To be fair, any time he got home early enough—with the exception of a night he'd gone over to Johnny's to play poker —Rhodes invited me over.

And of course I went.

Sitting as close to him as possible on the two nights we'd

watched a movie with Amos sprawled in a recliner. We'd smiled at each other from across the table on another day when, after dinner, we'd played an old version of Scrabble that no one knew where it had come from. But the most special part was how he walked me back to the garage apartment every night we spent time together and he gave me a long, lingering hug afterward. Once and only once, he kissed me on the forehead in a way that made my knees tingle.

I didn't think I was imagining the sexual tension every time my breasts got pressed against his chest.

So all in all, I was happier than I'd been in forever, in so many different ways. The hope that I'd gotten so many glimpses of over the last few months had grown bigger and bigger in my heart with every passing day. A sense of family, of rightness, wrapped around just about every part of me.

But on the 23rd of December, when Clara and I were closing up the shop, she turned to me, seriously, and said, "I don't think you're getting out of here tomorrow."

Covered in a down jacket I'd had forever that didn't have enough filling for the temperatures we were having, I shivered and raised my eyebrows at her. "You don't think so?"

She shook her head at me as she turned the lock on the door; we'd already set the alarm right before heading out. "I saw the radar. It's going to be a big storm. I bet they'll cancel your flight."

I shrugged but didn't want to worry about it. It had been snowing a lot, and tourists were still coming into town. Plus, it wasn't like I could do anything about it. My superpowers didn't extend to controlling the weather.

Pulling down the security gate that went over the door Clara still wasn't looking at me as she said in a funky voice, "I forgot to tell you... someone... some... charity, I think... paid off my dad's medical bills for Christmas." One dark brown eye caught mine before she focused back on the gate. "Isn't that a miracle?" she asked, sounding just a little funny.

"Wow, that is a miracle, Clara," I answered her, trying to keep my voice even and steady. Normal. Totally normal. Even my face was blank and innocent.

"I thought so too," she said, peeking at me again. "I wish I could thank them."

I settled for nodding. "But maybe they don't need any gratitude, you know?"

"No," she agreed. "Maybe not, but it still really means a lot to me. To us."

I just nodded again, averting my eyes until she wrapped me in a hug and wished me a safe trip and a Merry Christmas. We'd exchanged presents yesterday. I had sent Mr. Nez and Jackie a gift too.

But that evening, after driving slowly home, I was upstairs in the studio apartment, folding some clothes so I wouldn't leave the place a disaster zone that would give neat-monster Rhodes a migraine, when there was a knock downstairs, a creaky door being opened, and an "Angel?"

I smiled. "Hi, Rhodes."

The sound of him on the stairs kept the smile on my face, but when he cleared the top and stopped right at the landing, it went a little bigger, about as big as I could muster.

The corner of Rhodes's mouth twisted. He was in his uniform, but he must have gone inside his house first, because instead of his winter work jacket, he had on a dark blue parka with a fleece hood. It was pretty chilly outside. "Couldn't fit your clothes into the suitcase balled up so you're folding them?"

I gave him a flat look. "I used to wonder if Amos got his sarcasm from his mom, but now I get where it came from, and *actually*, I was folding them so you wouldn't go into cardiac arrest if you came up here while I was gone so...."

He walked over and stopped beside the table, his cold bare hand settling on top of my head. He eyed my small stacks of clothes—underwear in one pile, bras in another, mismatched socks over there.

I tipped my chin up and earned myself a rare smile. I swore he was handing them out to me left and right lately, and not like the precious currency they'd once been.

"What?" I asked.

"You're something else, Buddy," he said.

I set the T-shirt I'd been in the middle of folding down and squinted. "Can I ask you something?"

"What do you think?"

I groaned. "Why do you call me 'Buddy'? I've never heard you call Am that, or anybody else."

His eyebrows crept up his forehead at the same time as his mouth stretched into an even more rare, supermoon of a smile. "You don't know?"

"Am I supposed to?"

"I thought you would," he replied cryptically, still grinning.

I shook my head. "No idea. I used to think you called me 'angel' because you thought that was my name, but now I know you just... whatever."

Rhodes chuckled, laying a hand on top of the table, the tips of his fingers millimeters from the lace trim of my green underwear. Those gray eyes were totally hung up on them for a moment before he glanced back at me, color rising along his throat as he said, "Because you are one."

My mouth gaped, and I was pretty sure I was just staring up at him blankly.

One side of his mouth rose a little higher. "Why do you look surprised? You've got the sweetest, kindest heart, Buddy. It wouldn't matter what you looked like, you'd still be my angel."

His angel?

Was my chin quivering?

Was that my heart losing its identity for a new one?

Did Rhodes literally just say the nicest thing anyone had ever said about me?

His expression was so fond, so open, all I could do was gape at him as he looked down at me. "You remind me of Buddy the Elf. You're always smiling. Always trying to make things better. I thought for sure you would get it," he explained.

My chin *was* quivering.

And the softest smile swept over his hard face. "Don't tear up. We have to talk. Have you seen the forecast?"

I blinked and tried to focus, wrapping up that explanation and setting it beside my heart because otherwise I was about to get naked right then and there. "The forecast?" I croaked, trying to think. "You mean because of the storm?"

He nodded, apparently over paying me any more compliments that could make me feel like maybe, just maybe... he might love me.

Because the truth was, I was totally in love with him.

Just looking at him made me happy. Being close to him made me feel calm. Safe. There was nothing about this man that was hesitant or withdrawn. He was quiet, yeah, but it had nothing to do with him holding parts of himself back. I loved how serious he was. How deep his thoughts and actions went.

No one in my life, other than my mom, had made me feel the way he did. Like I could trust them completely. And it was when I'd accepted that—seen it for it what it was—that I'd understood the depth of my feelings.

I was in love with him.

"Yeah," I confirmed, making sure my mouth was closed and scrubbing under my eyes even though I was pretty sure no tears had actually come out. They'd just hung out right at the rim. "Clara told me, and I looked too when I got home."

He dipped that chin with its cute cleft. "Your flight is supposed to leave early, isn't it?"

I confirmed it was, swallowing hard once to make sure I was keeping it together and not blubbering—much less telling him that I was stupid in love with him.

"It's supposed to drop ten to twelve overnight," he kept talking, his words careful.

"The plane is supposed to leave at six."

He didn't say anything, but those hard, blunt fingers went to my jaw, touching from right behind my ear to the center of my chin and back.

"You think it's going to get canceled?" I managed to ask, mostly to distract him so that hopefully he'd keep touching my face. He hadn't been shy about touching my shoulders or my wrist. Sometimes he'd touch my fingers, and I'd swear it was better than anything I did to myself at night in bed.

He did—keep up his touching that was. "I think you should be ready for the possibility it will," he answered quietly, his lids heavy over his eyes.

"Oh, that would suck, but it's not like I can do anything about it if it happens. I have—"

Those gray eyes met mine, and he dropped into a crouch at my side, bringing that handsome face and beautiful hair to basically eye level with me. "Come stay at the house with us."

"Tonight?" I pretty much croaked.

The hand that had been on my throat for all of thirty seconds landed on my thigh. "I'll drive you in the morning if your flight is still on. You won't have to walk back and forth across the driveway," he said, like it was a half-mile walk from the garage apartment to his house.

My own mouth twitched. "Sure."

Rhodes stood and set that same palm on top of my shoulder. "Want to come over now? I'll help you carry your things."

"Sign me up."

His warm expression fueled my spirit. I really was totally in love with him. But the most surprising part was that the knowledge and acceptance of it brought no terror into my heart. None. Not a fragment of fear. Not a whisper of it.

This knowledge, this feeling, reminded me of concrete in its endurance, in the strength of it. I had told myself a hundred times that I wasn't afraid of love, that I was ready to move forward, but the future was scary.

But Rhodes had earned every inch of what I felt with his attention, with his patience and overprotectiveness and just... with everything that made him up in general.

Feeling pretty damn ballsy, I leaned forward and kissed him on the cheek quickly and then started getting my stuff together. It didn't take me long to get another change of clothes and pajamas together while Rhodes took the initiative and *finished folding my laundry*. When we were done, he carried my big suitcase down the stairs, not crying at all about how heavy it was even though I was only leaving for two days, as well as the grocery bag I'd stuffed with my extra clothes for tonight and tomorrow. I had already hidden their presents inside the hallway closet by Amos's room yesterday when I'd gone over there before work. I had planned on calling them Christmas Day and telling them where to look for their gifts.

We were crossing the driveway when Rhodes carefully said, "This storm is going to be big, sweetheart. Don't be too disappointed if your flight gets rescheduled, all right?"

"I won't," I assured him. Because I really wouldn't be.

"ARE YOU SAD?" Amos asked the next night as we sat around the table. Rhodes had pulled out a set of dominos an hour earlier, and I'd played one game against him before Am had wandered out of his bedroom and apparently decided he was bored enough to join in too.

"Me?" I asked as I stretched my arms over my head.

"Yeah," he asked before taking a quick sip of his strawberry soda. "Because your flight got canceled."

The notification had come in the middle of the night. The beep of the app had woken me up, and I'd rolled over—in Rhodes's bed, where he'd slept on his side and I'd slept on the other because he'd reminded me about the mice and the possibility of bats again—to find that my flight had been rescheduled from six in the morning to noon. By nine in the morning, it had been rescheduled to three, and by ten thirty, it had been totally canceled.

If I had felt even a little bit disappointed, the way that Rhodes had massaged my nape when I'd given him the news would have made up for all of it.

That and how he'd stripped down to his boxers in front of me before crawling into bed mere inches away, his fingertips brushing mine more than once before we'd fallen asleep.

I wasn't sure how much longer we were going to be able to sleep in the same bed together—even though it had only happened twice—but I was ready for something. And from the look in his eye, I could tell he was ready for something too. Something deeper than a three-letter word that hung between us even though we had barely kissed each other.

But that was something to ponder over later when Am wasn't sitting across from us at the table.

"No, it's okay. As long as you don't mind me hanging out with you guys...." I trailed off.

He made a face behind his can. "No."

"Are you sure? Because my feelings won't be hurt if you just want to hang out with your dad and your mom's family."

"*No*," he insisted. "It's fine."

"It's fine" from him was pretty much a blessing that I wouldn't close my eyes to. "Are you two sad your dad had to cancel coming because of the snow?" I asked Rhodes.

Father and son looked at each other.

I hadn't heard much about Randall Rhodes, but I did know that he had been invited to come over and spend Christmas Eve with them, since he definitely wasn't invited to the get-together on Amos's other side of the family, which might also be canceled now depending on road conditions. Personally, I thought it was a small step that the man had called and apologized for not being able to make it. But I was pretty sure I was the only one impressed by it.

He was trying. I thought.

"I'll take that as a no," I muttered. "Maybe we can find a scary movie to watch after this?"

That perked Am up, and I didn't miss the slight snort out of Rhodes's nose at the idea of watching something scary on Christmas Eve. I glanced at him and smiled. His sock-covered foot nudged mine beneath the table. I swore that was better than most kisses I'd gotten over my life.

"Yeah, I guess," Amos said, also in a way that was pretty much a "hell yeah" from him.

"Do you care?" I asked Rhodes with a hopeful look on my face, fluttering my eyes at him.

The older man side-eyed me. "Quit being cute. What do you think?"

I thought he wouldn't, and I was right to think so. We all sat around the television and watched *Brightburn*, and they ignored me when I closed my eyes or pretended to have something really interesting to look at beneath my finger-nails. By the time the movie finished though, it was midnight, and I couldn't wait until morning any longer. We had always celebrated Christmas at midnight—with my mom, at least. That tradition had seemed to be the only one she'd kept from her Venezuelan family.

On the couch, besides Rhodes where I'd watched the whole movie, I scooted forward and asked, "Can I give you two your presents now?"

Am said, "Okay," at the same time Rhodes asked, "You got us something?"

I eyed Rhodes again. "You saw how much garland I had up in the garage apartment. This can't surprise you."

He shrugged, and I believed him. He'd looked genuinely surprised when boxes from his brothers had arrived with Christmas presents for him and Amos. The only box that he hadn't been too surprised by was the one that had made it from Amos's parents.

"Of course I got you something. Wait, wait, wait, let me go get it. I love giving presents on Christmas Eve, sorry if this is messing everything up, but I just get so excited. I love Christmas."

"Your mom celebrated Christmas?" Rhodes asked as I got up.

I shot him a smile. "She probably would have hated how commercialized it is now, but she didn't back when I was a kid, or if she did, she hid it from me." I had a lot of fond memories with my mom on that holiday, and just thinking about it made me miss her a lot, but not in a bad or sad way. More grateful that I had those moments to look back on.

Because Christmas was about spending it with people who mattered, and even though I wasn't with my Florida family, I was still doing that.

And truth be told, I was glad I was with Rhodes and Amos. It felt right.

It took a minute to haul the huge box out and set it in the

doorway into the living room; then I had to go back and grab the two bags I'd stuffed behind all their old jackets and vacuum. They eyeballed me as I moved everything else closer in trips.

I went straight to Am and set the heavy gift on the floor in front of him. "I hope you like it, but if you don't, too bad. All sales were final."

He gave me a weird look that made me laugh but ripped the paper off.

He gasped.

I knew Rhodes had bought him his guitar because I'd helped get him a discount. And pick out the woods and the stain. He hadn't asked questions about how I'd gotten the discount or how I knew so much about guitars, and I wondered, not for the first time, if he truly had no idea who Yuki was when they'd briefly met. Amos had brought her up a few times in his presence, but he hadn't batted an eyelash.

Anyway, Am didn't know he was getting a guitar yet.

"This is *vintage*," he gasped, running his hands over the weathered orange leather around the amp.

"Yeah."

He looked at me, gray eyes wide. "For me?"

"No, for my other favorite teenager. Don't tell my nephews I said that."

Am's shoulders slumped as he ran his hands over the amp that I'd bought from a small shop in California and had shipped here, which had ended up costing as much as the amp had.

"Your other one is a little buzzy, and I thought it would be nice to have matching stuff," I told him.

He nodded and gulped a couple of times before looking back at me. "Wait a minute," he said, getting up and disappearing down the hall toward his room. I met Rhodes's eyes and made mine go wide.

"I wanted to give him his gift before you give him you-know-what and he doesn't care," I whispered.

"You spoil him. Even Sofie said it."

Sofie was his mom, who as I'd learned the day of Thanksgiving, was just a lovely fucking woman who loved her child more than I could have ever imagined. She had whispered to me no less than three times that Amos had been conceived artificially and that she loved her husband very much and Rhodes was a wonderful man.

I shrugged. "He's my little buddy."

He smiled.

"I'm sorry for messing up your traditions...." I trailed off, and he shook his head.

"Billy and Sofie both celebrate Christmas on Christmas Eve. I've only gotten to spend a couple with him, but he's seemed pretty happy to me today considering I know he's missing his mom and dad. He's only been trying to act like he doesn't."

"At least he's got one dad here though."

His face went somber. "I didn't mean to make you sad."

I'd almost screwed that up. "You're not making me sad. I'm okay." I stopped talking when Amos came back out, holding something in a Happy Birthday bag in his hand. I recognized it as the one that Jackie had given him his present in months ago.

He held it out to me. No warning, no explanation, no nothing. Just: here it is.

"You thought of me," I said, even though in the back of my head I wondered if he'd run into his room to get something old he didn't use anymore and regift it. But honestly, I wouldn't care. I had just about everything, and if there was something I wanted, I could buy it. It was just rare that I did. I had traded in my car out of necessity; I hadn't even splurged on buying the "right" winter clothes or shoes yet, despite Clara giving me a hard time when I complained about my toes being cold from my too-thin hiking boots.

I opened the bag and took out a heavy yellow leather notebook with an A on the front.

"So you can write new songs in it," Am explained as I traced my finger over the engraved letter.

I swallowed.

My chest hurt.

"But if you don't like it—"

I raised my gaze to his, telling myself I wouldn't cry. I had cried enough in my life, but these tears wouldn't be ones of grief. I wouldn't mourn the words I had lost, the ones that had arced through my head for years, nearly endlessly... until they hadn't.

Amos had no idea. Because I hadn't told him yet. I had to. I would.

A tear pooled right at the corner of my eye, and I wiped it with my knuckle. "No, I love it, Am. I love it a lot. That's so thoughtful of you. Thank you."

"Thanks for my amp," he replied, watching me closely like he was expecting me to lie or something.

"Can I get a hug?"

He nodded again and stood up, wrapping me up in the tightest hug he'd ever given me. I kissed his cheek and he surprised me by kissing mine back. Am took a step back, his face more than just a little bit bashful.

I almost cried, but I didn't want to embarrass him. When I was able to, I bent down and handed Rhodes the two bags I'd gotten for him. "Merry Christmas, Tobers."

He took them with a lift of his eyebrows at his nickname before saying in his bossy voice, "You didn't need to get me anything."

"You haven't needed to do half the nice things you've done for me, but you did, especially today. It's snowing, and dinner was so good, and we played dominos, and I think this might be the best Christmas Eve I've ever had. But don't be disappointed because your present isn't as cool as Amos's."

Those gray eyes met mine as he shoved his hand into the first bag and pulled out a frame.

"I hope you like it. You're both so cute. The other one I took off your Facebook page," I explained.

His Adam's apple bobbed, and he nodded. The first picture was the one I'd taken of him and Amos on the hike to the waterfalls so many months back. They had been standing close together at the bottom of the falls and had grudgingly agreed to let me take a picture of them being too cool to purposely be shoulder to shoulder. But still good enough.

"I didn't know what to get you, and you don't have any pictures of you two together in here."

He slipped his hand back into the bag and pulled out a second frame. This one I hadn't been sure about. I didn't want to overstep my boundaries. It was a photograph of a young Amos with a dog.

Rhodes swallowed hard once, those eyes lingering over the photograph for a long moment. He pinched his lips together, then got up and pulled me up and into his arms so quickly and tightly, I couldn't breathe.

"There's a gift card to the shop too. I had to give the store your business," I managed to mumble out around his sweater and pectoral muscle.

Then I stopped talking and let myself snuggle into that incredible body holding mine hostage. My cheek was against his chest, arms wedged against my body from his hold. He smelled just like his laundry detergent and clean man.

I loved it.

I loved *him*, this quiet man who took care of the people around him. In little ways. In little actions that meant everything. He had a heart bigger than I ever could have imagined.

It wasn't like it had snuck up on me. It didn't hit me on the back of my head. What I felt for him had walked right up to me, and I'd watched it happen.

"Thank you," he murmured, smoothing his hand from the crown of my head down my back to settle right at the small of it. His chest filled with air, and then he released it. It was a content sigh.

And I loved that too.

"I'm going to my room. What time are we leaving tomorrow?" Amos asked.

He was referring to his aunt's house. "We're *leaving* at eight. If you want breakfast before we go, get up early enough, Am."

He wasn't going to, and I was pretty sure we were both well aware of it, but Rhodes wouldn't be a dad if he didn't remind him anyway.

The teenager huffed. "*Okay*. 'Night."

"'Night," Rhodes and I both replied, and I took that as my moment to pull back a little. Just a little. Tilting my head up, I smiled at the bristly face aimed down at me.

"Thank you for letting me spend Christmas with you two."

His hand did that thing again where it cupped the back of my head and went down my spine, except that time, I think it might have gone a little lower, a little closer to my butt.

I didn't mind. I didn't mind at all.

"I know you wanted to see your aunt and uncle, but I'm glad you're here. Real glad," Rhodes admitted in that tough, quiet voice. His eyes were on mine, intense and hooded, as he said, "I've got your Christmas present upstairs. Come with me."

Upstairs, huh? The tingling was back... just not exclusively in my chest anymore. Was this happening?

I wouldn't know unless I went with him.

I nodded and followed, watching him flip off the lights downstairs as we passed them. They hadn't put up a tree, and Am and I had trudged back to the garage apartment to grab the tiny one I'd bought and decorated with dollar-store ornaments, and we'd propped it up on top of some books besides the TV. The lights were battery-operated, and neither of us bothered turning them off.

Rhodes kept holding my hand as we got into his room, but it was me who kicked the door shut behind us. He glanced at me with surprise, and I smiled at him.

"Sit. Please," he said after a second, before ducking into his closet.

I took a seat on the edge of the bed, tucking my hands between my thighs as he rooted around and produced two boxes. He'd wrapped them in brown paper, all nice and neat just like his ironing. He held out the smallest one first, stopping to kneel directly in front of me with the other box in hand.

"Here," he said.

I smiled at him and slowly tore the paper, pulling out the gift inside and noticing the name printed on the top. My mouth formed an O.

"Since you won't buy your own," he explained as I opened the box, moved the tissue paper aside, and pulled out the tall, slip-on boots with fleece-like lining around the tops. "Now your toes won't be freezing every time you leave the house."

I hugged the boot to my chest. "I love them. Thank you."

"Make sure they fit," he said, already reaching down for my foot and lifting it up. I didn't say a word as I handed him the shoe and watched as he slipped it on me, giving it a couple jiggles to get it over my heel.

His irises flicked up. "Good?"

I nodded, my heartbeat starting to pound away in my throat, and he did the other one. I scrunched up my toes to make sure they had the perfect amount of room, even though I was having a hard time paying attention to anything other than him kneeling on the ground in front of me, putting my boots on for me. "Perfect fit. Thank you so much. I love them," I breathed, giving him another smile.

He reached to the side and handed me the second box.

"You really didn't have to," I told him, already opening it.

"I only got you things you need," he explained.

I smiled at him as I finished ripping the paper off and then the tape holding the box closed and opened it to find something tangerine-colored inside. It was a down jacket. I recognized the brand as one of the most expensive ones we carried at the shop.

"It's winter here a third of the year, and you're always shivering when you come rushing in since that jacket of yours is too thin," he said quietly. "We can return it if you'd rather get something else."

I set the jacket aside.

And I threw myself at him.

Literally.

My arms went around his neck so fast he didn't have time to brace, but somehow managed to, my cheek to his, my legs straddling his hips from where he'd been kneeling. And I hugged him. I hugged him just as tight as he'd hugged me after opening his frames.

The jacket wasn't a diamond bracelet or a ruby necklace. It wasn't some expensive purse picked blindly just because it was expensive. It wasn't a new laptop I didn't need because my old one was only a year old.

These were things I needed. Things that he knew I needed. Things to keep me warm because that mattered to him.

They were two of the most thoughtful gifts I'd ever been given.

"What's this big hug for, huh?" he asked against my cheek as his arms went around the middle of my back, holding me steady on his lap as he rocked back to rest on his heels like we'd been in this position a hundred times before. "Are you getting upset?"

There were tears in my eyes, tears that snuck onto his neck and the collar of his sweater. "I'm getting upset because you're so nice. It's your fault."

He hugged me a little tighter. "It's my fault?"

"Yes." I pulled back a little, took in the heavy lines of his bone structure, his brows, that adorable chin, and I kissed him.

Not like before, when they'd been pecks that had fed my soul with their sweetness, but really did it.

Rhodes groaned as he kissed me back—our first real-real fucking kiss. His lips were as soft and perfect as I remembered, and I doubted there was a mouth in the world better than his. Tilting his head to the side, Rhodes kissed me slowly, softly. Still so sweetly. He took his time, his warm lips plucking at my bottom one, sucking the tip of my tongue and starting all over again, the palms of his hands going up and down my back, holding me to him and touching me all at the same time.

There was no awkwardness. No hesitation. His hands mapped my body like they already knew it.

We kissed and kissed, and that big palm slipped up the back of my sweater, fingers stretched wide, touching everything possible. So I did the same, sneaking my hand up under his side, palming the solid mass of muscles there and the skin over his ribs, earning a soft groan that I swallowed because I sure as hell didn't want to stop kissing him again any time soon.

Or ever, if I had the choice.

I knew Rhodes cared about me like I knew the sky was

blue, and some part of me thought he might be at least a little in love with me right back. He was affectionate in his own way. He taught me how to do things. He went out of his way to spend time with me. He never hid that he cared about me in front of other people. He supported me. He worried about me.

If that wasn't love, then I could still easily settle for all that the rest of my life.

But for now, today, in this room, stroking his warm skin, all those hard muscles… with two of the most practical and sweet gifts I could have ever asked for… I wasn't going to worry about more than what I had then. Which was more than I'd ever had.

He wasn't my ex. This man wouldn't lead me on or use me. He liked having me around, because he liked *me*.

And he just made me happy. His subtle smiles. His touches. Even his bossy britches voice. It all meant the world to me.

He made me happy. And I had decided I was ready. More than ready.

And I whispered those exact words to him as that callused palm snuck so deeply under my sweater his fingertips brushed that tender spot right between my shoulders.

Rhodes growled, tilting me back in his lap just enough so he could look right into my eyes as he said, with that ferociously serious expression from the first night I'd walked into his life, "You have no idea."

Then he kissed me again, slow and deep and sweet. Not asking me if I was sure. Not hesitating. Showing me again that he trusted what I felt and what I wanted.

And I had no idea that kiss was going to be the last of the sweetness.

"Can I see you?" he asked, all husky and ready.

I glided my hand as far up his back as I could possibly reach, his skin smooth. "You can do more than that."

His growl was deep in his throat as his other hand went to the bottom of my top, and he pulled it over my head. Those lips went straight from my mouth to my neck, leaving open-mouth kisses and nips there that had me instantly rolling my hips against his.

Against his hard, hard dick.

I'd felt... traces of it before, all sleepy or semi-sleepy in his jeans and sweatpants when he would give me a hug, but never... never like this. Ready. Waiting. Excited and fully awake.

It had been so long. We had taken our time. Built this up.

Because he sure wasn't indifferent at all as he groaned while I pressed against him as his mouth gave a hard suck at a spot between my neck and collarbone that had me whimpering. Rhodes leaned away for a moment, his throat bobbing, his breath heavy, that gaze moving from my face down to my breasts, held up by the green balconet bra I'd thrown on that pushed my breasts up to the top. The underwire sucked, but I'd never been gladder to have put that specific bra on in that moment until then.

"Jesus," he whispered. "Take it off." His throat bobbed. "Please."

"You got it," I whispered back, letting go of all his soft skin to reach back and pluck at the hooks, shimmying my shoulders to let the bra drop between our bodies.

I was ready, I was so fucking ready.

And I was pretty sure he groaned "fuck" under his breath a split second before his hands were at my waist, and he was lifting me up just a little off his lap at the same time his mouth dove down and those pink, wonderful lips sucked a nipple between them.

I moaned and arched my back, pushing my breast deeper

into his mouth before he gave it another suck and moved over, suckling at that nipple too, hard and then softly, two hard pulls and then one gentle one. Not wanting to break our contact but wanting to see him too, I grabbed at the bottom of his sweater and pulled it over his head.

He was just as beautiful as I remembered from the times I'd perved on him through the window. His stomach was flat and hard with muscle, his skin tight and covered with a V-shape of light hair across his pecs and down to his navel. I wanted to lick him right there, but instead, I ran my hands over his chest, over his shoulders, lowering myself back down onto his lap so that I could settle on top of him again. On top of his dick.

His mouth met mine at the same time my breasts brushed his chest, and I swore my nipples got even harder when they grazed the hair on his pecs. I touched him everywhere, and he touched me everywhere. And at some point, my hands went to the snap of his jeans and the zipper, and his snuck under the layer of my leggings and underwear, grabbing a handful of my bare ass and squeezing it, pulling me in even closer to his erection.

Sneaking my hand down into his underwear, my finger-tips brushed hair there. The wide, hard base. The smooth, smooth skin covering it all, and he grunted, his laugh unexpected and rough. "Not too much of that."

I kissed the line of his jaw, the tip of his chin, and gave him a squeeze anyway.

He pulled out one of the hands he had inside my underwear and cupped my breast with it, taking its weight. "How am I so goddamn lucky?" he groaned. "How can you feel this good already?" His mouth gave my neck a soft kiss that had me shivering.

"I've been thinking about this for so long," I told him, stroking both hands up and down his spine, nipping at his chin in a way that had his hips rolling straight against the seam of my body. "You don't even know how many times I've made myself come thinking about you sucking on my nipples."

He groaned, broken and loud.

"Or just pushing deep, deep in me."

He panted as I circled my hips into his.

"And pictured you coming in me, every inch of you stuffing me full."

He growled.

Those big hands went to my butt, and then we were up and he was dropping me in the middle of his bed. He yanked my leggings off and threw them over his shoulder before sneaking his fingers beneath my undies and pulling those right off too.

I smiled at him, arching my back and reaching for his jeans when he crawled over me. I kept on smiling at him as I pushed his pants down over his butt, copping a handful on the way back up, and then doing it again, but this time under his boxers, stroking once, twice.

He groaned deep at the touch, then groaned even deeper when I wrapped my hand around him too.

I wasn't sure who was more surprised, him or me.

Because I looked down at what I had my fingers on. I'd only gotten to touch the base of him. I hadn't gotten... the whole thing.

His laugh was husky as he dipped down and kissed me before saying, "I've thought about this every night too."

It was my turn to gulp as I risked a glance down at the thick cock I was holding.

It was perfect.

I gave him a squeeze, and he gave me another groan, a dreamy look in his eyes. He kissed me again, and I gave him yet another squeeze that had him swiveling his hips like he wanted me to do it again.

So I did.

"I've got places I want to put my mouth… my fingers…." He dipped his mouth back toward my breasts and sucked a nipple softly, slowly. "It'll be so damn good for you…."

Patience had never been a virtue of mine.

So as he sucked and licked at my breasts, I stroked up and down the thick cock bobbing between our bodies, rubbing my thumb through the drop of precum that pooled at the deep-red tip I wanted to put into my mouth at some point, and jerked him off slowly, kissing the parts of his head I could reach. His hair. His ear. My other hand stroked his back as he kept on sucking the tips of my breasts before eventually easing a hand to the side of mine and stroking the pads of his fingers up and down the seam of my body.

The words came out of my mouth before I could stop them. "Is it terrible that I hate knowing other people have seen you like this? That I'm jealous I'm not the only one who knows how big you are? What you feel like in my hand?"

The noise Rhodes made in the back of his throat was fucking savage. His breathing was deep, his fingers not stopping their petting movement up and down my lower lips. But his voice was harsh and deep as he said, serious, "They don't matter. They're never going to again. Understand me?" Rhodes pulled back and met my gaze with his stormy, bright one. "And you're not the only one jealous."

"There's nothing for you to be jealous about," I promised.

That must have been the perfect thing to say because then we were kissing again, and I'd licked my palm before going back to teasing him slowly when one of those big fingers finally dipped between my lips and pushed inside. I'd been wet from the moment he started kissing me, groaning as he pulled that long finger out and pushed it back in, pumping slowly, steadily.

"I'm on birth control," I whispered. "I went to the doctor and I'm good," I told him, needing him to know.

His voice was hoarse as he replied, "I go every year, and I haven't done anything in a long time...."

"Good." I bit his throat. "Then you can come in me as deep as you want."

Rhodes growled in his throat before he slid another finger deep, his sawing motions consistent before they started scissoring. And finally a third finger joined the rest, and I whimpered at the stretch, at the fullness that somewhere in the back of my mind I recognized was necessary for what we both wanted.

Rhodes whispered into my ear what he was going to do to me—telling me all about how he was going to bottom out, about how good he knew we were going to be together, about filling me up with more than just his dick. But what I loved the most was what he said about how much he wanted me, how good I made him feel, about me molding to him. With that bristly face between my thighs, my hand buried in his soft, brown and silver hair, his tongue dipped as deep into me as possible, lapping and twisting, his lips sucking and possessive. And Rhodes told me all about how he loved the way I tasted, and how he already couldn't wait to do it again.

Eventually, his hips dipped down between my legs, and I wrapped them around his hips, and with my hand around his root, guiding him where we both wanted him, he pressed all of those inches in me.

I was grateful for those three fingers he'd used, but I was more grateful for the gift he'd been given because, even though it took a minute to get used to the magnitude of his girth and how long he was... it was incredible.

His dick twitched the second his slow pumps had our

groins completely meeting, and he groaned against my neck, his body covering mine completely except for where my legs anchored him to me. Rhodes was breathing hard as he pulled a couple inches out and pushed back in. The mattress squeaked lightly. His voice was savage as he growled, and his hips pumped him in to the root.

I squeezed his sides tight, wrapping my arms around his shoulders and tilting up my hips a little. The mattress squeaked again, and I swore I'd never heard anything so erotic in my life. That soft *creak, creak, creak* burned itself into my brain, especially when he moaned into my ear. His breath was hot, his body hotter.

Dragging my palms up and down his back, I loved everything about him.

And that's what I told him.

His dick twitched in me, and he breathed heavily. "You want to end this before we've even really started?"

"It sure feels like we've started," I panted as he retreated and then pushed back in with a smack of his balls against my ass, earning another louder creak of the mattress. And that was how he moved, slowly, then hard, teasing me with the girth of his tip before pushing fully in and then starting all over again.

We kissed and kissed. I bit his neck, and he sucked hard at my shoulder, at my ear. The hair on his chest abraded my nipples, and I loved it. At some point, he slipped his hands under my ass and tilted my hips up even more, his pelvic bone hitting me perfectly. We were sweaty and quiet; I muffled my mouth against his shoulder, and he kissed his groans across my lips.

"You're incredible," he said.

"You're perfect," he whispered.

"You feel so damn good," he growled as his hips picked up

speed just as I started to feel the heat building and building at the center of my body.

Rhodes pounded inside of me, holding me off the bed and on top of his thighs, and I squeezed my legs tight around him as he ground and ground right against where I wanted him. I cried out my orgasm against his cheek. His hands gripped my butt hard as his hips became erratic and he came, pulsing and groaning so deep from his chest, I felt it against mine.

That big, sweaty body slumped against mine as he lowered us onto the bed, still inside of me, between my thighs. Rhodes laid his cheek against the top of my head, his lungs pumping for breath. I wrapped my arms around him, sliding over his slick back, breathing hard too.

"Wow," I panted.

"Jesus," he said, kissing me right above my breast.

"Merry Christmas to me."

Rhodes's sudden laugh filled my chest and heart, and I swore he cuddled me closer, lifting my head to brush his lips against mine. His gaze met mine, and he was smiling, this bright thing that made my chest fly, that made those three little words flare deeply in my chest. "Merry Christmas, Aurora," he whispered tenderly.

"Merry Christmas, Tobers," I repeated, and in some small part of my heart, I hoped this would be the first of many. "You're the best, you know that?"

I felt the curve of his mouth, felt the smile he made against my skin.

It really was the best Christmas I'd ever had.

CHAPTER 28

"Please, for the love of all that is holy, stop, Am," I moaned from the passenger seat the very next night.

Our student driver, who was currently behind the wheel of my car, didn't even bother looking at me as he shook his head in dismay and said, "We left half an hour ago!"

He was totally right. We'd left his aunt's house exactly thirty minutes ago. I'd even peed right before we'd walked out of her doors. But what he didn't know was that I'd chugged a cup of coffee right before all that just in case I'd had to drive home since Rhodes had drunk a couple of beers. "You know I have a tiny bladder. Please, you don't want me to have to pay you to clean my car because I peed in here."

From the seat behind mine, Rhodes made a sound that had to be a bark of a laugh.

"You don't want to smell pee for the next hour."

The teenager finally glanced over with an alarmed expression.

"Please, Am, please. If you love me—and I know you do—stop at the next station. At the next pull-off. I'd be happy going just over to the side of the road right here, and I'll be fast."

That time, Rhodes definitely didn't muffle his laugh or what came afterward. "No peeing on the side of the road. A state trooper will drive by, and I won't be able to talk him out of giving you a ticket for indecent exposure."

I moaned.

"Am, there's a gas station coming up in about five or ten minutes. Can you hold it 'til then?" Rhodes asked, leaning forward between the seats.

I squeezed my muscles—noticing again how sore that area in general was from last night—and gave him a tight nod before pressing my legs together even closer.

His hand came up and settled on my forearm, the thumb rubbing along the sensitive skin there. I grinned at him, which more than likely looked like a sneer from me squeezing my muscles again to ease the urge to pee.

Today had been a great, great day. We'd left right at eight in the morning, with Am saying five words until eleven mostly because he'd been passed out in the back seat. Rhodes and I had talked about Colorado and some of the things he'd learned while in training, explaining how there was a game warden, or a DWM as he called himself when he was being fancy, that handled all the areas closer to Montrose versus the southwest of the state like he did. We listened to some music, but mostly, he talked and I ate up every word and especially every sly smile he sent my way.

He didn't need to actually tell me, but I could tell he was thinking about last night too. Hopefully thinking about how we should have a repeat ASAP. I'd settle for draping myself over his bare chest again like we'd done afterward, too.

Am's aunt had been just as nice as I remembered from Thanksgiving, and I'd had such a nice time crashing their party, talking a ton to Rhodes, a little to Am who mostly hung out with his Uncle Johnny and his dad, and helped out in the kitchen as much as possible. I'd ducked outside in the cold for a little while to call my aunt and uncle and wish them a Merry Christmas, and talked to my cousins for a bit too.

We'd left right after four, because Rhodes had to work tomorrow. He'd asked if it was okay if we let Amos drive, and I'd been all about it—at least until he started to get stingy with the stops thirty minutes in. The roads had been plowed that morning, and the temperature had warmed to a pretty perfect forty-five degrees, keeping the roads free of ice, so it hadn't felt like a safety hazard to let him drive. Rhodes had only complained a little when I'd begged him to stop twice on the way up.

I was just about panting though when I spotted the sign for the gas station in the distance, having kept quiet because it was taking all of my effort not to pee myself, period.

"Finally!" I moaned when he turned right and headed for the pump.

"We're going to get gas," Rhodes said as his son parked.

"Okay, I'll pay you back. I gotta go," I hissed as I threw open the door, having taken my seat belt off while he'd been turning, and flew out of there.

I heard them both laugh, but I had better things to do.

Luckily, I'd been in so many gas stations by this point in my life, that I had an inner magnet for where the bathrooms were and spotted it instantly, pretty much waddling toward the sign because every step got that much harder. It wasn't a huge travel center, but the station was a surprising size with a full-sized bathroom with stalls. I peed about two minutes straight, or at least half my weight in fluid, and got out of there as fast as I could. The employee behind the counter looked away from where she'd been focused outside and nodded at me. I nodded back.

And it was then that I noticed what she'd been looking at.

There was a huge class-A bus that had pulled into the offset section where I figured 18-wheelers in the area stopped at.

The door was open, and people were filing out of it, yawning and rubbing at their faces. It was too many people to not be a tour bus, I recognized.

Rhodes or Am had moved the car one pump over, and they were both hanging outside of it, Am staring at the pump and Rhodes leaning against the car, gaze on me.

I waved at him.

He shot me one of those low-key, devastating smiles that made me want to hug him.

And that was when it went to shit.

"Ora?" the unfamiliar voice called out.

Looking to my left, maybe ten feet away from the two men I loved and was in love with, were two other faces I recognized. Why wouldn't I though? I'd known them for ten years. I thought they'd been my friends. And based on the pale expressions that had taken over their features, they were just as surprised to see me too. I was so caught off guard I froze and blinked, making sure I wasn't imagining Simone and Arthur.

"It is you! Ora!" That was Simone who called out, tugging at Arthur's jacket.

Arthur didn't look all that excited.

I couldn't blame him. I was sure he knew he was on my permanent shit list. And even though I thought I was a pretty decent person, I felt my facial features drop into a blank expression.

And I guess I decided to ignore them because I managed another two steps that brought me closer to Rhodes and Am before Simone's hand wrapped around my inner arm just as she said, "Ora, please."

I didn't snatch my arm out, but I did glance at her fingers before meeting her dark brown eyes and saying, calmly, perfectly fucking calm, "Hi, Simone. Hi Arthur. Nice to know you're alive. Bye."

She didn't let go, and when I met her gaze, there was something in hers that looked desperate. I didn't even bother glancing at Arthur because I'd known him a year longer than Simone—*I'd been in his wedding party for his first marriage*—and I wasn't about to let them ruin what had been a wonderful Christmas.

"I know you're mad," Simone said quickly, keeping her hand on me. "I'm sorry, Ora. We're both sorry, aren't we, Art?"

His "yes" was so sad maybe I would've played a tiny violin if I'd been in a better mood. If this had been any other day. Just maybe if I had been by myself.

One glance up had me meeting Rhodes's frown. Amos I guess was watching too, wondering who the hell I was talking to at a random gas station in the middle of nowhere. I knew then in that moment, that I had to tell them about Kaden. That I couldn't just keep giving them, especially Rhodes, vague details about my life. I knew I'd gotten lucky so far that he hadn't poked at the huge holes in my life story considering how much we'd nudged at just about every other painful thing in our lives.

"Okay, I'm glad you feel bad. There's nothing for us to say to each other. Please let go of me, Simone," I said, giving her a long look.

She looked tired, and I wondered who she was on tour with now, who they were on tour with. Then I reminded myself it didn't matter.

"No, please, give me a second. I was just thinking about you earlier, and it's a miracle you're *here*. Someone said you'd moved to Colorado, but what were the chances?" she rattled off, and I just kept on staring at her, but noticed out of the corner of my eye that Rhodes started heading over.

I lifted my arm and snuck it out of her grip. "Yeah, a coincidence. Bye."

"Ora." Arthur's voice was quiet. "We are sorry."

I'm sure, I thought, almost bitterly, but I really genuinely didn't care much anymore. What I cared about was wasting my time talking to them when I could be around people who hadn't turned their backs on me. People that wouldn't just start ignoring my phone calls when their boss and I broke up, even though I'd technically been their boss too in a way. Because always, *always*, I had thought we were real friends. At some point over the years, I'd ended up spending more time with Kaden's band than I did with him because his mom started to complain about how flimsy my excuse of being his assistant was.

These people, Arthur and Simone included, had... they had taught me how to play their instruments. They had told me when things didn't work with my songwriting. We had gone to movies together, the theater, out to eat, birthday parties, bowling....

Even when we hadn't been on tour together, they had still texted.

Until they'd stopped completely.

"Kaden just told us you two broke up, and then Mrs. Jones sent out an email saying that if she caught any of us communicating with you, that would be the last day we worked for her," Arthur started to say before I gave him my own flat look.

"I believe you, but was that before or after I'd tried calling you with my new number and left voice mails and texts you never replied to? You knew I would never rat anyone out to her."

He closed his mouth, but apparently Simone decided it was a good idea to keep talking.

"We're sorry. We didn't find out until a few months ago what all happened, and Kaden's been a mess. He's asked all of us if we'd heard from you, and he canceled his tour, did you hear? That's why we're out here with Holland."

I raised my eyebrows. "I know that Mrs. Jones had told you all we were breaking up *before I knew*. Bruce told me." He was the roadie I had stayed with in Utah. "You could have warned me, but you didn't. Both of you know I'm not a snitch. If it would have been one of you, I would've said something. Like I told you, Simone, when Mrs. Jones was whispering about firing you when you gained weight, remember? Didn't I warn you?"

"But Kaden—" Simone started to say.

"I don't care anymore, and that's the truth. You don't need to feel bad either. At least I can say thank you for not giving them my number... even though you didn't say anything so you wouldn't risk getting fired if Mrs. Jones thought you were lying about actually talking to me, huh?" I snorted. "You know what? Good luck on tour," I said as calmly as possible before turning around and coming face to chest with Rhodes, who had snuck behind me.

Beside him was Am.

And they were both looking at me with guarded, huge eyes that instantly sent panic piercing through my chest. Not much, but enough. More than enough.

Shit.

I didn't want them to find out like this. Well, I hadn't wanted them to find out period, but I'd planned on eventually telling them anyway. Admitting the last piece of the Aurora's ex puzzle.

And now these two "friends" that I'd used to have, who

had stopped answering my calls and texts, had taken that away from me.

I opened my mouth to tell them I'd explain in the car, even as a dull ache of shame filled my chest, but Rhodes beat me to it.

"Your ex's name is Kaden?" he asked slowly, way too slowly. "Kaden... Jones?"

And before I could answer that, Amos's mouth pressed together so tight, his lips went white and his eyebrows dropped into a confused and either hurt or angry expression.

Fucking hell. This was my fault, and yes, I could blame Simone and Arthur, but at the end of the day, it *was* my fault for putting Rhodes and Am into this position. There was nothing to do but tell them the truth. "Yeah. That's him," I answered weakly, that same wave of shame flowing over me.

Just one of the biggest fucking country artists of the decade.

Thanks to me partly.

"Your ex is the country guy on the insurance commercials? The one with the song for Thursday Night Football?" Rhodes asked in that ultra-serious voice I hadn't heard in forever.

"You said...." Am started to say before shaking his head, his throat and cheeks turning pink.

I had no idea if he was mad or hurt, maybe it was both, and I suddenly felt terrible. Worse, honestly, than a year and a half ago when life as I'd known it had gotten pulled out from under me. Fisting my hands, I tried to get my thoughts together. "Yes, that's him. I didn't want to tell you who he was because—"

"You said you were married," Amos muttered. "I know he's not because Jackie used to talk about him all the time."

"We were, technically. Common-law marriage. I could've

taken him for half his things, I have the proof. I went to a lawyer. I had a case, but…."

It was Rhodes who opened his mouth and shook his head, the tendon along his neck rising out of nowhere. "You lied to us?"

"I didn't lie to you!" I whispered. "I just… didn't tell you. What was I supposed to say? 'Hey, strangers, guess what? I wasted fourteen years of my life with one of the most famous people in the country? I wrote all of his music and let him take credit for it because I was dumb and naïve? He dumped me because his mom didn't think I was good enough? Because he didn't love me enough?'" That familiar shame seemed to squeeze down on my chest.

Out of the corner of my eye, I saw Simone and Arthur begin inching away with an "I'm sorry" that I didn't care enough about to acknowledge.

"You wrote his music too?" Am genuinely whispered, using that same voice I hadn't heard since the first time we'd met and his dad had busted us and his plan. "And didn't tell me?"

"Yeah, Am, I did. That's why they paid me off. I told you both I got money from our split. I just never told either of you his name…. I was embarrassed."

The teenager set his jaw. "You don't think we deserved to know?"

I glanced at Rhodes and felt my heartbeat over my neck and face. "I was going to tell you at some point, but it just… I wanted you to like me for me. For who I am."

He shook his head slowly, eyebrows knitting together. "You didn't think it was important that you were married to some rich, famous guy? That you made us think you were some sad, divorced woman who had to start all over again?"

Anger and hurt suddenly punched me right in the chest. "I was sad, and I was technically divorced. He used to call me his wife in private. Around very close friends. He didn't legally marry me because it would ruin his image. Because single men sold more records than married ones. And I did have nothing. The money doesn't mean shit to me. Besides your Christmas presents and a little money here and there I've spent on things and other people, I haven't spent it on anything. And I did have to start all over again, like I told you. He came home, said it was over, and the next day, his lawyer sent me a notice to leave the house. Everything was under his name. I had to move in with Yuki for a month before I had the strength to go back to Florida," I explained, shaking my head. "All I left with were the same things I brought here."

Rhodes lifted his head toward the sky and shook it. He was pissed. Which, fine, okay, if he had dated... Yuki, I would want to know. But I hadn't lied. And I'd just been trying to protect what little pride I had left. Was that so wrong?

"You wrote that football song, didn't you?" Amos asked in that tiny voice that felt like a kick to my sternum.

My heart fell, but I nodded at him.

His nostrils flared, and his cheeks went even more pink. "You told me my songs were good."

What? "Because they are, Am!"

My teenage friend looked down, and his lips pressing together so hard they went white.

"I'm not lying," I insisted. "They are good. You knew about Yuki. I told you I'd written things that people had recorded. I tried to hint at it. But I just didn't want you to be nervous, that's why I—"

Without looking at me or his dad, Amos turned around, walked toward the car, and got into the passenger seat.

My heart crashed to my toes, and I forced myself to glance at Rhodes. "I'm sorry—" I started to say before he met my gaze, that stubborn chin a hard point on his face.

He blinked. "How much money did he give you?"

"Ten million."

He flinched.

"I told you I had money saved," I reminded him weakly.

One of those big hands came up, and he scrubbed at his head through the knit hat he'd put on. He didn't say a word.

"Rhodes...."

He didn't even look at me as he turned around and got into the car.

Fuck.

I swallowed hard. There was no one to blame but myself, and I damn well knew it. But if I could just explain. I just hadn't told them Kaden's name or been specific about how much songwriting I'd done... at least for who. I'd hinted. I'd never *lied*. Was it so wrong that I didn't want to admit I hadn't written anything new in forever? I didn't even worry about that anymore. I didn't think about it.

We were just going to need a little time. Once they stopped being mad, I could explain all over again. From the beginning. Everything.

It would be fine.

They loved me and I loved them.

But even having a plan didn't help when neither of them said a single word to me, or each other, the entire ride back to Pagosa.

CHAPTER 29

*C*lara was looking at me as I sighed and rubbed my eyes.

"What's wrong? You've looked sad today," she said as I reorganized the shoe display for the third time. It still didn't look right. It made more sense to have the taller winter boots at the top than at the bottom, but the whole thing still looked off.

"Nothing," I told her, hearing the weariness in my tone and reminding me I was a bad liar. I had slept awful last night, worse than the nights the bats had terrorized me. But instead of taking the day off like I'd originally requested, I had decided to come in and not leave her short-handed instead.

She had to have heard the BS too from the expression she made that was all concern. Part of me expected her to let it go, but she didn't. "You know you can tell me whatever's bothering you, right?" she asked, slowly and carefully, trying not to tread on my toes but obviously concerned enough to risk it.

And that's why I set the shoes down and looked at her and then sighed so deeply, I didn't know how I still had air left in my lungs afterward. "I fucked up, Clara."

She came around the counter, walking right past Jackie who was renting some tubes out to a family, and came over to squat beside me, her hand resting between my shoulder blades. "If you tell me, I can try to help. Or I can just listen."

Love and tenderness filled my entire soul, so much of it that it almost made up for the ache I'd been feeling since last night, and I found myself hugging her close for a second before pulling back and saying, "You're such a good person. I hope you know how much I appreciate everything you've done for me, but even more for your friendship."

It was her turn to hug me back. "It goes both ways, you know. You've been the best thing to happen to me in a long time, and we're all so glad you're here."

Wasn't that nearly word for word what Rhodes had said once?

When he was talking to me.

When he wasn't ignoring my text messages like he had that morning. All I'd wanted was to talk to him, to explain better. I still hadn't gotten a reply though.

I sniffled, then she sniffled, and I told her the truth. "I hadn't told Rhodes or Amos about Kaden, and they found out last night. I feel terrible, and they're so mad at me." What I didn't say was that they hadn't even tried to stop me when we'd gotten back, and I went into their house to grab my things and go back to the garage apartment.

Her eyes had widened with every word out of my mouth but somehow circled back so that she ended up grimacing but making a thoughtful expression at the same time. "But you didn't tell them about him because you're embarrassed about it." I wasn't positive even she knew about how I'd written his songs. Jackie did because she'd overheard comments Yuki had made, but Clara had never brought up anything about it. Had Jackie told her? Had she put it together? I had no clue.

So I nodded and told her as quickly as possible about it, stressing mostly on how I hadn't written anything new in nearly two years and how I hadn't brought it up because I wouldn't be able to help Am with his music in that way anymore.

She tilted her head to the side, and her expression wasn't sad, but it was close. "You know, I get why they'd be upset, but at the same time, I understand why you didn't want to tell them too. If I were in your shoes, I don't know that I would either. At the same time, I always thought it was pretty cool you knew him in the first place, that you were together."

I shrugged.

"But you told them about him in general, didn't you?"

"Yeah, just never the specifics." I blew out a breath and shook my head. "They wouldn't even look at me, Clara. I know I kind of deserve it, but it really hurt my feelings. They found out because we stopped at this gas station and two of Kaden's band members happened to stop at the same one and they tried to apologize for turning their back on me. It was so dumb, and I feel like crap. The only reason I waited so long to tell them was because I wanted them to like me for me. And they did. And now it backfired."

"I'm sure they are upset. He's... Kaden Jones, Aurora. I saw him on a commercial last night. I think my jaw dropped when he had that first big hit and I realized you were together."

I grunted, knowing exactly what song it was. *"What the Heart Wants."* I'd written it when I was sixteen and I'd missed my life in Colorado so much still.

Clara reached over and grabbed my hand. "They'll get

over it. Those two love you. I don't think they know how to function without you anymore. Give them some time." I must have made a face because she laughed. "Why don't you come over tonight? Stay with us? Dad was upset you didn't come over Christmas Eve even though it wasn't like anybody was able to go anywhere because of the snow."

"Are you sure?" I asked, not wanting to picture myself sitting in the garage apartment all by myself for hours. Not with this feeling in my soul.

"Yes, I'm sure."

I nodded at her. "Okay. I will. I'll go get my things and then come over. Do you want me to bring anything?"

"Just you," she answered. "Don't beat yourself up too much. Nobody who knows you would ever believe you'd do something malicious." Clara paused. "Unless they really asked for it."

That was the first time I smiled all day.

～

My heart kept on feeling pretty heavy, despite Clara's assurance I'd be forgiven.

I knew it was my fault. My pride had kicked the shit out of me, and that was the most frustrating part, that I couldn't blame anybody else.

And my heart kept on hurting even more as I turned into the driveway and saw the ruts in the snow from wide tires. Because I knew what it meant. Rhodes was home.

As in, he'd literally just gotten home too. Seconds before me.

I knew that because I found him getting out of his truck as I pulled into the area that he'd plowed around my car Christmas morning when he'd dug us all out of the snow since the forecast hadn't called for much more.

Reluctant hope kind of sprouted inside of me as I put my car into park and reached to grab my bag. But just as quickly as its little roots had sprouted, they shriveled up. He didn't look at me. Not once as he slammed his door closed and stubbornly kept his attention straight ahead, refusing to focus down... or on me. I waited in my car, watching, hoping and praying he'd turn around and just... glance over.

But that wasn't what happened.

I swallowed.

He didn't need to do anything he didn't want to.

He was mad at me, and I just had to live with it. Clara was right. He would eventually forgive me. I hoped. Amos, I wasn't so sure about but... we'd figure it out. I hoped too. I really did owe them time at least to accept it and hopefully see things from my perspective... even if this was just about exactly what I'd wanted to avoid.

Up the stairs I went.

I put some things into my duffel bag for tonight and tomorrow morning. I knew it was a little immature, but I hadn't put the jacket that Rhodes had bought me on that morning, instead using my thinner one, and I left it where it was on top of the mattress. And yeah, I hadn't worn the boots either, and I left them on the side of the bed too.

They could be mad, but I could have my feelings hurt too, right? I was tired of people just... not talking to me anymore. Just letting me leave. It sucked, plain and simple. Maybe I'd gotten over a lot of things over the last year and a half, but the betrayal of not just the Joneses but my "friends" too stung the hardest.

So yes, chances were I was being extra sensitive, but there wasn't much I could do about it. There were only so many emotions you could talk yourself out of, and this ache wasn't one of them.

Finally ready to leave, I clutched my keys as I circled

toward my car and tossed my bag in the back. I happened to look up toward the deck and found Amos standing there, watching me through the window. I lifted my hand and ducked into the car. I didn't wait for him to greet me back; I couldn't handle having him blatantly ignore me.

Then I left.

CHAPTER 30

J'd be a lying son of a bitch if I said that a couple of tears didn't sneak out of my eyes on the way to Clara's.

Wiping at my face when one of them brushed the side of my mouth, I listened to the navigation warn about an upcoming right turn and immediately get cut off when a call came through.

The screen showed "TOBER RHODES CALLING."

Was he calling to tell me bad news? To tell me to move out? Dread wrapped its fingers around my stomach, but I forced myself to hit the answer button. I'd already learned the hard way what happened when I tried to avoid bad things.

Might as well embrace them and get them over it.

"Hello?" Even I could hear the uneasiness in my soul.

"Where are you?" came the rough voice.

"Hi, Rhodes," I said quietly, more quietly than I thought I'd ever talked to him before. "I'm driving."

He didn't say hi back; what he did say was a curt, "I know you're driving. Where are you going?"

His Navy Voice was back, and I didn't know what that meant. "Why?"

"*Why?*"

I sucked in a breath through my nose. "Yeah. Why are you asking?" I had to just... face it. If he wanted to tell me to get my things and leave, even though I didn't think that was something he'd want to do, might as well find out now.

That made my stomach clench painfully.

He took a breath so loud and haggard, I was surprised it didn't blow me away even over Bluetooth. "Aurora...."

"Rhodes."

He muttered under his breath, then seemed like he pulled his phone away from his mouth to say something to who I could only imagine was Amos before coming back on the line and repeating the same question. "Where are you going?"

"To Clara's," I told him, still speaking quietly. Then I decided to take advantage of the call because why not? "I'm sorry for not telling you the truth, but I love you and Am and didn't want you to think I was a loser, and I hope you'll forgive me. I don't really want to cry while I'm driving, but we can talk some other time. Okay, bye."

Like the chickenshit I didn't know I was, I hung up. I wasn't sure if I expected him to call me back or not, but he didn't. And I realized when my heart started hurting again, that I kind of had hoped he would. I'd fucked up.

I was so stupid.

But I couldn't bear the thought of hearing him say something hurtful. Maybe it was for the best that we hadn't spoken until now. The more time he had to cool off, hopefully the less my chances were of getting my feelings hurt more.

That still didn't make me feel better though. Not really. I'd rather get into an argument than get ignored. I really would. I would have rather heard him tell me that I'd hurt *his* feelings and say he was disappointed that I'd kept the truth from him than getting brushed off.

Parking in Clara's driveway, I got out with an even heavier heart at the same time the front door opened, and she was there and waving me in.

"Come on," she invited, her smile gentle and welcoming.

"Are you sure everyone's fine with this?" I asked, going up the steps.

Her smile stayed the exact same. "*Yes.* Come in."

I hugged her and Jackie, who I noticed was standing behind her, peeking over her shoulder with an anxious look on her face. "Hi, Jackie."

"Hi, Ora."

I stopped and cursed. "I forgot my bag. Let me go grab it real quick."

"Dinner's ready. Come eat and then get it."

I nodded and followed them in, giving Mr. Nez a hug too. He was already at the kitchen table, gesturing toward the seat beside him. Clara was right, dinner was done—apparently they adhered to Taco Tuesday, and I was all about that. We ate, and Mr. Nez asked questions about the store, and then they told me how Christmas had gone the day before. They hadn't left the house, but one of Clara's brothers had come over, so they hadn't been alone.

I was just finishing off my second taco, which if it had been any other day, it more than likely would have been my fourth, when a knock on the front door had Jackie getting up and disappearing down the hallway.

"Did you hear that she and Amos are going to do the talent show at school?" Mr. Nez asked.

I set the last bit of my taco down on the plate. "Am told me. They're going to do great."

"She won't tell us what they're singing or anything."

I didn't want to ruin the surprise and lifted a shoulder. "I'm sworn to secrecy, but we should all get there early."

"I can't believe Amos would agree to it," Mr. Nez commented between bites. "He's always struck me as such a shy young man."

"He is, but he's tough, and my friend has been giving him advice." I hoped he forgave me.

"The one that Jackie hasn't stopped talking about? Lady... what's her name? Lady Yoko? Yuko?"

I laughed. "Yuki. Lady Yuki, and yeah, that's—"

A shout came from the front door. "Aurora! It's for you!"

For me?

Clara shrugged as I got up. Heading toward the front door, Jackie purposely avoided my eyes as she went around me, heading back into the kitchen.

I knew who it was. It wasn't like there was a long list of people who would come looking for me.

But there wasn't anyone on the deck when I got to the door. What there was were two people by my car. I'd gotten into the habit of never locking my car anymore unless I was at the store. The trunk was open, and I couldn't see their heads, but I could see the bodies.

"What are you doing?" I hollered, going down the steps, my stomach twisting with all the bad reasons why they'd be digging around in there. And possibly a little bit in surprise as well.

It was Rhodes that moved first, hands going straight to his hips as he looked at me. All broad shoulders and full chest. Big and imposing, looking like more of a superhero than a normal man. He was still in his work uniform. His winter work jacket was open, his beanie was pulled down on his head, and he was scowling. "Getting your things," he answered.

I stopped walking.

Amos moved around to stand beside his dad. He was in a baggy hoodie, and he crossed his arms over his chest in the exact same way the man beside him did. "You gotta come back."

"Come back?" I echoed like I'd never heard those words before.

"Home," they said at the same time.

That one word felt like a Superman punch to my very soul, and it must have been apparent to them too, because Rhodes's expression went into his harsh one, his ultra-serious face. "Home." He paused. "With us."

With them.

That wide chest that I'd found comfort in time and time again rose with a breath, his shoulders lowering at the same time, and he nodded—to himself, to me, I didn't know to who—watching me with those incredible gray eyes. "Where do you think you're going?"

What? "Going? I'm here...?"

It was like he didn't hear my answer because his scowl went nowhere and the lines on his forehead deepened as he said slowly, sounding resolute, "You're not leaving."

They thought I was *leaving*?

My poor brain couldn't understand because it repeated their words, because they didn't make sense. None of it—none of this, even them being here—made any sense.

"You had your bag," Amos tag-teamed into the conversation, glancing up at his dad for a second before focusing back on me. He seemed to be struggling with something because he took a deep breath and then said, "We... we thought you lied. We were just a little bit mad, Ora. We don't want you to go."

They really thought I was leaving them? Forever? I'd only grabbed my little duffel.

And it was then that I noticed what Rhodes had tucked under his arm. Something bright orange.

My jacket.

He had my jacket with him.

Suddenly my legs went weak, and the only thing my brain could process was that I needed to sit down, and I needed to sit down right then. That's what I did. I plopped down on the ground and just looked at them, the snow instantly wetting my butt.

Rhodes's eyes narrowed. "You can't run away when we get into an argument."

"Run aw*ay?*" I choked out in surprise, and honestly, more than likely astonishment.

"I should've talked to you last night, but...." Rhodes's jaw worked, and I could see his throat bobbing from where he stood, legs planted wide. "I'll work on that from now on. I'll talk to you even if I'm mad. But you don't get to leave. You don't get to walk away."

"I'm not leaving," I told them in a whisper, stunned.

"No, you're not," he agreed, and I swore my whole life shifted.

Then I remembered what the hell had gotten us to this point and focused. "I texted you and you didn't text me back," I accused.

His expression went funny. "I was mad. Next time, I'll text you back regardless."

Next time.

He'd just said *next time*.

They were here. For me.

I'd been gone an hour... and they were here. Pissed off and hurt. I felt my lower lip start trembling at the same time my nasal cavity started to tingle. And all I could do was look at them. My words were lost, buried beneath the tidal wave of love filling my heart in that moment.

Maybe it was my lack of words that had Rhodes taking a step forward, eyebrows still knitted together, his bossy voice the roughest I'd ever heard it. "Aurora—"

"I'm sorry, Ora," Amos stuttered, cutting his dad off. "I was mad that you've been helping me with my shitty songs—"

"Your songs aren't shitty," I managed to say weakly, mostly because all of my energy was shifted toward not crying.

He shot me a pained look. "You've written songs that are on TV! That asshole won awards for *your* music! I felt stupid. You said stuff, and I didn't take it seriously." He lifted his arms and let them drop. "I know you wouldn't do something on purpose to hurt anybody's feelings."

I nodded at him, trying to gather my words again, but my favorite quiet teenager kept on going.

"I'm sorry I got so mad," he said solemnly. "I just... you know... I'm sorry." He sighed. "We don't want you to leave. We want you to stay, don't we, Dad? With us?"

So this was what it was like to have your heart broken for good reasons.

It was only from the sincerity in his eyes and the love I had in my heart for him that I was able to say, "I know you're sorry, Amos, and thank you for apologizing." I swallowed. "But I'm sorry I didn't just tell you both. I didn't want you to feel weird around me. I wanted you to be my friend for me. I didn't want either of you to be disappointed. I can't write anymore," I admitted. "I haven't been able to in a really long time, and I don't know what's wrong with me, but I don't mind it, actually, and I guess I was scared that you'd find out and only want me around for that... and I can't. I can't do it anymore. I can only help now, for the most part. Nothing comes to me randomly on its own like before. It ran out after I helped Yuki.

"All I have left are a few notebooks, but Kaden took all the best stuff." I swallowed. "That's the only reason why he and his family kept me around for so long. Because I could help them, and I couldn't bear to go through that again." I shook my head. "All those songs… they were about my mom. You'd be surprised how easily you can turn just about anything into a love song. I wrote them when I missed her the most. When my heart felt like it couldn't keep beating much longer. The best things I ever wrote were while I was hurting, and decent stuff came while I was happy, but it's all gone now. All of it. I don't know if it's ever going to come back. Like I said, I'm fine with it, but I don't want anyone else to be let down. Especially not you two."

Their eyes were wide.

"And I wasn't leaving-leaving. I was only planning on spending the night. All my stuff is still over there, silly," I admitted, looking at Rhodes too, who was staring over like I'd magically disappear. "I thought I screwed up and you both weren't going to want me around anymore, or at least not for a while. I was sad, but I know it was my fault, that's all."

I pressed my lips together, feeling the tears pool in my eyes, and lifted a shoulder. "I keep losing the people I consider my family, and I don't want to lose you guys, too. I'm sorry."

Rhodes dropped his hands about halfway through me talking. Just as I was finishing, those big, booted feet led him over, and from one blink of an eye to another, he was crouching in front of me, his face right there, those intense eyes boring a hole straight into me. Two hands I didn't see coming were on my cheeks before I could react, keeping me there as he said in a voice rougher than I'd ever heard, "You're mine. Just as much as Am is. Just as much as anybody will ever be."

A tear slid down my cheek, and he wiped it off, his eyebrows dropping low.

"You are a part of us," he said gruffly. "I told you before, didn't I?" One of the hands on my cheeks moved, and he took my earlobe between his fingers. "I don't know how anybody would let you walk away, and it isn't going to be me. Not today. Not tomorrow. Not ever. Are we clear?"

I leaned forward and let my forehead drop to his shoulder, the weight of his words settling around me. The hand he had on my ear fell away and dropped to my back. He stroked it.

His breath tickled my ear as he whispered, "I'm not some rich guy, Buddy. I'm never going to be... I can't imagine what you were used to—no, don't start shaking your head, I know now that I had time to think about it, that that doesn't matter to you... but I've got a lot more I can give you than that moron ever did. I know it. You do too. No, don't cry. I can't stand it when you cry."

"You're using your bossy voice again," I said into his shirt as more tears slid out of my eyes, and I swore some went down my throat, and it was okay because those arms of Rhodes's closed around my body and pulled me into his chest. Into him.

His voice dropped. "I'm sorry I was jealous. I don't give a shit about your money or your notebooks or if you never write a single word down again." Rhodes's arms tightened around me, and I was pretty sure all of the muscles in his upper body did too as his voice got even more quiet. The soft puff of his breathing tickled my ear as he whispered, "We love you—*I* love you—because you're mine. Because being around you is like being around the sun. Because seeing you happy makes me happy, and seeing you sad makes me want to do anything I have to to get that look off your face.

"I want you to come home. I don't want you thinking

these things that aren't true at all, about us not wanting you around or wanting you to be with us for the wrong reasons. You matter, angel, and I want you here with us. You decided, remember? You don't get to change your mind anymore. I'm not your ex, and you don't get to leave. We go through things together, we don't give up on one another, and not over something like this. Isn't that right?"

I nodded against him, swallowing back my tears before sliding my arms around his neck. He kissed my forehead and cheek, the stubble on his chin rubbing my face in a way I loved.

"Are we back on the same page?"

I sniffled and nodded again.

"Did you finish dinner? Can you come home?" he asked, his palm moving up and down my spine.

Home. He kept saying it, and my soul gobbled it up. I pulled back a little and nodded up at him. "I can come. Let me just—"

I turned around to see Clara and Jackie at the door, looking at us. Clara held my purse out with a sweet smile on her face.

Rhodes helped me up, his hand touching my lower back briefly before I made my way toward the front door, where Jackie handed me my jacket and Clara gave me my purse and keys. Her eyes were shiny, and I felt so bad.

But she started to shake her head the second I opened my mouth. "I've had something special like this before. Go home. Trust me. We'll have a sleepover another day. That out there matters more. I'll see you tomorrow."

I hugged her tight, having a small figment of an idea of how she had to feel saying those words. Of losing someone you loved very, very much. But she was right.

I should go home.

Smiling at Jackie, I backed up and turned around to find

Rhodes standing in the same spot. I didn't imagine the faint, pained smile that took over his mouth as he looked at me.

The second I was close, his hand slid over my hair. Just as smoothly, it moved over my face, swiping under my eye as he frowned. "I don't like to see you cry." The pad of his thumb moved again, over my eyebrow before sliding back over my head once more and curving down my back. "I would ride with you, but Am—"

"Only has his permit, I know."

That finger of his swept over my eyebrow again. "I'll follow you home," he told me in a grave voice.

Home. There was that word again.

I shivered, and he held out my brand-new jacket and let me slide one arm and then the other through the sleeves before he zipped it up for me. I smiled at him when he finished. He leaned in and brushed his lips over mine. Pulling back, he met my eyes again and then did it again, pressing his lips just a little heavier against mine. Then he stepped away, his face about as open and unguarded as I'd ever seen it.

Amos was waiting next to my car when we got over, and I hesitated a second before taking my keys out of my pocket and holding them up. "Do you want to drive?"

"For real?"

"As long as you promise not to run through any stop signs."

His smile was small, but he took the keys, and we got inside. Neither one of us said much as he pulled out of the driveway and his dad pulled over to let us go around and go first. It wasn't until we were on the highway that he said, "Dad loves you."

I unclenched my fingers from around my purse and looked at him. Rhodes had said it so fast, I hadn't absorbed the fact he had said exactly that. "You think so?" I asked anyway.

"Know so."

I saw him let go of the wheel with one hand. "Two hands, Am."

He put it back. "He's not good with words. You know? His mom used to hit him and do other stuff, say mean stuff, and I've never even seen Grandpa Randall hug him. I know he loves me... he just... doesn't say it a lot. Like, ever. Not like my dad, Billy. But Dad Billy told me a long time ago that, even if he doesn't say it a lot, he shows it doing other stuff." Amos glanced at me. "So you know. It's like he's learning now. How to say it."

"I understand," I told him seriously.

Amos glanced at me again before staring forward, hard. "I want you to know, so you don't think he doesn't."

He was trying to console me, or prepare me, or even tie me to his dad even tighter. Maybe all three. And I couldn't say I didn't love it because I did.

"I get it," I said. "And I won't forget, I promise. I don't think I need to hear it all the time anyway. You can show people they matter better by what you do than by what you say, I think at least."

The teenager nodded but kept his attention forward. Things still felt just a little off, like we were both unsure, like this frustration was still so new, we wanted to get over it but neither one of us knew how to kick it off.

But it was him that brought it up. "I don't care you can't write anymore, you know." He was totally serious. "But... you'll still help me with my songs?"

Pressure built up in my chest. "I kind of have to," I told him. "We've done this much. I might as well stick around and see what you can do with more time."

His smile was faint, and he glanced at me again. "I was thinking about the talent show again, and I was thinking about doing another song instead."

I bit the inside of my cheek and smiled. "Okay, tell me more."

~

AMOS PARKED my car in front of the house, not by the garage apartment, I noted but kept my mouth shut. All I wanted was to savor this. Whatever this was. Being accepted into their home and lives even more so?

They wanted me back.

They wanted me close.

And for me, that was more than something. It was everything.

We got out, and I caught Rhodes's face as he waited by the hood of his truck, watching me closely. Part of me still couldn't believe they'd come to get me. No one had ever done that before. Not my ex when he'd hurt my feelings beyond belief and I'd gone to stay with Yuki, and not after I left the house when he'd officially broken things off. He'd never even texted to check up on me and make sure I was fine and not in a ditch somewhere.

Just as I started to get mad at myself for everything that had led up to my relationship with him and how long I'd let it go on, I remembered that if it hadn't been for him and what he'd done, I might have never come back here.

Because as much heartache and tears as I'd wasted in my previous life, the happiness I'd found here balanced it. And maybe with time, it would more than make up for it. Maybe one day it would overshadow that period completely.

I could only hope.

"You coming?" Amos asked as he rounded the hood of the SUV.

I nodded at him and smiled.

But still, he hesitated, a frown forming over his lean features. "I really am sorry, Ora," he told me again.

"I'm sorry too. I'm disappointed in myself for believing that the music thing would be a deal breaker. Give me a hug and we'll call it even."

He seemed to freeze for a second before rolling his eyes and coming over. Amos wrapped a loose arm around my back, which was pretty much the equivalent of the warmest hug from anyone else in the world, and patted my spine twice—letting me hug him back—before he pulled away. He gave me a tiny mouth twist that was also the equivalent of a great, beaming smile from anyone else before he shook his head, looked away, and went up the steps to the deck.

Rhodes was still in place, looking, waiting as his son disappeared in the house, closing the door behind him. Leaving us alone. "All right. Come here," Rhodes said in that low, quiet voice, lifting his hand.

I took it. I slipped my fingers over his calloused palm and watched as his long ones curled around my own, tugging me toward him. Those purple-gray eyes were steady. "Now tell me one more time. Why didn't you say anything about who your ex was before?" he asked so tenderly I would've told him anything.

I answered, aiming for tender too. "There are a few reasons. A) I don't like talking about him. Who wants to tell someone they like all about their ex? Nobody. B) I told you, it embarrassed me. I didn't want you to think there was something wrong with me and that's why we split up—"

"I know there's nothing wrong with you. Are you kidding me? He's an idiot."

I had to fight a grin. "And for so long people just pretended like they wanted to get to know me because they thought I worked for him. I mean, I didn't take you to be a fan of his, but I just got used to not talking about him,

Rhodes. It's a habit. There were very, very few people I could ever talk about him to. And I didn't want to bring him up. I was trying to move on."

"You did move on."

My heart jumped, and I agreed. "I *did* move on. You're right."

He took a step closer, his body right there. "I want to understand, Buddy, so I know his level of stupidity."

That made me grin.

"You broke up because he had to pretend you weren't together? And that's why you didn't have kids?"

"Right. Only band members, people on tour, and close friends and family knew. Everyone had to sign a nondisclosure agreement. We pretended like I was his assistant to explain why I was always around. At first it was fine, but eventually... it really sucked. They were so paranoid about kids, his mom used to count my birth control pills. I would hear her asking him about fucking condoms all the time. It was so hurtful now that I think about it. And I don't want to talk about him, Rhodes, because he's the past and not my future in any way anymore, but I'll tell you whatever you want to know." I wouldn't mind knowing everything about him some day.

"There's a lot of singers who get married and are still successful, aren't there?"

I nodded. "Yeah, there are. But I told you, he's a momma's boy and she insisted things would never be the same. He valued his relationship with his mom more than his relationship with me, and that was fine. Not really, but I tried to be fine with it. With being the lie. Being a secret. With living a life that made me feel way too often that I wasn't good enough, because maybe if I had been, it would have been fine for everyone to know. All I wanted was to be important to someone again, I guess. So I put up with it.

"Then at one point, she talked him into doing 'publicity' and being seen going out with this other country singer, and I told him if he did, he could go fuck himself. He said he had to, that he was doing it for us because there were rumors going around that he might not like women—like there's something wrong with that—because he didn't have a girl-friend and was never seen with anybody. And I left. I was gone a month. I stayed with Yuki. He did it. That's when I told you that we'd split up and he'd kissed someone else. And eventually, then he came looking and begged me to get back together.

"Things were never the same after that. About a year later, he and his mom decided they were going to try and 'do something else' with his music, so they hired some producer instead of going through me... and that was the official beginning of the end. I think about it now, and I guess they figured out I was writing less and less. I bet they, or at least his mom, were trying to phase me out. A year after that, it was over. He had left for some 'business meetings,'—which I later found out had really been him staying at his mom's—came home and said things weren't working anymore, reminded me that the house was under his name since his mom wouldn't let me be on the deed because 'someone might find out,' and he walked out. The next day, she discon-nected my cell. It's kind of messed up, but I think that both-ered me more than splitting up did."

Rhodes just blinked at me. One long, slow blink, and all he was able to say was "Wow."

I nodded at him.

"If he hasn't already, he's going to wake up one day and think, *that's the worst mistake of my life,*" he said in surprise.

"For a long time, I hoped and prayed that exact thing would happen, but I told you, I just don't care anymore." I squeezed his hand. "When his mom showed up, that's what I told her too. So you know, he has tried emailing me. Months ago. I never replied to him."

The surprised expression on his features disappeared, and his serious face was back on as he dipped his chin once. "Thank you for telling me."

"Also, so you know, I've talked about it with Yuki and my aunt, and we all agree he's only trying to get back in contact because the two albums he did without me did so bad."

Rhodes's eyes roamed my face, and he softly said, "That's not the only reason, sweetheart, believe me."

I shrugged. "But it's not like I can write anymore anyway. Or that even if I did, I would ever go back to that bullshit."

"You know that doesn't factor at all between us, yeah? You know I don't care even a little bit about that, don't you?"

I pressed my lips together and nodded.

His gaze caught mine and held it, the lines on his forehead there and fierce. "I almost feel bad for the idiot."

"You shouldn't."

Rhodes's mouth and words softened. "I said almost." His hand squeezed mine. "He really gave you all that money?"

"He had to or I would've gone after him in court, and then everything would've blown up in his face," I explained. "I'm not dumb. After his little fake relationship, I thought of what my mom would say, and she would've told me to take care of myself first. So I kept proof, pictures, and screenshots that would have been more than enough to screw him over in court. I figured I deserved it. I'd worked for it. It's mine."

I knew I didn't imagine the pleased and proud glint in his eyes. "Good."

"It won't bother you then?" I asked after a moment.

"What?"

"The money."

He looked right into my eyes as he said, "Is it going to

bother me that you're rich? No. I always wondered what it would be like to have a sugar mama."

I grinned and knew I had one more thing to say to him before I hoped we never talked about Kaden again. "This is the happiest I've been since I was a kid, Tobers. I want you to know that. This is where I want to be, okay?"

He nodded solemnly.

"I love you, and I love Am. I just... want to be here. With you two."

Rhodes's hand went to my face, his thumb under my jaw. "And that's where you're going to be," he said. "Never in a million years did I ever think somebody—somebody other than Am—could make me feel the way you do. Like I'd do anything, *anything*, for them. I can't even look at you when I'm mad because I can't stay that way." He lowered his face, so his lips hovered inches from mine. "I've only had a few things in my life that were really mine, and I'm not the type of man to give things away or throw them away. And I mean it, Aurora, and it's got nothing to do with your notebooks or your face or anything other than that heart you've got in your chest. Are we clear?"

We were clear. We were clear all right, I told him, hugging him close.

We'd never been clearer.

CHAPTER 31

"Whoa, man! That was awesome!" I clapped and whooped where I was sitting in my favorite camp chair about a week or two later.

A *wonderful* week or two later. Who was keeping track?

Am flushed like he always did, holding the last note on his guitar, but the second he lowered it, he huffed. Things between us were back to normal, fortunately. The awkwardness had only lasted about two days before the elephant in the room decided to walk away on its own. "I thought I was off-key at the beginning."

Crossing one leg over the other, I tilted my head. "You were a tiny bit flat, but I mean a *tiny* bit. And it was only once when you went into the chorus. I figured it was only because you were nervous. I can really tell you've been working on your vibrato by the way."

Setting his guitar in its stand, he nodded, but I could tell he was pleased. "I was, but I did what Yuki said."

She had happened to video call me the other day while I'd been with Amos in the grocery store parking lot, and she'd asked him how the nerves were going. *"Fine,"* he'd responded sheepishly. Knowing he wasn't being completely honest, she had given him some suggestions. I wasn't going to tell him that hours later, she'd messaged me asking for a video of his upcoming performance so she could watch too.

"And I told myself it was only you," he went on. "You'd tell me if I did something wrong."

My little heart ached, and I nodded at him. We had come such a long way, and his trust meant so much to me. "Always."

"Do you think I should move around more?"

"You've got such a beautiful voice; I think you should focus on the singing part for now. You're going to be nervous, so why put more pressure on yourself? There's only one Lady Yuki anyway."

He slid me a side look and asked, way too nonchalantly, "Did you help her write that 'Remember Me' song?"

I knew exactly what song he was referring to, obviously, and I grinned. "It's a pretty good song, isn't it?"

His squawk didn't even insult me. *"You did?"*

I didn't get a chance to answer because we both turned toward the driveway at the sound of tires on gravel, and part of me expected to see a UPS truck because I'd ordered some mats for my car. The ones that came with it weren't meant for snow and slush. But when the pickup pulled up into its usual spot, I frowned. Rhodes had just texted me a couple hours ago saying he'd be home around six. It was only four.

"What's Dad doing here?" even Amos asked.

"I don't know," I answered as the man in question parked and got out, that long, muscular body moving so well in its uniform it almost put me in a trance. The memory of him coming over to my apartment last night filled my head. I'd asked him what excuse he'd given Am, and he'd laughed and said I was going to show him my old photo albums. Apparently, from the disgusted expression on the teenager's face, he didn't believe him, but that was exactly what had happened.

At least until we'd ended up taking each other's clothes off and I'd wound up on his lap, sweaty and shaking.

It had been a good night.

Most nights since the day they'd gone to find me at Clara's had been very nice nights. On that first one specifically, Rhodes had asked me more questions about Kaden once Amos had gone to bed.

How we'd met—through a mutual friend my first semester of college. I'd been studying to get a degree in education while he'd been in school for music performance. Rhodes said he could see me being a teacher, and maybe I could have been, but my heart wasn't into the idea at all anymore.

What the stipulations were for the money I'd gotten—that I wouldn't go after them in court for royalties or songwriting credit, because God forbid there be something in writing about divorce settlements.

There were so many things for us to talk about, and I didn't want us to waste our time on that topic. But I would if there was something bugging him. I just hoped there wasn't.

The past was in the past, and I hoped more than anything that my future was walking toward me right then.

"Hi!" I yelled at Rhodes from where I was still sitting. It was forty-eight degrees out, but not windy, so we had the garage door open. My aunt thought I was nuts when I told her I'd been wearing a T-shirt the last few days, but no one understood just how nice it could be, even with snow on the ground. That was low humidity life for you.

"Hi," he greeted me right back.

Did he sound weird, or was I imagining it? What I knew I wasn't imagining was his stiff gait as he made his way over, hands clenching open and close at his sides. His head was just a little too down.

I glanced at Amos and saw that he was frowning as he took in his dad too.

"You okay?" I asked the moment he stepped inside the garage.

"In a way, yes," he said in what was definitely a weird and tight voice that alarmed me even more.

I stood up. "What's wrong?"

He raised his head then. The fine lines branching from the corners of his eyes were deeper than normal as he said, "Aurora... I need to talk to you."

Someone meant business busting out my first name like that. "You're scaring me, but okay," I said slowly, glancing at Am. He was looking at both of us warily.

Those gray eyes were on me as he took my hands, very, very gently. "Let's go inside."

I nodded and let him lead me across the yard and up the stairs to the deck. It wasn't until we were going in that I realized Am was following behind. Rhodes must have just then noticed it too because he stopped.

"What? You're scaring me too," the teenager said.

"Am, this is private," he said seriously, that terribly sober expression still on his face.

"Ora, you don't care, right?"

What was I going to do? Say no? Tell him that I didn't trust him? "It's okay." I swallowed before eyeing the man who had talked me into going back to his room to sleep in his bed last night. "You're not going to break my heart or anything, right?"

Rhodes tilted his head to the side, and his throat bobbed, scaring me even more. His eyes though were totally stricken. "For what it matters, I don't want to."

I balked.

His shoulders fell. "It's not the way you think," he went on gravely.

I felt sick, and he sighed.

Rhodes scrubbed at the back of his neck. "I'm sorry, angel. I'm screwing this up already."

"Just tell me. What's wrong? What happened?" I asked. "I'm not kidding, you're scaring me. Both of us."

"Yeah, Dad, tell her." The kid made a sound. "You're being weird."

Rhodes shook his head and sighed. "Shut the door, Am."

The kid shoved it closed and crossed his arms over his chest. My hands were starting to shake just a little as fear rose up inside of me as I tried to think of what he could possibly be this freaked out about. I'd seen him go face-to-face with a bat. He'd been up like twenty feet in the air with no problem. Was he sick? Did something happen to someone?

Rhodes blew out a breath and looked at the floor for a second before lifting his head and saying, "Do you remember me telling you a while back about those remains a hiker had found?"

I suddenly went cold inside. "No."

"The day you picked up that eagle, I told you," he reminded me gently. "There were some articles in the paper after that. People were talking about it in town."

That didn't sound familiar at all.

Then again, any time that conversations about missing people came up, I usually tuned them out. Any hope I'd had of having closure, of having *answers*, had died a long time ago. Maybe it was selfish, but it was easier for me to keep going, to not get weighed down by those cement blocks of grief, by not focusing too much on cases too similar to what had happened to my mom. For so long, I'd barely been able to handle my own pain, let alone taking on anyone else's.

Some people came out of trauma with thick scar tissue. They could handle anything. They had been through the worst and could take any kind of hit because they knew they could survive.

On the other hand, there were people like me, who survived but with thinner skin than before. Some of us ended up wrapped in an organ even more delicate than tissue paper, with bodies and spirits buoyed only by our will to keep going. And coping mechanisms. And therapy.

"This hiker was out and came across some bones. He happened to be a trauma surgeon and thought he recognized... some of them as human. He called it in, and the authorities took what he found."

"Okay...."

Rhodes licked his lips and squeezed my hands a little tighter. "They matched the DNA."

A memory of that time about three years after my mom had gone missing, when remains had been found and they'd thought it might be her, filled my head. We'd been so disappointed when, after I'd provided DNA samples, it had come back that it wasn't a match. A few years ago, the same thing had happened. A search party trying to find a missing hiker had come across a hand and a skull partially buried, but nothing had come of it either. The remains had been of a man who had gone missing two years before that. That had been the last time I'd had any hope of ever finding her.

But I knew. I knew before he said anything what was about to come out of his mouth next. My skin started prickling.

"The coroner's office is going to be calling you soon, but I hoped you'd rather hear it from me first," he said carefully, calmly, still holding my hands. I'd been so distracted I hadn't noticed.

I pressed my lips together and nodded, my lips suddenly

feeling numb. My chest started to tingle. "Yeah, I would," I told him slowly, knowing… knowing….

He blew out a breath, that square jaw moved from side to side before he gently said the last words I would have expected and, at the same time, the only thing I could have imagined, "They're your mom's, sweetheart."

He'd said it. He'd really said it.

I repeated his words in my head, then again, and again.

I bit my bottom lip and found myself nodding, fast and for too long. I was blinking quickly too as my eyes started to get watery. And I almost didn't hear the tiny choking whimper that bubbled out of my throat unexpectedly.

My mom's.

My mom's.

Rhodes's face fell, and the next thing I knew, his arms were around me and he was pulling me in tight, pressing my cheek against the buttons of his shirt as another choke worked its way into my throat. I tried to suck in a breath, but my whole body shook instead. I was trembling. Worse than the day of the Hike from Hell.

They'd found her.

They'd finally found her.

My mom who had loved me with her whole heart, who hadn't been perfect but had always made it known that being perfect was overrated. The woman who had taught me that joy came in all different shapes and sizes and forms. The same person who had battled a silent illness as best as she could for longer than I would ever know.

They'd found her. After all these years. After everything….

The memory of the moment twenty years ago, when I'd realized she wasn't picking me up, kicked me right in the very center of my existence. I had cried. Screamed. I'd howled my throat and my soul raw. *Mom, Mom, Mom, please, please, please, come back—*

"You can put her to rest now," he whispered right before a big, wailing cry got muffled against his shirt. "I know, sweetheart, I know."

I cried. From the deepest place in my body, I pulled the tears. Over everything I'd lost, over everything she had lost too, but also, maybe in a way, in relief that she'd didn't have to be alone anymore. And maybe because I didn't have to be alone anymore either.

~

HOURS LATER, I woke up on the couch in the living room. My eyes felt puffy and crusty, and they hurt as I squinted. My head was in Rhodes's lap. He was slouched against the couch, head resting against the back of it. One of his hands was on my ribs, and the other was on the back of my head.

My throat hurt too, I realized as I sniffled. The television was still on, softly, some infomercial playing. But I focused on the recliner, on the boy passed out on it. The same one who hadn't left my side since Rhodes had broken the news. Since the coroner's office had called and the woman's words had gone in one ear and out the other because my brain had been ringing.

And that made me sniffle again.

I had always felt like I'd lost so much. I knew nobody got through life without losing something, sometimes everything. But the knowledge brought me no comfort then.

Because she was still gone.

I was never, ever going to see her again.

But at least I knew, I tried to reason with myself for not the first time. At least I knew now. Not all of it, but more than I ever would have expected. A huge part of me still couldn't believe it though.

It felt so final now, her loss.

Nearly as fresh and painful as it had been twenty years ago. My body and soul felt cracked open, with all the vulnerable soft bits out for exposure. It was like I'd lost her all over again.

I tucked my cheek against my Rhodes's leg and grabbed his thigh. And I cried a little more.

~

I WOULD HAVE WANTED to believe that I took the news as well as could be expected in the days afterward, but the truth was that I didn't.

Maybe it was because it had been years since I'd last let myself feel a shred of hope of finding her. Maybe because I'd been so damn happy lately. Or maybe, just maybe, because I'd felt like everything that had led me here had been for this. For these people in my life. For this hope of a family and happiness, and while I'd give anything to have my mom back, I'd been at something close to peace finally.

But I hadn't been prepared for how hard I handled the days that came.

In those first few days after Rhodes's confirmation, I cried more than I had since she had initially gone missing. If someone had asked me to tell them what happened, I would have only been able to recall pieces because everything became so foggy and felt so desperate.

What I knew for sure was that after that first morning, waking up again in Rhodes's living room with exhausted, swollen eyes, I'd sat up and gone to the half-bathroom to wash my face. When I'd come back out, feeling stiff and almost delirious, Rhodes had been standing in the kitchen yawning, but the second he'd spotted me, his arms had dropped to his sides and he'd given me a flat, level look and asked, "What do you need from me?"

That itself had been enough to set me off again. To force me to suck in a shuddering breath through my nose a moment before even more tears welled up in my eyes. My knee had started shaking, and I'd bared my teeth at him and said, in a ragged, tiny whisper, "I could use another hug."

And that was exactly what he'd given me. Wrapping me up in those big, strong arms, holding me against his chest, supporting me with his body and with something else that I was too heartbroken and numb to sense. I spent that day at his house, showering in his bathroom and putting on his clothes. I cried in his bedroom, sitting on the edge of his bed, in his shower while the water beat down on me, in his kitchen, on the couch, and when he tugged me outside, on the steps of his deck while that long, solid body sat beside me for who knows how long, lined up completely against my side.

Rhodes didn't let me out of his sight, and Amos brought me glasses of water randomly, both of them watching me with calm, patient eyes. Even though I didn't feel like eating, they pushed small things at me, nudging me with their gray irises.

I knew for a fact I managed to call my uncle to give him the news, even though he hadn't been all that close to my mom. My aunt had called almost immediately afterward, and I'd cried some more with her, remembering when it happened, that it was possible to run out of tears. I spent the night at Rhodes's house, sleeping on the couch with him as my pillow, but that's all I was able to process other than the finality of the news I'd been given.

But it was the day after that, that Clara came over, sat beside me on the couch, and told me all about how much she missed her husband. How hard it was to keep going without him. I barely talked, but I listened to every word she said, soaking up the tears that spiked her eyelashes, soaking in her mutual grief at the loss of someone she had adored. She told me to take as much time as I needed, and I barely said a word. I hoped the hug we shared had been enough.

It wasn't until that night, when I was sitting on the deck after texting Yuki back and forth while Rhodes showered, that Amos came out and squatted on the step beside me. I didn't feel like talking, and in a way, it was nice that Rhodes and Amos weren't big talkers in the first place, so they didn't push me, didn't force me to do anything I didn't want to do other than eat and drink.

Everything was hard enough as it was.

My chest hurt so bad.

But I glanced at Am and tried to muster up a smile, telling myself like I had a thousand times over the last couple of days that it wasn't like I hadn't known she was gone. That I had gotten through this before and I would get through it again. But it just hurt, and my therapist had said that there was no right way to grieve.

I still just couldn't believe it.

My favorite teenager didn't bother trying to say anything though as he sat beside me. He just leaned over, put his arm over my shoulders, and gave me a side hug that seemed to last ages, still not saying a word. Just giving me his love and support, which made me want to tear up even more.

Eventually, after a few minutes, he got up and headed over to the garage apartment, leaving me there by myself, in my tangerine jacket on the deck, under a moon that had been around before my mom and would be there long after me.

And in a way, it made me feel better. Just a little as I gazed up. As I took in the same stars that she had to have seen too. I remembered being a kid and lying out on a blanket with her while she'd pointed out constellations that years later I'd learned were all wrong. And remembering that made me smile to myself just a little.

None of us were promised tomorrow, or even ten minutes from now, and I was pretty sure she'd known that better than anyone.

My head hurt. My soul hurt. And I wished for about the millionth time in my life, at least, that she was here.

I hoped she was proud of me.

It was then as I was sitting there with my head tipped back, that I heard the chords to a song I knew well.

Then Amos's voice started carrying lyrics that I knew even better.

The cold air filled my body just as well as the words to the song did, with tears I didn't know I was still capable of wetting my eyelashes as I listened. I took in the message I had a feeling he was trying to share with me, absorbing it into my very essence. A memory I myself had shared with all the people who had ever downloaded Yuki's version of it.

A tribute to my mom, like every song and most of my actions had always tried to be.

Amos pleaded to not be forgotten. To be remembered for what he'd been, not for the pieces he'd become. And his beautiful voice belted out for the one he loved to be whole, and one day they'd be together again.

ALMOST A WEEK AFTER THE NEWS, when I was in my garage apartment going through my mom's oldest journals, even though I had them memorized at this point, someone knocked on my door. Before I could say a word though, it opened and familiar heavy footsteps made their way up, and then Rhodes was there. His face even, hands on his hips. He looked somber and wonderful as he stood there, as steady as a mountain, and said, "We're going snowshoeing, angel."

I looked at him like he was fucking nuts because I was still in my pajamas and the last thing I wanted to do was leave the house, even though I knew that I should, that it would be good for me, that my mom would have loved—

My throat burned. I shrugged at him and said, "I don't know if I'd be good company today. I'm sorry…."

It was the truth. I hadn't exactly been good company lately. All the words that usually found their way so easily into my mouth had mostly evaporated over the last few days, and though our silences hadn't been awkward, they'd been foreign.

It had been so long since I'd felt the way I had lately, that even though I knew I would get through it and was fully aware it wasn't some overnight thing I'd randomly wake up from feeling fine, it was still like treading water against a changing tide.

I couldn't find my way out of it.

It was grief, and some part of me recognized and remembered that there were stages of it. The one no one ever told you about was the final one when you felt everything at once. It was the hardest.

And I didn't want to put that on Rhodes. I didn't want to put it on anyone. They all knew me as being cheerful and happy for the most part. I knew I'd be happy again just as soon as the worst edge of this faded—because it would, I knew it and I'd been reminded of it—but I wasn't there yet. Not with my mom's loss feeling so fresh again.

I was exhausted on the inside, and that was probably the best way to describe it.

But this man who had slept beside me every night the last week, either on his couch when we'd pass out in silence, or who would coax me into his room, tilted his head to the side as he took me in. "That's all right. You don't need to talk if you don't want to."

I blinked. I swallowed hard before I snorted, which even that sounded sad. Wasn't that exactly what I'd told him months ago? When he'd been upset with his dad?

Rhodes must have known exactly what I was thinking because he gave me a gentle smile. "You could use the fresh air."

I could. Even my old therapist, whose number I'd found a couple days ago and had only hesitated for about an hour before calling—she remembered me, which wasn't surprising considering I'd gone to her for four years—had told me it would be good for me to get out. But I still hesitated before glancing back down at the journal in my hands. Rhodes had been beyond great, but I'd been feeling all kinds of ways. He'd been there enough for me lately; I didn't want to push it either.

Rhodes tilted his head to the other side, watching me closely. "Come on, Buddy. If it was me, you would tell me the same," he said.

He was right.

And that alone was enough to get me to nod and get dressed.

Before everything that had happened, I'd told him I wanted to try snowshoeing someday. And part of that pierced through my mood, reminding me of how lucky I was to have him. Of how lucky I was for a lot of things.

I had to keep trying.

Rhodes didn't leave; he sat on the bed while I changed my pants right there in front of him, too lazy to even bother going into the bathroom. He didn't say a word as he nodded at me to ask if I was ready, and I nodded at him back that I was, and we left. True to his word, he didn't talk or try to get me to either.

Rhodes drove toward town, turning left down a county road and parking in a clearing that I was familiar with because I'd driven by it before when I'd gone for hikes. Out of the back of his Bronco, he pulled out two sets of snow-shoes and helped me put them on.

Then and only then did he grab my hand and start leading us forward.

We moved quietly, and at some point, he handed me a pair of sunglasses he must have had in the pocket of his jacket because the only things he'd brought in his backpack were bottles of water and a tarp. I hadn't even noticed I was squinting with the sun reflecting off the snow, but the sunglasses helped. The air was so crisp it felt cleaner than ever, and I filled my lungs with as much of it as I could every chance I had, letting it soothe me in its own way. On we went, and maybe if I'd been feeling any better, I would have appreciated more how well the snowshoes worked or how pretty the field we were going through was... but I was trying my best. And that was all I could do. I was here, and some part of my brain was aware that that mattered.

About an hour later, we finally stopped at the top of a hill, and he stretched out the tarp on top of the snow and gestured me onto it. I had barely sat down when he took the spot beside me and said in that husky voice of his, "You know I wasn't around for any of Amos's firsts."

I crisscrossed my legs under me and looked at Rhodes. He was sitting with his long legs stretched out before him, hands planted a few inches behind him, but most importantly, he was looking at me. The sunlight was reflecting off his beau-tiful silver hair, and I couldn't think of a single man I'd ever seen that was more handsome than him.

He was the best, really, and that made my throat hurt in a way that wasn't bad.

"I wasn't there for his first word or the first time he

walked. The first day he used the toilet on his own or the first night he didn't have to wear diapers to sleep."

Because he'd been gone, living on a coast far away from Colorado.

"Am doesn't remember, and even if he did, I'm not sure if he'd care, but it used to bother me a lot. It still does bother me when I think about it." The lines across his forehead deepened. "I used to send money to them—to Billy and Sofie. For things he might need, even though they both said they had it, but he was mine too. I used to come and visit him every chance I had. Every vacation, any time I could swing it, even if it was only for a whole day. They told me I did enough, said I didn't have to worry about it, and maybe that should've been good enough for me, but it wasn't.

"It took him until he was almost four to start calling me Dad. Sofie and Billy corrected him every time he'd call me Rows—he couldn't pronounce Rhodes, and that's what they called me—but it took a long time for him to start calling me something else. It used to make me jealous when I'd hear him call Billy Dad. I knew it was stupid. Billy was with him all the time. But it still kind of hurt. I'd send him presents when I saw something he might like. But I still missed birthdays. I still missed his first day of school. I missed everything.

"When he was nine, he complained about them going to visit me during the summer instead of going to 'do something fun'. That hurt my feelings too, but it mostly made me feel guilty. Guilty that I wasn't around enough. Guilty that I wasn't trying hard enough. I had wanted him. I thought about him all the time. But I didn't want to leave the Navy. I didn't want to move back here. I liked having something reliable in my life, and for the longest, that was my career. And that made me feel guiltier. I didn't want to give up one or the other, even if I knew what was more important, what really matters, and that's my son, and it's always going to be him. I thought me knowing that was enough."

Rhodes blew out a breath before glancing at me, part of his mouth going up a little into that twist I knew too well. "Part of me hopes that I'm making it up to him. That it'll be enough that I'm here now, but I don't know if it will. I don't know if he'll look back on it and think that I half-assed being his dad. That he wasn't important to me. That's why I'm trying, so at least I know that I did. That I did everything I could think of to be there for him, but how am I ever going to know, right? Maybe he'll be an old man when he decides. Maybe not.

"My mom didn't even try to be a good mom. I can't think of a single positive memory of her. My oldest brother does, I think, maybe the one right after him too, but that's it. I'm never going to look back and think of her fondly. I don't feel like I missed out on anything with her, and that's shitty. I feel bad for her, for what she had to have gone through, but I didn't ask for it either, and I got it anyway. But Amos, I asked for. I wanted him. I wanted to do better than what I'd known."

I reached behind him and took his palm in mine, and when that didn't seem like enough, I cupped the back of it with my other hand too, cocooning it completely with my own.

He squeezed it, his gray eyes roaming over my face. "Maybe that's the thing about being a parent: you can just hope what you've done is enough. If you care. You hope that the love you gave them, if you really tried, will stay with your child when they're older. That they can look back on what you did and be content. You hope that they know happiness. But there's no way of knowing, is there?"

This man... I didn't know what I would have done without him.

Pressing my lips together, I nodded, tears filling my eyes. Slowly, I lowered my head, until his fist rested against my cheek, and I told him in a croak, "He loves you, Rhodes. He told me not too long ago that he wanted you to be happy. I could tell from the moment I met you both, that you loved him more than anything. I'm sure that's why Billy and Sofie didn't hound you about stuff or tell you that you needed to worry. If you hadn't been doing enough… if you hadn't been there for him enough… I'm sure they would have said something." I tried to suck in a breath, but it came in choppy. "Good parents don't have to be perfect. Just like you love your kid even when they're not."

The choke that gripped my throat was sudden and harsh, the slide of several more tears wetting my cheeks. I hiccupped; then I hiccupped again. And something—his hand, it had to be his hand—stroked the back of my head, his fingers combing through my loose hair; I hadn't brushed it since I'd showered. His words were soft as he said, "I know. I know you miss her. Just like you could tell I love Am, I can tell you loved your mom."

"I really did. I really do," I agreed, sniffling, feeling my chest crack with love and grief. "It finally just feels… final, and it makes me sad, but it makes me mad too."

He stroked through my hair then my cheeks, over and over, my tears eventually spilling through his fingers, over the backs of his hands as he touched my face. Opening a dam with so many of the words I'd shared with my therapist over the last few days. But it was different with him.

"I'm so fucking angry, Rhodes. At everything. At the world, at God, at myself, and sometimes even at her. Why did she have to go on that stupid fucking hike in the first place? Why couldn't she have done the trail she'd planned on taking? Why hadn't she just waited for me to go with her? You know? I hate being mad, and I hate being sad, but I can't help it. I don't get it. I feel so confused," I told him in a rush, taking one of his hands and squeezing it tight.

"At the same time, I'm so glad she was found, but I miss her, and I feel so guilty again. Guilty about stuff that I've worked out, things that I know I shouldn't feel bad about. That none of what happened was my fault, but... it hurts. Still. And it's always going to hurt. I know that. It's supposed to. Because you don't love someone and lose them and keep on going the rest of your life complete.

"I wonder too... did she know? Did she know I loved her? Does she know how much I miss her? How much I still wish she was around? Does she know that I turned out okay for the most part? That I had people who loved me and took care of me, or did she worry about what was going to happen? I hope she knows everything ended up okay, because I can't bear to think that she worried." My voice cracked over and over again, most of my words rambling and probably unintelligible, my tears soaking into the skin of the hand that was still touching my cheeks.

Rhodes tilted my face up and met me with those incredible gray eyes. When I tried to dip my chin, he kept me there. Everything about him so focused, so intent, like he was leaving me no room to misinterpret him. "I don't know about some of that, but if you were anything like the way you are now when you were younger, she had to know how you felt about her. I'm sure it had to have lit up her life to be loved by you," he whispered carefully, his voice hoarse.

I swallowed hard for a moment before I sagged, before I leaned over and rested the side of my face against his shoulder. And Rhodes... wonderful, wonderful Rhodes, slipped his arms under me and pulled me onto his lap, effortless, so effortless, one arm banding itself low on my back while the other curled around my side. And I settled in, right there, on top of him.

"It's okay to be sad. It's okay to be mad too."

I pressed my nose against his throat. His skin was soft. "My ex used to get so frustrated with me when I'd have bad days. When I was extra sad. He'd say I'd suffered enough and that my mom wouldn't want me to be so sad anymore, and that would make it worse. Usually I'm okay, but sometimes, I'm just not, and it's random things that set me off. I want to live, I want to be happy, but I miss her and I want her back."

One of his big hands cupped my hip, and I could feel the steady beat of his heart against my nose. "I thought we'd decided your ex was a moron," Rhodes murmured. "I hope someday that if I'm gone, someone loves me enough to miss me for the rest of their life."

He killed me. He really, absolutely did. I snorted a little into his throat, sagging even more into the warm wall of his frame.

"My dog, Pancake, died a few years ago, and I still get choked up when I think of him. I tell myself I can't get another dog because I'm not home enough, but between us, considering it in the first place makes me feel like I'm being disloyal to him." I'd swear he brushed his lips across my forehead as he held me even closer. "You don't ever have to hide it—your grief. Not from me."

Something painful and wonderful pricked my heart. "You don't either. I'm sorry about your Pancake. He was the one in the picture I gave you, right? I'm sure he was amazing. Maybe, if you ever want, you can show me some more pictures of him. I'd like to see them."

Rhodes's voice got tight. "He was, and I will," he promised.

I pushed my face even closer to his throat, and it took me minutes before I could get more words together. "My mom would want me to be happy, I know that. She'd tell me that it wasn't like I didn't already know she didn't want to leave me.

She would tell me not to spend more of my time being upset and live my life instead. *I know it.* I know in my heart that whatever happened was an accident and there's nothing I can do to change it. And I really am happy with where I am now. It's just hard...."

"Hey," he said. "Some days you pick up eagles like they're chickens, and some days you run screaming away from innocent bats. I like you both ways, angel. All ways."

A choke that was a mixture of pain and laughter exploded out of me, and I'd swear his arms got even tighter.

I couldn't help but hug him tight right back. "I just... I really just wish... I hope she knows how much I love her. How much I wish she was here. But also, that if all these shitty things were supposed to happen... I'm glad they brought me here." My fingers curled around his forearm. "I'm glad you're here, Rhodes. I'm so glad you're in my life. Thank you for being so good to me."

His hand stroked my hair, and his pulse beat under my cheek, and I could barely hear him as he said, "Any time you need me, I'm here. Right here."

I clung to him and lowered my voice, "Don't tell Yuki, but you're my best best friend now."

His throat bobbed against me, and I didn't imagine how hoarse his voice came out as he said, "You're my best best friend too, sweetheart." His next swallow was just as harsh, his voice even more rough, but his words were the softest, most genuine thing I'd ever heard. "I really missed hearing you talk, you know that?"

And it was then, with my face against his throat, his body warm beneath and around mine that I told him about some of my fondest memories of my mom. Of how beautiful she was. Of how funny she could be. Of how she hadn't been scared of anything, or at least it had seemed that way to me.

I talked and I talked and I talked, and he listened and listened and listened.

And I cried a little more, but it was okay.

Because he had to be right. Grief was the final way we had to tell our loved ones that they'd impacted our lives. That we missed them so, so much. And there was nothing wrong with me mourning my mom for the rest of mine, even as I carried her love and her life in my heart. I had to live, but I could also remember along the way.

The people we lose take a part of us with them... but they leave a part of themselves with us too.

IN THE DAYS THAT FOLLOWED, with my grief still curling around my heart but with a knowledge and strength that I'd pulled from the bottom of my soul, I tried my best to keep my chin up. Even if it wasn't easy. But every time I started to feel that drag pulling me down to a place I'd been at before, I tried to remind myself I was my mother's daughter.

Maybe I was a little cursed, but it could be worse. In some ways, I was one of the lucky ones. And I tried not to let myself forget it.

The people I cared about and loved didn't let me forget it either, and I was pretty sure that's what helped me the most.

When the time came, I had my mom's remains cremated and spent a lot of time thinking about what to do with them. I wanted to do something to really honor her spirit.

And that came in two forms.

The idea to turn her ashes into a living tree had been Amos's idea. He'd come up to me one day and slid a printout of a biodegradable urn across the table and headed back into his room as quietly as he'd left it. And it had felt right. My mom would have loved being a tree, and when I'd told

Rhodes about it, he'd agreed we could easily find somewhere to plant her. We made plans to pick somewhere during the summer and do it.

The second idea had come from Yuki the very next day. She found a company that would send a family member's ashes into space. And I knew without a doubt that my fearless mom would have absolutely loved it. I figured my blood money couldn't have been spent any better than on that. I could even go see the launch.

My heart and my soul ached, but there couldn't have been two more perfect ways to say goodbye to my mom's physical body.

So I hadn't been expecting to get home from work one day to find a bunch of cars parked in front of the main house. At least seven of them, and other than Rhodes's, I only recognized Clara and Johnny's. She had left early and let me close, claiming she had to do something with her dad. I'd taken off almost two weeks of work after finding out about my mom and would have managed the shop by myself all day every day, I'd felt so guilty for leaving her with that kind of load. I hadn't thought twice about it.

But seeing her car with Johnny's, and then five other cars with various license plates, completely threw me off.

Rhodes wasn't the kind of man who invited anybody over other than Johnny, and even that wasn't often. His work truck and the Bronco were both there too, hours earlier than they should have been. He'd told me that morning as he'd gotten ready for work that he would be sticking around close by and would be home about six.

I parked my car closer to the garage apartment I'd barely spent any time in lately and grabbed my purse before crossing over to the main house, confused. The front door was unlocked, and I went in. The sound of several voices talking surprised me even more.

Because I recognized them. Every single one.

And even though I'd been crying a lot less recently, the tears instantly welled up in my eyes as I crossed the foyer and into the main living area.

That's where they all were. In the kitchen and around the table. In the living room.

The TV was on, and there was a picture of my mom in her twenties scaling some rock formation that would have made me pee myself. The image changed to another one of both of us. It was a slideshow, I realized before even more tears boiled over, falling down my cheeks in absolute surprise.

I was overwhelmed.

Because in Rhodes's living room, in his house, were my aunt and uncle. All of my cousins, their wives, and a couple of their kids. There was *Yuki* and her bodyguard and her sister Nori and their mom. There was Walter and his wife, and Clara and Mr. Nez and Jackie. And just beside Johnny was Amos.

Moving toward me from that same direction was Rhodes, and I don't know if he pulled me into a hug or if I threw myself like I seemed to always be doing, but there we were a second later. With me tearing up in a bittersweet sense of joy, straight into him.

After a lot more tears and more hugs than I had ever remembered getting at once, I got to celebrate my mom's life with the people I loved the most in the world.

I really was one of the lucky ones, and I wouldn't let myself forget it. Not even on bad days. I promised myself that then.

And it was all because of my mom.

CHAPTER 32

"Good luck, Am! You can do it! You can do anything!" I yelled out of the car at the retreating figure we had just dropped off at the side of the auditorium of his school.

He waved but didn't glance over his shoulder, and behind the driver's seat, Rhodes chuckled almost distractedly. "He's nervous."

"I know he is, and I don't blame him," I said before rolling up the window the second he went through the double doors. "I'm nervous for him." I almost felt like I was performing too. I might have been more nauseous than Am.

But I welcomed the butterflies I got for Amos because they weren't bad.

The last month and a half hadn't been easy, but I was surviving. More than surviving actually. I was doing pretty well for the most part. I'd been having good days, and I'd have days where this new sense of grief over my mom made it hard to breathe, but I had people to talk to about it, and that same hope I'd had in my heart for the future had resumed blooming, slowly but surely.

It had been Mr. Nez who had said something to me the day of her life celebration that had really stuck around in my thoughts. He'd said the greatest way I could honor her life was by living mine, by being as happy as I possibly could.

My heart hadn't been ready to accept it in that moment, but my brain had. Slowly but surely the truth in them had seeped into the rest of me. It was a small, waterproof Band-Aid for a large wound, but it had helped.

"Me too," Rhodes agreed before turning the wheel and heading back to the lot where we were supposed to park. Not for the first time, I noticed he glanced in the rearview mirror with a scowl on his features.

I loved all of his facial expressions, even if that one specifically I didn't understand.

We were an hour early for the start of the talent show, but neither one of us had seen a point in driving all the way back home only to turn around fifteen minutes later. His phone beeped, and he pulled it out of his pocket and handed it over to me as he kept on driving.

"It's your dad. He says he's on his way and will be here in fifteen," I told him as I sent the older man a reply.

Rhodes was going to wring my neck for promising to save his dad a seat for the talent show, but Randall was trying and I'd give him credit. Rhodes still wasn't totally on board with putting in effort in return. But I had a feeling he'd wear himself down eventually, for Am's sake. For him to have another grandparent. You couldn't erase years of a rocky relationship with just a few examples of effort.

Part of me hoped he didn't find out that I'd been the one to tell Randall about the talent show when we'd run into each other at Home Depot in Durango, but it was worth the risk. It wasn't like he would really actually get mad at me. Not for that, at least.

Rhodes grunted as he parked and then took his time

looking at me, a tiny dent forming between his eyebrows. Those gray eyes roamed my face like they did pretty often, like he was trying to read me. He was real subtle about it, but if he could tell I was feeling down, he tried to cheer me up in his own ways. Some of those ways had included showing me how to chop wood when he'd had two full cords delivered. Another time had been taking me to snowshoe up to ice caves. But my favorite way was when he used that incredible body at night to get my endorphins going. It was comfort and bonding all rolled into one.

I loved him so much that not even my grief could mute how I felt about him.

And I knew without a doubt, that my mom would have been so happy I'd found someone like him.

"How are you feeling?" he asked.

I didn't have to think about it. "I'm okay."

Those gray eyes moved over my face. "Just making sure." He took my hand. "I saw you looking out the window in the kitchen before we left."

I had been doing that. I'd caught myself doing it less over the last couple of weeks. My body and brain had gotten some time to cope. The surprise visit from my loved ones had really helped too. It had reminded me again of how much I still had, so much more love than some people would ever know. "No, I'm okay, I promise. I was thinking about how funny things work out sometimes. Like maybe if I had waited to book your garage apartment, someone else might have and we would have never met."

"And here I grounded Am for six months and it was one of the two best things to ever happen to me."

The other being Amos, I knew. And I smiled. There was a lot worth smiling for. "You scared the shit out of me that day, by the way."

His mouth twisted. "You scared the shit out of me too. I thought you were breaking into the house."

"You still scared me more. You were like two steps away from getting pepper sprayed," I told him.

Rhodes's mouth pulled into a beautiful smile. "Not as much as you scared me that day you were screaming your lungs out in the middle of the night all because of a sweet little bat."

"*Sweet?* Are you high?"

His laugh sent my heart pumping.

I leaned over and kissed him, and that ridiculous, full mouth opened and he kissed me deeply in return. We pulled apart, and I smiled at him as he looked at me with tenderness, but the moment he could, his eyes flicked to the rearview mirror.

"Are you okay?" I asked.

Rhodes's mouth went tight. "I think someone has been following us."

I turned in the seat to look out the back window but didn't see anything. "You think? Why?"

"Yes. It's a black SUV. I noticed it right when we pulled out of the driveway. They were coming toward us and pulled a U-turn almost immediately. It's been following us since," he explained. "It might be a coincidence, but it doesn't seem like it."

I touched his hand. "I don't have any stalkers. Do you?"

That got one corner of his mouth to hitch up at the same time his fingers landed on top of mine. "None that I know of. Keep close, will you?"

I agreed, and we got out. The weather had taken a turn for a couple of warmer days, but I still had my down jacket on—the tangerine one he'd given me for Christmas that he'd said made me look like walking sunshine. Rhodes rounded the hood and came over to where I was waiting for him in the middle of the parking lot. He slipped his arm over my shoulder and kept me right there, next to that long frame that made me think of safety and home and love.

But mostly of the future.

For such a quiet, private man, he wasn't stingy with his affection. Part of me thought that he knew how much I needed it and that's why he sprinkled it on everything. I'd even caught Am looking a little funny sometimes when he'd randomly put an arm around his shoulder or tell him he was proud of him for the littlest things.

I loved him so much.

And I was totally on to the fact that he'd been slowly moving my things over to his house. I wasn't sure if he was trying to be sneaky or just giving me room to get used to the idea, but it had made me choke up when I'd noticed little things appearing over there that I hadn't brought myself. He rarely used the L-word but he didn't need to. I knew how he felt like I knew my own name.

And that was exactly what I was thinking of when I heard the last thing I ever would have expected in my life.

"Roro!"

My brain instantly recognized the voice, but it took my body and nervous system a second to catch up. To *accept*.

But I didn't freeze.

My heart didn't start pounding.

I didn't instantly start sweating or get nervous.

Instead, it was Rhodes who slowed down first. Him who, once we were over the curb and onto the sidewalk that ran around the school, came to a stop and slowly turned us around. How he seemed to know that the "Roro" was for me, I had no idea, but he did.

And I was pretty sure we both spotted the figure jogging across the parking lot with a huge man behind him at the same time.

It was my eyes that were the last to process who had called my name.

Kaden. It was Kaden running with his bodyguard, Maurice, behind him. I didn't know Maurice well, he'd been hired right before I'd been freed, but I still recognized him.

In a bulky parka jacket and jeans, I'd bet he'd spent a thousand dollars on, the man I'd wasted fourteen years of my life with came running over.

How the hell he recognized me now that I'd let my natural hair color totally grow out again, I had no idea. Maybe his mom had told him. Maybe Arthur or Simone had.

He looked the same as he always did. Made up. Dressed nice. Fresh and wealthy.

But the moment he was closer, I noticed the bags under his eyes. They weren't normal bags like the rest of us humans got, but for him, they were something. Something about his expression was anxious as well.

The black SUV Rhodes had spotted. That had been him. I just knew it.

"I'm sorry, Rhodes," I whispered, leaning into him just a little, trying to tell him that it was *him* I wanted, who I was here for.

I knew Rhodes knew who he was.

"There's nothing for you to be sorry about, angel," he replied just as Kaden huffed and slowed down as he approached.

He was looking at me with wide, light brown eyes, panting. "Roro," he said, like I hadn't heard him the first time.

The arm around my shoulders went nowhere as I asked him like he was a customer we'd banned from the store, "What are you doing here?"

Kaden blinked slowly, surprised, or... you know what? I didn't give a shit. "I came... I need to talk to you." He sucked in a breath. His bodyguard stopped short just a couple of feet behind him. "How are you?" he panted. His gaze tried to eat me up, but I wasn't edible anymore. "Wow. I forgot how beautiful you are with your natural hair color."

I definitely wasn't going to pick at that hypocritical comment with a ten-foot pole. He'd never stuck up for me once when my roots would start to grow back in and his mom would nag me about making an appointment at the salon. If I'd given enough of a shit to go back through my memories, I would have picked up on the fact that he never had stood up for me with her period.

I didn't have it in my heart to be bitter or angry or even be a bitch. I just didn't care anymore. "I'm great."

Seeing him was... just weird. Déjà vu like, I guess. Like I'd lived another lifetime and knew I should have felt something for him but didn't. There was nothing in my heart as I took in his clean-cut face and styled hair. And I sure as hell felt nothing as he did the same back to me.

But I didn't want to be here. I didn't want to have this conversation. Not even a little bit. And I needed to nip this in the bud ASAP. "Why are you here, Kaden? I made it really clear to your mom what would happen if I ever saw any of you again." I tried to keep it simple, even though I couldn't believe he was really here.

But he took a step forward, his gaze *finally* flicking to Rhodes. His throat bobbed. Then it bobbed again as he took in the arm resting over my shoulders. Noticing the way I was facing the man at my side, leaning against him. Kaden's inhale was quick and sharp. "She doesn't know I'm here. Can we talk?" he asked, deciding to ignore my comment.

I blinked.

And that blink must have said exactly what I was thinking —*no, I don't want to talk to you*—because he rushed out, breathlessly, "I came to see you."

It only took him nearly two years, I thought and just about laughed.

Two years later and he was here. Here! God bless America! I should be so lucky!

I knew better now than I had even six months ago that life was way too short for this shit.

I tried my best not to make a face; I wanted this over. "So did your mom, and I told her I have absolutely no interest in seeing or talking to either of you ever again. I meant it. I meant it then, I mean it now, and I'm going to mean it years from now. We aren't friends. I don't owe you anything. The only thing I want to do is go inside," I explained about as calmly as I possibly could.

Kaden's head jerked back, looking genuinely wounded. I had to fight not to roll my eyes. "We aren't friends?"

I didn't know what it said about me that I almost laughed at how ridiculous this conversation was. I'd been through so much and this... this was so stupid. "I'm going to say this without the intention of wanting to hurt your feelings, because I just don't care enough to even bother doing that, but *yes*, we aren't friends. We stopped being friends a long time ago. We're never going to be friends again, and honestly, I don't know why you're here after this long. Like I told your mom, there is *nothing* I want to hear from either of you."

"But I—"

I cut him off. "Don't."

"But—"

"No," I said. "Listen. Let me live my life in peace. I'm happy. Go be happy or don't be happy. It's none of my business anymore. I don't care. Leave. Me. Alone."

Kaden Jones, Country Music Star of the Year twice in a row a decade ago, frowned in a way that reminded me of a little boy as his features formed into a stunned expression. *"What?"*

How could he manage to still act surprised? What did he expect? Just when I didn't think anything could shock me anymore, it happened.

Today had been a pretty good day after a string of pretty shitty ones, and I wasn't going to let it go to hell.

"You heard me, Kaden. Go home. Go back on tour. Go do whatever it was you were doing before you came here. I don't want to talk to you. I don't care to see you. There's nothing you can say or do that will get me to change my mind. I meant it, all of you need to *leave me alone*. I'll take you, your mom, and everyone you know to court if you don't let me live my life in peace."

It was like he remembered his bodyguard was watching, or maybe he cared that Rhodes was seeing this happen, but Kaden's pale face flushed in anger and embarrassment. He took a step closer, gaze wide, looking damn near desperate for the first time ever. "Roro, you can't mean that. I've been trying to reach you for months."

For months. It had been *months* since he had last messaged me. Months since they found out where I was, and he was just barely getting around to come and see me? Didn't that just say more than any of his words ever could?

Rhodes's hand rubbed at my upper arm, and I glanced up to see him looking at me with an extremely blank face.

"I've been trying and trying." Kaden kept talking as Rhodes's mouth twisted down at me a little. "I fucked up. I know I did. It's the biggest mistake of my life. Biggest mistake of anybody's life."

One corner of Rhodes's mouth went up just a little.

Hadn't those been his exact words?

"I miss you. I'm sorry. *I'm so sorry*. I'll spend the rest of my life making it up to you," Kaden pleaded, genuinely sounding heartfelt.

But his words were going in one of my ears and out the

other, especially when Rhodes was looking at me the way he was looking at me.

"*Please*. Please, talk to me. You can't throw away *fourteen years*. You can't. I'll forgive you. None of this has to matter. We can put it all behind us and forget about it. I can forget you being with somebody else."

Only then did Rhodes's little smile disappear at the same time his head lifted and his gaze landed on my ex.

Rhodes was in his old Levi's, this crazy cute zip-up wool sweater that Amos's aunt had given him for Christmas that was maroon, and dark gray boots. He hadn't even bothered with a jacket, but there was one in the car. And he was the best-looking man I'd ever seen as he reared up to his full height, holding onto me just as tight as ever, and said in that voice of his, "She's going to be forgetting someone, and it's not going to be me."

The flush on Kaden's face went even deeper, and to give him credit, he looked pretty determined. "Do you *know* how long we were together?"

This shallow chuckle bubbled out of Rhodes's chest, and the hand he had been rubbing over my upper arm halted as he turned his arm to let his wrist dangle over my shoulder. But I knew that expression, and there was nothing casual about it. "Does it matter?" he asked, stone-cold and serious. "Because, to my thinking, it already doesn't. You're the past. And I've got no problem with making sure you end up being some guy that broke her heart before I took over and put hers in mine for safekeeping."

For someone who wasn't used to being so loving, he really did say the sweetest things. And if I had ever doubted that I loved him, which I hadn't, I knew then that I'd chosen right. Chosen *best*. There were going to be no mistakes here.

Not ever.

By the time I focused back on him, Rhodes's facial

features had morphed even more into one of his most serious expressions. "I love her. And I will gladly give her all the things you were too stupid not to give her. You wouldn't even hold her hand in public, right? Or kiss her?" he basically taunted him. "I'm fine not being the first man she's ever loved because I know I'm going to be the last."

Kaden's gaze flicked to mine like he was stunned. He'd asked for it. And honestly, I was getting turned on by what Rhodes was saying, big-time.

"That's the difference between guys like you and me. If she needed something, you'd give her a hundred dollars from your wallet even if you had more and think that was good enough. I'd give her everything that was in mine." His voice went hard. "The only person you can blame is yourself, dumbass."

My heart soared. It might have even got straight to the moon. Because Rhodes was right.

Kaden would have a roll of bills in his wallet and part with a hundred, easily. And Rhodes would give me five dollars if that was all he had. He would give me everything at any cost. And Kaden.... It didn't matter. And it never would again. He had killed anything and everything I'd ever felt for him, and there was nothing there. Not a speck. There never would be again.

And now it was my turn to tell him the same so there was no miscommunication.

Love could be about money. It made things easier, that was for sure. But the best kind of love was about so much more than that. It was about giving the person you loved *everything*. The easy, effortless things, but also the hardest intangible stuff, the uncomfortable. It was about telling someone that you loved them by giving them everything you had and everything you didn't because they mattered more to you than anything material ever would or could.

I caught his gaze and told him as seriously as possible, "I told your mom, and now I'm going to tell you too. There is no amount of money in the world that you could ever give me to get me to go back. Even if we could be friends, which isn't going to happen"—Rhodes grunted beside me—"I wouldn't work for you or help you again. You need to understand that. I will *never* change my mind."

Hurt, clear and bright hurt, flashed across the good-looking face staring at me. "This isn't about you writing for me, Roro. *I love you.*"

The arm over my shoulders stiffened, and Rhodes's voice dropped as he grumbled, "Not enough."

I focused on this man that I had known so well for so long and made a face so he would know I wasn't exaggerating, that I meant every word out of my mouth. "Bye, Kaden. I don't want to see any of you again. I mean it. I'll make you regret the day you met me."

I was done.

Rhodes glanced down, and I focused on him, and without looking at my past, we turned and walked away, leaving him behind. To stand there, to stare, to walk away; I didn't know and I didn't give a single shit. Not a fraction of one.

And what had to be about a minute of walking later, I suddenly stopped. Rhodes stopped too, and I threw my arms around his neck. He bent down and put his arms around my lower back, pulling me into that body, cuddling me close.

"You're the best," I told him seriously.

His hand snuck beneath my jacket and shirt and palmed my lower back as he whispered, "I love you, you know that."

Pulling him down so that he was ear level with my mouth, with goose bumps on my skin and a warmth that could have started a wildfire, I whispered back, "I know."

Rhodes's breath was a puff against my throat, and I felt him let out a deep sigh a moment later. He shifted and his cheek nuzzled mine. After a moment, with my face tingling from the rub of his stubble, he pulled back and aimed that purple-gray gaze at me. "Ready?" he asked.

I grabbed his hand and nodded. "Let's go save some front row seats to see our star-in-the-making win."

The man I loved squeezed my hand, and we went inside to do just that.

EPILOGUE

"**Y**ou look like a princess, Yuki."

Yuki bounced her shoulders from her spot in front of the mirror that had been set up in her room by the designer who had loaned her the dress she was wearing tonight, ignoring the squawk of disapproval from the stylist who had arranged everything. My dress. Her dress. The makeup and hair people that had been hired to take her from a "seven to eleven."

She was ridiculous, but she really did look like an eleven.

The woman the world knew as a pop star, but I knew as my great friend preened as she turned around. "I've got eight layers of makeup on, I'm not going to be able to breathe for the next six hours, and I'm going to need help peeing, but thank you very much, my love."

I laughed. "You're very welcome, and it would be my honor to hold up your dress while you go pee. If you have to take a poopy, I'm out of there though."

It was her turn to laugh. "No poo, but we have peed in front of each other a lot over the years, haven't we?" she asked with an almost dreamy expression on her face.

I knew exactly what she was envisioning: all the awesome hikes we'd gone on, which included the dozens of times we'd had to keep an eye out for each other when other hikers came by. We'd had a lot of fun over time, and it made me so happy that she genuinely enjoyed all of our adventures back home.

My friend shrugged and took her time eyeing me up and down. "And you, my glowing angel, look like a fifteen." She wiggled her eyebrows and ignored the noise her makeup artist made at the movement. "I'll forgive you for cheating."

I rolled my eyes. "Cheating. Right."

"It's the hormones. You got that natural glow this half-inch of highlighter and bronzer can't compete with." She whistled, and I curtsied about as much as I could, which wasn't much considering how tight this dress was. "I bet Kaden's going to shit himself when he sees you."

His mention surprised me for about a split second. I hadn't heard his name in... a year? One of his songs had come on while I'd been in the car with Jackie and Amos, and the two had started instantly booing before changing the station. That had been the last time I'd thought of him too, and that had been brief.

"If he shits himself, I hope someone catches it on camera," I joked, adjusting the strap of the dress I'd been fitted for two months ago when Yuki had originally invited me.

She cackled, and we high-fived. And not for the first time, I thanked my mom for giving me such a good friend—such good friends, in general. With Yuki being one of those at the very top of the list.

We'd seen each other a ton over the last four years. She'd spent Thanksgiving with us once, New Year's twice—even though I'd warned her we just went a couple towns over to see fireworks if it wasn't a drought year—and randomly throughout the year, she dropped by when she could. She'd rented out a yacht that second summer I'd been in Pagosa Springs, and we had met her in Greece and spent one of the best weeks ever. Even her sister, Nori, had come too.

The following year, she invited us to do the same in Italy, but... I hadn't been allowed to fly at that point. I hadn't regretted it either. Neither had Rhodes. Am had huffed and puffed, but he'd hung out with me the whole week we would have been gone, and he'd even rubbed my feet once.

He hadn't huffed or puffed at all when I'd told him we were driving to Los Angeles for the awards ceremony though. He'd hitched a ride down with a friend from school and volunteered to come along to "help out." Uh-huh. I missed him a ton now that he was gone at college for most of the year, and I'd take any of the excuses he made to visit.

He was still writing music and even performing from time to time at small businesses around his school. If Rhodes wasn't busy, we drove up to watch him. He still caught me up on what he'd worked on, but school, in general, took up most of his time, even though he was planning on majoring in musical composition.

"Thank you for inviting me," I told Yuki for about the tenth time, moving my hand along my stomach.

She tilted her head to the side. "We wrote the whole album together, Ora. And you're the best-looking date I could have brought."

"You did most of the work; I only helped a little," I told her. The words, the lyrics, hadn't come back to me over time. Once or twice, I'd felt a hint of a word or two float onto the tip of my tongue... but they had disappeared instantly. I didn't think or worry about it at all, though. No one cared, and that was pretty damn nice.

Then again, I had let Amos look through my notebooks a few years ago, and he'd stared over at me with wide eyes. *"This is your bad stuff?"* he'd demanded like he couldn't believe me. So maybe they weren't that bad. The only notebooks I still opened on my own from time to time were my mom's, so we could squeeze in one of her favorite hikes. We did that pretty often on the days my heart hurt and I missed her the most.

Yuki, though, gave me a look that reminded me of how many times I'd found her passed out on the couch that Rhodes had eventually put in the garage apartment for guests. Of which she was one of them. My family in Florida, her sister, and his brothers being our other main visitors.

A knock at the door had her manager standing up from where she had taken a seat on one of the couches. The woman opened it, said a few words, and stepped back, gesturing the person on the other side in.

It was only my favorite man in the entire world.

Part of my heart in another person's body.

I grinned and instantly went toward the silver-haired man. It had been all of two hours since I'd left them in the suite that Yuki had gotten for us—she'd ignored me when I insisted I could pay for it—but it felt like a whole day instead. It was different when we weren't separated by work. Even then, he'd drop by during lunch if he was close or on his way home if he had an early day after protecting Colorado's wildlife.

Rhodes's gray eyes moved up and down the length of me as he came forward too. His mouth formed an O. "Wow," he whispered.

"Too much makeup though, huh?"

He shrugged as his hands went to my shoulders for possibly the ten-thousandth time. "Way too much, but only you are even more beautiful without makeup on than with it." His hands squeezed me. "Nice dress though, Buddy."

"It's 'borrowed,' and I don't know how I'm going to pee in it." The dress I'd been loaned was emerald green, heavy with embroidery, and weighed close to fifteen pounds—or at least that's what it felt like.

"Pee yourself so you don't rip it," he said with a straight face.

I laughed and stepped in close to wrap my arms around his middle. I still hadn't gotten used to having unlimited access to him. To his rock-solid body that I still perved on every night and every morning, even if I was half asleep when he got home or left.

He'd told me once he worried that I'd get fed up with him working such long hours, and I'd taken my time explaining that was the absolute last thing he had to worry about. In some ways, I'd waited my whole life for him. I could wait a few hours. It wasn't like he was gone because he enjoyed being away. That was the thing about being confident with what you had. I'd never doubted him, not even for a second.

"I wasn't sure if I could hug you," he said, squeezing me back.

"You can always hug me."

His mouth drifted across my hair, and I knew he was just trying not to kiss my face because of the insane amount of makeup I had on.

"Yuki's dad invited us to go get dinner. He wants to talk fishing," he said quietly.

"Is Am going?"

Pulling back, he nodded, his gaze raking down me again.

Yuki cleared her throat way too loud from across the room. "Ora, it's time to go. Rhodes, do you want to walk her down?"

With his hand settling on my lower back, he ducked his chin in agreement.

We smiled at each other before heading out the door, followed by Yuki's bodyguard and manager. Security was tight at the hotel as we made our way through the lobby, trailing behind Yuki who was whispering about something to her manager the whole time. This whole experience was just a little surreal, and I didn't miss it at all.

Rhodes ducked in close, his voice basically a whisper. "Are you okay? You're not too tired?"

I shook my head. "Not yet, but hopefully I won't fall asleep because that would be real embarrassing."

Mr. Overprotective shot me a side look.

We'd gone to my OB-GYN before planning our trip, but I knew he was still apprehensive about the whole thing even though we had driven. Because of my age, I was at high-risk, but luckily I was healthy in every other way, and it was still early on. I wasn't planning on going anywhere for a while after this. My aunt and uncle were planning on visiting us next. They visited every year.

We stopped at a fancy car I was sure I'd been in before, and he gave my back a little rub. "Have fun."

"I will. I want to do this just this one time and never again. I'll probably have enough makeup left over on my face for the next decade anyway."

His twisting mouth lit up my world like it always did. "You deserve it, angel." He leaned in and lightly brushed his lips across mine. "Love you."

And just like it had the first few times he'd said those words, my body reacted the same way: like his verbal declaration of love was some kind of addictive drug it needed to survive. The truth was, I didn't think I'd know how to keep going without it anymore. For a man who hadn't used the L-word very often in the past, he wasn't stingy with it any longer. I heard it every morning and every night. I heard him say it to Azalia in quiet little whispers. He said it to Amos on the phone. My favorite lately was when he mouthed it against my stomach.

So it was second nature to pull him back down to me and

tell him I loved him right back. Because a man who could spread so much of it out with not just his actions but with his words too, needed to hear it right back. And that was a job I would gladly take.

A loud whistle had us pulling away to find Yuki there, shaking her head. "You two, you make me sick with happiness."

I snickered and went up to my toes, kissing him again. Rhodes smiled. "Text me when you're on your way back."

"I will."

I smiled back at him and ducked into the car, clutching my purse as Yuki slid in after me, giving Rhodes a hug on the way. She smiled as she settled in, her manager squeezing in as well. "I love seeing you this happy, Ora."

My exhale was choppy with the joy in my chest. "I like feeling this happy."

The last few years had been the happiest of my life. It was Rhodes, Amos, and Azalia, of course, but it was also the whole town in general. My life in general. I'd settled in. It was home. I had family and friends. And I got to see them all the time when they came to visit the shop.

I still worked there.

I owned it now actually.

Mr. Nez had gotten even more ill about two years ago, and Clara had admitted that she needed money for his treatment—adding in a sharp look when I'd opened my mouth to offer to help financially, so I'd closed it immediately—but also admitting that her heart wasn't in the store anymore and she was considering selling it. She wanted to go back to nursing. I loved working at the store, and I figured, why not?

So that's what we did. I bought it. Jackie was commuting to school in Durango and helped me. I hired Amos when he was home. And I'd hired a couple more people who moved into town.

Buying it had been a terrific decision.

Just like having an addition built to our house had been.

Then again, just about every decision I'd made since that night in Moab when I had decided to drive to, and possibly settle in, Pagosa had been a great one.

～

"Your face when you won was priceless," Yuki's dad chuckled hours later.

His daughter laughed, pushing her chair back. "We were both half asleep when they announced the category, and I had no idea what was going on until I saw the screen with my name on it," she admitted.

It was the truth.

We had gotten dropped off at the sports bar where the men in our lives had hung out during the awards ceremony. I had assumed she would want to go to one of the after-parties, especially after winning album of the year, but she had shrugged me off with a look of horror and said, "I'm starving, and I'd rather see my daddy."

And I'd rather see my family, so we'd left; we went straight to the bar slash restaurant in our stupid expensive dresses with Yuki promising to pay for them when I told her I was worried I'd get it dirty. I'd had fun at the ceremony, but nothing was better than walking into the restaurant and seeing Mr. Young with his arms crossed over his chest, laughing at something Rhodes had said. My perfect Rhodes, who was leaning back against the booth with Azalia standing up and bouncing on his lap while Am stared hard at a table across the room. One quick glance had me recognizing the girl he was staring at. She had been at the ceremony too and won something about fifteen minutes before Yuki had.

I'd gone and given them all kisses and hugs, taking Azalia

and play-eating her cheek before my daddy's girl had reached out for her older brother, who took her without hesitation.

Azalia was a miracle who'd made her tiny, tadpole-sized presence known a little over a year after Rhodes and I had gotten married. My eyes had teared up, his had too, and if I'd thought he'd been protective before, it was nothing compared to after that. I'd thrived on it too.

But focusing back on the present and not on the two-year-old passed out in Am's arms, I still couldn't believe that Yuki had won. Actually, I could, but it was still surprising and amazing. She'd thanked me twice in a nervous rush of gratitude onstage, and I'd cheered as loudly as I wanted, annoying the people around me.

She promised to send me a plaque, and I had just the perfect wall to put it on. In our bedroom. Beside the last one she'd given me for that fateful album we'd written together at a low point in both our lives. Yet here we were, better than ever.

It was late as we all got up to leave, and I watched Yuki slide her arm through her dad's as they exited the restaurant and started the walk a block down back to the hotel. Her bodyguard trailed behind them.

The rest of us followed him. The night was cool, and there were a lot more people than I would've expected at nearly midnight on a Sunday, with just about everyone doing a double take at the view of Yuki, obviously recognizing her.

Rhodes squeezed my hand. "I think I saw you when they were showing the nominees and zoomed in on Yuki," he said.

"Did you see us both staring blankly forward?"

"Oh yeah."

I laughed.

"I thought that sort of thing was fun?"

"It's not. It's so boring. We played rock paper scissors and tic-tac-toe on her phone." I squeezed his hand. "I brought two granola bars, and she had two packs of gummy bears, and we took turns bending over and eating them so the cameras wouldn't catch us."

He laughed so loud before releasing my hand and slipping it over my shoulders, pulling me into him. My favorite position.

"We had to help each other use the bathroom," I admitted too.

He squeezed me even harder. "That doesn't sound like fun at all."

"I'm good never doing it again, that's for sure," I said, peeking over my shoulder to find Amos holding his sleepy little sister behind us. He tipped up his chin just like Rhodes did.

He had matured so much over the last few years; he wasn't as tall as his dad, but I thought he was going to get close. To me, he looked a hell of a lot more like his mom, but when he smirked or rolled his eyes, I swore he was a mirror image of his dad. His Dad Rhodes at least. He'd gotten his laid-back attitude from his Dad Billy, I'd discovered.

Just as I opened my mouth to ask them what they wanted to do tomorrow, out of the corner of my eye, I spotted two familiar figures coming in through the hotel's other set of automatic doors.

One of them was Kaden.

In a black tuxedo just like the one I'd seen him wearing a hundred times before when he'd leave me in a hotel room. His shirt white, his bowtie still on. And beside him, his mom was there in a stunning gold gown.

She looked pissed. It was funny to see some things hadn't changed. Wow.

Kaden had managed to stay "relevant" enough to still be invited to awards shows and win sometimes, thanks to whoever he was hiring now. He'd been nominated for something or another tonight but hadn't won. I hadn't seen him in person, just the image of him that had appeared on the stage's massive screen.

Peace like I hadn't felt in forever filled my heart and, honestly, my whole body.

There was no anger in me. No pain or resentment. Just... indifference.

Like he could sense my gaze on him, Kaden's eyes moved toward us, and I could tell the moment it landed on the very soft swelling at my stomach. I was four months along now, and the dress did little to hide the second baby we were having. Another little girl. We hadn't settled on a first name yet, but since Azalia was named after my mom, we were thinking about giving baby number two Yuki's middle name: Rose.

Rhodes and I were so excited. So, so excited. Am was too. He'd put up one of the ultrasound pictures in his dorm room. Beside it, he had one of Azalia the day she'd been born. After all, he'd been the one to drive me to the hospital, and he'd hung out in the room with me looking green and letting me squeeze the shit out of his hand until Rhodes had shown up literally two minutes before I'd given birth. Amos had been the third person to hold his baby sister, and that, I'd guessed, explained their closeness perfectly.

We'd called him right after we'd left the doctor's office, and he had let out a noise that made us both laugh. "Holy shit. We're gonna be overrun with girls now, Dad."

The man sitting in the car beside me, still holding my hand, had grinned forward through the windshield with bright eyes and said the best thing he could have ever come up with, "I'm not complaining."

He meant every word of it too.

God knew I could never forget the way that Rhodes's

whole body had trembled after the doctor had confirmed that I was pregnant. How his eyes had filled with tears, how his mouth had pressed against my cheeks, forehead, nose, and even my chin after I'd given birth to Azalia. I couldn't have asked for a better partner, father, or a better man than him to spend the rest of my life with. He lifted me up, believed in me, and filled my life with more love than I ever could have asked for.

"Are you good, angel?" Rhodes asked, running his palm up and down my upper arm warmly, saving the day like always.

Moving my gaze away from the people that I used to know—I had a feeling it would be the last time I would ever see them—I nodded at Rhodes. At my husband. The person who would go through heaven and hell to get to me if I was ever lost. The man who had given me every single thing I had ever wanted and more.

This one ceremony had been enough. I hadn't missed out, not even a little bit. I was ready to go home. Ready to continue living my life with these people that I loved with my entire soul.

And it was as we were walking toward the elevators that Am snickered. "You know what I just thought about, Ora?"

I glanced at him. "No, tell me."

"Hear me out. What would have happened if I wouldn't have rented the garage apartment out to you? I almost chickened out. Would Dad have ever met you? Would I be going to school for music? Would you own the store?" he asked with a thoughtful expression. "You ever wonder?"

I didn't have to think about it, so I told him the truth.

I told him that I had before, but it had been a long time since then.

Because I had ended up exactly where I should have,

where every decision that had been made before me and made by me had led.

I *was* one of the lucky ones, I thought as a flicker of a thought brushed through my head; there so effortlessly, it stole my breath away. I grabbed Rhodes's arm in shock, and he glanced down at me curiously, with so much love it was just one more thing to steal my breath away.

And the thought, the words, came to me again.

I found a place where I belong,

A place with love that feels like home again.

ACKNOWLEDGMENTS

This book wouldn't exist in the first place without you—thank you so much to my incredible readers for your love and continued support.

An enormous thank you to the greatest designer in the world, Letitia at RBA Designs; my wonderful agents Jane Dystel and Lauren Abramo, and everyone at Dystel, Goderich and Bourret.

Judy, I can't thank you enough for always answering all of my audio questions and for just being wonderful. Thank you to Virginia and Kim at Hot Tree Editing and Ellie with My Brother's Editor for your editing skills. Kilian, thank you for all your help.

As always, Eva, I don't know what I'd do without you and your memory. And your suggestions. And your GIFs.

To my friends who have helped me in some way (who I know I'm forgetting): thank you for everything.

To my Zapata, Navarro, and Letchford family, you're the greatest families a girl could ever ask for.

To Chris, Kai, and my forever editor and angel in the sky, Dorian: I love you guys so much.

ABOUT THE AUTHOR

Mariana Zapata lives in a small town in Colorado with her husband and two oversized children—her beloved Great Danes, Dorian and Kaiser. When she's not writing, she's reading, spending time outside, forcing kisses on her boys, or pretending to write.

MarianaZapata.com

Facebook:
facebook.com/marianazapatawrites

Book Store:
marianazapata.bigcartel.com

Merchandise Store:
marianazapata.threadless.com

ALSO BY MARIANA ZAPATA

LINGUS

UNDER LOCKE

KULTI

RHYTHM, CHORD & MALYKHIN

THE WALL OF WINNIPEG AND ME

WAIT FOR IT

DEAR AARON

FROM LUKOV WITH LOVE

LUNA AND THE LIE

THE BEST THING

HANDS DOWN